61-6857

Date Due

THE BELLS OF ROME

GÖRAN STENIUS

The Bells of Rome

translated by
ISABEL AND FLORENCE McHUGH

1961
P. J. KENEDY & SONS
NEW YORK

Original title *Klockorna i Rom*, published
by Söderstrom & Co, Helsingfors, 1955
This translation was made from the
German version *Die Glocken von Rom*
translated by Rita Chquist
First published in Great Britain 1961 by
Eyre & Spottiswoode (Publishers) Ltd
22 Henrietta Street, London W.C.2
English translation © 1961 by Eyre & Spottiswoode (Publishers) Ltd
and P. J. Kenedy & Sons, New York
Printed in Great Britain
Library of Congress Catalogue Card No.: 61-6857

CONTENTS

5

AUTHOR'S PREFACE

This book is not a novel about a real priest's life, in the ordinary sense. It is, rather, a modern "legend" on the presence of the Lord in the Most Holy Eucharist. In this legend some of the characters fulfil a function which is different from that of the ordinary characters in an ordinary novel.

The persons in the book are purely fictitious.

The novel makes no claim to be a novel of Rome in the accepted sense. The legend of Saint Linus and his Church of San Lino and the whole story of Santa Presenza and the burned El Greco painting, are all pure fiction. The same applies to the Vicolo dei Pecorai, Santo Spirito in Gattafogata, Sant' Eusebio in Casaletto, and Santa Maria degli Ulivi.

Neither Monte Lino, Settevetri, nor Castelpendente are to be found on the map of Italy. The account of Santissima Trinita, on the other hand, is based partly on reality. And the prayers used in the celebration of the Eucharist in the Inn of the Good Shepherd are freely adapted from the Primitive Christian text, "The Teaching of the Twelve Apostles".

GÖRAN STENIUS

Prologue

THE VICOLO DEI PECORAI

❧❧❧

In the heart of old Rome, half-way between the Flea Market and the first Roman pawnshop, lies the Vicolo dei Pecorai, Shepherds' Lane, a drab back street that winds its way through a dreary maze of slums where the windows, half hidden by lines of ragged washing, stare like empty eye-sockets from the drab grey walls. Copper-smiths, bicycle mechanics and the like have their grimy workshops in the sunless back yards. Little grocers and hucksters have set up in the alleys, rough as cart tracks, which lead down to the Lane. The smell of poverty and decay is almost stifling. It seems as though the street-sweeper can hardly cope with his job of keeping the ground free of refuse and rotten vegetables. The penetrating smells of machine oil, sour wine and decayed animal refuse mingle together in the fetid air.

The whole quarter consists of ugly stone houses of indeterminate age planlessly crammed together on the site of a labyrinth of ancient ruins. A solitary baroque façade and, here and there, a noble doorway lost amid the general squalor, provide the only evidence that the district once knew better days.

The Vicolo dei Pecorai is so called because the shepherds from the mountains and the Campagna used to pass the night in the little inns here when they came to Rome. To this day in the Lane one can see their descendants – solemn-looking, thick-set people, dark-skinned as gipsies, dressed all in black and wearing heavy boots.

San Lino, the Church of the Shepherds, stands in a little piazza just where the Lane begins. It is one of the oldest churches in the

9

district, though nothing remains of the original building except a few time-worn blocks of Travertine stone in the outer foundations. During the seventeenth century, that age of bold enterprise, the church was completely rebuilt. The old shepherds' entrance from the Lane was done away with and replaced by a new main door-way from the Piazza. One of the side walls was hidden under a showy stucco-covered baroque façade, and an apse was built into the other one, thus changing the whole direction of the nave. The old wooden roof was pulled down and a resplendent dome was perched on top of the ancient, much-maltreated structure. Soon the breathless age of baroque filled the austere interior with its ecstatic exuberance, smothering the architectural deformities. Today the gilding has peeled off the moulded medallions on the walls, and the ornamental stucco-work is falling off in bigger and bigger lumps, but San Lino still opens motherly arms as wide as ever to all the wretched creatures who stream in past the holy water fonts with their greyish, murky water, or kneel on the rough stone floor before the confessional with its faded silk cur-tains smelling faintly of garlic.

The little square in front of the church is called the Piazza delle Pecore, Sheep Square, and originally it was merely the one spot which happened to be left unbuilt upon in the midst of the huddle of houses. In the seventeenth century, however, San Lino had a powerful patron, one Cardinal Terrasanta. He had first cleared a tidy space in front of the new entrance to the church, where up till then the pigs and goats of the neighbourhood had been in the habit of taking their siesta, and wandering shepherds halted to fodder their flocks on the way to the markets. Then the cardinal built a tasteful little baroque palace for himself opposite the church. He paved the new square with even flag-stones and placed in the centre a small fountain with a procession of little frolicking black marble goats round the edge. The Piazza was really supposed to be called after the man who had made it, but it still kept its old name in the popular mouth, a name which seemed incarnated, moreover, in the graceful little goats. The piazza probably did not turn out quite as the cardinal had meant, instead of a real square it seems more like a widening of the Lane of the Shepherds, which stops here to take breath, as it were, on its tortuous way to the Tiber. The patina of centuries has blotted out the contrasts but has not improved the general appearance of the place. And so, with its broken lines and its perspective all askew, the Piazza delle Pecore is rather like a bad caricature of Roman baroque.

The Church of the Shepherds still has a little parish of its own, which continues to exist as an historical curiosity among its bigger neighbours in the great bishopric of Rome. In former times it had been in the charge of a strict penitential brotherhood which had carried on a hidden but intensive missionary activity in the spirit of Saint Philip Neri. They were called the *Frati della Santa Presenza*, Brothers of the Holy Presence, and their particular apostolate was to foster an intensified devotion to the Real Presence of Christ in the Sacrament of the Altar. The first brethren had been plain uncultured men with the broad speech and accent of their native mountains. Their religious habit consisted of a thick grey shepherd's cloak and boots with wooden soles, and their patron was Saint Linus, the first successor of Saint Peter as Pope and Bishop of Rome. Pope Sixtus V, who was from the mountains himself, had approved their constitution, and in the course of the centuries the Church of the Shepherds had developed into a centre of Eucharistic revival among the humble folk of the quarter.

The old monastery of Santa Presenza, a massive, prison-like building with its pilgrims' hostel and its few small windows, still stands in the Lane of the Shepherds and almost gives the impression of being an organic part of San Lino's. But there is no longer a community of Brothers of the Holy Presence. Their silent, self-effacing existence was brutally engulfed by the turbulent nineteenth century. After the fall of Papal Rome the old pilgrims' hostel was turned into a municipal poorhouse, and during the following decades the monastery itself was gradually reduced. A few years after the First World War the last Brother Superior passed away. By then the brethren were already so few that the necessary chapter could not be assembled to choose a successor and the congregation automatically dissolved itself in accordance with its own statutes. The archives and library were rehoused in the chapter-room, and the rest of the building was given over almost entirely to the poorhouse.

The house itself is of a very peculiar structure. Behind its austere façade a pompous pillared hall opens on to a courtyard. Today it houses only a lot of half-blind and deaf old men – the former friendly and good-humoured, the latter sour and suspicious. They sit on the mossy stone benches in the ivy-grown quadrangle, but none of them seems to feel quite at ease in these historic surroundings. They all complain that it is too close and sultry in the hot months and too damp and sunless in the cold ones. Indeed, the place gives the impression that the architect, having gone to such extremes in the construction of the massive monastery itself, could think of nothing for the garden but an entirely unimaginative paved quadrangle surrounding a solitary fountain with slimy green rain-water in its basin.

But a three-foot high plaster Madonna in a pale blue robe and golden shoes and with a halo of electric lights around her head still stands in a glass-roofed niche in the outer wall of the monastery. The people of the Lane call her " the Madonna of the Shepherds ", though actually the name is not correct because the real Madonna of the Shepherds is a very ancient picture which is kept inside San Lino's and has been there since the very first days of the Brotherhood of Santa Presenza. The later counterpart outside in the niche is said to have an original somewhere up in the mountains, but this ancient Madonna has been long lost in the timelessness of the Alpine pastures. There is, however, a persistent tradition still current in the Lane of a prophecy that the Madonna of the Shepherds would one day lead another wandering Brother to the old monastery of Santa Presenza.

Book One

THE MADONNA OF THE SHEPHERDS

❦

PADRE BARNABA AND HIS LIBRARY, 1939

Padre Barnaba, the last survivor of the former Brotherhood of Santa Presenza, still acted as parish priest of San Lino's, and had continued living on in his old monastery cell. He was a rugged-looking figure, his square, deeply furrowed face surmounted by a mighty lion's mane of greyish hair. Although he had entered the brotherhood while young, the fetid air of the Vicolo dei Pecorai had failed to take from his cheeks the blooming colour which was a heritage from his native Abruzzi. His worn, faded soutane hung like a dried sausage skin around his lanky body. As he walked through the lane in his noisy hobnailed boots, glancing about him menacingly with his dark burning eyes, he looked like a robber in disguise from some folk comedy.

Life had made him very taciturn. Outside of church he seldom spoke except about the most everyday things. Anyone who approached him on questions that went deeper generally received the modest advice to examine his own conscience more fully. And if the conversation drifted on to politics or other worldly subjects, Padre Barnaba moved off with a little deprecating smile. He felt absolved from the duty of showing a personal interest in the future. Having neither relatives nor descendants in the world, he lived like an elderly bachelor on his old-age pension. He felt happiest when in his church. There, with his rosary beads in his hand, he knelt hidden away amid the faded baroque splendour,

13

before the altar of the Blessed Sacrament with its little red lamp.

One day a slight young man with flaxen hair arrived in the Vicolo dei Pecorai and knocked on the massive monastery door. The cut of his suit immediately betrayed him as a foreigner. He examined the massive building with a keen but almost suspicious glance as if he feared he might walk into a trap behind those thick walls. Yet there was something attractively straight and modest in his expression, and his deep blue eyes had an earnestness which made it difficult to rebuff him. He presented a whole bunch of letters of recommendation and asked permission to see the library.

No outsider had asked about the library of Santa Presenza within living memory. True, it was said to contain quite a number of rare theological works, but the learned world seemed to have forgotten this long ago. Padre Barnaba tended to regard the library as a kind of monument that had to be cared for and guarded, but preferably not touched.

He dutifully spelled out the name of the stranger, but with a shake of the head gave up the attempt to pronounce it. " German? " he asked politely.

"No, Scandinavian," replied the foreigner.

A vision of vikings, bloody raiders and intractable heretics flitted through Padre Barnaba's mind. Then he remembered having heard that the modern civilization of the Scandinavian countries was one of the most dangerous miracles of antichrist. He eyed the foreigner with curiosity and noted that he was very young. It was not difficult to detect an inner uncertainty behind his arrogant and instinctively defensive manner. The young man strongly resembled a terrier, but he was obviously a terrier without a master, looking for human help in his suspicious, awkward way.

Padre Barnaba's heart melted. " Va bene," he said, opening the door to the library.

It was an old chapter-room of majestic proportions. On the vaulted ceiling faded baroque angels frolicked in a graceful round dance that gave the impression of playful ecstasy to the whole composition. Below the frieze a series of faded frescoes ran the whole way round the room. They represented the legend of Saint Linus, but they were in such a bad state of deterioration that it was difficult to follow the story. The shutters of the tall deep-set windows were closed and the room was in semi-darkness. All the tables were covered with plain grey cloths, and the dust lay thick on the old wall cupboards. The summer heat had melted the candles on the librarian's desk, and the wax had dribbled in shapeless lumps down the candlesticks.

The stranger gave an almost frightened glance round the room. Obviously nothing had been touched for years.

"May I work here?" he asked.

"Yes, of course. Why not?" replied the priest kindly, and began opening the shutters. "The light seems best here," he added, drawing the dust cover off one of the tables by a window. "The catalogue is there to the right, and if you want anything you will find me in the church."

He started to go, but noticing that the young man wished to speak he stopped. "Is there anything not quite clear to you?" he asked.

On the wall opposite the door, above the former dais of the chapter, hung a huge oil painting. It was a naïve representation of the Sacrifice of the Mass at the moment of the consecration. The priest, surrounded by a deeply attentive congregation, was kneeling before the altar holding the sacred Host, around which danced rosy cherubs. On the altar one could make out the lightly sketched outlines of a figure that had originally been marked out in light brown, but had become darkened with age and now looked like a monk's habit which had been flung down. It obviously represented the shadow of an invisible form, the presence of which the painter had indicated by means of a mystic light that seemed to come from outside the picture.

The foreigner stood and stared at the painting as if confronted with a sudden revelation.

"The 'Holy Presence'?" he asked in a low voice.

Padre Barnaba gave an embarrassed little laugh. "Some unknown artist was commissioned by the chapter to paint that picture, and it has been left hanging here since out of reverence," he answered.

"Are there others of the kind here?"

"Others?" repeated Padre Barnaba, surprised. "Why, this is not a picture gallery!"

The stranger would not be put off so easily. "Isn't the famous El Greco here?" he asked.

"The what?" asked Padre Barnaba, with visibly increasing astonishment.

"I'm looking for a well-known painting by the famous Spanish-Greek painter, El Greco," the foreigner explained politely.

"It's not here," said Padre Barnaba.

"That's strange. I've been told for a fact that it is."

"Indeed?"

"I was also told that it's the most wonderful representation of the Eucharist that has ever been painted."

Padre Barnaba seemed to soften a little. "I suppose you mean *Il Santissimo*," he said. "It was never in this room. It used to hang in a little chapel near the refectory."

"Is one allowed in there?"

"No, that's impossible."

"But perhaps I could just look in the door?"

"The chapel no longer exists."

"I don't quite understand. . . ."

Padre Barnaba hesitated. "It was completely destroyed by fire and rebuilt in a different form," he muttered evasively. "There's nothing at all to see there."

"And the El Greco?" asked the foreigner tensely.

Padre Barnaba eyed him intently. "The El Greco no longer exists either," he said.

A hot flush spread over the fair-skinned face of the stranger. "Surely you don't mean to tell me that it was burned too?" he asked in a tone of tense horror.

Padre Barnaba laid a hand soothingly on his arm. "No doubt our Lord has willed it so," he said. "You see, He is letting the whole monastery gradually crumble away."

The foreigner shook his head. "Please forgive me," he muttered, "but how can such a masterpiece as that simply be burned without anyone knowing about it? Wasn't it under any sort of State control?"

"The picture belonged wholly and solely to the Brotherhood. There were only a very few outsiders who understood it. Ordinary tourists never asked to see it."

The foreigner looked suspiciously around the dusty room. "Isn't there even a reproduction of it here?" he asked.

"There's nothing, as far as I know."

"But perhaps there is some literature – a catalogue, for instance?"

"I hardly think so. You see, this is a purely theological library."

"But surely there must be some notes about the picture in connection with the history of the monastery?" persisted the stranger.

Padre Barnaba glanced once more at the letters of recommendation brought by the visitor. "The library is at your disposal, Doctor Cinnelius," he said with a shrug.

During the next few days the young man frequented the library diligently and Padre Barnaba had an opportunity to know him better. He had a Christian name, Thomas, and seemed a nice young fellow and exceedingly clever. Like most Scandinavians he had read an incredible amount, though for the most part rather worthless literature apparently, for he was prone to betray surprising gaps in his education. However, he spoke several foreign languages and knew a great deal of the world, though clearly he was not one bit the happier for that. Already Padre Barnaba felt almost sorry for him.

The most noticeable factor in the spiritual state of this young Thomas was definitely religious doubt, but it was doubt of the kind that borders on faith. The young fellow himself confused this with an honour complex which kept him in continual inner conflict with his environment and his work. It was as though he had put his natural conscience into a dark prison and set up in its stead, as the arbiter of his little human weaknesses, an exaggerated sense of justice.

It was not difficult to see that, in his general philosophy of life, he followed basically Christian principles though he tried to explain these away as though his soul's salvation depended on it.

But there was one really disquieting thing about the boy: he

B

seemed incapable of a spontaneous smile. The better Padre Barnaba
got to know his new friend, the more worried he became about
him. The boy probably had a sense of humour, perhaps quite a
keen one, but he certainly never showed it. One could see quite
clearly that he was doing himself a great deal of violence. He
burrowed among his books like a treasure-hunter, and when it was
time to close the library in the evening he had to be actually
wakened up to consciousness of his surroundings. This was not
normal industriousness – it was sheer obsession. Padre Barnaba
decided that he really must intervene.

He found Thomas seated at his library table, which was covered
with dusty volumes.

" Well, what are you reading now? " he enquired, as if he were
asking a schoolboy about his lessons.

The young man looked up furtively from between his stacks
of books for all the world like a terrier peeping out of a fox-hole.
" I'm engaged on a special study," he replied.

" El Greco? "

" No, on religious art in Italy, or to be more exact, on the
Eucharistic motif in Italian art."

A flicker which might have been involuntary alarm came into
the priest's eyes. " That sounds rather complicated," he remarked.

" There's plenty of material at hand," explained Thomas, " but
it's the choice which is difficult. Of course everyone knows the
great Last Supper pictures from Leonardo da Vinci to Tintoretto.
But there are also other pictures, very interesting representations
of the Sacrifice of the Mass. The vision of Gregory the Great
inspired Fra Angelico, Borgognone and Sacchi. There's Paolo
Uccello's painting of the story of the desecrated host in Urbino,
also Simone Martini's painting in Assisi of a famous episode from
the life of Saint Martin. On the façade of the Cathedral in Florence
there's that fascinating bas-relief of the priest holding the Host
at the moment of the consecration. And of course there are the
Stanza of Raphael in the Vatican. Outside of Italy, too, quite a
number of painters have treated the subject of the Sacrament –
van der Weyden, Dürer and Rubens, to name but a few. Then, as
regards El Greco . . ."

But this flood of information did not impress Padre Barnaba. "Most distinguished names," he admitted, not without an effort, "but they don't say very much to me."

"Of course the names are not what matter," continued Thomas indulgently. "Actually, I'm looking for artists who have depicted the Eucharist as concrete reality. What I require most of all is documentary material, if such exists."

Padre Barnaba glanced absently over the titles of the stacks of books on the table. He shook his head thoughtfully but made no answer.

"I don't wonder you shake your head," said the young man. "I know well that I'm sitting here playing about with non-essentials instead of seeking the essential thing."

"I'm afraid you will not find any original in this library," said Padre Barnaba.

"El Greco came very close to the original, didn't he? Perhaps you could recall something about it, Padre Barnaba. . . ? "

"How could I do that? " asked the priest, astonished. The hint of hidden reproach in the other's voice had not escaped him.

"You were the last person who saw the picture, were you not? Therefore, you must know more about it than anybody else ! "

A glimmer of antagonism had come into the eyes of the young man. Wounded dogs often try to bite the hands of those who want to help them, thought the priest. His first impulse was to take the youth firmly by the arm and lead him down to the church, and there, before the altar of the Blessed Sacrament, bid him think over his own words. But one might as well take a blind man out to look at the sunset.

"The best place to study the Eucharist is in a church," he said, "but it's difficult to understand it without personal experience of the Most Holy Sacrament."

"Thank you for being so frank with me," said Thomas bitterly. "For a moment I had thought, in my simplicity, that I knew your Church, for I have studied it from various angles. But now I see that I have been wrong. No admission for unauthorized persons."

The old priest groaned inaudibly. The discussion was getting nearer and nearer to the kind of subjects he disliked touching on outside of the confessional. "Really, that can hardly be called art history," he remarked.

"No, it certainly isn't, but I have stumbled upon a metaphysical problem behind a purely aesthetical matter. Now I am trying first of all to reduce the equation, so to speak. But such a mathematical operation is not possible without coming upon the unknown third factor which is always present when two like-minded persons come together, isn't that so?" With a little forced laugh he continued: "But I'm not wanting to be initiated into any mysteries which are not for outsiders. I would like to know only how one should set about treating of this unknown third factor in a work of scholarship, if only as an algebraical symbol. It was really to find an answer to this problem that I came to Santa Presenza."

Padre Barnaba looked around the room for some helpful inspiration. He had served the Blessed Sacrament all his life without question or explanation, and here came this young pagan coolly demanding that he should embark on an academic discussion of it. He stood up, went over to one of the bookcases, and came back with a little volume in his hand – a popular selection of the writings of Saint Augustine.

"Well, here's one answer at any rate," he said, opening the book at a page which was already marked with a faded silk ribbon, and pointing to a passage: *Non intratur in veritatem, nisi per caritatem.*

"There is no way to the truth except through love," read Thomas.

"I do not know what *caritas* is called in your language, Doctor Cinnelius," said the priest, "but as far as I can understand, you are really looking for a synonym of this word for your scholarly treatise. Hence it may be as well for you to know that even Augustine himself could see no other way to the truth except through what we call love. I do not think that you will find a greater truth than this in the whole library of Santa Presenza. And I'm afraid that there's really no use in discussing the Eucharist until you have learned this lesson, my son."

"How are you, Doctor Cinnelius? You look awfully tired!" said the little porter in his glass-encased booth, as Thomas passed through. The kindly old man followed the goings and comings of every reader with fatherly interest.

"Oh, I've only a bit of a headache," muttered Thomas.

"Yes, you work too hard, you know. In Rome we have to take life quietly, *adagio, adagio.* In our climate the body won't put up with being driven – or the soul either."

And while Thomas was entering his name in the register the porter continued roguishly: "Yes, indeed, that's the way! God didn't create hurry. Do you know how they say that in Latin?"

"*Festina lente,*" suggested Thomas, but the old man shook his head emphatically and, leaning out of his box with a sly twinkle in his eye, he reeled off triumphantly a tag which some joker had evidently taught him: "*Roma sedendo vincit.*"

Thomas smiled wanly and hurried through into the catalogue hall with its dull green metal filing cabinets. He took down a few catalogue numbers and, hoping to avoid any more remarks about his sickly appearance, handed his order to the librarian without a word. The big tables in the reading-room were almost all fully occupied, but at last he found a vacant place by a half-open window, and sat down to wait for the books he had asked for.

Many familiar sounds reached his ears from outside – the murmur of the fountain, the crunching of the sand under the passing cars, the half-whispers of some students who were enjoying a smoke and a rest on the steps, and German words of command from the officer of a troop of Swiss Guards drilling somewhere in the distance. Below the window lay the largest inner courtyard of the Vatican, and opposite the oldest papal palace reared its irregular façade, grey and forbidding-looking as a steep mountain wall. A few galleries ran round the top, directly under the parapet. The whole edifice gave the impression of a sombre foothill behind which Saint Peter's, the central massif, as it were, of this mountain range, reared its sunlit dome, dominating the whole. The Vatican was not only a palace, it was a little self-contained State as teeming with life as an ant-hill.

The vast reading-room was an airy Renaissance hall with brightly-coloured grotesques on the vaulted ceilings, and tall windows that flooded it with light. Scholars were working at the long tables. There were prelates from the Curia and teachers from the papal institutes, foreign scholars and Italian university professors, sandalled Capuchins, close-cropped Benedictines, portly Dominicans, Jesuits in their long buttoned-up soutanes, and nuns in white head-dresses. A few young students were searching through the treasures of the reference library, and up in the gallery a picturesque figure – a white-robed Carmelite Father – stood immersed in an immense volume that he was holding propped against the balustrade.

From time to time some higher official of the library emerged from amid the labyrinth of book-shelves – the Prefect, a Spaniard, rotund, blue-eyed, and rosy-cheeked, in his severe black Benedictine habit; the stout little Prefect of the Archives with his gold-mounted pince-nez, beaming with fatherly benevolence on all the young disciples of learning; or the Cardinal-Librarian, the simplest of the lot, with his plain soutane, long grey beard, and expression of innocent wonder – a modern hermit in a forest of seven hundred thousand volumes of which none knew the secrets better than he.

A bald Benedictine Father, who was sitting opposite Thomas, gave him a friendly nod. He was a rugged, thick-set man with a mighty cranium and a flaming red face which was further accentuated by a chronic flush around the temples. Dom Andrea Macdonald, a Scotsman by birth, was an antiquarian and archaeologist, and had made a name for himself as an authority on the Last Supper in art. Some years back he had been appointed to Sant' Eusebio in Casaletto, a special institute for conducting research on the Catacombs, established by Pius XI in the Campagna a few miles due south of Rome.

From another table two brown pepper-corn eyes, surmounted

by a thick mop of black hair, twinkled at Thomas. They belonged to Dr Samuel Mach, an authority of international repute on Catholic sociology. He had been obliged to leave Germany because of his Jewish ancestry and he now led the peaceful life of a scholar in the shadow of Saint Peter's, making no attempt at all to exploit the rank of monsignor which his distinguished services to the Church had earned him.

Both these men of learning had lent a helping hand to Thomas in his studies from time to time, but in his present state he did not dare to come to them with his problems. He just sat there surreptitiously eyeing Dom Andrea's knit brows and Dr Mach's long overgrown tonsure. What did these two really think about the mystery of the Eucharist?

His eyes wandered over the long lines of silent readers. There was the Norwegian Dominican who was working on his thesis in moral theology; the little Chinese monsignor who was studying aesthetics; the dark-skinned Brazilian art historian, an expert on Roman Baroque, and the Swiss Jesuit who specialized in the critical study of cultural problems. Of course Thomas was already used to working in their company; he had exchanged a few words with every one of them at one time or another, and he thought he knew them all. Nevertheless he could not put a single one of the questions that were burning his soul to any one of these men. A suspicion bordering on certainty told him that the answers he would get from all of them would simply amount to a personal variant of Padre Barnaba's quotation from Saint Augustine.

Have I no right of domicile here? he thought bitterly. And from the living his thoughts groped out yearningly to the dead. It was strange how the barriers of time seemed to fall away when one lost oneself among the bookshelves and their occupants. A mighty discussion, which spanned hundreds of years, was going on within these myriads of pages. One had only to listen to the multifarious voices.

Taken all together, these men who surrounded him represented an enormous body of learning. Thomas had only to formulate the questions he wanted to put to them. But he suddenly discovered that he no longer had any desire to learn what they knew. What he wanted was to know what they believed – not their official profession of faith, but their personal witness as philosophers, historians or artists. But it seemed to him that they had all kept silence on just this one point. Or was it that one who did not share their faith could not understand their language either. . . ?

Padre Barnaba's parting words rang in his subconscious mind. But now they spoke a new language. . . .

Thomas's father had been a teacher of mathematics – for him mathematics were a matter of faith – and he had passed on his modest experience of life to his only son in somewhat the same way that he explained to his pupils the simpler physical associations. On more intimate questions he remained silent. It was not customary for men to speak of these things.

Thomas's clearest recollection of his mother was her loud voice, which she had never really tried to tone down to the suppressed atmosphere of the home. There was often an undertone of desperation in it, for instance when she tried in vain to convince her husband that man does not live by bread alone. The immediate occasion was usually some unnecessary purchase that had aroused his moral disapproval. And when she had had her say he always answered in his timid, somewhat asthmatic voice:

"I'm afraid, my dear, that that was a very foolish purchase of yours. It's mere rubbish ! "

And equally inevitably the tremulous voice of his mother answered: "But I think it's so pretty, Nicholas ! "

To this his father would reply only with a tolerant little laugh which left the small son with the impression that his mother had said something very silly.

After her death the temperature of the home had dropped almost to zero. The son grew up in a world of purely practical things, the sheer weight of which threatened to crush him. The one exception was a sentimentalized painting of Mary Magdalen by some unknown master of the Venetian School which hung in the drawing-room. It was a strange and entirely superfluous heirloom that seemed reprehensibly akin to luxury. When Thomas grew older he sometimes imagined there was some mystery behind the beautiful sinner, but his father ignored her existence completely. One day, however, the boy picked up courage and asked his father where the picture had come from.

"It's from your mother's home," answered Professor Cinnelius. "She loved it more than anything else in the world."

This was the first time that Thomas had heard the word "love" used in a profane connection. He felt almost embarrassed. Obviously, then, what it was not right to say about people could be said about paintings. From that moment onwards he regarded the shrinking penitent figure on the drawing-room wall almost as though a living person were behind it. And even as an adult he still retained the tendency to look for some life-mystery behind every work of art that he came across.

He felt a hand on his shoulder. "So you're here again? Welcome back!"

Behind him stood a handsome, distinguished-looking elderly prelate with the air of a man of the world. He was Monsignor Szarnicki, a former Polish diplomat who had become a priest late in life. He was now an archivist in the Papal Secretariat of State but devoted two hours each day to his researches on the missionary history of the Baltic countries.

He had always shown an interest in the work of his "young Finnish colleague", in the Vatican Library. "You know, we're almost compatriots," he sometimes said. "Our forefathers had much in common in the past – more than people think. . . ."

It was not only their forefathers. Thomas's one real friend at school had been a boy of mixed Polish and Russian parentage who had been cast ashore at Wiborg by the storm of revolution. His name was Boris and, on leaving school, he had gone to America and so dropped out of Thomas's life. But before doing so he had been able to do more for his friend than anyone except his mother had ever done. For he had opened Thomas's eyes to a world outside the walls of the old Swedish-Finnish fortress town – a world inhabited by people who thought and believed differently, a world suffused with a more genial light than that which fell from the cold wintry skies of the North.

Boris had often spoken of a famous uncle who had become a

Catholic priest and who used to send him books and picture postcards from Rome. It later turned out that this uncle and Monsignor Szarnicki were identical. The Polish prelate was obviously pleased when he learned of the coincidence, and whenever he referred to it his eyes shone with affection for the nephew far away in America.

Now Thomas looked up embarrassed. He still felt a little unsure of himself in the Polish priest's company, for he had never really succeeded in obliterating from his mind's eye the halo with which Boris had invested his famous uncle.

"Were you away?" asked Monsignor Szarnicki.

Thomas shook his head. "No, I've only been consulting another library," he murmured; then, with exaggerated nonchalance, "It was in an old dilapidated monastery – Santa Presenza," he added.

"Santa Presenza! What on earth brought you there? I've never been in the monastery library, but there's a very ancient Madonna in the church. Very rare indeed – of Byzantine origin. I have found traces of the same one in Eastern Europe. . . ." And he looked at the young Finn enquiringly.

"I don't think I've seen it," replied Thomas somewhat shortly. "Madonnas are not in my line."

"They're one of my little weaknesses," said Monsignor Szarnicki. "But tell me, *cher ami*, how is your own research going? Were you looking for anything special in Santa Presenza?"

"No," answered Thomas; then, seeing the other's face clouding at the brusqueness of his tone, he added with a feeble attempt at jocularity: "Perhaps one might say, for the philosopher's stone."

Monsignor Szarnicki straightened his pince-nez. "*Comment?*"

Thomas flushed. The Pole looked at him intently. "Are such stones still to be found today?" he asked.

"I had hoped so. But doubtless one must first believe in them oneself."

The clever eyes of the prelate became a shade more intent. "I do hope you have not been meeting with any difficulties?" he asked.

Thomas shrugged his shoulders. "Perhaps I am too lacking in faith," he said.

Monsignor Szarnicki seemed not to know quite what he was
driving at. Bending down, he laid his hands on the younger man's
shoulders. "If I can be of any help to you, do please let me
know," he said. "You're studying religious art, are you not? "

Thomas swallowed hard. "You're very kind. Yes, that's what
I'm supposed to be doing," he replied in a distraught tone, "but
God only knows what I'm really looking for."

Monsignor Szarnicki stared at the thick copybooks crammed
with notes which were lying on the table. "*Tiens!* What on earth
are you making all those notes about? "

Thomas looked up at him with a comical expression of desperation. "I imagined I could piece together a whole, somewhat as
one does a jigsaw puzzle. But I cannot achieve any pattern."

The other smiled, but the touch of compassion in his smile
made it less pleasing to Thomas than it might have been. "I'm
afraid you are making far too high demands on your scholarship,"
he said.

"But surely that's a fault in the right direction? "

The conversation was beginning to disturb the readers. Monsignor Szarnicki patted Thomas encouragingly on the shoulder
once more, then moved off to his own table, where a stack of thick
volumes awaited him. Making a discreet sign of the cross, he
opened them and became immersed in his studies, all with a
natural harmony of deportment and an expression reminiscent
of a Canova sculpture. Thomas's eyes followed the old diplomat
with envy. He did not feel that he himself would ever achieve this
perfect balance, even in his work.

Once more he found himself overcome with a sense of strange-
ness. People and books turned their backs on him. In his youth
he had read somewhere in the works of a German Philosopher –
probably Hegel – that Minerva's owl only takes to the wing when
twilight falls. His quest for the mystery of art certainly had not
led him to the friendly stars and smiling landscapes dreamed of
by so many of the great masters. If his work was to bring him
to a Golgotha like this, he would never have the courage to be a
witness to the truth. To make a sacrifice one must have faith, but
works of art did not seem to bring him to this faith.

A library attendant carrying an armful of books came quietly up to the table. "*Il dottore* ordered these books, did he not?"

"Oh, yes, I did!" murmured Thomas absently.

"They have been lying on the delivery counter for the past hour," said the man. "Aren't they the ones you wanted?"

Thomas stared vaguely at the titles of the books. "Yes, that's all right, thank you," he said.

He opened the books and started scanning them. Why had he ordered them? He could see nothing but words, words, a whole sea of words, but never an answer to his questions. At least not until, following up some trivial clue, he stumbled on a quotation from the First Epistle to the Corinthians: "And though I have the gift of prophecy, and understand all mysteries, and all knowledge; and though I have all faith, so that I could remove mountains, and have not charity, I am nothing."

Once more his eyes wandered over the long rows of silent scholars at their tables. There was something very special about most of these people working here. They were not only diligent and learned and in some cases magnificent scholars. They were more than this – they were happy men. They prayed and they worked, and obviously they did both with the utmost devotion. A person who came here merely to collect sterile notes, on the other hand, was a pitiable adventurer without the real rights of a citizen in this Christian republic of the spirit. The hidden power which was capable of reconciling faith and knowledge – this was what he lacked.

❧

III SOR ANACLETO'S OSTERIA

Every morning at eight o'clock sharp Sor Anacleto, who kept a little *osteria* at the corner of the Piazza del Pecore, trotted across the street with a jug of coffee and a roll to the parish priest, and just as regularly Padre Barnaba was to be seen crossing over to the *osteria* as darkness fell. Every evening Sor Anacleto was in the habit of setting a few tables outside his café, facing the market square. Padre Barnaba sat at one of these and sipped his quarter of a litre of cheap wine. There, for half an hour or so, he chatted with the people on the piazza as peacefully as any village pastor, while the odours of wine and roast meat flowed out of the open door of the *osteria*.

Sor Anacleto was a genial Neapolitan with a squinting, dog-like expression of face and a drooping moustache. His restaurant consisted of two rooms with bare unpainted tables, and dreadful coloured prints on the walls. But this was just what his customers liked. On festive occasions he could produce dishes of roast lamb and artichokes that could bear comparison with the tasty menus of the celebrated restaurants in the near-by Jewish quarter. The art of serving his fellow-men with good food was natural to him and the fact that his fame had not spread all over Rome was solely due to his many other interests.

Actually, he ruled the Piazza delle Pecore like a little tribune of the people. After Santa Presenza had been dissolved he had succeeded in gaining a foothold within the old monastery walls as well. His wife, Sora Michela, took over the housekeeping for the one remaining priest, Padre Barnaba, and he himself officiated as sacristan and Mass server as required. In short, he became Padre Barnaba's right hand in all practical matters. Sarcastic tongues asserted that, if only it were permitted, in a pinch he could also carry out the other duties of a parish priest. Anyhow, he dispensed religious instruction lavishly all round, and knew at least as much of everything bad that went on in the parish as any father confessor. He operated, in addition, as a private money-lender and was said to be an adept at getting back his money with due interest. In spite of all this he was a good Christian personally and thoroughly enjoyed his role of number one pillar of the parish church.

One evening in May, as Padre Barnaba was sitting at his usual table outside the *osteria*, Sor Anacleto nudged him discreetly, saying: "Look who's coming, Father!"

Thomas Cinnelius, looking more forlorn than ever, was walking across the piazza.

"My! Isn't he a sight!" cried the innkeeper. "Anyone would think he had slept in his clothes this last week. And look at his shoes! What would his poor mother say if she saw him now?"

"Sometimes I wonder if he ever had a mother," murmured Padre Barnaba. "Anyhow, there's one thing she never taught him – to laugh!"

As Thomas passed by the *osteria* he nodded stiffly and showed no sign of stopping, but Padre Barnaba beckoned to him in a friendly way.

"Who are you looking for?" asked the priest. "Is there anything I can do for you?"

"Oh, no, thank you, Father. I only came over to have a look at the Byzantine Madonna I hear you have in your church," said Thomas. He tried hard to sound casual, but the excuse was so obviously invented that he flushed hotly as he spoke.

Once more Padre Barnaba was struck by the young man's resemblance to a dog without a master. The poor young pup had apparently been thrown out on the street again. He looked starved and the worse for sleepless nights.

"The Madonna is only taken out on festive occasions, so what about sitting down and having a glass of wine with me instead?" suggested the priest.

Sor Anacleto bustled along with a glass and Padre Barnaba filled it from his own small carafe. "It's not a particularly good wine," he continued, "but all the same it's the best and healthiest drink the good God has given us – next to spring water, of course." And, leaning back in his chair, he took a long pull at his chicory-black Tuscan cigar.

"Thomas . . . ?" he said thoughtfully. "I suppose that's the same as Tommaso?"

"Yes, indeed, Padre Barnaba," answered Thomas, showing no surprise at the unaccustomed form of address.

"*Ecco Tommaso*," said the priest, raising his glass and smiling, "I'm glad to see you again."

Thomas flushed to the roots of his hair. "It's very kind of you to say so," he murmured.

But Padre Barnaba's eyes remained fixed on him. "By the way, do you believe in the Madonna? " he asked in the same friendly way.

Thomas looked up with a defiant gleam in his eyes. " Unfortunately she only interests me in my capacity of art historian," he said.

Padre Barnaba looked away but it was impossible to say whether he was hurt or only slightly nonplussed.

" She it was who took the Divine Love in her own arms," he remarked with assumed casualness.

Thomas remained silent.

" She is our greatest witness for the faith. To no other being was our Lord so near in this life."

" I have read all that."

Padre Barnaba stole a glance at the dark rings round the young eyes, and shook his head. " My dear Tommaso," he said, " I really think you should lay aside your books for a while and try to digest what you've been reading. Allow yourself a little rest like other people."

The young man shrugged his shoulders. " What would I do with myself? " he asked.

" Well, what about going into the country somewhere and having plenty of sleep and rest, instead of running round the churches of Rome looking at pictures of things which, after all, you don't even believe in? "

" Where do you think I should go? "

" There are lots and lots of lovely places," said Padre Barnaba, standing up to go. " You have only to choose."

" Sunsets don't interest me."

Padre Barnaba looked at him, amused. " Going to bed early would be good for you too. But I think a few days climbing in the mountains would be best of all," he said.

" I'm not accustomed to mountains."

" Then why not go to the seaside? " replied the priest. " Well, I have to go now. Let me know when you're back. Good-bye, Tommaso ! "

Sor Anacleto looked after him with an expression of dog-like devotion. " *Simpaticone!* " he murmured.

"Yes, he's awfully nice," agreed Thomas politely.

"Do you know, he's like a father to our whole quarter," continued the innkeeper. "Helpful and kind as a saint, he is."

"I quite believe you," Thomas assured him, but his enthusiasm was several degrees cooler than Sor Anacleto's. The latter saw that he would have to touch other chords if he were to awaken an echo in the unresponsive heart of the foreigner.

"And he's one of the most learned men in Rome besides," he remarked.

Thomas reacted immediately. "What's that you say?" he asked.

"*Sissignore, dottissimo,*" continued Sor Anacleto triumphantly. "He's quite amazingly learned.

The young fellow's blue eyes, those uncannily blue eyes, gazed at the innkeeper, full of astonishment. "Pray what is his subject?" he asked.

"His subject?" repeated the innkeeper uncertainly. "Why, books, of course! He has read an enormous number of them, not only in Italian but also in Latin and French, they say. You have seen the library yourself, haven't you? And all the books that are in it! They are all his subject, you may say."

"He must have been here a long time?"

"Yes, it's going on thirty years since he came to the monastery. I was little more than a child then. The Brothers of Santa Presenza died off one after another. Padre Barnaba alone has remained behind. And now he has really become like one of ourselves here in the Vicolo dei Pecorai. But, as I have said, he's a holy man, and people never know how long they will be allowed to keep one like him in their midst . . . *Momento!*"

He disappeared with a nod, only to reappear the next moment with a fresh jug of wine. "It's a great honour to see Padre Barnaba's friends in my place. Allow me to offer you a glass of wine. *Alla sua salute!*"

"Thank you," answered Thomas shyly, "and to yours. I'm really very pleased to have met Padre Barnaba."

"You have every reason to be. There are not many of his kind about nowadays. There he sits, all alone in his monastery, but he never complains. He lives for others and he's ready to do anything for those who need him. And that's a good many, in this poverty-stricken quarter. Believe me, Padre Barnaba has helped many a soul into heaven from his old monastery – I mean the poorhouse. And I can tell you it's not only God's best children who live hereabouts. But Padre Barnaba never spares himself. If it comes to that, he'd go through fire for . . ."

Seeing the astonished expression returning to the young man's eyes, Sor Anacleto went on quickly: "You can take my word for that because there really was a fire here some years back. If Padre Barnaba hadn't been there I can tell you it would look very different here today. The community was still there in those days, but they weren't up to much. Actually, Padre Barnaba was the only one who was fit for anything – the only able-bodied man in two old men's homes – the monastery, where he lived himself, and the poorhouse adjoining. And you see, it was just in the wall between the two that the fire broke out. Well, that night Padre Barnaba risked his life many times over. . . ."

"I seem to have heard something about it," said Thomas hesitantly, "but I had no idea it was as bad as that."

"It's only thanks to him that it wasn't as dangerous as it might have been. When the fire broke out it looked as if most of the monastery would be destroyed before the fire brigade arrived, because there were a couple of lumber-rooms on the ground floor near the refectory, and they had been crammed to the ceilings with junk for donkeys' years. All that stuff burned like paper, you can understand, and the fire threatened to spread on all sides, but Padre Barnaba succeeded in hemming it in. So in the end only the old lumber rooms were destroyed, and a little chapel beside the refectory."

"Could nothing be saved from the chapel, then?"

"Nothing – except of course the *Santissimo*."

"The Most Holy? Do you mean the altar-piece?"

"No, not that. I mean the Sacred Host itself."

"The Host was saved," repeated Thomas, knitting his brows. "So that means that it was possible to get into the chapel?"

"Padre Barnaba forced his way in but when he opened the

door the flames beat out against him from the burning lumber-room, which was collapsing, and he couldn't see his hand in front of him for smoke. But he knew exactly where the altar was, of course, so he made straight for it, took out the Sacrament, and rushed out again. And he was just able to slam the door behind him against the flames. So the refectory was saved."

Thomas seemed to find the story difficult to follow. "You don't mean to say," he said slowly, as if he were dictating a police report, "that Padre Barnaba was in the burning chapel and actually standing before the altar, but instead of saving El Greco's picture Il Santissimo, he allowed it to be destroyed in the fire?"

Sor Anacleto shook his head. "How could he have taken both at the same time, the Host and the picture? And of course it was quite impossible to get into the chapel again because, you see, he had shut the flames in there."

"But he could have saved the picture if he had wanted to . . ." persisted Thomas.

"Haven't I been trying to explain to you that he couldn't?" replied Sor Anacleto.

"He had the choice of saving either the Host or the picture."

"Choice. . . ? He hadn't any choice."

"No?"

Sor Anacleto could not suppress a smile. "But would anyone seriously hesitate between the Most Holy Sacrament and its representation by a human hand?" he asked.

"What's that you say? Pardon. . . ?"

Suddenly the innkeeper got a bright idea. "Momentino!" he said. Then with a gentle, paternal air he sat down at Thomas's table and began delving in his pockets. At last he drew from somewhere in the region of his heart a worn little prayer-book, and from the prayer-book a memoriam card yellow with age with a faded photograph of an old woman on it.

"Ecco la Mamma!" he said, and when the other did not understand at once, he added apologetically: "It's the only photo of my mother I possess. I'm sure you have a much nicer picture of your mother, perhaps even a real oil painting!"

"What a beautiful face!" murmured Thomas, completely bewildered.

"Yes, she was a lovely woman right enough, even in her old age," said Sor Anacleto solemnly. "I'm glad I have this little photo of her, but of course it's no substitute for my mother herself, if you understand what I mean?"

"Well, to be quite candid, I don't. I feel you're trying to get round the question."

"What do you mean? I'm trying, on the contrary, to make you see it from the only right side," replied Sor Anacleto with an almost affronted air.

"Please let us not dispute about religious matters," Thomas said. "I only think you're a little unjust to the picture as such. It was a work of art of inestimable value."

"I don't know anything about that. Didn't you ask the Bulgarian what it cost?"

"Whom?"

"Well, the Greek or whatever he was, who painted the picture? He should know what it was worth."

"He's dead long ago. But I think he would have been very angry with Padre Barnaba if he had heard what happened."

"I can believe that. It's certainly not pleasant to hear that something you made with your own hands has been burned. But the poor fellow was a Christian, wasn't he?"

"Yes, a very devout Catholic as far as I know," said Thomas a trifle acidly.

"Oh, well, then he would have calmed down when he had really considered the matter properly," said Sor Anacleto nodding.

Thomas looked up. "Surely you don't mean to say that El Greco himself would have approved of what Padre Barnaba did?" he asked.

A few newly arrived customers beckoned to Sor Anacleto, who grabbed his napkin and stood up.

"I'm only a simple innkeeper, Doctor," he said, as he wiped a little spilt wine off the table, "but if that Greek was really a devout man and sincere about what he painted, he would most certainly have acted just as Padre Barnaba did."

Thomas would have liked to protest that at least one Host was consecrated in every Catholic church every morning, whereas the painting was absolutely unique and irreplaceable. But when he himself looked for a suitable analogy he could only think of the story of how angry Judas was with Mary Magdalen for using a whole pound of costly ointment to anoint the feet of her Lord and Master.

IV SANTA CRISTINA

The May sun, blazing down on Bolsena, was parching the dusty vineyards and olive plantations on the shadeless hillsides and driving swarms of humming insects into the little town from the gardens and fields. In the narrow streets it was oppressively hot. Only on the shores of the lake a light morning breeze was still blowing. Like the breath of a sleeper it passed through the green barrier of plane trees behind which the huge inland sea shimmered in opalescent calm. The heat had already begun to obscure the clear blue of the sky, and a milk-white haze, which irritated the eyes with its uncertain light, lay over the quiet glistening waters.

The holiday season had not yet really begun. Only one solitary visitor was walking up and down on the strand promenade. He was a young man of exceedingly gentlemanly, in fact elegant appearance. But obviously he was intent on avoiding rather than impressing his fellow-beings. Anyone who chanced to speak to him met a pair of shy blue eyes that betrayed the torture of many headaches.

"What a Pinocchio!" the little housemaid had sighed when the foreigner had left his room in the morning. "He's so wooden, his father must have been a furniture-maker!"

"Perhaps he'll have warmed up a bit by lunch," said Signora Angela, the proprietress of the little *pensione*. "And he's sure to be back early because he's bored stiff."

Signora Angela was a motherly soul in the fifties, and she really cared about the spiritual and physical well-being of her guests. Her small but pleasant guest house was much appreciated by priests and other people of sober habits. Her ability to sum up her guests was not particularly shrewd but quite adequate. In the case of the well-dressed young foreigner her prognosis proved correct. After an hour he was back again, exhausted and yawning, in Signora Angela's little garden.

"Have you been to our little church yet, Doctor Cinnelio?" she enquired pleasantly.

"Not yet," he replied, looking slightly annoyed.

"In your place I would have done that first thing. It's really well worth a visit, but naturally, as a student of such matters you must know that better than I do."

"To tell the truth I came here only to rest."

But Signora Angela chattered away undaunted. "All the more reason to go there. You won't find a more peaceful spot in all Bolsena than the church. When you go in you feel yourself lifted into another and a better world. It's almost like visiting some dear old friends in heaven. Most of our guests visit our own dear little Cristina first thing. . . ."

"Cristina – who's that?"

"Santa Cristina, our brightest ray of sunshine."

"Do you mean the saint?"

"Yes, of course. The whole town adores her. Little Cristina is still living among us today, as it were, though you would have to live here for a time to understand that properly. But you should come here on the 24th of July, Doctor. Then you would see the whole town turning out to honour her."

"That's very interesting."

"Little places like Bolsena haven't so much to take pride in," continued Signora Angela eagerly. "That's why it means such a lot to them to have a saint of their very own, as you can understand. Little Cristina is mother, sister and daughter to us, all at the same time. I couldn't imagine Bolsena without her." And she sniffed, so deeply moved was she by her own eloquence. "You mustn't be surprised because I stand here preaching to you as if I were a priest," she continued, "but if you had a *pensione*, as I have, and saw how people stream here from far and near day after day, all on account of that blessed young girl, her image would become imprinted on your heart. I can only tell you this: the greatest treasure a little town can possess is its own saint. That's the only thing that makes it different from a rabbit farm!"

"Your guest-house should really have a saint of its own," said Thomas ironically, but Signora Angela was far too much carried away by her own enthusiasm to be offended.

"Santa Cristina has time for my guests too," she said.

Thomas stood up with a sigh. "Well, I might as well go and look at the church," he said. "It's not far."

"Just a few steps, and good luck to you! When do you want your lunch?"

"I'll let you know later, if you don't mind."

"A nice plate of hot soup will certainly do you good after visiting the crypt. And the fish today is particularly good, a speciality of Bolsena. The wine . . ."

"No alcohol, please."

"But Doctor Cinnelio," she protested good-humouredly, "Santa Cristina never grudged anyone a glass of wine. And when you have been down there a while . . ."

But her visitor was already on the way to the church. He did not want to listen to any more panegyrics on the little daughter of a Roman officer who, he had read somewhere, had died for her faith in this town towards the end of the third century. As an historical personality she was almost unknown and even her mortal remains had been taken away somewhere else. Moreover, a wild crop of popular myths had overgrown her authentic legend; the genuine core was only a tradition more than seventeen centuries old which had found a fruitful soil in the popular soul and had kept the cult of the little martyr alive.

Though the façade of the church left Thomas cold he automatically took out his sketching pad as he entered. Wiping away the perspiration standing out in drops on his forehead, he made straight for the chapel of the saint. Struggling against an attack of cold shivers, he went down to a cellar-like crypt hollowed out of limestone rock and forming a kind of ante-room to the cata-

combs which lay behind. A deep niche in the rear wall contained
the former burial-place of the saint. He recalled that a terracotta
figure by Della Robbia and the remnants of an ancient sarcophagus were to be found beneath the modern monument, but he
did not get as far as investigating these.

On the immediate right of the entrance to the alcove he saw
an old worn stone table surmounted by a Carolingian baldachin,
shaped like a sugar-loaf and supported on ancient, austerely
chiselled columns. This was the famous Altar of the Blood. It stood
alone in the background of the crypt, dominating it with its lofty,
ancient severity. But it could just as easily be a druidical stone
which had come out of the mountain in primeval ages when
primitive man, filled with awe, had fashioned this cave as an
ante-chamber to the underworld. . . .

Here, if anywhere, miracles could happen. True, later generations had embellished the walls of the crypt with bas-reliefs and
erected gleaming marble columns and delicate wrought-iron work
around the worn podium, but these were only lifeless trappings
surrounding the mystical reality which the old stone seemed still
to enshrine. Down here in the crypt the darkness lay thick and
heavy as it had probably done on that morning nearly seven
hundred years before when—so the story went – a foreign priest
had ascended the steps of that altar to celebrate the Sacrifice of the
Mass with doubt in his heart. But when the time had come for
him to break the white bread that he had changed into the Body
of Christ by the power of his office, drops of living blood flowed
from the Host and fell down on the stone. This happened, so the
legend ran, to convince the unbelieving priest of the truth of the
real presence of his Lord and Master in the Sacrament.

According to a much-disputed tradition, this grotto had become
the cradle of one of the greatest religious revivals, in the second
thousand years of Christianity, the veneration of the Body of
Christ in the Eucharist. The recollection sent a stream of vivid
pictures flowing through Thomas's mind: sun-drenched processions; nocturnal vigils; Corpus Christi celebrations in Germany
and mystery plays in Spain; Raphael's Stanze in the Vatican, and
the Cathedral of Orvieto. And suddenly, at the end of them all,

Padre Barnaba kneeling silent and alone before the red lamp in the dark apse of San Lino's. . . .

When the old priest had given him advice that evening at Sor Anacleto's he could hardly have intended that his young friend should spend his holiday in Bolsena of all places. Thomas had made this choice himself. He might know nothing as yet of the religious experience of El Greco and his brethren in the faith, but he felt instinctively that he had found here a place where their hidden God had manifested His presence in historic times, and moreover, in such a way that a memento of His action was still visible. Thomas stared at the primitive altar as though it were a living creature, a mystically latent organism from primitive ages with a petrified heart, but a heart through which the Creator's blood had once flowed, and which could begin to beat anew at any time. He tottered. There was a buzzing in his ears. And suddenly he found himself on his knees.

He looked around him timidly to see if anyone could have noticed him and he perceived a few people kneeling on the prie-dieus in front of the saint's shrine. They were obviously waiting for a Mass to begin. He got hold of a dilapidated kneeling chair and drew it nearer to the light, then stood motionless, as if absorbed in prayer, while a small congregation gradually assembled. When the Mass server came at last to light the candles on the altar, Thomas mechanically opened a prayer-book that he found lying on the chair, and tried to decipher the text by the feeble flickering light. But the words danced before his eyes.

A quiver passed through his nerves when he heard the priest reading the opening psalm: "I will go unto the altar of God. . . ."

The ritual obliged him to kneel down again. The priest was in a hurry. He muttered the prayers in breathless haste, slurring over the final consonants in such a way that it was impossible to distinguish the words.

Thomas knelt the whole time with his face in his hands, his heart vibrating with an emotion so intense that it amounted to an almost physically painful tension. Now, if ever, he would learn to know personally that mysterious power that had forced him to his knees. . . .

The acolyte rang his bell, chairs scratched the ground, the priest knelt quickly and nimbly as a boy, then rose and raised the Host above his head. The whole congregation suddenly froze into absolute silence and immobility. Thomas waited, not daring even to breathe. The silence seemed almost uncanny. Then the bell rang again, and immediately afterwards an inaudible sigh, a perceptible release from tension, passed through the little gathering. Thomas noted with wonder that his nerves too relaxed now. Something had been surmounted. What it actually was he did not know, but he had undoubtedly become, for the first time, part of a community.

The thought filled him with satisfaction. When he saw the faithful preparing to go up to the altar to receive the Sacrament he decided spontaneously to do the same. To be sure Padre Barnaba had said that it was not permissible for those outside the Church to receive Holy Communion in a Catholic church, but it almost seemed to Thomas that he had received a personal call to do so. Formally, perhaps, he would be committing an unlawful act, but was he not doing it with God's blessing, like Jacob when he took Esau's birthright by stealth . . . ?

He stole up to the altar and took his place in the last row of devoutly waiting communicants. When he bowed his head at the Confiteor, however, his eyes fell on a block of black basalt on the topmost of the three altar steps. According to the legend, Saint Cristina had been thrown into the lake bound to this stone, and the two small footprints which were said to have remained behind when the saint was miraculously floated ashore on this stone, were still to be seen on it.

Thomas was suddenly seized with a desire to stand up and protest. What was this crude forgery doing on the steps of the altar of the miracle? How could they dare to dispense the Body of the Lord over such a phantasmagory? It cost him an intense effort to chase away his rebellious thoughts and concentrate on the reception of Communion, for the faint footprints were literally forcing themselves between him and the Sacrament. Half consciously he heard the words of absolution being pronounced from the altar. They glided past his ears as if they did not concern him personally at all. When the Host was carried down the altar steps he had to shut his eyes. Suddenly an astonished question flashed through his mind: Had the doubting priest of the altar of the miracle legend also caught sight of those confounded footprints? This idea undoubtedly opened up new perspectives. . . .

"*Deo gratias*," croaked the voice of the acolyte. "For what is he saying thanks?" thought Thomas irritably. At this he suddenly became aware that he had waited too long. He opened his eyes. The priest was up at the altar again and the communicants were all back in their places way behind in the crypt. The server answered his glance with a deprecating gesture which seemed to say: Too late!

Thomas, abashed, remained hidden in his corner while the sacristan extinguished the candles on the altar. The church emptied slowly, and he slipped out last. Only when he got into the sunshine did he notice how cold it had been down in the crypt.

The sun was at its height and almost all shadow had disappeared from the landscape. The light fell with pitiless harshness down on the lake, which was becoming bluer and bluer. The chalk-white islands, shimmering in the heat, looked as though they were rising up in the air. On the northern shore a chain of hills, silver as fairy mountains in a dream landscape, gleamed in the noonday sun.

Thomas had really meant to visit the old fortress of the town before lunch but the strong light hurt his eyes and brought back his agonizing headache, so he decided to return to the *pensione* instead. Giovanna came running from the kitchen with a napkin in her hand, but he waved her off wearily and went up to his room.

"Santa Cristina!" cried the girl. "Now he won't even eat! What am I to do with the fish . . . ?"

But Signora Angela took the matter more placidly. "Leave him alone," she said. "He belongs to a race who have camels' stomachs. It's all the same what he eats. He has only a tank in his belly. I thought as much when he said he wouldn't have wine. We'll let him lie down and sleep if he wants to."

Thomas slept for six hours and when he woke it was already evening. He had a temperature, and pains in the back of his head.

The next morning Signora Angela informed him that she had taken it on herself to send for the doctor.

"We have a very clever doctor here," she said, "a Ravenna man named Romolo. He used to have a fine practice in Rome and was very well known there, not only as a doctor but also on account of his – er – opinions. And now he's here. That's how it is these days, if you understand?"

Thomas was too ill to bother to understand. The doctor came and diagnosed a severe internal chill.

"It's nothing at all to worry about," he assured the patient. "With a rest in bed and proper diet it will be over in a few days. Most foreigners get it here sooner or later," he added reassuringly. "I take it that you're not used to our food yet."

Doctor Romolo, who was still fairly young, was obviously of humble origin. He had thick, strong hair and coarse features, and his small, close-set eyes had an expression of mingled suspicion and simplicity. For an Italian he was extraordinarily ungraceful, but his broad peasant face gave a pleasing impression of reliability and ready helpfulness.

Ill though he was, Thomas could not refrain from protesting against the diagnosis. "I've been living in Italy for a long time and there's no question of this being due to errors of diet," he said.

"Perhaps you're right," laughed Romolo. "You certainly speak far too good Italian to be the victim of a tourists' malady."

The expression of suspicion in his eyes had given way to a boyish candour – as Thomas noted with growing liking. "And now, since we can talk like two Italians, tell me what's really wrong with you," the doctor continued jocularly. "For a chill like this doesn't come without some cause. Have you really not been drinking too much iced water in the heat?"

"No, I haven't been drinking iced water at all."

"Hm! And no other vices, I take it?"

"No, I can't think of any."

"Even that can make people ill too," remarked Romolo sarcastically. And he scrutinized the patient with gay nonchalance. "By the way, what's your profession."

"Art historian."

The doctor whistled. He was an expert whistler. "Aha! So of course that means that you have been snooping and squatting about in that confounded crypt."

"Yes."

"I thought as much. It should be closed down."

"But why?"

"You can ask that!" exclaimed Romolo beginning to put away his instruments. "Do you think that you're the first case? That crypt is a veritable plague-spot."

The youthful gaiety had disappeared from his eyes and the earlier grim suspicious expression darkened them once more.

"Surely that's a bit far-fetched?" murmured Thomas.

Romolo threw him a glance over his shoulder. Now he looked like a very young, somewhat stubborn boy who had been deeply offended. "I can never make out what draws people down into that crypt," he said. "Surely there's more than enough superstition above ground. But of course one dare not say things like that aloud nowadays. . . ."

Thomas felt a healthy combativeness surging up in him. "Why not?" he asked.

Romolo threw him a meaningful sidelong glance. "So you haven't been in this country long enough after all, Doctor," he said.

Thomas sat up in bed and replied in a lecturing tone: "Naturally, I've come on a good bit of superstition, in the streets of the cities, for instance. You find that all the world over, just as you find mud or dust on the street. But it should not be allowed to propagate unnecessarily. . . ."

"That's just it!" interrupted Romolo. "And when you've been here a few years longer you'll notice how widely it has been propagated. So much so that one finds it's time to settle down in the country to preserve one's health."

He placed his arms akimbo and lowered his head as if to parry an expected attack, but when none was forthcoming, he continued in an almost lamenting tone: "I can stand anything but moral duress. I refused to become a fetish worshipper, and that's why

I'm parked here. Politics, of course! But when the clergy start to carry on their hocus-pocus underground – well, that's enough to turn Carlo Romolo anti-clerical!"

As the patient still remained silent, Romolo gradually concluded that his words had been misunderstood. So he suddenly turned back, came up to the bed, and, grasping Thomas by the hand, said with a hearty grin: "I'm a nice doctor indeed! Standing here jawing with my patient. But you know, the atmosphere here is positively poisonous. I hope you realize that my ranting was not directed in any way against you personally, in fact, the contrary. You're a man of science as I am, and it is your task as it is mine to fight superstition and ignorance. And when you actually go so far as to risk your health for your work – well, even though I'm a doctor, I can only take off my hat to you!"

He scanned Thomas's face eagerly and when he saw the shadow of a smile, sat down on the edge of the bed with an air of relief.

"Tell me, have you read Sinclair Lewis's *Arrowsmith* by any chance? Well, that's my ideal. The book is hard to come by here but I can lend it to you if you like. Besides, it's as thrilling as a detective story."

Thomas summoned up all his strength. "There's something I should really have told you before, Doctor," he said. "I don't want any misunderstanding between us, but the fact is that I caught cold simply . . ."

He hesitated. He had meant to say "during Mass", but the words stuck in his throat. What had made him want to confess this to the doctor? It had no bearing whatsoever on the medical diagnosis. "I caught cold examining certain footprints," he continued hurriedly, then sank back on his pillows.

"I understand," nodded Romolo, "and again I can only emphasize my respect for your zeal in research. But if you will allow me to advise you as a doctor, I would say that it's better not to take unnecessary risks. And don't forget to put on something warm, preferably a wool pullover, the next time you go underground. And avoid as far as possible kneeling too long on the floors of crypts and the like – it causes rheumatism and internal complaints."

Then, with a knowing wink at Thomas, he stood up. "I must go now," he said, "but I'll look in again in the afternoon – with *Arrowsmith*. He was a martyr to science too."

For quite a while after he had gone his laughter resounded from the well of the stairs and Thomas noted, with relief, that there was not a trace of malice in it.

V THE PALAZZO BRANCACCIO, 1939

Surrounded by the intoxicating luxuriance of the Roman spring-time, Felix Letterman, blond and narrow-chested, stood at his easel painting from memory a Norwegian mountain pasture. He had a predilection for subjects far removed from his surroundings. Indeed, sarcastic tongues whispered that he had made his *début* as an artist in the Eternal City standing on the Roman Forum painting an ice drift. His own explanation was that he found this practice conducive to concentration.

Letterman had settled in Italy because he could not stand the social climate in his own country. He was wont to say that all Scandinavia was a small provincial town seething with under-hand gossip, envy and spite. Down here in the South the environ-ment was more congenial to him. True, he seldom had his park bench to himself, but on the other hand, he had complete liberty to eat, love and paint just as he liked within the four square yards or so of living space which he had staked out as his private domain. And now and then, when he wanted a change, he could invite himself to the little Swedish Institute in the Via Merulana, where he was always a particularly welcome guest, for there were few Scandinavians who knew Rome, and Italy as a whole, as well as he did.

A rather stout, red-faced young man with full, curved lips and wearing a white linen suit and dark sun-glasses, came into the gardens. He was Fabian Arnesson, an archaeologist. Wiping the perspiration from his unusually high forehead, he threw himself down under a tree, puffing and panting, for a strong sirocco was blowing.

"I'm afraid the 'Church militant' has run aground," he remarked, staring glumly at the painter.

Swallows, intoxicated by the spring, were whizzing like swarms of flies over the Esquiline, but above Felix Letterman's head the air was clear as he stood there, like a scarecrow in dirty grey, with his incredible straw hat pulled down over his ears. Rumour had it that he had stolen this famous hat of his from a Calabrian peasant's donkey.

"Who's run aground?" he asked.

"Our catholicizing friend, of course. He has been in a bad way ever since he came back from Bolsena. A most peculiar malady."

"Hang-over, do you think?"

"Definitely not. Cinnelius never drinks too much. His present illness is clearly psychological in origin."

Letterman took the pipe from his mouth and pointed it disapprovingly, stem foremost, at some blatantly gorgeous roses. This was a favourite gesture of his when something irritated him.

"Your damned subtle language is a bit above my head, I'm afraid. What's that you called him?"

"The Church militant. Naturally I was thinking of his book."

"What book?"

"On the Art of the Crusades."

"What's that? Never heard of it."

"The work earned its author a scholarship," said the archaeologist, mildly surprised. "It is really outstanding, but only from a Catholic point of view."

Letterman aimed another spit at the rose bush, which seemed to be blushing with shame.

"I should have thought that even the Catholic Church fights with different weapons nowadays," he remarked.

Fabian Arnesson turned his high Olympic forehead, glowing with perspiration and wisdom, towards the painter. "Well, everyone has to seek his own salvation in his own way, and apparently that's Tommy's way," he said.

"What makes you think that?"

"He has always had very much of a mind of his own. His father's people were Karelian country parsons, his mother's were in the Smaland timber industry. Well, these two ingredients produce a very particular flavour of their own. Then, he himself grew up in old Wiborg, near enough to the Russian frontier to give his character a meditative bent. When his parents died he came to relatives in Stockholm. I got to know him at Uppsala, where he took his degree. He's a clever boy, and he has amassed quite an incredible amount of knowledge. But it's unfortunate that he was born so far out on the edge of the world. For one needs influence and money, quite a lot of money, to carry through such a colossal work of scholarship as he has embarked on. . . . But for Thomas the whole undertaking has the character of a personal pilgrimage."

Letterman laughed. It started with a feeble piping sound, somewhat like the chortle of an angry turkey-cock and ended in a series of short, convulsive cough-like sounds which came quicker and quicker, like the spluttering of an internal combustion engine.

"Oh, poppycock! You will tell me next that the Crusades were that too!"

"Don't be sarcastic. I think, actually, that the Catholic religion is getting a hold on him."

The spluttering noise started again. "At his age? Rot!"

Arnesson winced. "In this case nothing could be more natural," he said. "After all, the subject of his research is leading him straight towards Catholicism."

"Quite a useful religion for an art historian."

At this remark the placid archaeologist became perfectly furious. He sat bolt upright, pushed his sun-glasses up on his forehead and fixed the other angrily with his red-rimmed, short-sighted eyes.

"If that remark was meant to be witty, I may tell you it has misfired. As Thomas Cinnelius's friend and colleague, I must protest. I'm a Lutheran myself, and a convinced one, but I can't fail to respect his honourable ideals. He's serious about everything he goes in for, whether it's a matter of religion or scholarship."

Letterman laid down his brush and, closing one eye, viewed his canvas critically. "There's something rather standoffish about him," he remarked.

"I imagine he has had none too easy a time so far in his life," continued Arnesson. "His relatives don't seem to have much sympathy with his pursuits. You know, we Scandinavians are a frightfully conventional lot, and in certain circles it's considered not quite the thing even to discuss art. And as for choosing it for a career – that is utterly taboo! Moreover, as far as I know, Thomas hasn't made any real friends since he left school. He has chosen his own career quite independently, and he's ploughing a very lonely furrow."

"Of course; he's afraid people will see through him."

"What do you mean by that?" asked the archaeologist suspiciously.

Letterman began calmly filling his pipe. "Very well, if you want to know what I think, I'll tell you: I believe Cinnelius is not what he professes to be."

"What on earth do you mean?"

"A genuine art historian would never, never behave as he is doing. A genuine art historian has no greater ambition than to become a professor and mount a pedestal – I mean of course a professor's rostrum. But there's nothing farther from our young friend's mind than that, if I know him aright."

"Why, then, do you think he has chosen the study of art as a career?"

"Because he apparently confounds this bent of his with the perfectly natural craving to live among real live people and to be treated decently."

"I'm afraid I can't quite follow you."

"But you yourself said much the same thing just now – that he didn't feel very happy at home because people there are so confoundedly disagreeable towards each other."

"Now, don't try to make Thomas out a Bohemian!"

But Letterman continued to pursue his train of thought undeterred. "Our people are so damnably enlightened. They have been taught that they belong to a highly civilized race and live

D

in a just and happy State. They believe as blindly in their own superiority as the Italians believe in the Pope. And this faith so fills their whole existence that there's no room left for such primitive feelings as common or garden love of one's neighbour. I mean a free, natural sympathy for one's fellow beings."

"You're wandering rather off the subject now, aren't you?"

"No, I'm not. I'm just trying to explain to you what poor Thomas is really out for. There's something which is called *caritas* in the languages of the civilized peoples – something which makes life worth living. But in Scandinavia the State has taken over all that too. And it has come to this: that if you meet *caritas* on the street in the form of a private individual, you feel you must send for the police. Many people, like myself, choose to leave their country. Others seek refuge in art. You don't have to look for any deep theological explanations for this reaction."

"There's probably something in what you say," admitted the archaeologist reluctantly, "but Thomas's religious convictions definitely lie deeper than that."

Letterman lit his pipe. "How long have you been in Italy?" he asked.

"Four years this autumn."

"Oh, that's not so long. I've been here twenty-three years." He meant to go on talking, but his pipe claimed his undivided attention.

At last Arnesson lost patience and asked: "What do you mean by that?"

"Oh, nothing except that one has to be careful about the word Catholicism, it's so often misused. And anyway, I don't believe Cinnelius will ever become a Catholic."

As he started putting his brushes and paints away, he asked: "Which Christian warrior is Cinnelius singing the praises of at the moment?"

"Oh, an insignificant painter named El Greco."

"El Greco? But surely he doesn't come under Italian art, does he?"

"No, not directly, but possibly in his quality as master."

"Hm! Then young Cinnelius will evidently have to shift his

field of action to Spain, because there aren't any of the more important works of El Greco here in Rome."

"Oh, yes, there's one."

Letterman looked up. "Which one are you thinking of? " he asked.

"The 'Most Holy'. Isn't that the name of it? "

The painter seemed astonished. "Do you mean ' Il Santissimo'? Have you seen it? " he asked.

"No, but Tommy has often spoken of it. It's said to be one of El Greco's greatest paintings."

The painter gave an impatient snort. "'Said to be', indeed! Why, my dear fellow, anyone who has ever looked at that picture once could never speak of it in that tone. I saw it only once – that's fifteen years ago. It was simply fantastic, absolutely stunning, I tell you ! "

"I'm quite ready to believe you. Isn't it a kind of Last Supper? "

"Last Supper, indeed! It's bathed in an emerald green light which could just as well have come from the glacial depths of hell as from the groves of paradise. In the centre some figures sit round a table, but what's actually happening at the table I don't know. And apparently El Greco didn't know either, or perhaps he simply didn't want to express it. Many say that he painted that part of the picture in a kind of trance, but of course that's super-stition. And yet I, who after all am a pagan, freely admit that before I saw that picture I would have said it was not possible to convey the conception of the Sacrament in paint. There's some-thing absolutely terrifying about it, and I'm sure it has made more people realize what poor frail creatures we mortals are than all the skulls in the catacombs of Rome. . . ."

"Your eloquence almost makes me feel I'm looking at the picture," remarked Arnesson with a smile. "But they say it's very difficult to get a sight of it. Isn't there a good copy somewhere? "

"Copy! " exclaimed the painter. "No, thank God, there's not a single copy ! In that respect ' Il Santissimo' is unique. It's one of the very few inviolate virgins among all the ravished master-pieces of painting. You can buy the Mona Lisa and the Sistine Madonna in a tuppenny-halfpenny souvenir shop, but not the

Santissimo! If you want to see the picture you must go and see the original. And before you do that you had best take off your shoes and socks and confess your sins!"

Arnesson nodded. "Tommy has obviously got the idea firmly rooted in his mind that God, if indeed He exists, comes nearest to us ordinary mortals in art. He works with a passion I have never come across in a scholar before. At times I feel I'm witnessing something far beyond the normal research work of a specialist. A real wrestling of Jacob, I would call it."

"Jacob wrestling in the Via Merulana," said Letterman. "You don't know what you're talking about."

"I assure you I do. Tommy has taken it into his head to follow up and demonstrate the Divine in art, and he's going about his self-imposed task with a superhuman exactitude and method. It's as though he were trying to cordon off the whole of Christian art in the hope of tracking down God the Father Himself, in an unguarded moment, in the creation of a work of art. To tell the truth I don't know what has actually happened. He seems to have suffered a very acute disappointment. But the real root of it lives far deeper, I believe."

Letterman had become quiet and calm. "Of course it does," he said as he carefully cleaned his last paint-brush. "Young Cinnelius isn't the first case of the kind I've met in my experience. I've been expecting him to hoist the SOS flag for quite a long while past. Catholicism can prove quite a dangerous malady at his age – I mean when he discovers the first crack in his splendid monolith. That hurts most frightfully, believe me, and it hurts us Scandinavians worst of all, naturally, because we take things so seriously. Italians get over these maladies at puberty."

"Oh, keep your witticisms for more suitable subjects."

"But, my dear fellow, I'm only trying to establish why the patient is in such a bad way. How's he sleeping?"

"He's not sleeping, he's not reading, and he refuses to answer questions. Normally he gets up at six and goes off to some church, but these days he's lying in bed till eleven and then complaining of headache all day. An extremely disquieting sign for anyone who knows him."

"Oh, the malady is curable all right," said Letterman, clapping his easel together, "but it's sheer torture while it lasts. You know, I suppose, that most children's maladies can be very unpleasant for adults. The only thing one can do is to take timely precautions against a relapse."

"What do you mean by that?"

"Young Cinnelius requires an inoculation which will make him immune for the future–a moderately mild dose of Catholicism which will give him just a little touch of superiority over us dechristianized Philistines, but on no account more than his heathenish nature can bear. The after-taste can be washed away with a few litres of Frascati."

The archaeologist could not suppress an ironical smile. "My word, Felix, you surprise me! I had no idea you were so expert in the practical cure of souls."

Letterman seemed slightly disconcerted. "Of course it's all nonsense," he said contemptuously. "The main thing is to get the boy out of the house here for a while. I'll see to the rest. If I'm not greatly mistaken in the symptoms, there will soon be an end to his papistry."

Arnesson eyed him curiously. "You almost sound as though you were speaking from personal experience," he said.

Felix Letterman pushed his straw hat back on his neck and grinned up at the sun like a heathen. Then he stuck his hands in his pockets and sauntered with an easy rolling gait down the sloping paths of the Esquiline, between the waving purple of the wisteria.

"We've probably all been a trifle bitten with Catholicism in our young days," he chuckled, smiling to himself at the recollection.

⤜⤛⟊⤜⤛

VI THE VIA MARGUTTA

"Should you feel an urge to penetrate the deepest meaning of art," said Letterman a few days later with gentle sarcasm to

Thomas, "you simply must make an appearance in Lillemor's salon. We others daub or scribble, as the case may be, to the best of our poor ability, but she knows exactly how the Lord wishes it all to be done."

Lillemor Steeg was what might be called an institution within the Scandinavian colony in Rome, and as such she stood in sharp opposition to all other institutions. At the turn of the century she had already made a name for herself by her researches in the art of the Late Antique Period, and had set up her headquarters in the Eternal City, where she had since constituted herself a kind of general agency for Scandinavian cultural interests. But increasingly sharp competition had forced her to retreat in the course of time to her main line of defence. So she rented one of the best studios on the Via Margutta and opened an intellectual salon for "old Romans".

Among the "old Romans" there were several Catholics and it was already being whispered that Lillemor's salon was strongly oriented in a Catholic direction. However, this gossip seemed only to amuse the lady, who regarded it as a splendid opportunity for irritating orthodox opinion at home. In the course of time, her good relations with the Papal academies and the Vatican had gained her a certain advantage over many of her Protestant colleagues and often enabled her to be very helpful to Scandinavian scholars. She strove methodically to foster and extend her contacts with clerical social circles generally. True, she never betrayed her own confessional standpoint, but she was always highly delighted when she succeeded in luring a Catholic prelate to her salon. Letterman said that this was just collector's mania in her case, for the monsignori were actually rather rare guests in the studios of the Via Margutta.

Ten days after Thomas's return from Bolsena, Letterman had walked in on him unexpectedly. "Still lying at anchor?" he asked.

Although Doctor Romolo had told Thomas that he could resume work with due caution, the convalescent said he was still suffering from his old headaches.

"It's world-weariness," said Letterman with a knowing nod, as he seated himself on the edge of the bed, puffing his inseparable pipe, and surveyed Thomas with paternal benevolence. "I can well imagine that life must often seem bristling with problems for a Catholic philosopher of art. It's easier for us painters. But you will find a good father confessor at Lillemor's."

"I'm not a Catholic," murmured Thomas.

"Well, thank God for that. And you needn't become a regular client of Lillemor's, but you can surely pay *one* visit to her salon without giving yourself away."

The spring twilight was spreading its gradually thickening veil over the city. The Via Margutta was as deserted as a back street. An abandoned handcart stood in front of Dottoressa Steeg's steps, barring the view. The house itself looked deserted too as Letterman led his young friend up fifteen creaking steps and through a labyrinth of corridors and galleries. The two groped their way over purring cats and between hanging washing until they reached a padded door behind which could be heard a hum of voices. When it opened the noise inside was so overpowering that Thomas fell back a step.

A small angular female in a blue check wool dress and low-heeled shoes stood on the threshold. Her smoothly combed hair lay in two thin plaited coils over her ears, and a pair of gold-rimmed, very masculine-looking spectacles sat on her sharp nose. Her pepper-brown eyes scrutinized the guests with the intent expression of the short-sighted.

"Hello, Lillemor," said Letterman. "I've brought along young Cinnelius."

The insignificant appearance of the painter's companion seemed to astonish Lillemor. A warm smile suddenly suffused her somewhat supercilious face. "So this is our scholar? What a child!" she exclaimed, grasping Thomas's hand and shaking it with exaggerated camaraderie. "Welcome, Thomas Cinnelius! I had heard so much about you that I had imagined you much older."

At first glance Lillemor's salon gave the impression of a better-class antique shop. Greek ceramics, Etruscan terra-cottas, Roman statuettes, Byzantine crucifixes, Gothic miniature Madonnas,

Romanesque bas-reliefs and Renaissance medallions were crowded together on the walls or on brackets cheek by jowl with modern experimental art, folkweave tapestries and a multitude of photographs with signatures and inscriptions. A gigantic bookcase occupied one whole side of the room; at the other side was a magnificent grand piano laden with piles of the latest books and journals.

For a newcomer the sight was overpowering. Lillemor observed her young guest and seemed amused at his obvious bewilderment. Her scrutiny was at the same time a surreptitious examination which he appeared to pass satisfactorily.

"There's nothing to be scared about," she laughed. "When you're a little more at home here, you'll find your way through it. All the things you see here are mementoes of a long and full life. Later on, if you like, we can have a closer look at them all. And I want so much to hear something about you and your work. We shall certainly have a lot to say to each other. Now let me introduce you to my other guests."

She drew him behind a gigantic Roman amphora, completely covered with white shells. "Monsignor Gold is here in Rome," she whispered. "You know – the Vicar-Apostolic of Lappland. He's coming here this evening and I have invited some of the Catholics of the Scandinavian colony to meet him. So you will find more Catholics than usual here with me today. But you yourself have probably lived long enough in Rome to know how useful these contacts can be."

A group of younger people were standing around the grand piano looking through the books. One of them was a priest of indeterminable nationality but the others were obviously Scandinavians. Thomas noticed that they were all wearing a discreet white bow on their breasts. A tall freckled girl with tortoise-shell spectacles gave him a smile of recognition. Lillemor Steeg beckoned her over.

"Will you please look after our young friend here for a moment, Beata Veronica. I see that some more people have just come."

The girl walked up to Thomas with outstretched hand. She was of a decidedly masculine type and had a deep voice and a rather colourless face. "I'm awfully glad to meet you here," she said, "though of course we've seen each other often at the Hertziana, because I'm studying art history too."

Miss Hörneberg, D.Phil., had received the name of Beata at her Lutheran baptism but had chosen the name Veronica herself when she had become a Catholic in maturer years. After this she had gone her own way with unusual consistency and determination. With her short red hair, Roman nose, Hapsburg underlip, and an expression which seemed to bid defiance to any and every tyrant, there was nothing whatsoever of the weaker sex about her.

She took Thomas by the hand and drew him firmly over to the group around the piano. "There's no need to tell my friends here anything about you," she said. "We have all read your writings and are simply overcome at your ability to penetrate to the inner meaning of Catholic art even though you're not a Catholic."

Letterman, who had been watching the abduction, hastened to the rescue. "Must you tread on his tenderest corn right away?" he protested. "After all, he's not the only heretic here."

"You can keep your sarcasm to yourself, Mr. Letterman," said Beata Veronica. Then to Thomas, "This is my friend Viveca."

Something cold and clammy touched Thomas's hand. He felt as though he were grasping a jellyfish. Not a muscle reacted to the pressure of his hand. He bowed, and when he raised his head he found himself looking into two dull fish's eyes which were regarding him with a horrifying absence of expression.

"Viveca is a poet. Just now she's working on an enchanting volume of lyrical verse, and she has come over quite recently," explained Beata Veronica.

"Viveca is a genius," whispered Letterman, "but unfortunately she has always had a raw deal, not least from the Almighty. Still, she's a good-hearted creature and she has forgiven Him long ago."

Thomas tried to slip away from her with a bow, but the fish's eyes hung on to him. There was something entreating in them. The strange creature was obviously expecting something from him as she did from every fellow-being who came into her vicinity. But Beata Veronica saved him for the time.

"Come, you two have been holding hands long enough," she laughed. "You can talk things over fully later, but now I want to introduce Mr. Cinnelius to Folke Frisk, our promising young literary critic."

Thomas had never heard the name before, but he bowed respectfully to a stocky, stoutish young man, who was hardly older than himself. The famous critic gave him an embarrassed but not displeased smile. He had black fuzzy hair, a milk-white, baby complexion and a veiled, dreamy expression behind his thick spectacles.

"Folke Frisk specializes in old Church music. He's given us a wonderful course of lectures on it. And he's our President, too, by the way," explained the indefatigable Beata Veronica.

Folke Frisk cleared his throat and blushed, but found nothing to say.

"Have you a special society here, then?" asked Thomas.

"One could hardly call it a society," answered the critic in a voice as high and clear as a choirboy's. "It would be more correct to say that it's a free association of intellectual Scandinavian Catholics living in Rome. We call ourselves the Olaus Magnus Circle."

"In other words, a Catholic Students' Guild," suggested Thomas.

"Well, yes, more or less," admitted Folke Frisk with obvious reluctance. "Our chief purpose is to gather together for study and companionship with others of our way of thinking."

"What do you study?"

"Catholicism, of course. At present we're busy on the Liturgy, and our members are tremendously interested. Do you notice, Doctor Cinnelius, that all those who are taking the course wear a little ribbon in the liturgical colour of the day? Today it's white because of the feast of Pope Gregory – if you remember?"

"Were there not several Popes of that name?"

"Certainly, but only one who triumphed at Canossa."

"So that's what you mean by people of your own way of thinking?" said Thomas, trying hard to keep calm.

The critic stared at him open-mouthed. "Well, you see, we're only a small, select company here," he began uncertainly, but was interrupted by Beata Veronica, who threw herself watchfully into the breach.

"Folke is speaking only of the liturgical studies," she said, "though of course our Circle has a much more comprehensive programme. But there are so few who have received the grace."

Thomas retreated into his shell again. "That is a formidable word," he remarked frigidly.

Beata Veronica's offensive was not to be stopped. "Yes, it is a very formidable word," she repeated, fixing her verbal opponent sharply.

Thomas shrugged his shoulders. "Do you assume, then, that all intellectual Catholics are of the same way of thinking?" he asked.

"Yes, certainly. In this case, definitely so. We build on an intellectual homogeneity which no outsider can really understand. To understand us you would need to be one of us. We feel we're soldiers in Olaus Magnus's company. You should come to one of our meetings."

"But I do not fulfil the condition of being of the same mind."

"That's not really necessary. If you like our Circle, the right spirit will come of itself. One cannot expect everything at once. And when it is a matter of making the Truth one's own, one must be ready to take it in small doses, like a strong medicine. I will not say anything more about grace, since you reject the word. But if you drop your prejudices you will soon find yourself looking at life with different eyes. You go through life with no idea of the load of Protestant complexes you are dragging around with you. And they keep you from seeing the reality. You have only to open the windows and let in the sunlight. Yes, indeed, it's as simple as that."

"Staggeringly simple," remarked Thomas enigmatically.

Beata Veronica gave him a searching look. "I do hope you understand that we're not just a lot of sectarians," she said. "We're only a little group of people who are working *ad majorem*

Dei gloriam, each in his or her particular field. For we regard it as our first task to use worthily the talent we have received – I mean to enrich our knowledge and develop our capacity for thinking in keeping with the obligation imposed on us by our status as intellectuals. Isn't that clear? "

"Very clear."

"So you see, it's natural that we should wish to meet as often as we can," continued Beata Veronica almost pleadingly. "For after all, we have most to say when we're among ourselves. We come eventually to love our Circle as a soldier loves his regiment. Anyway, most outsiders would not have the necessary qualifications for taking part in our discussions."

As he showed no sign of agreement she hurriedly went on: "Naturally I'm referring to our Protestant fellow-countrymen in general. In our part of the world intellectual Catholicism still remains something extremely exclusive."

Letterman had quietly reappeared and was standing beside Thomas. "How is it that that little word Christian never turns up any more? " he asked suddenly.

"What do you mean? " asked Beata Veronica, astonished.

"I've been told that Catholic means much the same as universal. Doesn't it? "

"Yes, certainly," she answered.

"Well then, I don't understand why you Catholics are so confoundedly exclusive. You say yourselves that you have really nothing essential to add to the good old Christianity. And nevertheless you go around preaching Catholic art, Catholic literature, Catholic youth, Catholic morals, as if you had a monopoly of all these things. So I merely ask myself what you mean by it. To my simple mind all this should be translated into art for all, literature for all, youth in general, and universally valid morals."

"Pardon me," remarked Beata Veronica sharply, "but it seems to me that it is you who are forgetting that little word 'Christian' now."

"No, I'm not; I'm starting out from it."

"That may be, but if that's so you have failed to understand what Christianity is."

"Hm . . . possibly not. But assuming that's the case, will you please tell me how I should set about understanding it."

"I have told you already: one needs grace for that."

Letterman snorted angrily and turned away. But Thomas's eyes flashed with a longing to argue which he could no longer suppress.

"I cannot say that you make the problem any simpler for a poor heretic," he remarked dryly.

"But, my dear man, surely you cannot expect to receive grace without asking for it?"

"Have you asked for it?"

"Yes."

"And you receive it?"

"Yes."

"Would you please tell me, then, in what this grace consists," continued Thomas, not particularly politely.

"It's the greatest gift that anyone can receive – the Faith."

Thomas shook his head. "We're speaking two different languages," he said. "Words such as faith and grace mean about as much to me as Chinese hieroglyphics, whereas to you they are obviously living realities."

Beata Veronica suddenly realized that the wisest thing was to remain silent. The prim little scholar standing before her was coming out of his shell, and it was a painful process.

"Realities which determine our action," repeated Thomas thoughtfully. "Realities which drive some people to go into monasteries and others to sacrifice their lives; and others again to build cathedrals over the tombs of those who have sacrificed themselves. . . . Would you do that?"

"Would I do what?"

"For instance, would you sacrifice your life for a consecrated wafer?"

Beata Veronica did not reply.

"I'm asking seriously," urged Thomas. "Yes or no?"

"If God gave me the strength – yes," she answered very quietly.

"Even if no one was looking?"

"Yes, even if no one was looking."

"Naturally you could hardly say anything else," said Thomas

bitterly, "but I want to know why you would be so ready to sacrifice your life?"

Beata Veronica shut her eyes. She had turned very pale.

Thomas repeated his question.

"Do you really not know why?" she whispered.

"No."

"Then – I'm afraid – I can't explain it to you, because I would have to use one of those outmoded words which you don't believe in."

"And that is . . . ?"

Beata Veronica opened her eyes. Something like fear and defiance flickered in them. "Love," she said tersely.

He became silent. She recovered her courage and said earnestly: "You should definitely talk things over with some understanding priest. There are so many things which I am not competent to discuss with you. Let me introduce you to one of our spiritual directors, a very clever young man who is working on his thesis for his doctorate? His name is Father Weber and he's to go to Scandinavia as a missionary. . . ."

Thomas got red to the roots of his streaky blond hair. "No, thank you," he answered brusquely. "I certainly don't wish to be produced as a potential project for some future Scandinavian missionary. . . ." But his words were drowned by a resounding call from the door. It was Lillemor announcing that the guest of honour of the evening had arrived.

Thomas saw a tall stout prelate with a luxurious crop of grey hair and a strikingly fresh complexion. He was wearing a violet cape, a red sash around his waist, and a cross with glittering stones on his breast. Standing motionless at the door he looked a splendid figure, but when he began to walk, his uncouth, heavy gait was in striking contrast to the light, gliding steps and elegant deportment of Italian prelates.

Monsignor Gold spoke a grammatically perfect Swedish marred only by some painfully guttural sounds. He greeted his hostess with exaggerated heartiness, and while he did so the other guests hurriedly ranged themselves along by the walls. Then, with a majestic and at the same time familiar and condescending manner, he made the round as guest of honour, rather as if he were inspecting a superior boarding school for young ladies. Deep bows, an occasional curtsey, and intermittent shy giggles marked his progress. He himself emitted at regular intervals great guffaws of laughter as unmodulated as blasts on a trumpet. His whole personality exuded a professional *bonhomie* that successfully bore down all obstacles in its path.

With sweeping gestures and a blatant glitter of gold teeth, he finally steered his way up to the little group by the piano. Thomas, seeing him coming, tried to beat a retreat, but was too late. Monsignor Gold was already standing before him, breathless with sheer benevolence.

"Oh, there you are, Catholics!" he wheezed. "Bravo! Scandinavian Catholics! But we're already acquainted, are we not? I see only old acquaintances! Splendid! Splendid! It is really delightful to meet old friends again on foreign soil – it really is! Isn't it now? Are you all studying here? Splendid! Where in all the world is there so much to study as in Rome, the Eternal City? Just think of its history... !" He rolled his eyes dramatically as if to lend emphasis to his words. "Of course you have all been in Saint Peter's, I take it? Magnificent, isn't it? Truly the greatest sight in Rome, the one all the non-Catholic visitors go to see! And for us Catholics Rome is always the wonderful, the unique city, the capital of the Church, the home of our Holy Father! " He raised his brows until they nearly touched his hair, and paused as though expecting a spontaneous outburst of applause. "Have you seen the Holy Father yet? You should try to do so. It is by no means impossible, my friends. And just think what a memory it will be to cherish for the rest of your lives! "

He raised his hand as if in benediction, but let the gesture stop at a discreet token blessing. As Thomas listened bewildered to this flow of rhetoric, he noted that Monsignor Gold changed his conversational tone as soon as he spoke Swedish. There was no attempt to carry on intelligent conversation, nothing but a noisy conventional fatherliness, as if he were speaking to adolescents.

"So that's the great white chief of your Olaus Magnus

Society?" said Thomas when the prelate had passed out of earshot.

Beata Veronica threw him an uneasy glance.

"A splendid missionary!" continued Thomas mercilessly. "'Let your communication be Yea, yea; Nay, nay.' That was more or less what he was trying to say, wasn't it?"

Her face clouded. Thomas noticed that she was hurt, but he could not bring himself to mitigate the harshness of his words. For he himself was far more deeply hurt. . . .

"Well, what did you think of Chrysostom?" asked Letterman on the way home.

"Chrysostom – what do you mean?"

"It's a title of honour given the Monsignor by his more distant admirers," explained the painter. "It means 'Golden Mouth', as you probably know."

Taking Thomas by the arm he turned into the Via Babuino. "Don't take it badly, old fellow. I know Lillemor well enough to take the liberty of saying what I think of her and her friends."

"I really didn't know that she was so interested in – er – active Christianity," muttered Thomas glumly.

But the painter broke out again. "May I point out a little peculiarity in the form of Christianity which is called 'universal'? It is considered very high-brow, let me say, to be a Catholic. Of course there are also Catholics who remember that they are just ordinary Christians. But not all do, and that is the rub! Catholicism is for us the most ingenious solution of the problem of how to be exclusive and popular at the same time. You simply turn the word popular into exclusive and all the little nondescripts from Naples to Cape North are happy."

"You're generalizing far too wildly," protested Thomas.

"Of course I'm generalizing. That's obvious. I'm not a caricaturist for nothing! And besides, I'm speaking of converts, the type you meet in Lillemor's nursery. Vanity combined with inadaptability drives them to change their religion. As compensation they find themselves accepted into a select circle with exclusive mysteries and communal love-feasts, where they sit and praise each other and look down on all outside the fold. They're too clever to consider themselves 'saved' and too farseeing to call themselves 'regenerated'. They're intellectual Catholics; and with this they shut the mouths of the rest of humanity. I know from personal experience how pleasantly all this tickles one's vanity and how completely it lulls to sleep all doubts as to the infallibility of the inner ring. For you see, I'm of the same kidney myself. . . ."

Thomas stopped with a jerk. "You don't mean to say that . . . ? " he began.

Felix Letterman seemed hugely amused. "Don't worry ! " he said. "I've never been a Catholic, though as a matter of fact I *was* once very near to becoming one. I still like the company of Catholics very much indeed – I mean real Catholics who don't have to wear an intellectual steel corset to keep their backs straight."

"And how does one recognize real Catholics? "

"By the complexion," said Letterman, lighting his pipe.

By now they had reached the Piazza di Spagna. An uninterrupted stream of cars was emerging from the Via Condotti. The evening strollers were thronging the open doors of the wine shops and the gay shop windows, and the Spanish Steps were brilliantly floodlit. The dark façade of the old missionary College of the Propaganda Fide formed the end of the perspective behind an austerely plain white pillar – the column of the Madonna of the Immaculate Conception.

"I gather, then, that you have no particular religion," observed Thomas, slightly irritated.

"Easy, boy, easy ! " said Letterman, stopping to buy a paper. "What makes you think I have no religion? " As he took his *Giornale d'Italia* he continued : "My religion has one thing in common with Catholicism, namely, exclusiveness. On the other hand, it is anything but popular, and I have never tried to teach it to other people. In other words, there's nothing of the apostolate about it. But please don't tell that to the gentlemen behind us there," he concluded with a jerk of his head in the direction of the College of the Propaganda.

"But surely there must be a second party in your religion," persisted Thomas.

E

"Who should that be?" asked Letterman, who had become immersed in the leading article on the threat of war.

"Do I need to say?"

The painter shook his head absently. "Do you mean the man in the moon? No, he doesn't come into it, nor any other god either. That's the grand thing about my religion."

"It is difficult to get at its content."

"How's that? It rests on a basic principle called tolerance. If I brought any single god into it, I'm not quite sure whether he'd allow me, for instance, to go into Saint Peter's. But as it is, I move freely, that is, with human dignity, wherever there is something beautiful to see."

"Ah, then your religion is based on the worship of beauty?"

At last Letterman looked up from his paper. "Now you probably think you've pinned me down at last," he said laughing. "In a certain sense you're right – I'm always looking for beauty, but preferably with the help of a mirror."

And with a wave of his paper he disappeared into the throng in the Via Due Macelli. Thomas remained standing under the solitary gleaming white pillar on which the bronze Madonna stood silhouetted against the starry sky.

The Immaculate Conception, he thought – for Northern Protestants an incomprehensible theoretical definition, almost repellent, in fact; but down here in the South a living reality to whom people erect a monument in the thick of the most frantic street traffic. The figure up there on the pillar symbolized such a titanic, challenging idea that Thomas did not dare to tackle it with his own logic. He felt in the grip of a bitter desperation. He had already been two years in the Eternal City, and now here he was, standing like a lost stranger in the Piazza di Spagna – a stranger among his own countrymen too – and unable to understand something which obviously was one of the primary associations of this environment.

It was an ordinary spring evening and the life of the city throbbed past him. The air was full of cries and laughter, but neither concerned him. People met, waved at each other, smiled. No glance sought his. They all seemed to be talking, talking, talking, to each other, but he seemed to understand nothing of what they were saying. He looked around him almost appealingly. Only the beggars took any notice of him. A dirty little urchin tried to persuade him to buy a set of perfectly horrible picture postcards; a girl of about ten, with dark rings under her eyes, tried to force a few withered chrysanthemums on him; a toothless old woman grabbed his trousers fast with her claw-like fingers as she whimpered for his pity. In Northern Europe this poverty would have been only utterly depressing in its effect. Here, however, it dissolved into the general picture, was carried along by the human stream, and mingled, like a sombre minor chord, in the tumultuous symphony played by the street itself around the Madonna of the Immaculate Conception.

Almost with shame in his heart Thomas raised his eyes once more to the Queen of Heaven. All of a sudden he felt overwhelmed by the realization that all these wretched creatures knew more about her than he did. And for all their misery, none of them was so deeply frozen within, so torn in spirit, as the art historian Thomas Cinnelius.

Non intratur in veritatem. . . .

He felt he could fall on his knees before the statue in the Piazza if only it would put an end to this intolerable loneliness.

❧

VII PADRE BARNABA IN HIS OFFICE

The parish hall of Saint Lino's was a great long room with a vaulted roof and narrow windows that overlooked the former monastery courtyard. In the past it had been the monastery refectory. Most of the furnishing dated from those days – plain long tables and wooden chairs as well as some cupboards, stained dark brown, which had formerly held the brethren's tableware but were now used to store the school library and the monastery archives. On the walls hung an enormous oak crucifix, a photograph of the Pope, and a banner of dirty green silk with a picture of Saint Linus embroidered in the centre; also a map of the Holy Land and a white screen for showing lantern slides. But the most striking decoration of the room consisted of a series of frescoes depicting the life of the saint and dating from the golden age of genre painting. An artist member of the brotherhood had painted them in vivid oils with admirable draughtsmanship for the community to feast their eyes on as they dined.

Padre Barnaba received Thomas in his office, which was next to the former refectory. It had really been the porter's room, and had one small square window in a deep embrasure overlooking the street. Inside it was just as it had been in the past century. Two narrow bookcases stood one at each side of the door; in front of the window was a high writing desk with a three-legged office stool before it and near it a wooden bench for everyday visitors. The more honoured visitors were asked to sit on a sagging, plush-covered sofa which stood against the opposite wall under a row of faded lithographs of Popes Sixtus V, Gregory XVI and Pius IX and Cardinal Secretaries of State Lambruschini and Antonelli.

"I hardly think all this really suits you, dear Tommaso," said Padre Barnaba with a vague sweep of the hand that included the paupers in the monastery courtyard and the whole of the Vicolo dei Pecorai. "You must be used to very different surroundings. All the same, it's more comfortable to have your instruction here than in the library."

Padre Barnaba would have much preferred Thomas to have turned to another priest. More than a fortnight ago Padre Barnaba had sent him off to take a rest, and here he was standing before him again with eyes pointed at him like pistols, demanding that he should open the way to the Church to him. Padre Barnaba could not turn him away. His experienced eyes perceived that the young man had undergone a change of heart. The finger of the Lord had touched him, and he was trembling to the depths of his being. It was easy to detect, under the mask of brusqueness, a hidden craving for human warmth and encouragement.

"Ah, yes, the ways of the Lord are wonderful," sighed the old priest, but he really felt very nervous himself because he had never had any experience in the instruction of foreigners.

"Have you been to the Brigettine nuns in the Piazza Farnese?" he asked. "I should think there is probably a Scandinavian chaplain there?"

"No, there isn't any, as far as I know," replied Thomas.

"As far as you know," repeated Padre Barnaba. "But there are so many foreign academies and colleges here in Rome! I'm sure the Scandinavians must have something for themselves. I seem to have heard of a Swedish academy or the like?"

"That's an archaeological institute. I've worked there myself."

"Oh, then the matter is clear," said Padre Barnaba, visibly relieved. "You can surely get instruction in your own language there. If you like I shall write a few lines to the director for you. No doubt there's some monsignor or other there . . ."

He stopped short, dumbfounded. His solemn young friend had suddenly burst out laughing. "I'm afraid there's no one in the institute who would be competent to instruct me in the Catholic faith," he said. "And for my own part, I shall be deeply grateful if I may learn it from you, Padre Barnaba, and from no one else."

Well, obviously there was no getting out of it, so Padre Barnaba began: "In the name of the Father, and of the Son, and of the Holy Ghost! I saw you making the sign of the Cross! So you have been baptized?"

"Yes, as a Lutheran, in Finland."

"Splendid. Do you know the Ten Commandments?"

"Of course."

"That's good." Padre Barnaba seemed agreeably surprised. "Then you probably know the six precepts of the Church too?"

"In a general way," murmured Thomas, "but I probably need to refresh my memory."

"Wait a moment."

Padre Barnaba went to one of the bookcases and began rooting in its dark depths. The hesitancy of his manner had by no means escaped Thomas. "If you're short of time perhaps I could manage myself, Father, if you will only give me a few suggestions as to what to read up on the subject. And I already know my way about the library pretty well, anyway."

Padre Barnaba threw him an astonished look over his shoulder.

"What do you know? "

"The library."

"Who said you should work in the library? "

"But I have already got through quite a lot of preparatory study," explained Thomas, equally astonished. "Perhaps it would be easier for you to work out a course of study for me if I gave you a list of the books I have read already? "

"That's unnecessary," replied Padre Barnaba, "because I know you have not read the most important book of all."

Thomas had pen and paper ready, but meanwhile Padre Barnaba had found what he had been looking for.

"I'll explain what I mean," he said, coming back with a little book in a plain brown-paper cover. "I know very well that you have read more books than I, and have acquired a great deal of knowledge of our Faith. But you have skipped the introduction, so to speak, and for that reason you cannot digest what you have learned."

"Is that the book? " asked Thomas suspiciously.

"Yes, indeed, but it's not to be found in the library."

"How is that possible? "

"Because I took it out."

Thomas shied like a frightened horse. "Is it something forbidden? " he asked.

A shadow passed over Padre Barnaba's face. "No," he said, "but I needed it in my daily work." And he laid the book on the table with an air of reverence. "Besides, it's hardly worth having it in the library because I don't think anyone can read it on his own. At least, I've never heard of anyone doing so. But you are welcome to try if you think it will work."

"Thank you for your confidence in me," murmured Thomas. "I'm very sorry if I hurt your feelings just now." He opened the book and stared at it nonplussed. It was an ordinary Italian catechism for children.

Padre Barnaba noted his bewilderment and nodded. Suddenly he became formidable, stern and authoritative. "Dear young friend," he said, laying his hand on Thomas's shoulder, "I shall be glad if this little book gives you some idea of the magnitude of your undertaking, because I very much doubt if you are clear about it yourself. But I can't give you any other literary introduction to the subject for a long time yet."

Thomas seemed about to protest, but the priest literally pressed him back on the sofa.

"Don't allow yourself to be repelled by the simplicity and childishness of the style," he said. "It is meant specially for little boys at the age when they think they can kill a bear with a toy arrow – which to my mind is no more childish than to imagine one can round up the Lord God Himself in a dusty library."

Thomas stuck the book in his pocket without further comment and went off. But the very next day he turned up again and asked for more literature.

"You don't say that you've read the catechism already? " exclaimed Padre Barnaba in an almost offended tone.

"Of course I have."

"Surely that's impossible? "

"Why should it be? "

Padre Barnaba stared at him solemnly without answering. He himself had once learned his faith from that catechism, and he had impressed the truths contained in it on all the youth of the Vicolo dei Pecorai. So it was a book which should be read with due humility and thought. However, as he did not wish to seem disagreeable he produced an introduction to the Catholic faith written in the pietistic style of the last century, and a small popular edition of the writings of Saint Augustine with commentaries. He refused to produce any further theological wisdom for the time being. However, seeing Thomas's obvious disappointment, he tried to allay it with a monograph on Saint Francis of Assisi and an illustrated book on the Abruzzi. All this was little more than a gesture designed to hide from his young catechumen the fact that he was almost afraid of him. . . .

One July day Padre Barnaba locked his door and set off to visit the former legal adviser of the monastery of Santa Presenza, whom he was in the habit of consulting on any really knotty problem arising between himself and the secular powers.

Commendatore Carlo Maria Tartaruga belonged to the old aristocracy of Vatican officials, but had also made a name for himself
as a lawyer in private practice in Rome. Now, in his retirement,
he devoted his time to charitable works. A dapper little gentleman
with a grey goatee, a waxed moustache, and shining velvety eyes,
he wore a wide black tie like an artist's, a high celluloid collar, and
a little cap on his bald ebony-coloured skull. He received Padre
Barnaba in the exquisite miniature drawing-room of his residence
in the Via Giulia and listened with the utmost attention to his
account of the case of Thomas.

"The young man's lack of spiritual balance does not surprise
me in the least," he said when the priest had finished. "He's from
north of the Alps—*ecco tutto!*"

Padre Barnaba sat balancing like a circus bear on the edge of a
dainty Venetian chair.

"Even if that is so, it does not make the matter any easier,
humanly speaking," he said. "How can one cope with a person
like that? He's as nervous as a racehorse, and that's hardly the
right frame of mind for a young man who's preparing for his
first Holy Communion."

The lawyer nodded solemnly. "My dear Padre Barnaba," he
said. "You must try to realize what a frightful inner upheaval
conversion to the Catholic faith means for a Scandinavian."

Padre Barnaba looked up, but said nothing.

"It is difficult for us Southern people to have any conception
at all of what it means," continued the lawyer. "Neither you nor
I have been through anything of the kind. We were born beside
the sacristy, so to speak, and pushed through the church doors as
a matter of course and without any choice. But for the average
Scandinavian, Rome is about as far away as the moon. We would
have to go back to the days of the martyrs, it seems to me, to
find a comparable spiritual achievement in our latitude."

Padre Barnaba had turned a shade paler. "I've never been
north of the Alps myself," he said, "but I suppose I must believe
you."

Signor Tartaruga nodded his round head like a toy mandarin.
"I'll tell you this," he said. "I was once on the Baltic coast of

Germany, only passing through, in the month of October. I shall never forget it ! The mere thought that there are people who live and die even farther north than that infernal sea, makes me feel quite dizzy to this very day ! As far as I'm concerned, the world might end at that coast. Believe me, Father, there are still martyrs up there ! "

"*Santissima Vergine!*" cried Padre Barnaba. "Am I making a martyr of young Thomas, then? I have been worrying only about his health. Surely he should gradually get past the crisis? It's more than two months now since he first came to see me."

The lawyer's head nodded still more sagely. "I have been observing the young man in San Lino's," he said. "He belongs to a race of people who live and react more slowly than we do – more slowly and more deeply. That also applies to their crises. . . ." He paused and looked up thoughtfully at the priest.

"Are you sure that he has not been called by God to Santa Presenza? " he asked.

This was a new shock for Padre Barnaba. "Surely God would not call anyone to a derelict monastery? " he asked. "Besides, it would be rather premature since the young man isn't even a Catholic yet."

The lawyer shrugged his shoulders. "Naturally you are a better judge of that than I, Father. But what can I do for you in the matter? "

At last the priest came out, if somewhat hesitantly, with the real purpose of his visit. "I believe young Tommaso needs company," he said. "He seems to me to be very lonely. Perhaps you could do something for him there? I mean, put him in touch with suitable lay people who would stand by him in ordinary life, don't you understand. I'm only a poor slum pastor, but you must know people of his kind, Commendatore. What he needs is a good Catholic friend of his own class. That's really what I've come to you about."

Signor Tartaruga had been sitting with his hands spread open. He now expressed his discreet bewilderment by making a series of graceful gestures, as if he were trying in vain to arrange a bouquet of flowers which would not come right.

"The situation is certainly highly complicated, Father. I understand your dilemma completely, but I scarcely think the matter could be materially improved were I to invite young Dr Cinnelius to dinner. Friendship cannot be forced. Besides, I'm convinced the young man knows enough intellectual Catholics here already to find as many friends as he wants – if indeed he wants them. But since he prefers to bury himself in Santa Presenza, that simply means that he does not wish to have anything to do with those you call his own kind. And I believe we shall not please him at all if we try to force intellectual companionship on him."

Padre Barnaba stared wide-eyed at his adviser. "But what on earth is to become of him, then?" he asked.

"The mills of God grind slowly. Let us wait and see how the grist turns out."

"Well, there seems to be nothing else we can do," said Padre Barnaba, standing up with a sigh. "But you will promise me, won't you, to bear the matter in mind – just in case . . . ?"

Avvocato Tartaruga clasped Padre Barnaba's right hand warmly between his two. "You do not have to ask me that, my dear Father," he said. "When the time is ripe I shall be very happy to introduce him into a suitable social circle. For of course we have our modest San Lino Society. It may possibly prove a suitable milieu for your friend later on. But first he must become really at home in the Church, eh?"

"Yes, he certainly must, but not in Santa Presenza. It is far too bleak and austere there," replied the priest, turning to go.

A few days later he came upon Thomas studying the edifying frescoes in the former refectory with such intense curiosity that he felt an unpleasant shock. For he himself regarded these old frescoes as the artistic property of the old brotherhood and he did not like to see strange eyes prying too closely into them. He was turning away with a silent nod when Thomas held him back.

"Please forgive this intrusion, Father," said the young man, "but I found a strange piece of information in the library just now and I came down here to have a closer look at the frescoes. No, I'm not thinking of El Greco any longer," he added quickly, with a deprecating smile when he saw the priest's face clouding.

"I'm just studying the Saint Linus legend now. This series here is more recent than the one up in the library, but these, on the other hand, are intact."

The frescoes consisted of two series of pictures. The first one depicted the life story of the saint. It began with a couple of commonplace pastoral scenes which carried the story as far as his baptism. These were followed by scenes from his life in the Roman community as assistant and then successor to Saint Peter. Finally, came his death in the arena and his triumphal entry into heaven. The second series, on the other hand, depicted only one single episode from the life of this saint of many miracles. It showed Saint Linus wandering through the mountains and meeting the Saviour, whom he does not recognize; deep in conversation with Him in the shade of leafy oak-trees, surrounded by peacefully slumbering lambs and amiable-looking wolves; then the evening meal together with a few poor shepherds, and its climax – the joy and astonishment of the company round the table when the unknown Guest reveals Himself; and finally a scene reminiscent of Raphael's "Transfiguration". The whole series was an illustration of familiar themes. The artist had obviously been so deeply gripped by his message that he had made a supreme effort to announce it to his unlettered contemporaries as graphically, sublimely and at the same time intelligibly as possible.

Padre Barnaba made another attempt to get away, but Thomas would not let him go. "Just one other question," he pleaded.

"Well, what is it?"

"I chanced to find some particulars in a seventeenth-century manuscript of a very old tradition, namely, that when Linus became Pope, he gave a special privilege to the village in which he had sat at supper with Christ. But unfortunately I could not understand quite clearly what that privilege was."

"I have never seen the manuscript," muttered Padre Barnaba, and his answer sounded like a rebuff.

"If I am not mistaken, the inhabitants of that village were authorized to celebrate the Eucharist for the rest of time in the manner of a primitive Christian agape. Have you never heard about it?"

"I may have," replied Padre Barnaba, looking away.

But Thomas continued enthusiastically: "It sounds very strange indeed to me. I wonder how on earth such a tradition can be regarded from the ecclesiastical point of view?"

Padre Barnaba only shook his head. "There are doubtless many peculiar traditions in Christendom, but nobody has bothered about this one for many a day. And when I am gone there will be no one, even in this house, who any longer remembers it."

"That's no answer to my question, Padre Barnaba."

"It is not meant to be one either. My task is to pass on to you the living tradition of the Church. All these things here are only dead memories." And, taking Thomas gently but firmly by the arm, he led him out of the refectory and locked the door.

The young man looked at him abashed and whispered, "Pardon me." He had suddenly realized that Padre Barnaba had sat at table with his brethren in this room for fifteen long years, and had seen them dropping off one by one, leaving their places empty. . . .

But the old priest betrayed no emotion. He only said: "There's nothing to pardon. I shall receive you into the Church in a few days. And I must ask you to keep your thoughts on the essential things during this time of preparation."

❧

VIII   PADRE BARNABA'S CONFESSIONAL

At six o'clock every morning the little bell of Saint Lino's emitted a shrill cry which gradually died away in a whimper. It sounded as though it had rung in its sleep and then fallen silent, frightened by its own discordant voice. But it was only that the porter had given one pull at the rope before opening the door. The signal was meant in the first place for the aged inmates of the poorhouse, and sure enough, the shuffling of slippers could soon be heard along the stone cloisters. Padre Barnaba habitually arrived in the church a good half-hour before Mass, to hear confessions.

In the right-hand aisle of Saint Lino's there was a large alcove. The shepherd's entrance had been here originally, before the church had been rebuilt. One side of the alcove was adorned with a black marble memorial tablet framing a baroque bust of white alabaster. At the other side there was a plain painted wooden statue of Saint Anthony with the Child Jesus on his arm, and a collection box with a porcelain inscription tablet at his bare, sandalled feet.

Inside the alcove stood Padre Barnaba's confessional, a massive stained-oak structure which had been made by a village carpenter somewhere in the Abruzzi. Penitents had given it to the church long years ago and carried it all the way down from the mountains on their shoulders. That was long before Padre Barnaba's time, but because of the memories which it held of his thirty years' care of souls in San Lino, the old priest loved his confessional as a seaman loves his boat. And entering the confessional was much the same as entering the boat of a fisher of men himself. The step was hollow and the floor swayed and creaked like a deck. The rail was worn from handling like the breast-rail of a ship, the wood itself was dark and hard and as if impregnated with constant salt spray. Nevertheless Padre Barnaba used to say that his confessional was the firmest structure in the whole district and indeed it was true that fiercer storms had raged against its blackened grill than any seaman could imagine.

When the first old men came shuffling along in their slippers, Padre Barnaba laid aside his breviary, drew the violet curtain across the door, and opened his little wooden grating for the big morning washing. As a rule, the poorhouse inmates of Santa Presenza did not give him much to worry about. His most trying penitents came from the Piazza. The folk of the Vicolo dei Pecorai were a good-hearted lot, and no doubt fundamentally Christian, but their moral hygiene was extremely dependent on Padre Barnaba's supervision and care. The great annual spring cleaning took place towards Easter when Padre Barnaba knelt in spirit before his flock and washed them clean, as Christ had washed the feet of His Apostles. Indeed, there were days when he had to toil like a charwoman in a hospital. At such times he felt that only his tried old confessional held him up.

He could have heard Thomas Cinnelius's general confession just as well in the office, but somehow he felt more sure of himself in his confessional. His attitude towards the task he had taken upon himself was still somewhat hesitant, and the appearance of the penitent was not calculated to allay his fears, for the young man looked pale and much the worse for sleepless nights. And he spoke far too loud. However, Padre Barnaba did not have to check him for this as he had thoughtfully instructed Fausto to keep the church shut while Cinnelius was making his confession. Who could know how a timid foreigner like this one would react if he suddenly discovered a whole queue of impatient people behind him at the moment when, for the first time in his life, he was laying bare the secrets of his soul?

At first, however, there seemed to be no question of any very private matters. By way of introduction Padre Barnaba received a brief report on certain misinterpretations of the Catholic faith common to persons educated in Protestant countries. Then the penitent passed on to the basic problem of moral responsibility, which he made the subject of a serious discourse. Padre Barnaba felt as though he were listening to a classical disputation on moral theology at which he himself played the role of objector and in the end had to place the laurel wreath on the brow of the absolved penitent. The moral question was further ventilated from various social angles, and finally a family and a problem of heredity – highly complicated, this – emerged out of the distance. By now Padre Barnaba felt more doubtful than ever of his ability to cope with this erratic soul. But he had once heard the confession of a German student, who had treated him to a long metaphysical dissertation before coming down to brass tacks about girls and such matters. The priest's hand was already clutching for support at his old confessional when at last he heard Thomas beginning to speak about himself.

"I was very unhappy, Father," he murmured, and suddenly his voice sounded different.

"Being unhappy isn't a sin," replied Padre Barnaba encouragingly. "On the contrary, it may well be a sign of grace. You know: 'Whom the Lord loveth he chasteneth.'"

"But I'm afraid I myself was responsible for my unhappiness," said the voice, "for I have denied the greatest truth in life."

"It is not given to all to possess the truth. You should be happy to have found it."

"I prided myself on being a seeker of truth – and different from other people in that respect – but in reality I was fleeing from the truth. That was my way ever since I was a child. And yet I never dared to admit it to anyone, even to myself."

"After all, we have all sinned from our childhood. You know that human nature . . ."

"But I have lied my whole life through. I have lied to you too, and my lying made me hard and unjust. . . ."

"I don't think God will reckon that against you," said Padre Barnaba appeasingly. "You know that it is of the essential nature of the Divine Love to forgive the youthful lack of understanding of the children of men."

"It was not only lack of understanding," continued the voice obstinately, "it was far more a matter of vanity. My studies had brought me nearer and nearer to the truth, but I found it embarrassing. I looked for an easy way out. I tried to track down my Lord and God through a keyhole, so to speak, in order not to have to bow my knee before His countenance. Do you understand what I mean?"

"At least the gist of it," muttered Padre Barnaba, though he was really not at all sure that he had grasped it aright. It was anything but easy to decide what lay under all this flow of rhetoric – inborn melancholy, faulty upbringing, or real sin? One single silent prayer rose from the depths of Padre Barnaba's soul: Merciful God, help him to express himself intelligibly!

"My work came to nothing," continued the penitent, "but I did not dare to turn back. There was no alternative for me but to go on with my eyes open – until the lie burst like a boil. . . ."

"How did that happen?"

"It was in a church in the country. I tried, like a necromancer, to force His secret from the Lord. . . ."

"In what way?"

"I tried to steal up to the table of the Lord, but I failed."

Padre Barnaba waited for a clearer explanation but when none was forthcoming he began slowly: "If I understand you aright, you are accusing yourself of an attempt to commit a sacrilege. That is a very serious sin if it is committed deliberately. But then, you say yourself that you did not want to accept the teaching of the Church; therefore you can hardly have known what you were doing."

"I don't know if I knew," answered the voice despairingly, "but I feel so loaded with guilt that my back seems as if it would break."

Padre Barnaba felt the perspiration breaking out on his forehead. If only I could speak to him in his own language, he thought. I could have helped an Italian to his feet long ago. But one can never be sure with these foreigners. They say one thing and mean another, speaking a foreign language. However, I must put an end to this dismal tale of his and bring some order into his confession! So he decided to take refuge in the catechism. If it applied in Rome it should surely be comprehensible even in Ultima Thule.

"Have you practised idolatry?" he asked.

His words were lost in a bottomless pit of silence, and he felt obliged to formulate the question more clearly.

"You know what that means, don't you?" he asked. "The first Commandment says: 'Thou shalt not have strange gods before Me.'"

No reaction.

"False gods are not only to be found in history and among aboriginal peoples. There are some in our modern world too. They emerge inevitably wherever man denies God, yet that has become so general that we hardly notice it any longer. But an upright, thinking person can hardly allow himself to be deceived in this matter."

Still no answer.

"So you have nothing with which to reproach yourself in this respect?" decided Padre Barnaba, and was about to continue with the Commandments when a faint whisper came through the grill at last.

"Yes, I have done so. But I did not admit it to myself."

"I understand," said the priest, discreetly. "But now you have certainly turned away from your false idols, eh?"

"It is difficult to see clearly," continued the voice, barely audibly. "I was probably too proud to apply that word to myself. I banished it from my own consciousness."

Padre Barnaba bent his head down closer to the grill. At last the words became intelligible. Even through the grating he could perceive the anxiety of the penitent, and he said reassuringly: "Well, the thing is to keep your eyes open in the future. You know that one of the most dangerous wiles of the devil consists in getting people to deny his existence?"

The answer came, slow and tremulous: "I promise to do my best."

"That's good. But you must be prepared to find it difficult at first. The devil will not give up without resistance. And he generally has the laugh on his side. But against good will he is powerless – never forget that. You are not one of those who *want* to believe in idols. It was probably through thoughtlessness that you accepted them, eh?"

Again silence.

"What did you see in your idols?"

"People," replied the voice, "and myself."

"I know, I know . . ." said the priest, but the voice interrupted him with sudden passion:

"I made my own mind my idol. I imagined that that was the meaning of existence. I believed in everything that flattered my vain delusion that I saw God's will. I persuaded myself that man's kingdom is God's kingdom. I wanted to bring paradise down to earth. I placed my own ideal on God's altar and knelt down before it and adored it. I . . ."

"*Basta, basta,*" interrupted Padre Barnaba. "You're trying to say that you served God's image instead of Himself. Isn't that so?"

"Yes."

"Listen . . ." he whispered, his mouth close to the grill, "if you had really known what you were doing, that would have been a very grievous sin. But I don't believe that you knew. It is in no way wrong to want to see the best in your fellow beings, and our Lord often makes use of our little weaknesses to teach us humility. He can even use our idols to achieve His purpose in us. There are certain people who find it incredibly difficult to bend the knee. Perhaps they have to be forced to do so by harder means than God's love can devise. God sometimes delivers such people over to their own false gods to make their knees more pliable. And of course that cannot happen without much weeping and gnashing of teeth, but it is the only possible way of bending stiff limbs. For every true relationship with God begins with bended knee – that is absolutely unavoidable. No one can receive God's grace standing. But when we go on our knees God helps us to our feet, if that is His Holy will. You have received a doctrine for which you should be truly thankful. Do you understand?"

He received for answer only a tremulous sigh which he interpreted as a "Yes". His trained ear told him that the burden of fear at the other side of the grating had lost some of its weight.

"*Bene*," he said. "Let us think no more about the matter. Have you anything else on your mind?"

"I have confessed the worst. But when one thinks of one's whole life, there is such a lot more that . . ."

"I don't believe that there is anything in your past life that our Lord has not already forgiven you. Have you ever had intimate relations with a girl?"

"No, never."

Padre Barnaba asked no more questions but leaned back wearily in his trusted old confessional and shut his eyes.

"I see that you are penitent, my son," he whispered. "Say for your penance one Our Father, and go in peace! God will take care of the rest. But do not forget: He is invisible, even here in Rome. *Ego te absolvo . . .*"

IX THE REFECTORY

Padre Barnaba dreamed that a young novice had come into his old brotherhood. It was a sultry midday in the worst heat of August, but in his dream it was a pitch-dark December evening, and frightful weather. The rainwater was flowing in streams along the Vicolo dei Pecorai and lay many inches deep over the Piazza, where the north wind, the *tramontana,* was howling like a mountain wolf round the forlorn little marble goats. Not a soul was to be seen out of doors and even Sor Anacleto had closed down. The ill-ventilated church reeked of wet wool clothing and inside the monastery the moisture was trickling down the bare stone walls which the few small braziers failed to warm in the least. The brothers were going about shivering, with little skull-caps on their shaven heads and mittens on their wrists, and their breath hung about like smoke in the cellar-like air.

The community had assembled for supper in the refectory, where two stout lay brothers, in blue linen aprons such as women wear, were serving up the meal. The lighting came from a few dim oil lamps that hung at wide intervals from the dark, vaulted ceiling. It was not easy to distinguish the different faces, but Padre Barnaba knew that the whole brotherhood was present, from the prefect, prior, confessor, parish priest, choirmaster, novice-master and procurator – all those who formed the council of the congregation and sat at the middle of the horseshoe-shaped table – down to the novices and lay brothers, including the sacristan and porter, who sat at either end. They all stood with bowed heads and sang their "Amen" with trembling voices when the prefect had said grace. Then there was a rasping noise of chairs as in a class, and petrified hands eagerly clutched at the steaming soup plates and the carafes of thin, sourish, home-grown wine.

The new novice had the task of reading aloud during the meal and it was his first appearance before the assembled brethren. One could see that he had awaited this moment with tense anxiety and had prepared himself in spirit for it. With shining eyes he took his place on the rostrum and eagerly turned over the pages of his manuscript, then began to read in a low, intense voice. His accent was foreign but his speech was completely intelligible. The text dealt with Santa Presenza and the history of the Brotherhood, and it was soon clear that the novice had composed the paper himself. Actually, it only consisted of a brief history of the monastery embellished with tales and episodes from various periods, but Padre Barnaba observed with some uneasiness that the youth spoke with a note of jubilation in his voice as if he were describing the heavenly Jerusalem. As he told of the golden age of the Brotherhood – Cardinal Terrasanta's magnificent buildings, the art collections and libraries, the mission, the charitable work, the instruction of the people, and the higher studies pursued within the monastery itself, all the things which in past ages had given the Brotherhood of Santa Presenza its particular stamp and its renown in the world – his enthusiasm was evident. He then proceeded to try to portray the particular spirit and task of the Brotherhood – the soul, so to speak, of Santa Presenza.

Padre Barnaba became more and more hot in the head. No one had ever before dared to write a history of Santa Presenza, still less to glorify the Brotherhood. From time immemorial it had been an unwritten law of the monastery to avoid everything that could be interpreted as an effort to extol its own excellence. Consequently, everyone had been persistently silent about the good deeds of the Fathers, pioneers and founders, and their work for the common good. And now, here was this young novice taking advantage of his *début* on the rostrum to try out his prose composition on this delicate subject, *ad majorem congregationis gloriam* – to the greater glory of the Brotherhood – before the assembled community.

Padre Barnaba felt a burning compulsion to shout out: "Stop! Santa Presenza is not what you think it is! It is neither a cultural institute nor an historical academy, nor a communal compensation for persons who flee the world, nor a beautiful garden where guileless old men have raised flowers and plants through the centuries instead of the posterity that God had forbidden them.

People are so ready to think that a monastery is a compensation for home and family and must be particularly nice to live in because it is a kind of tenancy held from the Church, a fact which lends it something of the fragrance of eternity. But that has never been so in Santa Presenza. This monastery is a burial chamber, or to be more correct, an ante-room to the grave, which lies hidden behind the altar. Here men prepare for death by prayer, work and silence – above all by silence. And the man who enters here does well to give up all hope, however modest and discreet, of earthly happiness. Our life in the monastery is nothing but a ceaseless watch before the sanctuary lamp which burns over the tomb of Christ – a constant preparation, in His presence, for the Holy Sacrifice, with the hope of gaining eternal life, with His help, when He shall come again. . . ."

But his lips could utter no sound, and the young novice continued his reading. Now he started reading out a programme of action, and painted a glowing picture of a future for the old Brotherhood. It was only a matter of preserving the valuable existing traditions and developing them further on modern principles. Santa Presenza must become an expanding centre for a new world mission. It must open houses in more and more cities, and found provinces in foreign countries. The Brotherhood must found dioceses, publish books and periodicals, erect schools and universities, secure bishoprics, and seats in the Curia. In short, the Brotherhood of the Holy Presence must reform the religious life of today and go down in history as one of the driving forces in the Universal Church, like Saint Francis of Assisi whom the Pope of the time had once seen in a dream supporting the collapsing Church on his shoulders. . . .

The words echoed, phantom-like, down from the vaulted roof, but no one reacted to them. Padre Barnaba looked around the table desperately – the prefect, the prior and the master of novices remained silent as the grave. The young man stepped down from the rostrum, his cheeks glowing. The meal ended. The brothers took their places two abreast and walked in procession, singing monotonously, to the little chapel from which came a distinct smell of burning. The novice walked ahead of them with devoutly clasped hands and ecstatically shining eyes. Padre Barnaba tried to jump up and grab him by the collar, as one would snatch a young dog away from a railway line, but his legs would not obey him. . . .

He woke up with a start to hear the door-bell ringing. The siesta time was over, but he remained lying where he was, waiting for someone else to go down and open the door. He had gradually become accustomed to having Thomas around the place. The mere knowledge that the young man was sitting up there in the library gave him the pleasant illusion that the house was inhabited.

The bell rang again. This time he jumped up in alarm. Of course it was Thomas, who had come to speak to him about his first Holy Communion. The Feast of the Assumption had been fixed for this. It should really have taken place immediately after his first confession, but Padre Barnaba had decided to defer it for a few days. The young man is a bit too strung up, he said to himself.

Thomas's first question confirmed his fears. "Don't you need some help here in the monastery, Padre Barnaba?" he asked.

"This isn't a monastery," answered Padre Barnaba quietly.

"Well no, perhaps not in the real sense of the word; but you must surely have more than enough to do, particularly with the books. Wouldn't a librarian be wanted here?"

At this moment Padre Barnaba came to a firm decision. "No, I don't need a librarian," he said. "In fact, I shall close down the library for a time. Indeed it would be best, dear Tommaso, if you would continue your instruction with another priest."

The young man looked utterly stricken. "Does that mean that you have no more time for me, Father?" he asked.

"I'm very sorry, but I believe it's the only thing to do."

"Have I offended you in any way, Padre Barnaba? If so, I hope you will forgive me."

"You certainly have not offended me, my dear friend. It seems rather that it is I who should ask you to forgive me, because apparently I have given you an entirely false idea of Santa Presenza. I should have realized that long ago and sent you away."

Thomas seemed desperate. "I simply can't understand what

you mean, Father. You have instructed me, you have received me into the Church, you have heard my confession. So why should you suddenly send me away now? Surely you can at least give me Holy Communion first? "

" I believe it is better if I do not do that. You must learn to see that the Sacrament is not bound to any particular person or any particular church."

" But there is no one who can dispense the Blessed Sacrament with such great love as you, Padre Barnaba. I thought that you were an expert on the subject."

" Expert on what? "

" On the Eucharist. Isn't that the original purpose of Santa Presenza? "

It was now Padre Barnaba's turn to feel desperate. " I'm afraid you have got the whole thing completely wrong," he said. " Santa Presenza was a house for the humblest of the servants of the Blessed Sacrament – poor day labourers in the Lord's vineyard. And even that came to an end. The only survivor is myself, a poor old mule no longer fit for service. You had best get this clear once and for all: Santa Presenza is dead. And now let us speak no more of it ! "

Thomas's old spirit of contradiction awoke anew. " Excuse me, Padre Barnaba, that's something I don't understand. Surely Santa Presenza represents one single tradition which today is more necessary than ever it was. If you close your altar shrine for ever, that will be a betrayal of the Blessed Sacrament – at least I see it as such – whether you call yourself a day-labourer or a specialist."

Padre Barnaba shook his head. " There is no question of closing down the altar shrine, as you call it. San Lino's is older than we are, and will survive us."

" I'm not thinking of San Lino's at all. I'm thinking of you. Not everyone can tend the old vineyard of Santa Presenza."

" Santa Presenza was only a vine stock which has borne its fruit," answered Padre Barnaba gently. " Next year new vines will grow in the vineyard. No one knows who will tend them. We only know that San Lino's will go on."

" We are speaking at cross-purposes now," protested Thomas.

"I only want to save what remains to be saved of the traditions of the house. Everything depends on you, Padre Barnaba. Why not do something while there is still a continuity to be maintained? You do not have to be alone. One must propagate the knowledge of these things as widely as possible – write articles, give lectures, seek novices, propagate the work in other countries. . . ."

But now Padre Barnaba stood up, determined and formidable. "Enough of this, Tommaso! You must not tempt God. Do not forget: He is invisible!"

He almost repented of his words when he saw their effect. Thomas turned white and departed without a word.

But Padre Barnaba went straight to the Brigittine Convent in the Piazza Farnese. There he learned that a distinguished Scandinavian prelate had been staying in Rome for some months past. Monsignor Gold himself willingly offered to administer the Sacrament to the young convert.

X   THE MADONNA OF THE SHEPHERDS

On the eve of the Feast of the Assumption Thomas found himself irresistibly drawn back to San Lino. It was right in the middle of the dead season, when everyone who could do so had gone to the seaside or the mountains. The town was hot and dusty, the streets almost empty. Only the Piazza delle Pecore seemed fully alive. The doors of the church, which were festively adorned, stood wide open, and a rhythmical murmur of prayer flowed out into the Square.

The interior of the church was almost in darkness, but Thomas could have found his way about it with his eyes shut. In the right-hand front bench were the Franciscan nuns from the Vicolo del Giglio, and behind them, as usual, the poorhouse inmates. The female pillars of the parish sat in the left-hand front bench, while behind them, in descending social scale, were the working people, the servants and the beggars. A number of chance visitors were kneeling on special prie-dieus in the background. As Thomas came nearer he noticed, much to his surprise, that one of them was Monsignor Szarnicki.

On the altar was a small Byzantine Madonna, dark with age, surrounded with lighted candles. Thomas had never seen it before, but now he remembered that it was the one Monsignor Szarnicki had spoken of. Here they called it Nostra Signora dei Pecorai, Our Lady of the Shepherds, and its history was just as obscure and difficult to follow up as most of the other legends in the Vicolo dei Pecorai. When it had actually come to Rome no one knew, but long before Santa Presenza had been founded it was an object of veneration in San Lino's; and this veneration had continued with undiminished fervour down the centuries. Outsiders could accept her as Queen of Heaven or not as they pleased – but she was undeniably the Queen of the Piazza delle Pecore.

The monotonous murmur of prayer filled the church like a soothing narcotic incense. Thomas allowed his eyes to wander discreetly over the bowed backs of the praying people, and up to the altar. Suddenly he realized that he was no longer an art historian. It was a matter of complete indifference to him whether the dark picture of the Madonna up there in the flickering candle-light was ugly or beautiful, old or new, vulgar or choice. A lump of wood with a crown of gilded paper, fashioned by children's hands to resemble a statue, would have served just the same. The picture was, in the last resort, an expression of the love which animated this whole poor parish – a love which was stronger than the contrast between the invisible original and her imperfect embodiment in this dark, cold world.

He clasped his hands and tried to join in the prayers, but got thoroughly mixed up with the verses and finally resorted to following in his thoughts the familiar rhythm of the Rosary. This rhythm led him back to the paths that formed a labyrinth under the everyday surface of life as do the catacombs under the poppy-fringed roads of the Campagna. The perspectives were lost in the gentle rise and fall of the prayer, but he felt himself drawn along by a force which was becoming more clearly perceptible to him the farther on he went. It was as intangible as an invisible centre of gravity, but its existence was just as obvious because of its own power of attraction.

The Rosary came to an end and Padre Barnaba mounted the altar steps. A heavy figure, powerful as that of a boxer, appeared in the sacristy doorway. It was Fausto the lorry-driver, who spent his free time doing odd jobs in the church for Padre Barnaba. Stepping gingerly between the rows of chairs, he picked his way up to the altar carrying a censer which Padre Barnaba took from him as he knelt down. The congregation started singing the *Tantum ergo Sacramentum* in a shrill chorus. Suddenly the same silence which Thomas had observed during the Mass in Santa Cristina fell upon the whole gathering. It was as though a living, observing, sentient Being filled the whole church. But now he did not need to ask who this Being was. It was the same supernatural Love which poor humanity, in its simplicity, associated with age-blackened Madonnas and crudely forged footprints of saints, or tried to conserve in ancient monasteries, like the man who tried to gather sunlight into his barn. . . .

Thomas bowed his head and received the sacramental blessing. When the service was over and the church had emptied, he still remained kneeling at his prie-dieu staring up at the Madonna. He had at last discovered the being behind the picture. It was easier to find this person behind an old picture in a slum church than to detect her behind a majestic statue that rose high above the crowd on the Piazza di Spagna.

This Woman had possessed the secret which he was seeking. What had happened first within her womb was fundamentally the same thing which was still happening on all the Church's altars. She herself was a living answer to the yearning of every poor earthbound mortal for a faith embedded in a reality with the warmth of life about it. She had passed this faith on to her fellow-beings in a manner all could grasp. That was why she was so greatly loved, particularly by the poor and humble; for them all the explanations of the theologians concerning the mystery of the Incarnation were but feeble commentaries on the glorious and joyful fact of Christmas night. . . .

He waited to see if Padre Barnaba would come back, but only Fausto appeared and began tidying up the church for the night. He took the chairs from the centre aisle and ranged them along by the walls, picked up forgotten prayer-books and rosary beads, and blew out the little wax candles beside the offertory box. Finally, rattling his enormous bunch of keys, he came up to Thomas.

"We're closing," he announced in a business-like tone.

Thomas did not understand right away. "Closing? Why?" he asked.

Only when the other began to laugh did he realize how silly his question had been. But Fausto understood him all right, and nodded roguishly. "Because the Holy Virgin must go," he said.

"Are you taking The Madonna away?" asked Thomas, taken aback.

"Yes, indeed," replied Fausto, "she has to go back to heaven tomorrow."

"What does that mean?"

Fausto became serious again. "There are many waiting for her, Signorino," he said. "You see, she has to listen to the prayers of everyone so that she can then explain their troubles to our Lord."

Fausto went up to the altar and knelt down before the Madonna. The light fell on his round, childish face with its small, expressive mouth and clear-cut profile, so out of keeping with his large and clumsy body. He was like an overgrown boy who was trying in vain to hide that he was secretly in love. His black eyes looked up, shining with devotion, at the Queen of Heaven, but instead of folding his hands in prayer he suddenly swelled his chest, puffed out his cheeks, and with one gigantic puff blew out all the wax candles at the foot of the picture.

"How long have you been with Padre Barnaba?" enquired Thomas.

"Me? Nearly ten years now."

"It's a good work you're doing, Fausto."

"Oh, that's nothing really. At home in the country I used to help our parish priest in his old age, and now I do all kinds of odd jobs for Padre Barnaba when I have time. You see, he's from my part of the country too."

"So you're from the Abruzzi?"

"Yes, I'm a real mountaineer," replied Fausto, not without a touch of pride, "but my wife is a Roman – she's from Trastevere."

"Have you any children?"

"Yes, one, a darling child. Only five years old and she sings like a nightingale already," replied Fausto, beaming. "Her name is Assunta. . . . You really must see her one day, Signorino."

It was now quite dark in the church. Apart from the red lamp before the altar of the Blessed Sacrament the only light was from a small bulb over the entrance to the sacristy.

"Isn't Padre Barnaba coming back here this evening?" asked Thomas.

"No. What would he want here?"

"I thought he spent all his free time in the church?"

Fausto laughed. "Yes, if he could do what he liked he would certainly sit here the whole night too."

He went up to the altar, took the old picture in his arms, and carried it into the sacristy with the tenderest care, as if he were carrying a newborn babe in his rough hands.

It had grown cooler outside and the Piazza delle Pecore had become crowded again. The first customers were already sitting outside Sor Anacleto's. Padre Barnaba's place was still vacant but Monsignor Szarnicki was sitting next it, obviously waiting for Thomas. He seemed to see nothing at all extraordinary in a Protestant art historian taking part in a popular service in honour of the Madonna of the Shepherds, and he greeted Thomas with genuine warmth.

"I haven't seen you for a long time, my dear fellow, but I've been thinking of you quite often lately."

Thomas looked away, embarrassed. Naturally he should have informed Monsignor Szarnicki of the step he had taken. But he soon found out that the Pole had something quite different on his mind.

"Have you had any news from home recently?" he asked.

Thomas looked up. Monsignor Szarnicki seemed worried, then, noticing Thomas's surprise, he continued: "Naturally I'm thinking of the international situation. It doesn't look very hopeful. You understand, of course, that we Poles must watch the development of events very closely. And your problems are rather similar, are they not? "

"I have not heard any disturbing news from Finland. As far as I know, everything is all right there."

"If that's so you have every reason to be thankful. . . ." Szarnicki hesitated for a moment, then leaned over and whispered: "They say the Germans are entering into an agreement with the Russians. You will realize that the result may be another Tilsit. If that comes to pass, God help our two countries! "

When Thomas was on his way to the Brigittine Convent the next morning to make his First Communion he caught sight of a familiar figure waiting on the Piazza Farnese. It was Padre Barnaba. He was visibly moved and quietly pressed a small prayer-book into Thomas's hand.

"A little souvenir of the Madonna of the Shepherds, and God be with you, *figlio mio!*"

The book was the office of the Blessed Virgin Mary. Across the flyleaf Padre Barnaba had written, in bold copper-plate, three laboriously composed aphorisms:

"Only one who stands on firm ground himself can help others.

"Mary is the first human-being who was physically taken from the world of shadows into the heavenly kingdom.

"Therefore she is our surest guide to the world of reality."

The Brigittine Sisters had decorated their little chapel with Alpine meadow flowers from their summer home in Genzano. A few members of the Olaus Magnus Society, who had been hurriedly mustered, occupied the small space and made the responses during the Mass with almost military precision. But the whole time Thomas knelt before the tabernacle with his face buried in his hands and neither saw nor heard anything of what was going on around him. Only after he had received Holy Communion did he open his eyes; as his gaze turned enquiringly, as though looking for a sign of approval or confirmation, towards the flower-crowned statue of the Mother of God that stood beside the altar.

Book Two

THE LORD PASSES BY

❦

XI THE ROME EXPRESS, 1940

As the sun was setting the train passed through Florence, which lay bathed in an unreal, golden light. The German professor's eyes greedily drank in the intoxicating picture. "How beautiful," he murmured, with almost childish delight.

Thomas only nodded. He had been travelling three days and three nights without a break, and was very tired. Moreover, the oppressive midday heat in the Po plain had brought back his old head pains.

The German grew quite lyrical. "Florence presents an almost sacred picture," he mused. "There are towns which are dominated by one single church, around which the whole commune groups itself in hierarchical obedience, as it were. Then again there are other towns in which one finds Christianity represented in a more direct form – purely national, you understand. When one comes into a town of this kind one feels instinctively that its citizens and architects were devout believers. There is not only one church, there are many. They have grown organically out of the commune and their dominating presence gives the whole vista a discreet but characteristic stamp. Does it not seem to you that the spiritual temperature in such towns is always several degrees higher? They have a popular, not to say democratic, atmosphere – here in Italy even more than in Protestant Germany. . . ."

"The churches here in Italy enshrine a Sacrament in which

the people still believe," interjected Thomas, "so if the spiritual temperature outside them is higher than elsewhere, the explanation is quite simple."

"Indeed! Let's hear it, then."

"The church doors are always open."

The German did not grasp the significance of the remark. He eyed his travelling companion with amused interest. "Yes, that may be," he said with a smile, and opened his evening paper.

Immediately north of Arezzo the darkness of night, which seemed to flow up from the south, enveloped the train. Thomas leaned his aching head against the dusty upholstered corner. The hammering in his neck was nerve-racking. He thought with horror of the coming night.

The German was reading the war news. He seemed immersed in an account of the destruction of Rotterdam. But suddenly he let the paper fall with a gesture of despair.

"It's frightful," he said. "And what is it all for? Surely our task is to defend civilization, not to destroy it."

"Against whom would you defend it?" asked Thomas caustically.

The German looked at him intently from behind his glasses. "How can you ask that?" he said.

"Pardon?"

"I understand you're a Finn?"

"That's right."

The German cleared his throat solemnly. "Your struggle has been the only positive and rational fight in all this slaughter. . . ." Leaning over to Thomas, he laid his hand on his knee, and continued in a lower voice. "Unfortunately you Finns had to fight alone, but I assure you that the whole civilized world, Germany included, was on your side at heart. You have almost rekindled the spirit of the Crusades, a spirit which Europe has never known since Sobieski's day. Therein lies the historical significance of your fight. But it is not yet at an end. Europe needs a spirit such as yours. You Finns have shown the way. European culture is essentially a culture of the Crusades. . . ."

Suddenly a long line of faint lights appeared, sharply delineated, high up on a mountain-side in the east. That must be Cortona, thought Thomas. So it's several hours more to Rome! Now the lights were snuffed out by a suffocating, moist darkness. The perspiration broke out on Thomas's forehead, and he felt sick. He knew the symptoms only too well. There was only one thing that could help him now – absolute rest and quiet.

He shut his eyes in a desperate effort to relax, and actually succeeded in dozing off for a while, but when he awoke his head was paining him so much that it was hopeless to think of getting to sleep again. The train was now passing through the verdant plain of Umbria. It was a May night, soft as velvet, lit by feeble starlight, but still warm. The German had begun talking again – or perhaps he had been talking the whole time. Now he was holding forth on Europe's common destiny. . . .

The landscape gliding past them was only faintly discernible, but suddenly, to the right of the track an immensely high rocky wall reared up. On its summit a row of yellow lights glittered like the eyes of beasts of prey lying in wait. The train slowed down and finally glided with screeching brakes into a well-lit railway station. Most of the travellers prepared to get out. Thomas stood up like a sleep-walker, took down his luggage, nodded to the German, and almost unconsciously followed the stream of passengers. He had no idea of where he was. He knew only that he could not last out any longer.

The station was noisy and crowded, but the fresh air gave momentary relief. Thomas laid down his luggage and looked around him. The lights up on the hill were more distinct now, but still he could not imagine what town lay behind them. The human stream dammed up in front of a notice board on which there was something about accommodation for pilgrims. At last he caught sight of the name Orvieto lit up by an arc-light.

An overloaded hotel bus brought him to the town on the mountain-side. Throngs of people were pushing their way through the narrow streets. Naturally the hotel was full to overflowing but the proprietor, out of pity for Thomas's sorry state, fixed up a bed for him on the sofa in a shabby drawing-room that bore its dusty, threadbare elegance of the eighties with comical dignity.

Obviously this was a favour, but the guest could only respond passively, for the shaky bus journey had increased his pains and he was on the verge of collapse.

With an ice-bag pressed to his forehead he lay as if unconscious, waiting for the frightful tension in the blood-vessels at the back of his head to ease off. A picture of Umberto the First hung over the sofa; the air in the room was fusty. A ceaseless uproar came in from the street – singing and laughter, the shouting of children, shrill whistling, tired tramping, and hurried steps, the tinkle of bicycle bells, and the violent clatter of motor-bikes. Each new wave of noise pierced his neck like splinters of glass, and the pain came back in heavy, hot waves. . . .

The words of the German in the train had awakened distorted, nightmarish memories – his headlong rush home to Finland in the late summer of the previous year when war became imminent; the melancholy beauty of autumn, with its mild and muted tints, as the war-clouds gathered over his unhappy country; the complete change which had gradually come over the populace – the selfless self-sacrifice and patriotism that had turned the wait in the condemned cell into a moral miracle. He suddenly found himself back in those days. A newspaper had employed him immediately to take the place of its foreign news-editor, who had been called up. For two months he had sat and read despatches and correspondence from all parts of the world. The distance between Finland and the countries of Europe outside seemed suddenly to have contracted; the rest of humanity seemed to have moved fraternally nearer to the small, forgotten nation in the north. He, Thomas, wrote his news paragraphs and set out the various columns with the firm conviction that the Lord had chosen his people to be his champions – until one morning the Russian bombs began to fall over Finland, and from that moment she was as alone as ever. . . .

Two days later a green form lay among the telegrams on the news editor's table. It was a call-up paper – Militiaman Thomas Cinnelius was ordered to report at once at the regional defence headquarters in his native parish of Kinnalax, Northern Karelia.

The Cinnelius family had been pastors up there for generations, and a brother of his father still held the old family farmstead of Kinnby. Thomas had spent several summers there as a child, and his town-bred mind had become fascinated by its wild, desolate beauty, though the austere spiritual atmosphere had oppressed him.

The poverty-stricken region in the north of the parish horrified him particularly. It was called "the Famine Pit" in the local dialect, and the wild backwoods population in that old moorland parish had always been resistant to the civilizing influence of the Cinnelius family.

Thomas arrived in Kinnalax on a dark December day. The familiar landscape seemed more desolate and barren than ever. The farmhouses lay as if devoid of life among the snow-covered fields; the woods stood black and wet around the cold, grey lake, and not a ray of sunshine lightened the monotonously sombre horizon. The population was already being evacuated. Not a soul was left in Kinnby. Thomas made a last tour through the old familiar rooms in which a military staff was just settling in, not for the first time in the history of the farmstead, he recalled. His forefathers had often had to give up their home to the armed forces and even join the ranks themselves, one with a sword, another with a Bible in his hand. But none of them had ever complained. For that had been the immemorial destiny of the frontier dwellers in a country whose national flag bore the emblem of the Cross. . . .

Suddenly he felt he could understand why everything had had to happen as it did, and why he was now standing here alone. For centuries the Church militant had carried on its struggle, forgotten and unnoticed, among his own people and in his own family; and the victims of that fight lay silent and forgotten in the cemeteries of Karelia under the poor wooden crosses. Now his turn had come to take up the cross his fathers had borne. But he must do so alone and without the moral support of others of like mind. He must offer his sacrifice to God, and God alone, for his native parish. . . .

He was still immersed in this train of thought when the

Russian bombers came flying low over the jagged silhouette of the northern woods. They flew right into the swampy pinewood region unsighted by the scattered anti-aircraft units. Thomas rushed out on the road hoping desperately to reach his quarters before the enemy got to the village. But suddenly the frozen ground under his feet heaved up, striking him on the head with such force that he lost consciousness.

It was late afternoon when the bombers came over. The village had been burning the whole night. From where he now lay helpless on the floor of the dressing-station, Thomas could see Kinnby being devoured by flames each time he came to between bouts of unconsciousness. Soon the flames spread to the neighbouring farmhouse, until finally, like hungry wolves, they flung themselves on the village church. When the pale grey dawn of morning lit the frozen waters of the lake, the whole village was literally level with the ground, and ominous fresh clouds of smoke were rising from the distant hills of " the Famine Pit ". Thomas, almost blind and deaf from pain, was taken to a field hospital in an Army ambulance. The doctor's words still rang in his ears:

" They will probably have to take you to a real hospital for examination, but whatever happens you must not get up for several days. If you do, anything may happen."

The clock in the hall of the Orvieto hotel struck twelve. It gradually became quiet in the corridors, and also in the streets. The ice in the ice-bag had melted, but the piercing pains in his head had eased. As if freed from a horrifying nightmare, Thomas dropped off to sleep.

❦

XII ORVIETO

The rest had restored Thomas's strength to some extent. The next morning he remained lying on the sofa until the hotel proprietor came and asked him if he wanted to see the procession. Only then did he remember that it was the Feast of Corpus Christi. He had never been in Orvieto before. Now it seemed as though a kind Providence had led him here just on the day of the famous procession of the Blessed Sacrament.

He opened the window and breathed in the warm, fragrant air of early summer. Then, after a cup of black coffee and a roll, he set out to find the way to the Cathedral, but the throng was so great that it was almost impossible to get through the narrow streets. Finally the crowds forced him against a house wall and he could move neither back nor forward. Waking up with a start from his day-dreaming, he looked around him.

This part of the town did not look very festive. He was standing in a back street between rows of mean houses decorated with tawdry paper garlands and in their windows pictures of Christ surrounded by candles. On his right was a dirty barber shop, on his left a low bar, and opposite a general store that sold ironmongery, cheap crockery, and hideous tourist souvenirs. Continuing on his way, he wandered through a seemingly endless slum quarter, with only an occasional Gothic church window or Renaissance façade to relieve the drab greyness.

Suddenly from the other end of the street came a roar that spread like thunder through the surging crowds, and finally emerged as a primitive, sentimental melody which was quickly taken up by all those around:

> " *T'adoriam, ostia divina,*
> *t'adoriam, ostia d'amor.*
> *Tu dell' Angelo il sospiro,*
> *tu dell' uomo sei l'onor . . .*"

> (*We adore Thee, Divine Bread,*
> *We adore Thee, Bread of Love,*
> *Thou art the joy of the angels,*
> *Thou art the honour of man . . .*)

Thomas remembered this Italian hymn from the Corpus Christi processions that wound their way between the flowering gardens of Tuscany and through the shady, wooded paths of the Alban Hills. Heard in such surroundings there was something of the romance of folklore about it, but sung in city slums or roared through loudspeakers from famous cathedrals, it somehow seemed less edifying. Slowly as a tortoise, it was now dragging its way through the sultry back streets of Orvieto.

"What on earth am I doing here?" Thomas asked himself as he wiped the perspiration from his forehead and looked about him for a way out. Every possibility of retreat was cut off.

Now he noticed that he was moving forward automatically with the mass of people who – almost as imperceptibly as a sand-dune – was being propelled forward by an invisible force. They were progressing only at a few yards per minute, and Thomas found this almost more exhausting than standing still, for he had by no means recovered from yesterday's fatigue and illness. His neck was getting painfully stiff, and the mounting rhythm of his blood was causing a buzzing in his ears. After a good half hour the slow pushing forward had sluiced him to the other end of the street. There was an ominous throbbing in the back of his head, but he summoned up all his strength, for it could not be much farther to the Cathedral now. Only one more corner to get round – and there he was tottering on to the sunlit, light-filled Piazza. Dazzled and stupefied, he stood still as if confronted with a revelation.

Before him rose the Cathedral, shining white like a marble cascade against the brilliant blue sky. The sight almost took his breath away. His eyes told him that he was standing before a perfect work of art – probably the most imposing he had ever seen. If architecture could be described as music in stone, this cathedral was an immortal expression of the Christian hosanna. His thoughts wandered back involuntarily to the crypt in Bolsena. He knew that the building of this Cathedral of Orvieto had been ordered by Pope Urban IV to enshrine the blood-stained chalice cloth of the miracle of Bolsena. So from the mystic ground with its dark stain of blood an orchid of supernatural beauty had sprung up. The miracle, the actual Miracle of Bolsena, had found its final confirmation here.

His pulse was still hammering wildly, but his fatigue had

vanished. The secret dreams of his youth which he had already almost forgotten, were they suddenly to be fulfilled? The overwhelming sight before his eyes seemed like the *Ecclesia triumphans* in concrete form. . . .

Accompanied by a deafening clanging of bells and a thunderous surge of hymns, the procession of the Blessed Sacrament slowly emerged and moved down among the seething multitudes on the Piazza. Thomas saw a white silk canopy rocking to and fro in the broad portal of the cathedral. Joy and enthusiasm swept over the Piazza like a spring storm. At each side of the canopy a double row of monks and priests and seminarists in white surplices walked with lighted candles in their hands. Above them rose a tall white mitre, and under it a thin, fine-featured face with bushy white eyebrows and penetrating eyes that might have served as a model for one of Simone Martine's Apostles. The bishop was carrying the reliquary with the original blood-stained corporal from the miraculous Mass at Bolsena, and as he passed the multitudes sank to their knees as if mown down.

The bells in the campanile continued their powerful pealing. With growing excitement Thomas listened to their message. They seemed to him to have something ineffably significant to announce. Could it be the Second Coming of the Son of Man in unimaginable glory? All creation seemed to be preparing to take part in the triumphal procession. The old town had suddenly assumed a golden radiance; hymns of triumph soared heavenwards from the rejoicing crowds. Even the Cathedral itself seemed to be waiting to take its place in the procession. And now – now it too started moving. But Thomas Cinnelius fell forward on his face like Moses on Mount Sinai. . . .

He was carried into the old bishop's palace beside the cathedral. Those around him had asserted that he had cried out like one who had seen a vision as the corporal was carried past. The rumour that a foreigner had seen a vision during the procession spread through the whole square and soon a curious crowd gathered in front of the palace.

But Thomas himself was not aware of any visions. The throbbing in his fever-ridden brain felt like the blows of a hammer. In spirit he was still lying prostrate before the house of the Lord. It was no longer the radiant Cathedral of Orvieto, however, but a poor little church in dark, wintry Wiborg.

The long train journey after the air-raid on Kinnalax had exhausted his last ounce of strength. They had finally taken him to the military hospital in Wiborg for a thorough examination. The wait there was long and painful. The Russian air force was attacking the town incessantly, fires were raging at various points, and the hospital was about to be evacuated. Thomas asked for a Catholic priest, but none came. He repeated his request and finally wrote to the rector of the little Catholic parish, but all in vain. In his overwrought state he imagined that the military authorities were denying him a priest through prejudice. He feared he would die without absolution, so he gathered his clothing together and slipped out of the hospital when nobody was looking. He got away without difficulty because no one could imagine any patient going into the burning town.

The church was in the centre of the old town, which had suffered heavily in the bombardment. It was a long way off, the air was bitterly cold, and there was no transport. Thomas wandered through ruins of the scenes of his childhood; past the massive eighteenth-century ramparts on which he used to play when the spring sun shone green over the sea and the water from the melting ice gushed out through the gun-ports. The harbour, smelling of machine oil and grain, shimmered here and there between the black hulks of freighters. He recalled the clear May nights filled with mysterious whispers. At last he reached the narrow medieval streets through which he used to wander with his friend Boris, immersed in endless philosophical discussions, on starlit winter evenings when not a sound was to be heard but the crunching of the snow under their feet.

It was a horrifying walk, but he became conscious of its utter frightfulness only when he fell down exhausted on reaching his goal. Once more he had the mysterious feeling that he had to tread the same path of suffering as his forefathers. Even his own father had never felt quite happy and at home in this town where he had always remained an exile. After the early death of his wife he had lived like a hermit, then, one dark January evening, he had fallen and broken his spine. He was found – a poor heap of humanity – crushed by the nemesis of mortality, on his own cellar stairs. The house and everything in it had come under the auctioneer's hammer, and the most positive legacy that Thomas had inherited from his father was a secret fear of life. . . . And now here he was himself, lying on the street like an old rag in the town of his childhood, watching it being shattered into ruins.

The little church was shut. He rattled desperately at the door, but it did not stir. He hammered, knocked, shouted, but all in vain. Then he slipped round the corner to the presbytery and rang the bell. No one opened. He noticed now that the snow was lying ankle deep and untouched on the steps. Fear gripped his heart again, and he began calling loudly for the priest.

At last an air-raid warden came out of a near-by building. "It's no good," he said. "There's nobody there."

"You're wrong," replied Thomas irritably. "It's the pastor's house."

"Do you mean the foreign priest?" asked the man contemptuously. "He cleared off in time." But, seeing Thomas's dismay he continued, more sympathetically: "I'm sorry, comrade, but this church hasn't been open since the war began. . . ."

He stopped short, for Thomas suddenly burst out laughing. "It's nothing," he says, waving the man off, "I only thought of a funny story."

"And what was that?" asked the man suspiciously.

"Something about crusaders' banners. . . ."

Those were Thomas's last words before he lost consciousness, and they left a bitter taste in his mouth for weeks afterwards. The man's answer, on the other hand, was blotted from his memory, for at that same moment hell broke loose again, in the air, in the air-raid shelter, and in his own head. He was taken back to the hospital where an aneurism of the blood-vessels of the brain was diagnosed, a condition complicated by severe inflammation of the lungs. Transfer to a hospital in Western Finland proved beneficial, but for a long time he lay hovering between life and death. When he finally returned to full consciousness life had completely changed.

Thomas heard a strange voice above him. "No, that's not sun-stroke. He's just completely exhausted."

He opened his eyes and found himself lying on a sofa in a white-washed room with a vaulted ceiling and deep window embrasures. A nun was sitting beside him cooling his temples with iced water. Behind him were two priests talking to a man in ordinary clothes, obviously a doctor. A tall, white-haired man in impeccable clerical attire had just come in. He returned the respectful greet-ings of the others with an almost youthful grimace. Thomas stared up bewildered at the thin, sharp profile and clever grey eyes. They seemed curiously familiar. Suddenly he remembered. Yes, of course. It was the prelate who had carried the Blessed Sacrament in the procession.

"Have you been able to find out who he is?" asked the new-comer with an unmistakably American accent.

"Yes, Your Eminence," replied the doctor. "It seems he's a poor pilgrim from Finland."

"From Finland?" repeated the tall man with an astonished laugh. "Is that possible?" He came over to the sofa and bent down to Thomas. "But, look, he's quite conscious! How are you feeling? Do you speak Italian?"

"I think I'm all right now, thank you," whispered Thomas, trying to sit up.

"Please don't stir. Obviously you have suffered a severe shock. Did the strenuous journey across the Continent make you ill, or what was it?"

"I was probably a little rash, for I'm still convalescent, but I shall be all right."

"Were you wounded in the war?"

"No, not exactly. I only got hurt in an air-raid."

"Where was that?"

"In Northern Karelia."

The questioner's face again showed the same little youthful grimace. He eyed Thomas with obvious sympathy, then, nodding to the others, he said: "Well, gentlemen! It seems we have a living specimen of one of Mannerheim's soldiers here. Take a good look at him because there are not many of them left."

"I'm not a soldier," murmured Thomas. "I was only a kind of territorial."

"That's certainly nothing to be ashamed of. What is your calling, then?"

"I am, or rather I was, an art historian."

"And are you not one now?"

"No, I'm going to study theology."

The priests exchanged significant glances.

"I didn't know that Finns came to Italy to study theology," said the tall man in his calm way.

"No, they don't normally, but I'm an exception. I'm a Catholic."

Silence fell in the room.

"How does one go about becoming a Catholic in Finland?" one of them asked in a subdued tone.

"I really can't say. I became a Catholic in Rome."

The tall man nodded. "I should have guessed as much," he said. "And now you're going back to Rome to become a priest?"

"Yes."

The sharp grey eyes became suddenly troubled. "The climate in Rome is trying. You should be very careful there with your head trouble." He turned to go, and added in parting a few conventional words which nevertheless disclosed a certain curiosity: "I take it that you have good friends who will help you down there?"

"I haven't got many, I admit."

"Where did you receive your instruction in the faith?"

"In a dissolved monastery where there was no place for me."

"That sounds rather odd. What was the name of the monastery?"

"Santa Presenza."

"What?" asked the other, visibly astonished. "You were converted in Santa Presenza?" He signed to the others to leave the room, then sat down on the edge of the sofa.

"Forgive my curiosity, but this interests me because I know that place quite well. Perhaps you may have heard mention of me there. I'm Patrick Norcus" – and this time the little grimace became a broad grin – "otherwise known as '*Il cardinal americano*'."

Thomas now recalled that Padre Barnaba had spoken several times of Cardinal Norcus. But in other quarters too he had stumbled on the name of that prince of the Church. Norcus had been living in Italy for many years. He practised philanthropy on a large scale and was extremely popular. Moreover, he was a highly individual person. His father had been an Irish immigrant, his mother a member of the French aristocracy, and through her he had been introduced into high society while still a youth. He had studied at Oxford, the Sorbonne, and the Gregorian University, and was well trained in political science. He had been made Rector of the Papal Academy of Diplomacy, had then been entrusted with various special missions on behalf of the Papal Secretariat of State and had received the red hat when he had just turned forty. That was in the second decade of this century, and he would probably have become Papal Secretary of State if he had not been closely identified with one of the belligerent powers. So he had remained only *il cardinal americano*, one of the most reliable counsellors of the Curia, and at the same time a colourful and remarkable addition to the unique collection of human originals in the Eternal City.

He listened in silence to Thomas's report. Only when the latter had finished did he ask casually: "What actually happened on the Piazza during the procession?"

Thomas drew his hand over his forehead as if he were trying to dispel an unpleasant memory. "I don't really know," he said. "I must have had an hallucination of some kind. Between the heat, the exhaustion and the migraine – it was all too much for me. It suddenly seemed to me that the Cathedral was beginning to move with the procession . . . and then I lost consciousness. Perhaps it was the mental excitement."

"What mental excitement?"

Thomas flushed. "Your Eminence, I was completely unprepared for the beauty of the cathedral, and the whole spectacle had an overwhelming effect on me. I regarded it almost as a miracle. And I saw it as an answer to my prayers, a confirmation of my vocation, a revelation of the Church triumphant. . . ."

The Cardinal raised his hand. "One moment, please. I must remind you that the Curia in Rome has a positive horror of visions. A disabled man may conceivably get permission to become a priest, a visionary never."

"But I haven't had any vision," protested Thomas.

"So much the better. But you must beware. There must be no repetition, under any circumstances, of whatever happened to you on the Piazza. You have caused a good deal of unnecessary excitement among the people – even though quite unintentionally. You understand what I mean, don't you?"

"Yes, and it will never happen again."

"I will take your word for it. But if I were you, dear Mr Cinnelius, I would get all those fantasies about the Church triumphant right out of my head once for all. We Catholics have got more than enough to do to help our suffering brethren in the faith. This is my advice to you, and if you take it I shall gladly put in a word for you in Rome, if ever you wish me to."

"I am very grateful to Your Eminence."

"But I have one other condition: if you have any recurrence of this, you must look me up. Will you promise me that?"

"Willingly," whispered Thomas, shutting his eyes to conceal his emotion.

"*Benedicat*," murmured Patrick Cardinal Norcus.

❦

XIII   PADRE BARNABA'S PARISH

The gathering dusk of the May evening was drawing cubistic triangular shadows over the irregular quadrangle of the Piazza delle Pecore. The hot season was just beginning and the chief function of the houses seemed to be to form a back-cloth to the open-air stage of the Piazza. Following its natural instinct, the entire population had foregathered in the market place, where life seemed to expand just as colourfully and luxuriantly in these early summer days as in a valley among the mountains. Barefooted children were playing marbles on the worn pavements; black-haired girls, with heavy copper jugs on their heads, were chattering at the fountain; and a gaily painted wine cart with enormous wheels and creaking axles, was rocking down the Vicolo dei Pecorai. In the background stood a couple of people who might have stepped straight out of an Abruzzi Christmas crib – Sor Anacleto with a white apron over his pot belly heartily clapping on the shoulder a sunburnt man in heelless shoes with a sheep-skin jacket over his arm and a leather sack on his back. There was nothing at all to indicate that any of the people in this peaceful, idyllic scene were aware that one of the most tremendous struggles of the War was raging at that time on the other side of the Alps.

Thomas had instinctively slackened his pace as soon as he caught sight of the black marble goats around the fountain. Was this not like walking into the middle of an early nineteenth-century genre painting? As he drew nearer the picture came to life and he himself assumed a part in it. He had to pass a whole series of faces that nodded friendly recognition. But he did not want to stop and talk before he had met Padre Barnaba; for he had great news for him.

On the other side of the square the old men from the poor-house were sitting ranged down both sides of the broad baroque steps of San Lino's, like sparrows on a telephone wire. The doors of the church stood wide open. Thomas noticed several people going in, evidently to the usual May devotions. He pushed the heavy leather curtain a little aside. A rhythmical murmur of prayer, like the hum from a beehive, struck his ear. The church was full. Padre Barnaba was kneeling before the alter, but bent so low that one could see nothing but his gold-embroidered cope. His voice sounded more indistinct and tired than Thomas had remembered it. Otherwise everything was as before.

As before – except for the fact that Thomas had now received a call. This call had begun to sound in his heart among the snow-drifts of Wiborg as a bitter-sweet yearning for all that lay hidden behind the closed church door. Even in the severest crisis of his illness it had lain in his subconscious, colouring the imaginary world of his delirious dreams. During the weeks of convalescence it had risen gradually into his conscious mind again, until finally it had become an imperious command which was to determine the course of his life. It caused him bewilderment and anxiety, but on the whole it made him happy, for it told him that in spite of everything his life now had a purpose.

Looking back on his illness, he realized that the force behind that yearning was his love for the living Sacrament. It had saved him from dying in the snow, kept him alive on his sick-bed, and given him back his strength. And like every great love, it demanded total self-surrender. From day to day the call had sounded more distinctly in his soul. Finally, he had literally taken up his bed and walked. The doctors had expressed their fears, but in the end, with many warnings regarding his future mode of life, they had consented to his returning to the South to convalesce.

Thomas had then visited the nearest Catholic priest and told him of his intention of studying for the priesthood. He was a young Dutchman who had been only a short time in Finland, and he did not know Thomas. He seemed sceptical, for there had not been a vocation to the priesthood from Finland since the turn of the century. But Thomas was insistent.

"I was very near death – perhaps even a little beyond the boundary. The world is no longer the same to me," he said.

The priest nodded sympathetically, though obviously by no means convinced. "Of course that is nothing to boast of," added Thomas. "I have had only a foretaste of damnation. I know what it is to stand outside when the gates of heaven seem closed for ever. That experience will determine the course of my life."

"But it is hardly an adequate reason for wishing to become a priest," objected the other.

"But don't you see that it was in this way I became aware of my vocation? I know that Someone heard my cry for help. I received an answer through the locked door of the church, and I have taken that answer as a call. Now I want to learn to open the door of the Church to others with my own hands. This is the only really essential task I can see as yet in my life. . . ."

After lengthy discussion and much hesitation the priest finally gave him a letter of recommendation, with the advice to get in touch first of all with the Italian priest who had received him into the Church. So he had set off for Rome and here he was, come to visit Santa Presenza. Now more than ever he needed Padre Barnaba's moral support.

Thomas found a *prie-dieu* behind the old confessional. The Litany of the Blessed Virgin was beginning. Up in front of the altar the priest was reciting the invocations, and the monotonous *Ora pro nobis* of the congregation came in rhythmic surges, like the wash of the waves round a ship's prow. He followed the text in his prayer-book:

> "*Janua coeli,*
> *Stella matutina,*
> *Salus infirmorum,*
> *Refugiam peccatorum,*
> *Consolatrix afflictorum,*
> *Auxilium christianorum* . . ."

Each new invocation set chords vibrating in his soul - chords which he had not dared to touch for many a day. He felt near his goal. With pleading eyes he looked up as if he hoped that Padre Barnaba would come down himself and lead him up to the altar with his own hands.

The litany ended. The priest walked forward and took up the monstrance to give the Benediction of the Blessed Sacrament, but when he turned round Thomas saw to his dismay that it was not Padre Barnaba at all.

As the church emptied he remained quietly in his dark corner lest he betray his disappointment. Only when Fausto reappeared, this time with his rattling bunch of keys, did he slip away towards the exit.

On the steps he met the old lawyer from the Via Giulia, who greeted him with a friendly smile.

"Good evening! Welcome back to Rome!"

"Good evening . . ." said Thomas hesitantly.

"I have seen you in Padre Barnaba's company," explained Signor Tartaruga, and was about to pass on with a nod, but Thomas held him back, saying: "Excuse me, Signor, but who was the priest at the altar?"

"That's the new parish priest. Haven't you met him?"

"No, I haven't."

"You'll find him over there in the parish office. You are more likely to find him in the morning, because he doesn't live here."

"Where's Padre Barnaba, then?"

"He has been moved. Didn't you know?"

"No. When was that?"

"Shortly before Christmas. I thought you knew all about it. You were such good friends, were you not?"

Thomas could only shake his head. "Where has he gone?" he asked at last.

The other hesitated. "I don't know," he said. "Somewhere in the country, I believe."

"But how was that possible? Who looks after Santa Presenza?"

"There's not much left to look after there. I presume the archives and books will be taken into the Vatican library in due course. The house itself will remain what it is already, a home for the aged poor. *Finito.*"

"But won't a tradition of centuries be lost then . . . ?"

"We have still older ruins in the city."

"My God! Then all the work which has ever been done in this house will have been in vain."

The lawyer looked thoughtfully at Thomas.

"Why should it have been in vain?" he said. "Don't you know the words: 'Except a corn of wheat fall into the ground and die . . .'? Only God can see the seed that will one day spring up round this old dead monastery, and not only in this district. Santa Presenza has most assuredly not been in vain. . . ." He stopped abruptly and stretched out his hand to Thomas. "Pardon

H

me, but I have to go now. I'm Avvocato Tartaruga. I hope we shall meet soon again. I come to San Lino's regularly."

"I'm very glad to have met you, but I'm afraid there will be nothing to bring me to San Lino's any more."

Signor Tartaruga's eyes suddenly became wistful and clouded with emotion. "*Caro mio,* you are not the only one who mourns for Santa Presenza," he said, raising his tremulous old hands to Thomas's shoulders. "We have a little circle here consisting of layfolk and secular priests, who try to preserve and cherish something of the spiritual heritage of the old Brotherhood. It is a purely private association and works in a hidden, silent manner. We call ourselves the 'San Lino Circle' and we meet a few times a month. You have probably never heard of us."

"No, never."

"I shall gladly introduce you should you care to join us. Get in touch with me if you would like to." And shaking hands once more, he nodded to Thomas and went off.

Sor Anacleto's pleasant grinning face hove into sight at the other side of the Lane. Waving his short, thick arms he cried: "Welcome back, Signorino! Do me the honour of sampling my new Frascati!"

Darkness had fallen densely, almost palpably, over the Piazza. The platter of the water in the fountain basin had suddenly become audible. The whole quarter seemed to be breathing a sigh of relief after the oppressive heat of the day, and a strange mixture of odours streamed out of the houses into the air, which was becoming cooler. There was the usual vapour of wine from the cellars, the smell of cheap perfume from the barber's shop, and from the *osteria* a delightful odour of food.

Sor Anacleto appeared with a half-litre carafe. "*Complimenti,*" he said, filling out a glass of yellow wine which foamed as new wine does.

"Please sit down a little while," pleaded Thomas, "and tell me where Padre Barnaba has gone."

The innkeeper produced a second glass as if by magic from under his white apron. "Padre Barnaba has gone back to his mountains. I was glad for his sake." He sighed and took a deep draught of wine.

"Why? Was it a promotion?"

Sor Anacleto smiled. "Padre Barnaba wanted to retire. He deserves a bit of a change of air in his old age, don't you think? And he has certainly been wearing himself out long enough in this hole of a place. But of course it's very sad for us. We shall wait many a long day for a better parish priest," he added, wiping his moustache with a green-spotted handkerchief.

"Where is his new parish?"

"Somewhere up in the Abruzzi, beyond Castelpendente. It's a long way from here."

"Have you never been there?"

"No, I'm not from that district, I'm from Naples. Cesarino!"

A tall boy of about fourteen emerged out of the darkness behind the fountain and came as far as the footpath. There he stopped, and his black eyes, glittering in the light from the *osteria*, looked warily around.

"My son," said Sor Anacleto with fatherly pride, laying his arm round the shoulders of the reluctant boy. "He works with a coach company and knows more of Italy than I do."

"At your service, Excellency," muttered Cesarino, trying to make off.

"Wait a minute," said the father. "I'm sure you know which bus line to take to Padre Barnaba."

Cesarino burst out into a rude laugh. "There aren't any buses to there – or anywhere even near there," he said. And, nimbly disengaging himself from under his father's arm, he disappeared into the sheltering darkness of the lane.

"He has a girl round the corner," said Sor Anacleto apologetically. "He used to be Padre Barnaba's best acolyte, but who is there now to see that he even lives like a Christian . . . ? It's not so easy for the young ones nowadays." He was obviously about to embark on a very delicate subject but suddenly stopped short and stood up: "Oh, there are more customers! I hope you won't forget us, Signorino, even though Padre Barnaba isn't here any more."

Thomas walked slowly up the Vicolo dei Pecorai, which was filled with shrill whistles and giggles. He could not help glancing up at Santa Presenza. The monastery stood there lifeless and dark, looking more like a prison than ever. The door into the garden stood ajar. He pushed it and slipped in. An odour of damp earth and living growth assailed his nostrils. Myrtles and ivy sprawled over the sparse bit of ground, rambling roses covered the pillars, and a chestnut tree near by was in full bloom. The cloisters themselves were desolate and deserted, but when he listened more closely he could hear the monotonous croaking of the toads from the half-ruined fountain in the garden.

⁂

XIV THE COLLEGE OF THE PROPAGANDA, 1942

Monsignor dei Palleschi was sitting in his office looking out the window at the little football field in the grounds, where a lively match was in progress between the students. Negroes, Hindus, Arabs, Malayans, Chinese and Japanese, all dressed in the long narrow soutanes of the college, were rushing merrily to and fro in clumsy efforts to get possession of the ball. There was a cackle and chatter as if from a duck-pond, and the Roman sun shone down, warm and friendly, on smart red braid, gleaming teeth, and dazzling white, rolling eyeballs.

Monsignor dei Palleschi was thoroughly enjoying the sight. Boys will be boys even if they are going to be priests. He noted with satisfaction that the different racial colours were divided impartially between the two sides. That meant that the prevailing spirit was Roman, brotherly and good. Any tendency to form cliques must be nipped in the bud even if it was only a matter of a football match. To permit it would be dangerous to the spiritual health of the college, for the fathers and brothers of these youths were fighting each other at this moment on the widely separated battlefields of this poor crazy world. Rome had soon become the only spot on the face of the earth where the difference between Jew and Greek remained obliterated.

One student, however, was not taking part in the game. He was a small, freckled, flaxen-haired young man with a somewhat haughty and reserved expression. Apparently oblivious of his surroundings, he was sitting on the grass under a fig-tree, buried in a book. The Rector's eyes took on an expression of slight annoyance. As usual, this young man was not in the humour for games. These Scandinavians – they were always intractable and different. . . .

Monsignor Giacomo dei Palleschi prided himself on being a true Roman, a *Romano de Roma*. His family looked back on an ancestry of four centuries among the Seven Hills. Several members of his family had chosen an ecclesiastical or an academic career, sometimes both. Giacomo's theological training had been supplemented by a broad education in the humanities, which had led in due course to a professorship in philosophy. His teaching post in the Papal missionary university filled his Roman heart with pride, for he regarded it as a gracious confirmation by Providence of his family's traditions. He had soon won a name for himself as an outstanding professor and wise educator, and had finally been made Rector of the College. A bishop's ring now seemed within sight; and a career which would bring fresh laurels to the name of dei Palleschi hovered over the horizon of his dreams.

The telephone on his desk rang.

" His Eminence requires a suite for the procession tomorrow," said a business-like voice. " Can you spare four students for a few hours? "

" Need you ask? Naturally, the whole College is at the disposal of His Eminence."

" Four will be enough; but four of different colours as usual, please."

" I understand," nodded the Rector, hanging up the receiver.

" His Eminence " was Cardinal Magni, Prefect of the Congregation of the Propaganda Fide. He was also Chancellor of the University, and for this reason the Rector was particularly deferential to him. It was one of the privileges of the College to provide him with a few students as suite when he appeared in public.

Monsignor dei Palleschi upheld this tradition very strictly. When they were required, he saw to it personally that the young men chosen were of the most strikingly different nationalities. This presented an impressive picture symbolizing the unity and universality of the Church.

His searching eyes wandered over the football field. There was no difficulty at all in finding Chinese and Negroes for tasks of this kind. The Negroes in particular were deeply stirred by any ceremonial they were permitted to take part in; and the Chinese were patient and submissive and as students absolutely splendid. A Hindu could also be enlisted, if necessary, if the matter were explained to him reasonably. As usual, the most difficult thing would be to get hold of a suitable white man. It would be really too lacking in imagination to provide one from the dark-skinned Mediterranean races. A really flaxen-blond Scandinavian with a milk-white skin would be best, of course, but unfortunately there was not much of a choice of these.

The eyes of the Rector had fastened on the solitary student under the fig-tree. Yes, he would fulfil all the requirements ideally. He was considerably older than the others, to be sure, but Northerns mature much later physically – and mentally never. He would be better a bit taller, of course. Compared with most of his compatriots he was on the short side, though otherwise a fine young fellow with a colouring one would never find in the South. Moreover, he was unusually quick and intelligent for one of his nationality, and the seriousness of his dark blue eyes was reminiscent of the intense expression in pre-Raphaelite paintings. Definitely good material, but alas, so difficult to handle.

Actually, most of the Scandinavians found obvious difficulty in conforming with the spirit of the College. True, this spirit might be regarded as childish in many ways, for in such a heterogeneous collection it was not always the most mature elements who gave the tone. A stern regimen was therefore necessary. Naturally this was not easy, but it was a very healthy treatment, particularly for these spoilt Scandinavians, who were far too prone to forget that we are all children in the eyes of the Lord.

The "odd man out" under the fig-tree was Thomas Cinnelius,

the first Finn who had ever studied at the College. He had come there a year after the outbreak of war, and was one of the most difficult cases in Monsignor dei Palleschi's experience. His head was crammed full with all sorts of knowledge collected in various secular universities, with the result that he imagined himself wiser and more experienced than his colleagues. When he became involved in an argument, he bit into it like a fierce little terrier that let itself be nearly beaten to death before it would give up its bone. To have a philosophy pupil of this kind was most infuriating.

This young man, Thomas, really had the most amateurish idea of the difficult art of studying. He insisted on reading books of his own choosing as well as following the academic course. The Rector tried to point out to him discreetly that it was the teacher's business to study the books and the pupils' to listen to him. What would be the result if one allowed immature young people free and unlimited access to literature of their own choosing? But Thomas seemed to cherish a superstitious faith in printer's ink and a most regrettable contempt for verbal exposition.

Monsignor dei Palleschi found this contempt for his personal guidance painful in the extreme. Why had he become a professor? Why had he learned to master the Latin language until it was like his second native tongue, and acquired by assiduous practice that eloquence which had made him famous all over Rome, if not to give to his pupils more than they could get out of books? His lectures were widely regarded as classical examples of the verbal method of instruction on which all higher education should be based. But Thomas was entirely lacking in appreciation for the lecturer's art. He declared with brutal frankness that he could acquire by himself in a few weeks, with the aid of a suitably graded text-book, all the knowledge that the Rector trickled into his pupils' heads over a whole year. He refused obstinately to take notes and instead crammed his room with literature about everything under the sun.

For quite a long while Monsignor dei Palleschi had turned a blind eye to this importation of literature. Scandinavians have to be given a somewhat looser rein than other people, he had heard.

But when Thomas's books turned up in the rooms of other students too, the Rector felt impelled to intervene. So one morning he quietly took an inventory of Doctor Cinnelius's private library and confiscated all the less desirable volumes. In their place he left on the young man's table some favourite volumes from his own library – *The Introduction to a Devout Life* by Saint Francis de Sales, a biography of Saint Philip Neri, and a magnificent illustrated volume on the Catacombs of Rome. But there was no sign of a change of heart in Thomas. He seemed, indeed, to be going his own way more obstinately than ever. Even now the Rector's sharp eyes could see from his office window that Thomas's book was *not* from the College library. Now, this was not only a question of his, the Rector's, authority. The fundamental principles of imparting education demanded that the young man should be led back to the right path.

Monsignor sent for his vice-rector, Don Gualtiero, who was responsible for the practical supervision of the students. He was a little Sicilian with a big heart, and was greatly loved in the College. In the course of two decades of adventurous missionary life in exotic countries he had gained a wealth of experience. He was blue-eyed, with a definite Norman streak, but his round skull was burnt brown by the winds of the Indian Ocean and shone like mahogany. Hence his nickname "Monsignor Mogano".

The Rector looked sharply at his right-hand man.

"His Eminence requires a Scandinavian for his suite tomorrow, Don Gualtiero. Whom shall we take?"

Don Gualtiero knit his brows, and his whole cranium looked like a withered apple. "Why precisely a Scandinavian?" he asked.

"Why precisely a Scandinavian? Why *not* a Scandinavian, pray? Why should these people always be made exceptions of?"

"They're not suitable for processions."

"Well, then, they must simply learn to be. Whom would you suggest?"

"I don't know. We haven't much of a choice."

"Hm. Where's young Pedersen?"

"Abroad."

"And the other Dane?"

"Ill."

"Ah, yes, that's true. Well, what's our Norwegian friend doing?"

Don Gualtiero writhed. "I'm afraid he's too deeply engaged politically. His presence might be interpreted as a show of sympathy."

"Perhaps so. And what about the Swede?"

"Ah, the poor Swede. . . ."

Don Gualtiero looked at his chief, shook his head and smiled. The Swede was a youth named Jonasson who had come to the College only a short time ago. The last Swede had acquitted himself very well indeed, but this poor fellow could not be entrusted with any official duty, he was such an awkward, confused boy, and seemed literally to stumble over his own feet. Once, when sent to a procession, he had actually mistaken a taxi for the Cardinal's car and handed the red hat to the driver, who had hung it over his taximeter with a mischievous grin.

"Oh no, we can't send him anywhere," decided Don Gualtiero.

The Rector nodded. "So there's only Cinnelius left."

The other remained silent.

"Well, I really think it would be salutary for the young man," explained the Rector. "He's a good fellow at heart, but unfortunately he reads far too much and so forgets the world around him. He needs some experience of real life side by side with his studies, and perhaps a little practice. We must see that he gets out oftener."

The Vice-rector still remained silent.

"Don't you think so too?" continued the chief encouragingly.

"I think one has to be very cautious there," replied the Sicilian gloomily.

"Why that? What are you afraid of?"

"We have had several of his kind in our College. They're not proper types for processions. You couldn't believe the inhibitions they suffer from. To be quite candid, I doubt very much whether it's at all possible to train them for such things."

"I'm afraid I really cannot follow you, my friend," replied Monsignor dei Palleschi sharply. "How would it be were *we* to adopt the attitude that we are incapable of training our pupils? Why do the missionary bishops of the whole world send their best youths to us if not because they wish us to educate them? I must request you, Monsignor, to reflect a little before asserting that one cannot civilize Scandinavians."

Don Gualtiero bore the reproof with apparent humility. "I meant only that they are different from ourselves," he said. "It is often very difficult to understand them, and still more difficult to help them. Generally they don't even understand their problems themselves. I'm sorry for them."

"I can well believe you. But surely that's all the more reason for keeping a sharp eye on them, eh? "

Don Gualtiero had not yet had his say, "Actually, to be a Scandinavian is synonymous with having a tortured soul," he went on, "in so far as Scandinavians admit the existence of the soul, which fewer and fewer of them do. Even Darkest Africa does not produce more spiritually unhappy people than Northern Europe. Too little sun and too much alcohol, polar hysteria and Puritanism – all in unbalanced proportions – no wonder that the people up there are pessimists ! They regard original sin as a joke; nevertheless they seem to have a chronically bad conscience about bringing children into the world. A vocation to the priesthood from such a milieu is a very delicate plant indeed. So delicate, in fact, that one must often ask oneself whether it can possibly survive. . . ."

The Rector could not suppress a smile. "Calm yourself, my friend," he said. "You doubtless view the problem in a much too lurid, Sicilian light. I don't at all get the impression that young Cinnelius is so frightfully unhappy."

"If he were a Sicilian he would have gone over to the Mafia long ago," replied Don Gualtiero dejectedly. "He's on the brink of revolt."

"He certainly doesn't show it."

"One can never see what's in their minds. That's part of their national character. But I know the symptoms and I can only advise you to be very cautious."

"What symptoms? "

"Insomnia, loss of appetite, and extreme nervousness, all of which arise from a general discontent and rebelliousness, not to say misanthropy."

"Well, well! Is that all?" And Monsignor dei Palleschi leaned back majestically in his rectorial chair. "I have noted those symptoms in other students here in the College, and I can tell you straight away what they mean. The young man in question feels unsure of himself. And that, again, arises from the fact that he hasn't yet got fully used to the garb he wears. In other words, he lacks the necessary practical experience of real Roman Catholicism. Kindly tell him to report to Cardinal Magni's secretary tomorrow morning!"

But Don Gualtiero still shook his head. He himself had something to say to Cardinal Magni.

⌘

XV   PALAZZO DELLA PROPAGANDA FIDE

Cardinal Magni, Prefect of the Roman Congregation for the Propagation of the Faith, was a Venetian of ordinary middle-class parentage. He had spent the greater part of his life in the Far East, where he had won the ardent gratitude of millions of Chinese Catholics and the undying hatred of all the great European powers who had political interests in the helpless Middle Kingdom at the turn of the century. He had come home from the East thin as a rake, with a wrinkled Mongolian face and a legendary halo. When he had received the red hat the joke had gone around that China had got her first cardinal. He had now been guiding the destinies of the Congregation for more than a decade, and was regarded by his colleagues as the greatest strategist of the missionary world.

As an old colleague of the Cardinal's South China days, Don Gualtiero had admission to the latter's private apartments at any time. The Cardinal resided in the historic seventeenth-century palace of the Congregation in the Piazza di Spagna, an extensive building that formerly also housed the College of the Propaganda.

The marble portals of the reception-rooms, magnificent furniture and old oil paintings gave it rather the impression of a princely Roman palace, and asthmatic lifts and stiff-legged lackeys did their best to blend with the old-fashioned style of the whole. Don Gualtiero found His Eminence sitting in a library with a high vaulted ceiling, at a desk piled high with papers. The "Red Pope" was wearing a plain black skull-cap and looked like a gouty old book-keeper in an eighteenth-century office of the East India Company.

"We have a Scandinavian in the College who would like to have his own latch-key," said the Sicilian brusquely.

His Eminence was immersed in a thick file of documents. Apparently their contents were not pleasant reading, for the lines in the wrinkled face were even sharper and deeper than usual. But a twitch of his eyebrows betrayed that Don Gualtiero's words had registered.

"What's his name?"

The Cardinal's voice was surprisingly clear. He had some difficulty in pronouncing his "r's" and this gave his speech an almost childish, lisping effect.

"Thomas Cinnelius. He has been ordered to attend on Your Eminence tomorrow."

The Cardinal laid his papers aside, but his face remained impassive. "Hm, that sounds rather like a punishment," he said.

"Yes, it almost seems so," admitted the Sicilian glumly.

"What has he done?"

"Nothing, as far as I know. He rather seems to me to be a victim of his race."

The Cardinal raised both hands in a weary gesture. "Race, race, nothing but race," he said. "Is one never safe from that word, even here in this house?"

Don Gualtiero hung his head. He had touched a very tender spot, and the Cardinal's angry reaction wakened an almost equally strong echo in his own breast.

"We were progressing very nicely indeed until this wretched war broke out," continued the Cardinal. "Have you been following what is happening in Canton, Manila, Singapore and Djakarta,

Don Gualtiero? The work of centuries seems well on the way to being destroyed."

"All that is only a storm on the surface, Your Eminence," replied Don Gualtiero. "Our influence is more deeply rooted than that. As soon as peace comes, we shall return – with or without Europe."

But the Cardinal shook his head. "Nonsense! I have spent my life persuading people to forget their colour. You know better than anyone else how difficult that is. Do you remember our experience in Canton thirty years ago? We have really done our utmost in this peeling off process, and a few times I actually had the feeling that we were succeeding. It is a very rare art and one quite unknown to the budding imperialists who are trying to set up their little empires all round the world these days. But anyone who has really mastered this art possesses the greatest treasure in the world. Hand on heart, Don Gualtiero, which race would you choose if you had to decide for only one? "

"I was born in Palermo, Your Eminence," replied Don Gualtiero with quiet dignity, "and I have worked for twenty years of my life between Durban and Shanghai."

The Cardinal nodded. "Yes, I know. And then you were posted to Dei Palleschi's institute. I was sorry for you at the time, but of course the Rector needed a man with practical missionary experience to help him. And now you're worried about some delicate example of this race problem. What's wrong with the young man – his stomach or his morals? "

"Definitely not his morals. Our friend Thomas is a most honourable young man, and he has more faith than most. But he's – highly individual – shall we say? "

"Doubtless a bit romantic – or perhaps merely overwrought? Young men easily get like that when they're confined to a house where nothing but Latin is spoken."

Don Gualtiero bored his chin into his chest and turned the palms of his hands outwards. "Of course he may develop into a dreamer, at the worst – but not necessarily so. . . ."

"So you're not quite sure yourself whether he is a suitable candidate for the priesthood? " remarked the Cardinal.

"I have never before come across such faith as his, Your Eminence. He literally clings to the altar. God definitely has some special plan for him. He may end up as a university professor, or in a martyr's cell. But he will certainly never make a parish priest of an ordinary parish, least of all in his own country."

"Hm . . . What's he doing in the College of the Propaganda, then?"

"I have often asked myself that. Our job is to train men to be missionaries, but Thomas will never be a missionary. He's a scholar and philosopher, and has a decided tendency to mysticism. There's definitely no place for a person like him in Scandinavia. He would simply freeze to death up there."

"How can you know that?"

"Because that is why he has fled down here. An abyss lies between ourselves and Scandinavia. It's not easy to step across it without burning the bridges behind one, so to speak."

The Cardinal looked at him keenly. "You are not the first who has spoken to me of this abyss," he said, "but no one has ever been able to give me an illuminating explanation of the phenomenon."

"It's a long way to Scandinavia."

"Do you think the way to China is shorter?" he asked.

"To be quite candid, yes."

A faint smile hovered round the ivory-coloured folds of His Eminence's cheeks. "We two are not precisely unbiased on this point, my dear fellow. But have you ever been to Scandinavia?"

"No, never."

"Neither have I – unfortunately. Indeed, I hardly think anyone from this house has ever been there for many years. Strange, isn't it?"

"Very few tourists go there from here."

"I'm not speaking of tourist visits. Many of us cherish a kind of unrequited love for Scandinavia which we don't even dare to admit. The deepest reason for this is that tragic state of things here which is certainly not the less present for never being openly discussed."

"The question would have to be taken up by the Holy Office

first," interjected Don Gualtiero, with a touch of sarcasm.

But the Cardinal was in no joking mood. "Is there any region on the face of the earth where public opinion and social morals correspond more closely with the natural Christian principles of justice? At any rate, looking at it from here, that is so evident as to be beyond all dispute. In the matter of safeguarding the elementary human rights, Scandinavia should probably be the surest ally of the Holy See. Yet instead of this, the one is hardly aware of the existence of the other."

"You are quite right, Your Eminence. But what do you think we should do about it . . . ?"

"There's nothing at all we can do. Neither you, nor I, nor anyone else whose visiting card bears the words 'Propaganda Fide'. I am well aware that the concept has acquired a completely different meaning there. We Catholics are irreparably stamped as indulgence-peddlars as soon as we show our noses. At the moment we must be content with stretching out a friendly hand to those of them who come to us – your young protégé from Finland, for instance. What do you think we can do for him?"

Don Gualtiero looked at his chief with a worried expression. "He feels an outcast," he said. "We should find a place for him where he would not be so galled by his racial difference. . . ."

His Eminence pretended not to hear the word. "Is he a university graduate?" he asked.

"Yes, and he's better educated than I am, and in many subjects better than Dei Palleschi."

"How many languages does he know?"

"At least six. Probably more if you count the various Scandinavian dialects."

"And what kind of a reputation has he among his compatriots?"

"Excellent, as far as I know. He had been studying in Rome before, and has friends here. He has also published something in the art history line. I don't know exactly what it's about."

The Cardinal nodded approvingly. "We shall certainly have use for him later. One could recommend him to the Secretariat

of State, for instance. But for the moment we shall certainly see
that he is dispensed as far as possible from the crude grind of
examinations. And if the College of Propaganda does not suit
him, send him to Sant' Anselmo or to the Angelicum, or anywhere else where he would feel more comfortable. I'm sure he
would have felt most at home among the English in the Beda
College if it were not closed just now. By the way, who sent him
to the College of the Propaganda? "

"The Vicar Apostolic of Finland, I presume."

"Then I can write to him, of course. But I think I remember
someone else telling me about this young man before . . . ? "

"He has a good friend in the Sacred College," said Don
Gualtiero respectfully.

"Indeed? Who's that? "

"*Il cardinal americano.*"

Magni raised his eyebrows but not as showing actual surprise.
"That's right. I remember now. It was about some little dispensa-
tion. Your young friend was wounded, was he not? War-wounded,
I think? "

"Yes."

"When did he come to the College? "

"Two years ago."

"You had best make out a Vatican pass for him at once. The
situation is changing from day to day, and none of us can guess
how this war may end. . . ."

XVI SANT' EUSEBIO IN CASALETTO, 1943

"Theology – yes, that's necessary of course," began Dom Andrea
MacDonald, "but in every college there must also be some
fatherly man with whom the students can discuss the things
a young priest requires to know about himself. I know of
no calling which makes such stern demands on a man and at
the same time gives him so much scope for bungling. The

Catholic priest is answerable, in the last resort, only to an invisible God. His superiors really know precious little about what he does or does not do. But how many priests have sufficient self-discipline to conduct their lives solely under God's eyes? How many become entangled in a self-deceit which only increases with the years! Oh, it begins quite harmlessly – a few little bachelor habits, a pardonable weakness for beautiful books or good cigars; a smugness or positive laziness, encouraged by our calling, in regard to physical exercise. Perhaps a certain tendency to be autocratic, a little jealousy, and a conceit fondly encouraged by devout female admirers. Ah yes, indeed, when all these little weeds are allowed to flourish freely and luxuriantly in the fertile soil of the pres- bytery, they turn into a glorious jungle of growth in the course of the years. . . ."

He stole a glance at Thomas to see how much more the young man could stand before he continued: "Don't be afraid, my dear boy, this phenomenon was known even to the Evangelists. The words, 'Many are called, but few are chosen', were probably directed in the first place to those followers of Christ whom we call priests. You only have to read the text. Francis and Ignatius of Loyola could probably supply a fine lot of supporting facts. . . ."

Dom Andrea never divulged, however, how he himself had come to be a priest. He had grown up in France, where he had entered a Benedictine monastery when already of mature years. His father had been an artist and had spent the greater part of his life abroad. This homeless, roaming existence had left a certain mark on the son's character. He liked to affect an exaggerated lack of sentimentality, and his sparkling wit and humour easily turned to cynicism. He had never succeeded in taking root in his native Scotland, but had sought and found his greatest earthly happiness in the bewildering world of the catacombs of Rome.

Thomas had looked up his old friend of the Vatican Library shortly after returning to Rome. The Scot had received him with a certain gruff, taciturn understanding which, though in no wise compensating for Thomas's lost attachment to Padre Barnaba, developed in time into a sort of friendship. Dom Andrea showed no particular surprise when his young friend told him of his plans for the future. But now his harsh verdict had a rather stunning effect on Thomas.

"Aren't you rather too pessimistic?" he asked.

Dom Andrea shrugged his shoulders. "We shall discuss it again in twenty years when you know the clerical profession better."

"That doesn't sound exactly encouraging for a future priest."

Dom Andrea knit his brows meditatively. "It seems one would have to be a woman really to understand what becoming a priest means. For a young man it is certainly a more delicate matter than being entrusted to a woman. That lies in the nature of things. In the latter case the man is the active party. For the priest, like the woman, must be resigned to the new partner taking hundred per cent possession of his person. In other words, a real life of his own no longer remains to him. At the best he can talk a little bit of shop with his clerical colleagues on the way to the sacristy. . . ."

He paused as if to give the other a chance to object, but when Thomas said nothing, he continued with an ironical smile: "Of course you think I'm exaggerating. A woman with the necessary strength of character can subject her husband to her own terms even if he's a perfectly normal fellow. But no one can impose his own terms on Christ. The priest is confronted with a demand for total self-surrender which can evoke almost feminine reactions in a man. He has surrendered everything to Christ and he feels that he has thereby acquired a certain right to precedence, even in a human sense, with his Saviour. He would prefer not to see any clerical colleagues at table with him. He cannot tolerate any rivals in his parish. His clerical jealousy can be just as torturing as any common or garden jealousy. I always give young priests the same advice: 'Love your God above all else, but do not imagine that you are His only love.' Perhaps it could be expressed more elegantly, but I haven't got the necessary verbal *finesse*."

At last Thomas picked up courage to protest. "I have always regarded this total demand as a happiness," he said.

"So it is."

"And one's first impulse is to share one's happiness with others."

"Quite right – in so far as there is something to share."

"Why should one not be able to pass on one's happiness to others? "

"Hm. Will you please explain to me in what this feeling of happiness consists? "

"I cannot say exactly," replied Thomas, embarrassed, "but I imagine it comes from the conviction that one has really come a step nearer to God."

Dom Andrea nodded. "And with every step nearer that one comes, the total demand grows greater, whereas the feeling of happiness does not. On the contrary, it becomes more and more difficult even to look cheerful. And then comes the day when one has nothing more of the feeling of happiness left to pass on to others. And there one stands with the Ten Commandments of God and a bad conscience. And one sees how poor and miserable one is. Do you understand what I mean? "

"Well, at least I hope I do."

"You will learn what it is in due course. If not sooner, at least when you have come to understand what it is to walk with the Lord day in, day out. When He revealed Himself to the Jews of long ago He generally did so in fire and smoke. If our bodies possessed a sense of guilt our innards would have been burnt out long ago as if with prussic acid. Instead of that we feel fine and develop a remarkable enthusiasm for dolling each other up in silk skull-caps and red sashes. . . ."

Thomas bowed his head. "Of course I've got awfully little experience in these matters," he said, "but I have learned this much at least – that this pessimistic feeling is only a station on the way of the Cross. Do not all authorities on the spiritual life speak of a period of discouragement and interior desolation in most people's spiritual development? "

Dom Andrea became more serious. "That is just what I have been trying to explain in my own way," he said. "But as for what follows, it is best to consult the prophets. I am only a little scribe who watches with great fear in his heart as the Lord passes through the courtyard of the Temple."

Sant' Eusebio in Casaletto, Dom Andrea's archaeological Institute, was situated half a mile south of Rome, near the Via Portuense, in a hollow between two crests of hills, on which a few isolated pine groves stood out against the horizon. At the bottom of the valley were strips of parched tillage fields dotted with withered vegetable stalks, and the neighbouring buildings were a few neglected farmsteads. The Institute itself stood at a dusty cross-roads, and was surrounded by high walls capped with protective coping studded with broken glass. Inside the walls there was a small fruit garden and a little primitive Christian chapel which formed the entrance to a rather small, half silted-up catacomb.

The modern Sant' Eusebio was a white-washed, factory-like building with a hooded bell-tower. A brilliant white originally, it had given the whole wretched region the cheerful air of better times coming, but finally the poverty-stricken environment had dragged the proud newcomer down to its own level. The walls had become grey, the clay soil had even invaded the entrance, damp patches disfigured the façades; and the whole premises had gradually become clothed in the drab garb of poverty. Still this wretched exterior was definitely not unbecoming; it only emphasized the fact that Sant' Eusebio was a monastery, but did not betray the fact that it housed scientific specialists and moreover harboured a unique set of microfilm archives.

Don Gualtiero had obtained permission for Thomas to visit there as much as he liked. His visits to Dom Andrea became increasingly frequent, and he soon made several other friends among the learned Benedictine Fathers. Times were becoming more and more difficult, but within the monastery walls one could breathe freely, and Thomas felt the pressure in his head easing when he was there. Dom Andrea succeeded moreover in getting a little cell at the monastery for him when the College of the Propaganda was closed for the holidays.

During the German occupation of Rome several English, American, French and Polish prelates took up their quarters in this

Papal Institute which enjoyed extra-territorial rights. Among them
was Monsignor Szarnicki. He greeted Thomas with a spontaneous
warmth which he had never shown before.

"I'm so glad that you're with us here. How do things look in
Finland?"

Thomas was slow to answer. Too much had happened since that
summer evening on which the Polish prelate had put the same
question to him outside Sor Anacleto's little *osteria*.

"I know no more than is in the newspapers," he replied
cautiously.

"That's certainly not much. But perhaps you read the foreign
newspapers?"

"No, I don't," admitted Thomas, almost ashamed.

"Of course it's practically impossible to get any here, but that
may be just as well. I'm afraid we two shall have to wait a few
years longer before we can go home." And when Thomas did not
answer, the Pole continued with forced lightness: "You probably know that a certain treaty has been signed in Teheran. But
don't be uneasy. An equitable arrangement will doubtless be
arrived at in the end."

As Thomas still remained silent, Monsignor Szarnicki felt
moved to give him a friendly pat on the back. "There will be
plenty for us to do down here," he said. "I trust that Sant' Eusebio
will prove a fruitful *milieu* for you also."

"Yes, I believe it will. There's such a lot to learn here if only
one has the time and the strength."

"I think the Institute is an ideal place to work, and the library
is exceedingly well stocked. But, besides that, you will have an
opportunity of making friends here with people who may be
useful to you later on, and not only in scholarly matters."

Thomas could not suppress a smile. Shortly before Dom Andrea
had remarked to him ironically that since the autumn the attraction to the monastic life had increased to a very remarkable
extent in the Eternal City. Sant' Eusebio, for instance, seemed to
be filling up in quite an astonishing way. In its silent corridors
one came unexpectedly on celebrated university professors, well-
known journalists, senior military officers and diplomats. They

all wore the black Benedictine habit, and the porter, on being questioned, explained that they had retired to the monastery to make spiritual retreats. . . .

Monsignor Szarnicki seemed to have misinterpreted Thomas's smile, however. "Just look around you," he said. "You're in most distinguished company. Do you realize that most of the people who are lying low here now will have great influence in Rome later – perhaps sooner than you imagine? " And bending down he whispered in Thomas's ear: "They're expecting an Allied landing in Italy at any moment. . . ."

He did not finish the sentence but made a circular gesture with his hand as if he were winding up a tangled knot of yarn, then nodded significantly, and went off.

The expected landing did actually take place, but hostilities were certainly not wound up. The Allied air forces bombarded railway stations and motor roads, and, instead of the Americans, famine entered Rome. At the same time the stranglehold of the Germans became still tighter on the city, and more and more people sought sanctuary behind the monastery doors. An enormous painted notice in yellow and white announced that the monastery was under the protection of the Holy See, and a member of the Papal militia, in field-grey uniform, was posted outside on sentry duty as an extra precaution.

One day as he entered the library Thomas met a lay brother who struck him as strangely familiar. Awkward in his movements and obviously unused to his long habit, his broad face with closely set brown eyes like pepper-corns looked out from the black cowl. It was Romolo, the doctor from Bolsena.

Thomas tried to salute him, but the other reacted only when he said who he was. Then, of course, Romolo remembered.

"Well, we're a fine collection here," he remarked with his broadest grin. "It was a grand idea to doll up in a seminarist's cassock. You're less obviously disguised than if you had chosen a monk's habit . . ."

"But it's not a disguise at all," replied Thomas.

Romolo's beaming face darkened. "What's that you're saying? " he asked.

"I'm not a refugee. I'm studying at the College of Propaganda."

"Is that possible? But aren't you an art historian?"

"I've given that up, at least for the present."

"Why?" asked Romolo in the tone of a cross-examining judge.

"I found it too strenuous." It sounded evasive, but Romolo thought he had got to the truth at last.

"You pitched into it too strenuously," he said. "I saw that in Bolsena. It's no good carrying on like that. One must know what one's health can stand."

"That's true. Unfortunately I still have some difficulty with mine."

An expression of sympathy came into Romolo's eyes. "You're not the only case of that kind in this town," he said. "But you'll see it will soon be better."

"Yes, we must hope so. And how are things with you?"

"Splendid. I've become monastery doctor, as you see." And his loud laughter echoed down the passage. "One must show one's gratitude somehow. The Germans found out that I'd patched up a whole lot of partisans whom they thought they had liquidated. So I'm obliged to lie low for a time. But it won't be for long."

"If I were you I wouldn't go out. You could get caught in a comb-out at any moment on the street," Thomas advised.

"There will soon be an end to that."

"I've been hearing that for the last six months, but the terror is only becoming wilder and wilder, and the starvation worse."

Romolo laughed. "You don't know the plan of operation," he said.

"No, that's true," replied Thomas, "but while the grass is growing the cow is dying."

At this Romolo came close up to him and repeated in a tone of deep conviction: "It will not be long now. And as soon as the situation becomes easier there will be bread again. It may be even tomorrow."

"You're an optimist."

"My dear fellow, I'm speaking of facts. One would have to be blind not to notice that the horizon is clearing."

"Then I must have very weak eyes. And may I ask where you see the silvery streak?"

"In the East, of course," whispered Romolo with a wink. "Why, even these monastery folk here are gradually tumbling to that."

"It has certainly escaped me."

"But you can surely see who is winning the war? You shall see, everything will be much easier once the Germans are gone. And for you up in Finland too. It will be our turn then, if you understand?"

"Who are 'we'?"

"You and I, the democratic masses. And first and foremost the Communists."

Now it was Thomas's turn to be flabbergasted. "You believe in Communism, then?" he asked.

"Naturally. The world is waiting for Communism like a parched field waiting for rain."

"And do you really think that Communism would make us happier?"

"Can you suggest anything better?"

"Well, what about Christianity, for example?" asked Thomas, allowing his eyes to wander over the monk's cowl.

Romolo smiled good-humouredly. "No, thank you, I'm not interested. I've more important things to do."

"Here in the monastery too?"

"One has to peg away doing what one can. Of course I'm losing a lot of time. But better lose that than my life."

"Are you so sure that your time here is wasted?"

"Well, I regard it as a holiday."

"And have you learned nothing at all?"

"No, not a thing. I've just walked about the place chatting. Having endless discussions about everything under the sun. You get the chatting habit when you're shut up. I notice that about the monks too."

"And have you noticed nothing else about them?"

"Oh, yes, I have. I've looked into the eyes and down the throats of most of them, so I know them quite well. A very nice lot of chaps on the whole, though not in very good trim physically, perhaps. That's the result of the diet. They won't find it too diffi- cult to adapt themselves to a productive political system as soon as they get enough meat to eat."

"Don't you think that the monks here are really perfectly happy with their own social order?" asked Thomas.

Romolo laughed uproariously again. "Oh, those? Why, they hardly know what happiness is, but we'll teach them!"

His ardent faith in the future was disarming. Thomas would have liked to contradict him, but he found no words. He could only say that Romolo was much happier about the future than he was.

❧❦❧

XVII THE BISHOP'S RESIDENCE, 1945

"Welcome, Signorino," cried Fausto, opening the heavy gate of Santa Presenza. "Assunta!"

His daughter, a young girl in her teens, came up behind him. She was bare-legged and sickly looking, but had magnificent brown eyes and thick black plaits.

"Mind the door while I take Signor Tommaso over to the Bishop's Residence," ordered Fausto, "and don't let in anyone who shouldn't come in, do you hear!"

The post-war depression had descended on the Vicolo dei Pecorai. It was unsafe to walk in the Lane after dark and thefts were increasing to an uncanny extent. The people were worn out and exhausted. Prices were rising from week to week. There was hardly anything to be bought on the market except greyish bread, old car covers, imitation leather articles, and cigarettes that were dangerous to health. The butcher had nothing but a handful of tough offal lying on his counter; the greengrocer had nothing for sale but turnips and chicory, and Sor Anacleto's menu card confined itself to grey-brown macaroni, sour wine and Bologna sausage of very doubtful composition.

Only two individuals in the whole quarter had benefited from the new state of things – Pietro, the porter of the Palazzo Terrasanta, who had gone into the black market, on which he was growing fat and thriving, and the newsvendor Ettore, who had suddenly established himself as a duly appointed Communist agent, with a cinema in a neighbouring quarter to provide him with an income. Among his disciples was Sor Anacleto's son Cesarino, now nineteen years of age, who had developed into an enterprising young man of independent views. He drove a coach for a private transport firm plying between the Piazza Venezia and Saint Paul-Outside-the-Walls, and hated the American soldiers as passionately as he loved their song-hits. The only being in the Vicolo dei Pecorai who still meant anything at all to him was Assunta, the playmate of his childhood. The girl's father did not conceal his horror at this attachment.

Fausto walked ahead with an electric torch to light the way through the cloisters, for the electric light was not functioning, and could not be repaired owing to lack of material and money.

" Is anyone here yet? " asked Thomas.

Fausto counted off deferentially on his fingers: " C'e l'avvocato, l'elefante, il poetino, la medaglia d'oro . . ."

These were some of the most faithful members of the San Lino Circle. Thomas knew them all. The advocate was, of course, Tartaruga, the elephant was Massimo Monti, an economist of slightly negroid type and a good six feet six tall; the little poet was one Bernardo Spaccalocca, whose faith in the arts could move mountains; and the holder of the gold medal for valour was a war-blinded air force officer who turned up at the meetings on the arm of a nurse.

" But to see you here again is best of all, Signorino," continued Fausto warmly. " It reminds me of the good old times when you were having instruction from Padre Barnaba. And now you will soon be a priest yourself, won't you? "

" Yes I will, if it pleases God."

" That it certainly will. And then you can become parish priest of San Lino's."

Thomas could not help smiling, but it was a feeble smile. " That would hardly do, I'm afraid. I'm too much of a stranger to the parish."

"*Non tanto*," was Fausto's spontaneous reply. "You're almost like one of ourselves."

"Thank you, Fausto, it's kind of you to say that. But you've got Don Achille, haven't you? You could hardly get a better parish priest."

"That's true, but Don Achille is wanted in so many places, he'll hardly be left for long in our little parish."

The so-called Bishop's Residence was on the first floor. It consisted of two rooms which had served the former priors of Santa Presenza as reception-rooms. Padre Barnaba had placed them at the disposal of the San Lino Circle. Thanks to Tartaruga's help, he had also obtained permission from the municipal authorities to divide off these rooms from the poorhouse.

The San Lino Circle consisted mainly of laymen of various professions who were interested in religious questions. It met on Friday evenings for the free discussion of every conceivable problem of the day, from astro-physics to causality, and from Benedetto Croce to Russian nihilism. In order to preserve its freedom of speech the Circle had always sedulously avoided publicity of any kind. As its President, Padre Barnaba had taken a quiet pleasure in these meetings but his own attitude was passive and non-commital. The Circle had grown in strength during the War. The moral pressure outside had intensified the need for exchange of views and mutual moral support among persons of like mind.

The new parish priest was also President of the San Lino Circle. He was a fair-haired, broad-shouldered North Italian from the Valley of the Aosta, and wore a black beret like a French priest. In his youth he had been an officer in the Alpine artillery but a fall in the mountains had put an end to his military career. His lameness had not diminished his fighting spirit, however, though its aim was no longer the protection of *la bella Italia* against transalpine invaders.

Because of his anti-Fascist attitude he had been obliged to spend the war years in a little village on the Maiella, the traditional mountain retreat of refugees, in Central Italy. When the guns had fallen silent at last he had come down from his mountain, like a second Moses, with the social catechism of the New Age under his arm. During his years among peasants, shepherds and partisans he had imbibed their ethos very fully. He now felt that his task lay among the proletariat of post-War Rome, and he threw himself into it with all the pent-up belligerence of his youth.

San Lino had not had such an energetic pastor for generations. Don Achille seemed determined to make his parish a model one. He modernized the religious instruction of children and adults, revived Catholic Action, and was full of practical ideas for renewing the religious life of the parish. He organized the distribution of American relief, set up a Community Centre in the Palazzo Terrasanta, founded a technical school in the neighbouring quarter and a summer colony in Fiumicino. He was a zealous preacher and lecturer, and wrote articles on social questions for a periodical edited in the Piazza del Gèsu. More and more frequently he had to leave his little parish in order to preach, at the request of the Church authorities, to large congregations in or around Rome.

His only recreations were music and the San Lino Circle, and he often said that he found both equally necessary for his spiritual equilibrium. He played the violin well and had even composed some modest pieces. With the help of his violin he kept his own life in tune.

"*Ecco il San Tommaso di Finlandia!*" he cried gaily as Thomas entered. "Our most faithful member! I'm glad you like our Circle."

"I can only be grateful for the patience you show a foreigner," replied Thomas.

"There are no foreigners in our Circle," said the priest.

Avvocate Tartaruga nodded and, putting his arm round Thomas's shoulder, said fervently: "No, we're all old Romans here!"

Thomas had been attending these meetings regularly for a couple of years now, and had found a spiritual climate that suited him. In the Scandinavian countries he had never come across such free exchange of thought on religious questions. It requires the

candour and warmth of the Italians, Latin schooling and the
Catholic spirit of unity, he thought to himself. Perhaps also a
certain simplicity of heart. . . .

"How are you getting on with your studies?" enquired Don
Achille.

"I'm to be ordained at Easter."

"Splendid! Then you will no doubt be able to produce some
really fresh views on today's subject. We are discussing the
cultural aspects of the training of the clergy."

A small lively Jesuit with merry eyes and sharp tongue opened
the discussion. His criticism was directed against the present-day
social education of priests, and it immediately evoked hot discussion. The second speaker, who taught chemistry in a Roman
university, was a bullet-headed man with friendly blue eyes that
wandered around as he spoke, and changed their expression
according to the turn of the discussion. The next speaker was a
tall, dark-complexioned gentleman with a noble profile and elegant
manners, a quite distinguished Roman historian, who held forth
in long, declamatory periods. Soon almost everyone had had his
say – the little poet, who almost shrieked in a shrill treble, a dry-
as-dust lecturer in philosophy, whose deep bass sounded like a
subterranean waterfall, the choleric political economist, whose
heavy body writhed as he spoke as if in torture, and old Tartaruga,
who nodded like a toy mandarin. . . .

Thomas alone remained silent in his corner and followed the
debate with an absent expression. The discussion had quickly
drifted to politics, and revolved mainly round the attitude of the
Roman clergy to the Communist danger. Thomas feared that his
silence might be misinterpreted and he wished that Dom Andrea,
with his biting wit, were there. But at this moment an old
Franciscan with a greyish lion's mane encircling his magnificent
Jupiter-like head, stood up to speak. He was a Croat, and taught
exegetics in the college of his order. With arms crossed and hands
hidden in his sleeves, he stood calmly waiting for the buzz of
voices to die down.

"It is not the priest's task to serve this world," he said. "He is
only a mediator between God and man, but it is God who has

chosen him, despite his weakness, to be His servant. Therefore we must not be too shocked if the priest does not fulfil the demands made on him. I am inclined to think, indeed, that God intentionally uses simple souls to reach simple hearts, and it is certain that a humble village pastor fulfils His purpose just as well as a university professor. Has not the Church preserved her greatest truths in old liturgical formulae, simple, repetitive prayers, and the hidden whispers of the confessional? Possibly the ideological fight against Communism gets greater results on this plane than in halls and parliaments."

The eyes of the professor of chemistry, which had been wandering to and fro between the speakers with an expression of growing excitement, took on a troubled expression now. He was contemplating a reply when a strange, hollow voice, which sounded as though it were rising from some subterranean world, forestalled him. It came from the war-blinded airman, who had been following the discussion with an impassive face.

"You're quite right," he said. "That is the only way. Let the world say we're a hundred years behind the times – that is only as it should be. Catholics have nothing to gain by seeking political influence in the atomic age. Our future lies under the earth, in the catacombs and in the underground, today as so often in the past."

This was too much for the historian. He raised his eyebrows as if he were trying to chase away an annoying fly. "No, that is not so," he cried. "We are in the midst of a significant phase in the history of Roman Catholicism. Greater possibilities than ever are opening up. Italy stands on the threshold of her special mission and ultimate destiny as an old classical democracy leavened by the spirit of Christianity. A dream of centuries is about to be fulfilled, and our race shall once more show mankind the way. . . ."

"That sounds very fine," laughed Don Achille, "but I'm not too sure that it sounds quite so well in the ears of all our friends." And his eyes wandered towards Thomas's corner, but once more rescue came from an unexpected quarter.

"Please let us leave the politics of the day alone," said a quiet voice. The speaker, Valentino Fortunato, a nerve specialist of international repute, was a fair-haired, florid gentleman with a keen, ironical expression in his protruding eyes. "We all know what happened when they tried to christianize the dictatorship, and there's no guarantee that the christianization of democracy will be any more successful. For here it is not a question of a system but of people. And if I may express my personal opinion, we cannot reach the masses from a university chair. . . ."

The gathering became visibly restless. The poet shot up as if bitten by a tarantula, the political economist spluttered like a volcano, and a sound almost like the crying of a child came from the direction of the professor of chemistry.

But Fortunato continued undeterred. "I myself question very seriously whether this great mission which we have in our minds should be undertaken from our level at all. At any rate, Christ and the Apostles did not do it that way. Paul tried it out once in Athens, but as we know, the experiment was not successful, and he never repeated it. The Roman Empire was christianized by the martyrs, and medieval Europe by monks and warriors – not by philosophers. In spite of this many Catholics still dream of con-verting Areopagus. But have we any evidence that our Lord and Master wishes to operate in this way? "

"For whom, then, did Aquinas write? " asked the historian with a disdainful little laugh.

"Definitely not for me," replied Fortunato promptly, "and, in fact, only for those who can stomach the decoction. At any rate, as a physician I would hesitate to prescribe it. And I know of cases in the papal universities too with whom the neo-Thomist patent medicine does not agree at all."

This sounded almost like blasphemy. The eyes of the professor of chemistry rested, round and uncomprehending, on the doctor. The Jesuit's shoulders writhed as if he were suffering from a con-striction of the chest, and the professor of philosophy swallowed hard and remained silent. Fortunato had shifted the discussion on to a plane on which no one was prepared to venture unprepared.

At this juncture a quiet old gentleman with a somewhat enig-matical expression, a wrinkled vulture's neck and big liver spots on his bald pate, rose slowly from the corner of the plush sofa. He was a retired professor of tropical zoology and the Nestor of the San Lino Circle.

In a mild, somewhat tremulous voice, he began: "The fault probably lies, not in the philosophy but in the philosophers, or to be more correct, with all those of us who go in for philosophy without really knowing what we are doing. For there is a certain kind of pride of intellect that bids fair to become the arch-sin of our generation. Moreover, it has a specifically Catholic form which one could call confessional pride, and it is a frightfully dangerous malady precisely because it is so difficult to diagnose. For it often carries many shining virtues like a shield in front of it – personal modesty, a spirit of sacrifice, perhaps even asceticism. Of course it is very pleasant to be one of the *élite*; and it is all too easy to imagine oneself cleverer than others. One feels, at any rate, that one's credit is so good with the Lord that it is not really dangerous to be a little remiss now and then in one's philosophical speculations. After all, there is no one here on earth who will even notice it."

He looked around the Circle with a paternal smile as if to show that he had addressed himself to all, named no one, and forgotten no one. The audience remained respectfully silent, and he continued in the same mild tone: "Someone has said that the most dangerous errors are ninety-nine per cent true. And these are precisely the kind of errors committed by confessional pride. Its convolutions are as imposing as Gothic cathedrals. Viewed from an earthly perspective, they appear perfect. But on closer inspection one may discover that they are surmounted, not by the Christian cross, but by an academic laurel wreath – probably from a famous Catholic university. The day will come when the whole proud edifice will collapse. And then it may be that our sons will have to begin picking up and collecting together in the catacombs the broken fragments of Christian wisdom. . . ."

Don Achille sat in the gilded episcopal chair doodling mechanically as if he were making private notes. It was his task as chairman to save the central theme from being lost to sight even when the arguments mounted in dramatic periods to a mighty *fortissimo*. But when he had at last succeeded in collecting the discussion into a synthesis which could have made it possible for it to end in a harmonious finale, he tapped the table with his pencil as a sign that the concert was at an end.

The company broke up and walked in little groups, under the echoing, vaulted ceilings and through the dimly lighted cloisters with their faint smell of lysol, down to San Lino's. Fausto quietly rang the bell for evening service, then went up to put out the lights in the Bishop's Residence. But he left one little light burning over the door in front of the monastery inscription, almost as though it were a votive tablet.

❦

XVIII   SAINT JOHN LATERAN, 1946

When the time for Thomas's ordination arrived, he went to Dom Andrea and asked if he might say his first Mass in Sant' Eusebio.

The Scotsman was flabbergasted. "Your first Mass . . . ? " he murmured, and his eyes wandered desperately around the room. "But why do you come to me? "

"For you to help me – naturally."

"Anything but this. . . ."

"Pardon? "

"Really, I think this is a little too thick, it amounts to a surprise attack," Dom Andrea grumbled pathetically. "How should I be able to help you? "

"Would that be so difficult? "

"Difficult? Not for a monsignor in a purple cape. But it's rather much to ask of a poor monk."

Thomas took up the other's tone with a twinkle in his eye. "Wouldn't you do it even for a double brandy? " he asked.

"No, nor for a case of whisky," snapped Dom Andrea.

But Thomas refused to be put off. "Name your price," he said.

"Once for all, it's really not possible."

"Then I'll smash your photoscope."

K

"Just what one would expect from a pupil of Dei Palleschi."

"Aha! So that's where the shoe pinches?"

"You're right there! I can't stick any kind of public show. Remember it's not for nothing I've entered a monastery, young man!"

"I too loathe any kind of public exhibition, and that's why I have come to you."

Dom Andrea became serious again. "So you really want to celebrate your first Mass here in the monastery?"

"Yes, I do. Is a special permission from the Papal Institute of Archaeology necessary?"

"No, the permission of the Abbot is enough, and you'll get that all right. Only – I'd rather not be there."

In spite of his years' acquaintance with Dom Andrea's oddities, Thomas felt slightly offended. "Oh, indeed . . . ?" he said. "At that rate I must apologize for having come to you with such a presumptuous request. But I didn't want to go to the Abbot about this purely private matter."

The screwed-up corners of the Scotsman's eyes twitched. "Please don't misunderstand me," he said. "You see, it's this way: I'm not keen on these first Masses. We have them several times a year, here as well as in the catacombs, and the whole monastery is on its toes for weeks beforehand. My more romantically inclined colleagues simply love these celebrations, but I usually shut myself into my cell as soon as I hear of them."

"But if someone nevertheless asked for your assistance?"

"I'd just clear away as far as I could."

"Where to?"

"Well – to Africa, for instance."

Having overcome his first dismay, Thomas returned to the attack. "I seem to have heard that you have a retreat house considerably nearer than that," he said.

"You mean Santa Maria degli Ulivi?"

"Yes, that's it. Where is it, actually?"

"Fifty miles up the Tiber in purely rural surroundings. But don't tell anyone."

"And how does one get there?"

"Aha! You're trying to worm a secret out of me, young man."

"It's hardly a secret. I have only to ask the porter."

"He'll just advise you to take a taxi, but we poor monks usually travel on a lorry that goes there twice a week."

"Is there no railway?"

"No."

"No tourists?"

"No tourists."

"And can one live in the house?"

"Yes, there's a kind of old watchdog there – a frightfully odd chap, in fact, an impossible fellow."

"All that sounds very attractive. Do you think I could say my Mass there?"

Dom Andrea's jaw dropped. "Are you in earnest?" he asked.

"It would be pretty well my ideal."

The Scotsman hesitated for a moment, then he began to smile as though a cramp in his neck were easing off. "I give in, if your ideal really isn't any higher; though I must warn you I can't guarantee you against rain in the lorry, Reverendo."

Early that Holy Saturday morning Dom Andrea appeared in the Lateran Basilica. The Scotsman's bushy eyebrows stuck out like cocks' combs and his shorn skull and big red ears towered up behind a crowd of well-to-do Italians who were giving vent to their emotions in floods of tears over a beloved nephew among the ordinands.

Cardinal Norcus conferred Holy Orders, but the rite of ordination was actually merged with the liturgical ceremonies of Holy Saturday, and the whole service lasted several hours. Eighty young ordinands represented the annual harvest of the seminaries of Rome. Entering the church in procession in their long white surplices, they prostrated themselves full length before the high altar. Above them, in the apse, the magnificent gleaming mosaics shone like the Heavenly Jerusalem, and the glorious Lateran choir almost drowned the ceaseless tramp of feet in the naves.

Thomas was already tired when he entered the church. The last few months in the College had been filled with enforced studies and strenuous spiritual exercises. Almost apathetically, he allowed himself to be helped into the alb by his assistant, a dark-eyed young Hindu from the College, who handled the liturgical vestments as tenderly as though he were dressing a sick infant. Thomas noticed that he himself was much less deeply moved by the solemnity of the hour. He could only think with tired surprise: Now, at last, I am really on the way to the altar. Almost mechanically he prostrated himself with the others and buried his face in his hands. Gradually his nerves relaxed and his weariness gave way to a feeling of peace as though he were dozing off. The Litany of the Saints wove its way to and fro above him like an invisible pergola of prayer. One tabernacle for the Lord, another for Moses and a third for Elias. . . . He felt only one wish – never to have to open his eyes again and see the blatant golden blaze of mosaics up there on the vaulted ceiling!

And suddenly it seemed to him that he had experienced all this before in the snow-swept streets of Wiborg. The art historian had died in those snow-drifts, but his yearning had remained alive. A merciful hand had opened the locked door of the church, and what was happening here and now was only the final, solemn confirmation of his death and resurrection. But when he looked into the church he saw nothing but darkness and loneliness ahead.

Almost like an answer to his thoughts came the voice of the old Cardinal:

"You are now about to approach the altar of the Lord. You hope for a pledge of that communion with God which is the goal of every human being's deepest yearning. In exchange for this you offer at the altar the greatest sacrifice anyone can make – yourselves. You are leaving behind you your homes, your pleasures, and all your old life. Perhaps the full implications of this step awaken fear in your hearts. Those who do not love God will never be able to understand this step of yours any more than the Jews could understand why Peter left all things and followed the Lord when He passed by.

"The force which has brought you to the altar was neither the gift of prophecy, nor that of speaking in divers tongues, nor thirst

for knowledge. It was the divine love – *caritas*, which Paul says
'*Omnia suffert, omnia credit, omnia sperat, omnia sustinat*'."

The young ordinands knelt in turn before the Cardinal, who
laid his hands on the head of each. Thomas returned to his place
with bowed head. His candle was lit for him, he was anointed
with oil, and linen cloths were wound round his hands. But
throughout the whole ceremony his heart trembled as if before
a threatening storm.

In the corridor leading to the sacristy the friends and relatives
of the new priests pressed around them to receive their blessing.
An overpowering perfume of flowers made the already vitiated
air even heavier. The throng pressed along as if in a catacomb.
In the wake of the Cardinal were Monsignor dei Palleschi and
Don Gaultiero, who were standing ready to offer their congratulations, and behind them, in a group to themselves, the Scandinavian students of the College. Thomas recognized other familiar
faces in the crowd too – Don Achille, Avvocato Tartaruga, Sor
Anacleto and Fausto, all with bouquets of flowers in their hands
and solemn, deeply moved faces.

Suddenly Cardinal Norcus was standing before him. "*Ad
multos annos*, Don Tommaso," he said, giving him a hearty
handshake.

Don Gaultiero's eyes twinkled gaily over at him across the
Cardinal's shoulder. Dei Palleschi, who was weeping with quiet
dignity, handed Thomas a choice little volume bound in Morocco
with a gilt monogram on the cover – a selection of his own Lenten
meditations in Latin, published by himself.

Then came the Scandinavians. Three of them had completed
their studies and were to return now to their respective countries.

"When are you going home?" they asked Thomas.

"I haven't had any definite orders yet," he murmured. He had
always deliberately avoided speaking of his future with his
comrades.

"Don't let them persuade you to stay here too long," warned
an athletic Norwegian who was known in the college as the Soccer
King. "This sirocco doesn't suit our constitutions at all."

Thomas could not help smiling. "That's evidently a matter of the individual," he said. "Actually, my health has been restored only since I've been down here."

"Yes, you've been in better form in the last few years," admitted Pedersen the Dane, who had already got his doctorate, "but generally speaking we are better in our own country. One could easily go crazy down here."

"Hm. And other people's brain boxes work better in a warm climate."

The Swede Jonasson stared at him with a worried expression in his blue eyes. He was not worrying about Thomas, however, but about himself. He had just been ordained too, and the heavy cloud of responsibility already rolling up on the horizon was visibly oppressing him.

"I hope we shall meet often at home," he said, giving Thomas a hand still clammy with excitement. "After all, it's not so very far from Helsingfors to Stockholm. You will be going back to Finland, I take it?"

"I haven't dared to think about it yet," replied Thomas, feeling not a little envious of the matter-of-course simplicity of outlook which marked his comrades' plans for the future.

When they had all shaken hands and congratulated him, Dom Andrea came stumping along. His patched habit with its plain black girdle was in striking contrast to the festive attire around him. With the expression of a convict seeking pardon he fell on his knees before Thomas who, with some emotion, laid his hands on his head and spoke the blessing over him. When Dom Andrea kissed the open palms of the newly ordained priest in accordance with custom, Thomas noticed to his astonishment that the snappy old bear was shedding a few tears over them.

But more surprises were to come. A stately prelate with aristocratic features and a beautiful, slightly greying head of hair suddenly hove in sight behind Dom Andrea. Thomas could hardly believe his eyes. It was Monsignor Szarnicki!

"I am sincerely glad that you have reached your goal, dear friend," he said, unobtrusively pressing a little ivory crucifix into Thomas's hand. "I wish you every happiness, and may I at the same time express my joy at the prospect of our keeping you here in Rome for the time being? I have been asked to convey to you the compliments of the Secretariat of State. But we shall talk about that later."

He nodded and turned to go. Thomas stared after him, bewildered. He had had no chance to answer, but now he caught an ironical little gleam in the eyes of Dom Andrea. After that he was caught up in a growing crowd who all wanted his blessing. Hardly conscious of what he was doing, he laid his hands on the heads of hundreds of people known and unknown to him. He was dead tired after the long ceremony, but his hands worked on quite uninterruptedly, dispensing blessings as if they had at last found their true use. Are these really my own hands? he thought.

Dom Andrea stood aside quietly observing him. When it was all over he remarked with a quiet little chuckle: "Baffling, isn't it, how much a pair of empty hands can give?"

⋘✦⋙

XIX   SANTA MARIA DEGLI ULIVI

In the evening Dom Andrea returned to the same theme. "Yes, there's much for the hand of a young priest to do," he said. "There's something wonderful about it, like a child's hand. But by now you've probably noticed that yourself?"

"Haven't I, indeed!" laughed Thomas. "But to tell the truth, my hands are so tired that they ache."

"You must save up some strength for tomorrow. After Mass all sorts of people may come along."

"How is that? I thought we would have peace from all outsiders out here?"

"It will be only the local inhabitants, the simple peasants, you understand. They have their own church several miles away, but when it gets out that a newly ordained priest is saying the Easter Mass here, no power on earth will stop them from coming. They may not attend the Mass, but they will definitely want your blessing. There's no help for that. It's a superstition common to the whole country."

"How is it a superstition?"

"What else can one call it? Of course it's a beautiful custom, but there is no documentary proof that the first blessing of a priest is of more value than any that follow. It is merely one more proof of man's predilection for the first of anything."

"Are you not a little too rigorous in your judgments, Dom Andrea?"

"Don't start hair-splitting, my dear boy. I didn't say I'd like to do away with this first blessing business. There are many folk customs and traditions which have been accepted by the Church, even if they have not found a place in the liturgy. A poor devil can lay his paper flowers at the feet of the Madonna! It doesn't worry me."

"But if you found a false coin in the collection?"

"It counts for just as much in the eyes of Christ as a good one. One cannot well assume it has been put in there with a dishonest intention, can one?"

"No, not if the generous donor is a self-deceiver."

Dom Andrea shrugged his shoulders. "Let him who is without sin cast the first stone," he said.

Santa Maria degli Ulivi was situated in a well-watered region among the Sabine Hills. It was a smiling landscape, with comfortable farmsteads in the valleys and little isolated towns up on the heights. The population was dependent mainly on agriculture and cottage industries, and was practically untouched by the spirit of the age. The neighbourhood therefore offered ideal conditions for rest and meditation, and prelates of the Roman Curia were in the habit of retiring to such remote places as this from time to time.

The rest house of the Fathers of Sant' Eusebio was an unrestored medieval monastery that had evidently been an offshoot of the monastery of Farfa. It had been built into the ruins of an ancient villa whose network of brick walls and arches were still visible. These now formed a system of natural terraces for the gardens and grounds, from the middle of which the old monastery reared its weathered walls and its round, grey apse, like a fortress. The terraces provided a desirable separation from the surroundings, for the Fathers were at least as well sheltered behind the vine-stocks, fruit trees and rose arbours that covered them as behind the high walls of Sant' Eusebio.

Santa Maria degli Ulivi was almost empty for the greater part of the year. Only one lay brother was stationed there to look after the house, garden and bees, to see that the peasants carried out their agreements, and to despatch wine, oil, honey, fruit and vegetables to Sant' Eusebio. He was a Savoyard and his name was Brother Boniface, but some joker, watching him pottering among his plants, had given him the somewhat Franciscan-sounding nickname of Fra Farfalla. This appellation was decidedly ironical for his exterior was rather repellant than otherwise. His figure was heavy and slouching, his hair bristly, his watery eyes squinty, his nose red and veined, and his chin usually covered with a week's stubble. Nevertheless this flattering nickname of " Butterfly " was justified in one particular at least, for the way to Fra Farfalla's heart was definitely *via* the flowers of the earth. Happily absorbed in his task, he pottered around the terraces in his enormous, disreputable-looking straw hat and his torn old working clothes, smelling of earth and dung and just a little of wine too.

He had laid supper for Dom Andrea and his young guest in the old refectory, a big room with a vaulted ceiling and stone floor, and bare walls which still exhaled the cold of winter. On the rear wall was a gigantic fresco, faded and mildewed, of the Last Judgment, which some local artist had painted towards the end of the Renaissance, obviously after having made a close study of the more famous models in Rome. Behind it was a deal table on which stood a couple of heavy metal candlesticks. Against the opposite wall was a decrepit cupboard containing plain crockery, a few tin beakers and spoons, and some tattered books.

The meal consisted of a thick bean soup, roast lamb and vegetables, fresh cheese made from goat's milk, and some dried figs. There was also a strong red wine.

"This is the best the house has to offer," said Dom Andrea,

"and but for you, dear Don Tommaso, it would be still simpler, because Fra Farfalla refrains on principle from serving up elaborate meals at Easter-time. An admirable principle in itself."

The shadow of a smile flitted over Fra Farfalla's sad features as he stood filling his simple bean soup into two rough chipped plates.

"I'm deeply moved," said Thomas, "but surely roast lamb isn't such a rarity here in the country?"

"I never eat Easter lamb," replied Fra Farfalla brusquely.

"Why not?"

"We offer the real Easter Lamb on the altar. Why should we celebrate the memory of Christ's sufferings with a feast?"

Dom Andrea laughed. "Fra Farfalla is a Puritan at heart. If he had his way he would force all Christendom to fast the whole year round, especially on the great feast days. He says he came out here because he simply couldn't endure any longer the way they celebrate Easter in Rome."

Fra Farfalla nodded glumly. "A peepshow for tourists," he said.

"I wouldn't go so far as that myself," replied Dom Andrea, "but I understand Brother Boniface's views on many points. Easter and particularly the weeks preceding it should be a time of prayer and penance. True, we still call that time Lent, but in practice it is observed in very different ways. In Rome it can be made palatable by various piquant spices, which are highly esteemed by authentic gourmets. To be sure, in order to appreciate these properly, one needs to have all sorts of gifts such as a sense of tradition, a trained taste, a knowledge of art history and perhaps a little experience of life too. But if one possesses all these things, one can prepare oneself in stages, during forty intoxicatingly delightful spring days, to celebrate and enjoy the Passion of Christ in a more subtle and refined way than anywhere else in the world. One of my Chinese friends assured me once that it was an incomparable aesthetic experience. He was not even a Christian, only a highly cultured philosopher."

"Naturally, you know Rome better than I do, but what you say does not correspond with my experience of the Romans, at least not the plain people."

"I'm not speaking of the Romans themselves. I'm thinking of

all the religious sybarites and mood hunters who muster round the bigger churches towards Easter. Just go to the Lateran or Sant' Anselmo on Good Friday! You will look in vain for any ordinary Romans there but you'll find a horde of tourists on the hunt for the most moving choral music. . . ."

"Yes, that's right," said Fra Farfalla.

Thomas looked down at his plate, from which the tempting odour of roast lamb rose. "You're spoiling my appetite," he said.

Dom Andrea laughed. "You needn't take it as seriously as all that," he said. "If you're hungry you have a right to eat, and a roast of lamb is as natural a food here in the country as it was once for the shepherds of Canaan. Besides, we're celebrating your wedding feast, so to speak, Don Tommaso! *Ad multos annos!*" And with a joyful smile, he raised his glass.

"*Auguri!*" beamed Fra Farfalla, promptly refilling the glasses.

"I hope Monsignor Szarnicki had good news for you," asked Dom Andrea casually.

"He didn't say what it was about."

"They're not likely to be thinking of burying you in your native place – what's this its name is – Karelia?"

"There would hardly be a place for me in Karelia now. . . . Most of it's been made a part of Russia."

"Oh, pardon! I forgot. . . . But after all, you've been trained as a missionary. Perhaps they're going to send you to some exotic overseas mission?"

"I do hope not!"

Dom Andrea raised his eyebrows. "I can understand your feelings. Nowadays most pagans have more natural Christianity than we have. Much better to stay here and search for the lost wisdom in the Scriptures. Have a good talk with your friend the Cardinal and persuade him to see that you are allowed to embrace a scholarly career."

Thomas shook his head. "I can't do that," he said. "That's all over for me."

"What's all over?"

"What I believed was to be my life-work. And my interest in scholarship has gone with it."

Visibly perplexed, Dom Andrea took refuge in a jest. "Then you had probably best stay here and help Brother Boniface with the bees," he said.

But Brother Boniface was obviously shocked. "Don Tommaso – he'll surely be an abbot one day," he said. And with an apologetic grin he left the room.

"I would have nothing against studying bee-keeping with Fra Farfalla," said Thomas, "but there's one thing I have had to learn – that no monastery has room for religious mood hunters and sybarites."

Dom Andrea flushed right down his neck. "My dear Thomas, surely you don't think . . . ?"

"No, I know well you were not thinking of me – luckily."

"Why luckily?"

"Because otherwise you would not have said what you said." And with his eyes fixed on the table, Thomas continued as if speaking to himself: "You needn't be afraid you have offended me, Dom Andrea. On the contrary, I have every reason to be grateful to you. You have certainly given me the best gift on my ordination day that anyone could hit on. One so seldom gets good advice just when one needs it!"

For the first time in their long acquaintance Dom Andrea felt unequal to his young friend. "Well, it's nice to hear that a muddle-headed old monk can be helpful to a highly promising young secular priest," he said. "But to be quite honest, I don't understand how I have been helpful to you just now. We have both merely come to the conclusion that every road is closed."

"Considered subjectively that's true. But I definitely believe God has a path waiting for me, though it may be hard to find. It's only a narrow path, I know; but one must tread it, even if it leads through a thorn-thicket, so to speak."

Dom Andrea looked at him suspiciously. Thomas smiled wanly and in an unsuccessful attempt to be jocular, continued: "Doubtless one must learn to plait one's own crown of thorns."

"I'm afraid you're going to find your crown of thorns on a desk in the Papal Secretariat of State."

Dom Andrea emptied his wineglass at one draught, filled it to

the brim again, and drank it off once more. Then he stood up and
shook himself. "It's time to go to bed," he said, "but come out
and have a look at the thorn thicket first."

It was as cold as in January, and pitch dark. The moon had not
yet risen, but the bare crests of the mountain shimmered with a
dull, silvery radiance in the pale starlight. The whole neighbourhood seemed to be asleep. There was not a light to be seen anywhere. The monastery lay as if in the midst of an enormous desert.
An indistinct murmur of water rose from the gorges, and somewhere in the distance a mill-stream babbled. Otherwise there was
nothing to be heard but the sighing of the wind in the tree-tops
on the terraces.

A strange sound came from the direction of a blossoming apple
tree to the south side of the house under which a big dark mass
was barely distinguishable. It looked almost like a sleeping animal,
but it was an uncouth human form, sitting on the ground, the
arms clasped around the drawn-up knees, and – now one could
see – the forehead beating against them intermittently.

"Who's that?" whispered Thomas.

"Fra Farfalla. He's celebrating Easter."

"But what's he doing there?"

"Keeping vigil. He says it's easier in the garden. He's waiting
for the Lord to pass – if you understand. . . ."

Thomas retired to his cell, a small, cold room with a north
window and whitewashed walls. The camp-bed was hard and
narrow and the torn straw mattress was clumsily stuffed here and
there with newspaper. He fell asleep at once and dreamed that he
was lying shivering on the bare ground, convulsively clutching
the much too thin felt blanket in which he was wrapped. He had
climbed up to a sheepfold in the mountains and found himself in
the midst of a flock of animals that were snorting and groaning
uneasily in their sleep. He himself was lying awake, listening to
the night voices of the woods. The wind was blowing through the
crowns of the oak-trees with a sombre roar which seemed to be
announcing to all the creatures in the mountain pasture that the
great Shepherd Himself was approaching. All creation seemed to
be holding its breath and trembling.

He was wakened in the grey dawn by the loud chatter of swallows. He opened the window and let the air stream in, pure and cold as a mountain spring. The sun was still hidden somewhere behind Monte Pizzuto, whose grey crown was powdered with snow. To the west a mighty monster had crawled out of the sea and lain down in the plain on the other bank of the Tiber. It was the Soracte, which, seen from here, looked like a giant prehistoric lizard.

Salva, magna parens frugum! Olive trees, olive trees, everywhere! As far as the eye could reach they spread like a silver-grey sea, up to the dark green forests and the steep cliff-like faces of the mountains. Isolated fields of corn, cabbage and root vegetables could be seen in the undulating valleys, and just where the highroad was lost in the green, shimmered the white-washed walls of a farmhouse, surrounded by its orchards and vineyards.

Not a soul was to be seen anywhere when Thomas went out. Once more he breathed in the fragrant country air. Then he went into the church which Fra Farfalla had opened wide to let out the damp, cellar-like smell. The altar was decorated with apple blossoms and pink cyclamens, and the ground strewn with fragrant branches of bay; otherwise the interior was just as austere as the refectory. The walls, which were devoured with dampness, showed traces of old frescoes; a few fragments of ancient sculptures were plastered above the door, and some memorial stones embedded in the floor bore half-obliterated inscriptions. For the rest, the decoration consisted only of a crude wooden cross above the altar and a simple Madonna casually perched on an antique marble capital carved with acanthus leaves. The whole bore unmistakable witness to Fra Farfalla's aversion to anything that savoured of tourist attraction.

Dom Andrea had already said his own Mass and was waiting at the altar to assist Thomas, but Fra Farfalla was kneeling on the threshold, where the swallows kept sweeping around him, almost colliding with the doorposts.

With a faint shock Thomas heard his own voice reciting the introductory prayer:

"I will go unto the altar of God . . ."

When he heard Dom Andrea's rough voice answering: "Unto God who giveth joy to my youth", it seemed like a faint echo of his own mood.

It required an effort of will to concentrate on the text. Behind his back he heard Dom Andrea murmuring the Confiteor, and he noticed to his astonishment that he himself had spoken the great words of forgiveness in God's own name. Then he found himself standing up at the altar. It seemed to him that Dom Andrea must have pushed him up there.

"Lord, have mercy on us," his lips spoke.

"Lord, have mercy on us," repeated Dom Andrea.

The angels intoned their canticles of praise of the Lord of Heaven, who was about to come down among His own. But for Thomas the prospect was too overpowering. He felt almost paralysed at the thought of the stupendous act before him. His trembling lips were to form the words which would call the Lord back to earth; his poor hands were to open the tomb from which the Risen Saviour would step forth. . . .

Dom Andrea moved quietly about the altar. He carried the Missal from one side to the other, poured out water and wine, presented a bowl of water and a towel. Thomas was almost completely unconscious of all this and had to pull himself together with a great effort before he could bring himself to touch the uncovered chalice on the altar under his raised hands. Mechanically he murmured his *Sursum corda*, not daring to stop to think of the meaning of the words. But once more Dom Andrea's answer came clear and precise, leaving no room for the slightest doubt. Once more it was almost as though he had pushed Thomas along. Now his bell rang warningly. Thomas raised his hands expectantly. Suddenly Cardinal Norcus's caution against visions sounded in his ears. Once more the bell rang, this time as a signal. Instinctively he shut his eyes, bent over the altar, whispered barely audibly, "This is my Body," hurriedly genuflected, raised the Host above his head. But he did not dare to open his eyes until Dom Andrea's eager little bell announced that the Consecration was over. It seemed to him that he dared not desecrate the mystery with his profane gaze.

In this way he had succeeded in forgetting himself completely. As the Mass progressed he became conscious of an increasing patter of footsteps behind him, but he drove away all distracting thoughts. The Lord was now really present in this chapel, and the priest was only a stone under His feet. The shepherds in the fields and the birds in the air were singing His praise, but Thomas's own personality had to be immolated on the altar like a victim of sacrifice. The chalice was waiting. Dom Andrea's little bell rang once more, this time more softly and almost apologetically. Thomas shut his eyes and drank the chalice.

Dom Andrea now began reciting the *Confiteor* for the second time and the shuffle of many footsteps became audible. When Thomas turned round to give the Absolution, he saw four rows of people waiting for Holy Communion. Dom Andrea took a ciborium of consecrated hosts out of the tabernacle. His forecast had proved correct: the rumour that a young priest was saying his first Mass in Santa Maria degli Ulivi had spread throughout the countryside.

Outside in front of the church an even bigger crowd was waiting for the new priest's blessing. Thomas stood there calmly as the long procession filed past him. The wonder still persisted; all of a sudden he had something to give. He had come down from the altar with an inexhaustible basket, and now he was distributing his gifts as a farmer sows seeds. He felt that his hands were already becoming accustomed to dispensing blessings. But he still kept his eyes averted as if he did not want to expose the work of his hands to his own gaze.

The sun had risen; the countryside lay bathed in light, and the hum from Fra Farfalla's beehives was becoming louder and louder. For one brief moment Thomas felt a warming stream of happiness flowing into his heart from outside. This is love, he thought, the redeeming love, visible from afar off, which lights up the mountains, the earth and the face of man, and draws from the air a thousand gentle sounds.

But his fear still remained behind in the depths of his soul, and for years to come he still shut his eyes every time the Lord came down to His altar.

Book Three

THE INN OF
THE GOOD SHEPHERD

ﾟ｡◦❀◦｡ﾟ

XX CORTILE DI SAN DAMASO

Dom Andrea had been correct in his prophecy – Thomas's path had led straight to the Curia. Immediately after his ordination Monsignor Szarnicki had him appointed to a papal office which dealt with aid to victims of the War. The Pole would not hear of his young protégé returning to his Finnish homeland. No, it was much too soon for that, he said.

Thomas settled down submissively to the unaccustomed work and performed it to the entire satisfaction of his superiors. But Szarnicki, who had taken him completely under his wing, insisted that he should study for his divinity degree at the same time. It was relatively easy to get together a thesis from the ample material he had collected while pursuing the study of religious art. The paper caused quite a stir among his friends. Dom Andrea alone dismissed it with a disapproving shrug.

" Of course it's only a sketch," explained Thomas modestly.

" It's very distinguished. All it lacks is a few edifying anecdotes incorporated into the text."

" It's not customary to bring anecdotes into scientific treatises."

" I seem to have heard you say that your interest in scholarly matters was a thing of the past? "

Thomas went red. "That's true," he admitted. "This monograph is only meant to be a little student's thesis."

"And what's its purpose?"

"To get me admitted as a scribe in the Court of the Temple."

But Dom Andrea only shook his head. "My dear fellow, no student's thesis is required for that. I thought you wanted a crown of thorns. Instead I see you've plaited yourself a very charming wreath of flowers. . . ."

Shortly afterwards Dom Andrea set out for the East on a rather lengthy archaeological expedition. He was never to see Rome again, for he died in the Holy Land.

Meanwhile the prelates of the Curia had become seriously interested in Thomas and wished to test his abilities with new tasks. He was to take an examination at the Papal Academy of Diplomacy in order to equip himself for a higher career.

But once more Monsignor Szarnicki intervened. "An examination is not necessary," he declared. "Don Tommaso knows as much as any of us, and what is more, he can apply his knowledge better than most."

Thereupon he went to the Under-Secretary of State, and got Thomas appointed as his assistant in the Archives. His official title was Attaché to the Secretariat of State, and Szarnicki gave him to understand that this was only a step to higher offices in the service of the Church. Whenever Finland was mentioned, he only shook his head and laughed. "'Slow and sure wins the race', cher ami. There are certainly good missionary priests in your country, but none who have had such training as you are getting here."

Thomas's office was in the Cortile di San Damaso, the famous central court of the Vatican. All the traffic to and from the papal receptions, the Secretariat of State and the administrative departments, passed through here. It was a uniquely international milieu, but thanks to his knowledge of languages Thomas gradually got used to it. He seemed to feel at home there, and he also made personal friends among the high prelates, the officials of the various departments, and the officers of the Papal Guard. However none of them could fill the place of Dom Andrea in his life.

On the other hand, he got to know Monsignor Szarnicki more

broke into a playful sparkle under the pious allegories on the ceilings. Thomas had got so used to the enchanting views from the Vatican Palace that beauty and harmony had almost become necessary conditions of existence to him. At times he felt that a mysterious atmosphere of happiness pervaded the Palace itself and had created a harmony in human hearts as in the very stones, yesterday, last year, and centuries ago. They had seen blood flowing and fists angrily clenched, these stones, but they had been erected by men whose desire was to build a home for a ruler who stood for peace on earth to men of good will. O *felix Roma!*

Thomas's eyes filled with tears. "I can never be thankful enough for the time I have spent here," he said, "and I only hope it has been of some use."

"You may be certain of that," Monsignor Szarnicki smilingly assured him, "and you must not forget that even here you are working for your own countrymen too."

When life in the Vatican returned to normal with the end of the Holy Year, Thomas was moved from Archives to the Department for Extraordinary Affairs in the Papal Secretariat of State. A year later he received the title of Monsignor. Shortly afterwards he was informed that he would be posted to the Papal Delegation in Ottawa.

He went straight to Monsignor Szarnicki. "Why should I go to Canada?" he asked. "Surely there was never any question of my going anywhere except back to Finland?"

"It is well to gain experience if one is to go abroad on official missions," replied Monsignor Szarnicki as coolly as if the other had asked permission to lunch in town. "There is a good old rule among diplomats that one should not make one's youthful errors where one is likely to hold high positions later. Don't you like the idea of Canada?"

Thomas stood there changing colour and blinking like a school-boy. "If it's at all possible, Monsignor," he said hesitantly, "I should like a little more time. You said yourself, didn't you, that I could serve my countrymen here in Rome too?"

"I shall willingly put in a word for you," replied Monsignor Szarnicki calmly. "But after all, it was you yourself who broached the question. Nobody in the Curia wanted to force a decision on you. Perhaps we shall discuss it later, when you feel clearer in your mind, eh? " he concluded with a smile.

Thomas never again discussed his posting with Monsignor Szarnicki. Shortly before the beginning of the Marian Year he resumed his work in Archives. Since his ordination a considerable change had taken place in his appearance. The lines around his mouth had deepened, his freckles had grown paler and his blonde hair thinner and less unruly. Clerical attire suited his slight but well-proportioned figure. His clothes were meticulously correct from the well-polished shoes and the close-fitting silk sash to the faultless white starched collar under the high neck of his soutane.

In the New Year he received a visit from Beata Veronica, whom he had not seen all winter. He had just been taking part in the great Candlemas Day ceremony in the Aula of Saint Peter's, and was passing back through the packed car park in the Cortile di San Damaso, when he saw her with head high and eyes cast down walking along between the shining American cars like a martyr between growling beasts.

"I'm coming to discuss an important matter with you, Monsignor," she called across to him.

He greeted her with a welcoming smile and her spirits rose instantly. "I have a favour to ask of you, Monsignor. Promise me you will not say no? " she said.

"I will try."

"It's a quite unique opportunity. You're invited to speak at the Institute."

"At what Institute? "

"The Cultural Institute. Ah, I should have told you first that I've been elected to the committee."

"Congratulations," he said, not very enthusiastically.

The Cultural Institute was one of the favourite meeting-places of Scandinavians in Rome. Thomas had frequented it a great deal before his conversion but the atmosphere there had become progressively less congenial to him. The Institute possessed a great tradition, a well-used library, and in its heyday had numbered a great many distinguished Scandinavian artists and writers among

its members. But the dust lay thicker and thicker on the old
bookcases as the decades passed, and it was becoming increasingly
difficult to preserve the fine cultural heritage from the all-devour-
ing spirit of the time.

"I must say I'm really glad that such confidence has been placed
in me," continued Veronica with becoming modesty. "Twenty or
thirty years ago it would have been unthinkable to elect a Catholic
to such a position, but there's a different wind blowing these
days. And now it's your turn, you deserter," she added, laughingly.

"Aha," said Thomas, arming himself with patience.

"We're working out the spring programme, and we're looking
for someone to give a lecture, founded on practical knowledge, on
the Cultural Aspect of Modern Catholicism. The Committee
decided to turn to you as the best Scandinavian authority on the
subject. Well – what do you think about it? "

Thomas was just able to suppress a spontaneous "No, thank
you ! " but he had not the heart to disappoint her so he only
said : "It is certainly very flattering. But do you really think the
Cultural Institute is a suitable forum for me ? "

"It will not be the first time that a Catholic priest has spoken
there. But this opportunity is so unique because you will be
speaking to people whom you could never reach otherwise. Just
now there are several parties of archaeologists and linguists from
Sweden, an art history university group from Denmark, and
various Scandinavian and Finnish artists and scholars. There are
two scholars in particular you definitely must meet : Professor
Kneipp from Denmark – you know, the theologian – and Oslok
Olsen, the Norwegian naval historian. I believe he's working just
now on the Battle of Lepanto. . . . And of course all the old
friends of the Scandinavian artists' colony will be there besides.
And the best of it all is that the initiative has come from the
Institute. There are a great many there who want to hear you."

"I don't know why they should," he murmured hesitantly. He
saw it was too late to back out; he should have cut short the
interview long ago.

"You must know better than I do how enormously the Church

has gained in authority in recent years. One notices that even in Scandinavia. Catholicism has become a problem for intellectual Protestants. These people are demanding enlightenment. You simply have to speak to them. Apart from anything else, mere politeness demands it."

"Well, I suppose I must make my Scandinavian maiden speech some time," murmured Thomas. "When shall it be?"

❧❧❧

XXI THE CULTURAL INSTITUTE 1954

Thomas had received the title of Monsignor at the age of thirty-six. Informed observers were firmly convinced that another star had risen in the firmament of the Curia. The Scandinavian colony in Rome had also long since detected its lustre.

So it was only natural that his lecture should fill the whole suite of rooms which served the Cultural Institute as a home. He had to speak standing in the doorway between the two largest reception halls, which were filled to capacity. In the outer rooms too a continually increasing throng of listeners were waiting, packed like sardines. The Chairman welcomed him with such polished and complimentary words that Thomas suspected Beata Veronica had composed his piece for him. The listeners signified polite agreement by their applause. In short, the curtain rose just as it should.

Nothing seemed to have changed in the decade since Thomas had been here before. He saw the same sagging chairs and rickety tables, the same shabby carpets and smoke-darkened wallpapers, the same dim lighting illuminating drawings yellow with age and marble busts that had grown darkish too. And the steep stairways were abuzz with illustrious scholars and artists, shy students, and rootless, roaming Bohemians just as they had been ten, twenty and thirty years ago. Thomas saw several familiar faces, which seemed to him as much part of the place as the furnishing; but the majority of the listeners were obviously of a later vintage.

The evening's programme developed in a direction which Thomas had not foreseen. He had agreed to his lecture being announced as " A Catholic Cultural Review "; nevertheless he had only planned a little impersonal talk that could offer no points for attack and would leave the more important arguments for possible discussion later. But he noticed very soon that he might just as well tackle the main questions at once. The audience had come for a candid discussion, and before them a pleasant impersonal causerie would have fallen absolutely flat; worse still, it would have amounted to positive rudeness. For he noted to his astonishment that he had immediately established with his hearers that direct contact which ensures the success of a speaker.

Perhaps Beata Veronica was right after all? Was it not his duty to fall in with the plain though perhaps not clearly formulated demand of these people for a sober explanation, and above all for human contact with a Catholic? Down here in Rome they found themselves daily and hourly confronted with Catholicism, but they had no one to give them a personal introduction in their own language and in accordance with their own mode of thought. Personal – that was the word. He ought to give himself absolutely or else keep silence.

Suddenly the prim young prelate with the red sash began to smile – at first an embarrassed and slightly enquiring smile. There he stood weighing the little roll of manuscript in his hand, while his eyes roamed appraisingly over the audience.

Unconsciously, he ran his middle finger round inside the narrow Roman collar – a gesture that made the metamorphosis still more complete; Monsignor Cinnelius was once more a little Finnish scholar.

"Pardon me," he began, still a trifle hesitantly, "I had brought some notes of my lecture, but your friendly welcome has made it clear to me that I should speak freely, as is usual among fellow-countrymen."

He was interrupted by applause.

And before he knew himself how it happened, he had laid aside his pince-nez and found himself launched into an account of his first encounter with the Catholic Church as a young man. The memories and experiences of those first years in Rome streamed into his mind. Once more he was a student, thirsty for knowledge, standing before the magnificent cathedral, wondering dreamily about the inspiration from which all this beauty had been born. Unconsciously he allowed himself to be carried away by his thoughts. He became eloquent. He painted his word-pictures with stronger colours than ever before.

Between historical parallels and present-day perspectives he brought to life a picture of the universal Church before his spell-bound listeners. It was only façade painting to be sure, but it had a perspective in depth that gave an indication of the essential principles. It was not difficult to bring out the disputed dogmatic central doctrines against this background; they fitted into his simplified picture as naturally as into the paintings of the primitive masters. It gave him a peculiar satisfaction to be able to speak in his own language about these questions before a highly educated audience. As he perceived the effect he became more and more daring. A global picture of Catholicism emerged, rich in colour, fertile, concrete and overpowering. And from the present he went on to the future and confessed to a burning faith in the *Ecclesia triumphans*, God's triumphant Church on earth.

The Church was only in the beginning of her earthly development, he said, and therefore held, hidden within herself, a vast potential power. Strange though it might sound, she was continually hampered in her growth by the armour – fear of criticism, exaggerated regimentation, clericalism and formalism – which past dark centuries had forced upon her. But he, Thomas, regarded all this as purely external. Once the time was ripe and the position of the Church firmly assured in the new political commonwealth, all this would disappear. Actually, work aimed at achieving the adjustment of the Church to the modern State had long been quietly and hiddenly in progress. Future generations would see the Church becoming progressively more democratic; but that could not happen until the whole human commonwealth was leavened through and through with truly Christian thought, and Catholic teaching had grown so strong in the consciousness of the masses that the Church could take root in democratic soil without having to fear distortion of her teaching. Rome would then have fulfilled her historical task and mankind would have crossed the threshold to the millennium that is destined to precede Christ's second coming.

When Thomas finished speaking he did not get quite the ovation he would have got had the audience been a Southern one, but the warmth and sincerity of the applause was unmistakable. No debate followed; it would have been scarcely possible to have one without touching on the person of the speaker. So the Chairman thanked him with a few complimentary words in which admiration for his courageous confession of faith was implied rather expressed. The audience rose and people began smoking. Gradually an interested circle, glad of an opportunity of talking things over frankly with a modern-minded Catholic priest who was also a Scandinavian, gathered round Thomas.

A stocky, bald-headed diplomat with tortoise-shell spectacles over his cool blue eyes, laid his hands warmly on his shoulders.

"That was most interesting, Monsignor," he said. "My service has brought me to several Catholic countries, so I am not quite unfamiliar with these questions. Moreover, I have the honour of knowing His Holiness since the time he was Nuncio. He is an impressive personality, undoubtedly one of the greatest minds of our age – though of course we usually converse only about neutral matters. But how different it is to be able to look behind the curtain of the Temple, so to speak, quite privately here among ourselves. It is a great and beautiful temple, and one must admit that – quite apart from its political significance – the world would be a great deal the poorer without it. . . ."

The ambassador thoughtfully took the cigarette from his mouth and blew one of his most perfect smoke-rings into the air.

But now another figure, greybearded, far-seeing, stern and omniscient, emerged from behind the diplomat's full-moon face. It was Oslok Olsen, war historian, political journalist, and spokesman for the collective Scandinavian conscience, six feet six in his stockings.

"Your Church represents a unique concentration of power," he said. "Opinions may differ regarding her politics but one cannot shut one's eyes to this fact – Washington, Moscow, Rome – there we have the political physiognomy of our century. However, it is interesting to hear that Catholicism counts upon developing to her maximum strength on a democratic basis."

Thomas was hesitating as to whether he should answer when a sculptor whom he knew, an ardent creature with long hair and an open shirt-collar, got in first. "To think that all this lies in the hand of one man!" he exclaimed. "To cope with the organization one must be a superman, but the present Pope is definitely big enough for his job. I would give anything to do a bust of him!"

"One sees a striking lot of fine heads among the Catholic clergy," came a familiar grating voice with a lightly ironical tone. Thomas swung round and caught sight of Felix Letterman, who gave him a conspiratorial wink over his puffing pipe. "I have often asked myself to what extent the outward qualifications weigh when it comes to a choice. By the way, doesn't the *Codex Iuris Canonici* contain something about the exterior of the priest . . . ?"

"A most reasonable principle," declared the sculptor, getting in before Thomas again. "The beautiful is worthy of the strong. Anyhow, Catholicism has an appreciation of beauty such as one finds nowhere else."

A murmur of agreement rose from the listeners. Thomas saw nothing but solemnly nodding faces round him. A well-known operatic tenor informed him that Gregorian chant expressed the deepest feelings of the human breast; a little philologist confessed that she always went into a Catholic church when she wanted to have a good weep, and a Finnish historian assured him confidentially that all experts were now agreed that the Catholic Church was the oldest vehicle of Western culture in the North.

A familar profile which Thomas had not seen for many years emerged outside in the corridor. It was his old fellow-student Fabian Arnesson, now a well-established lecturer and leader of a successful archaeological expedition to Corfu. He tried to go over and greet him, but this was not so easy. The artists were still storming him with their questions – about the art theories and musical teaching of the Catholic Church, the keys in which the Mass is sung, the technique of stained-glass painting in the Middle Ages, whether Fra Angelico was still considered the most saintly painter, and why the Catholic Church had not canonized Raphael and Michelangelo. . . .

Then the company sat down at the long tables, where wine and sandwiches were served. Thomas tried cautiously to change his company, and found to his joy that Arnesson came literally half-way to meet him.

"Well, old boy," said the archaeologist, "it's a long time since we've seen you on the Forum Romanum."

"Yes, it's certainly a long time," said Thomas, smiling. "I have another sphere of activity now."

"But I have heard that your title hasn't made you any different," said Arnesson laughingly putting his arm familiarly round Thomas's shoulders. "It's really grand to see you again, Tommy. Drink a glass of wine with me!"

Fabian was just the same. His forehead was a bit higher, his figure a bit heavier, and on the whole he had become a little more porcine in appearance, but the eyes which shone behind his spectacles had the same kindly, anxious expression as ever. Thomas murmured some conventional words about his well-preserved youthful appearance, but the archaeologist interrupted him quickly.

"Let's stop swopping compliments! We have both changed. How could it be otherwise? I've got stout and slow, and sleep badly, but you look splendid. And that's not a mere outward impression – one can see that you have kept your old elasticity. That was noticeable in your lecture too. Catholic priests can keep their form longer than other mortals. You needn't take that personally. I know plenty of other examples. How on earth do you people do it?"

"We don't do anything in particular. It goes with our calling," said Thomas, smiling.

Arnesson nodded. "I can understand that," he said. "If a man has once found his true vocation in life, the very knowledge of this must be a constant source of strength. That goes without saying."

Thomas pressed his old friend's hand impulsively. "You're right there, Fabian," he said.

"I'm very glad of that. I know how you used to rave about Italian church art even in our student days in Uppsala. Even then you wrote some fine things, brother, but now I understand that your heart was yearning for something else. One should have seen that at once."

"You're right. But I found my way rather late."

"Your future biographers will probably break their heads over that, but the main thing is that you *did* find your way and you courageously took the first step. When I heard your lecture just now I realized that you absolutely had to go away and leave us. You are undoubtedly in your right place here. Do you know that many envy you your choice?"

Thomas flushed. "How do you mean?" he asked quickly.

"I mean that it is very rare for an art historian from our part of the world to have the courage to surrender himself completely to a particular call. But you have done so, dear Tommy, and we all respect you for it, and, as I say, envy you a bit too. Certainly, it must be wonderful to devote oneself undividedly to such a subtle object of art study as your Church offers. For only Catholic priests can really do that. We others have to worry about expeditions and collections of specimens, and enquiries. But you can meditate the whole day long if you want to and, when all is said and done, that must be an intense artistic delight to an expert. We are expecting a book from you, dear Tommy, an important book. You owe that to your old friends – do you hear?"

Thomas swallowed a drop of wine down the wrong pipe. His head was burning frightfully. With a few polite words he excused himself, hoping to slip out unseen. A suffocating, indefinable fear was coming over him. But a little gentleman with smooth fair hair, good brown eyes and a firm chin, barred his way. His face betrayed a solid calm of conscience which was too evident to be wholly attractive.

"I'm Kneipp," he said, bowing and stretching out his hand. It

was the celebrated Protestant theologian. Immediately a respectful
circle formed around the two.

"It's a great pleasure to meet you," murmured Thomas.

"The pleasure is entirely mine. I should like to thank you for
your lecture. It was simply magnificent. But it would be very
pleasant to discuss these questions more thoroughly. We have so
much in common that it would be really too bad if we did not
seek every opportunity to strengthen the contact between Pro-
testantism and Catholicism. Don't you agree?"

"Definitely. I am always glad to be of help to anyone."

"You can certainly be that, Monsignor," replied the Dane.
Then, sticking his thumbs in his armholes, planting his legs apart,
and looking up at the ceiling, he cleared his throat emphatically,
and went on: "I at least am firmly convinced that a convergence,
if not actually a union, between all the Christian Churches will
come to pass sooner or later. By union I mean a co-operation on a
common Christian basis in which all partners are permitted to
preserve and develop their own individual character. This last
point is certainly particularly important to the Catholic Church,
which, of course, is the oldest ecclesiastical community. We no
longer want to do away with the Pope" – here he made a rhetori-
cal pause to give his listeners an opportunity for a discreet little
laugh – then continued: "You Catholics have your place and we
have ours. Your strength lies in your monumentality, not to say
monolithism, and, in the interests of all concerned, that should be
allowed you. For if I may say so, you Catholics must look after
the outward defences. You must build the temple walls and create
the solid organization. You have the tradition and the experience
as well as the technical and material sources at your disposal for
this. It is nothing more than Rome's historical destiny, as you
emphasized in your lecture. We of the Evangelical communions
shall devote ourselves, on the other hand, to prayer, meditation,
theological development, and the moral education of the individual. In this way we should gradually arrive at an apportion-
ment of work such as we see indicated already in the Gospels in
the story of Martha and Mary. Is that not so?"

A second pause was respectfully filled with applause by the

M

bystanders. But Thomas could bear no more. "It would certainly be very interesting to discuss all that some other time," he assured him as the cold sweat gathered on his forehead, "but unfortunately I must go now."

Out on the landing Beata Veronica was waiting for him, with glowing cheeks. "Deo gratias," she whispered, grasping his hand. "You were splendid. It was an immense success."

If I don't clear off quickly she's quite capable of kissing me, thought Thomas desperately, tearing himself away. But as he walked down the stairs he heard her calling after him: "Victoria! You have laid the world at the feet of Christ!"

She means her own feet, he thought bitterly. But the words of the Danish theologian kept ringing in his ears: "It is nothing more than Rome's historical destiny. . . ."

It was already night. The streets were empty. Thomas wandered by shuttered shop windows and empty bars. His thoughts were whirling through his head like leaves in a storm. He felt tired to death, his steps made a strange hollow echo, and he surprised himself wondering dreamily how many times he would have to tread these same steps to leave a footprint like Santa Cristina's behind him on the pavement. . . .

Shaking off his thoughts, he looked around him. He was standing in front of a little church behind the Piazza Navona. The emphatically gesticulating figures on the dark, blackened baroque façade looked spectral, daemonic in the feeble night light. The faces grinned at him like death-masks on an unreal horror stage.

So these were the temple walls which the Catholics had built and were to go on building until the end of time, if Professor Kneipp had his way! He stared at the convulsively strained muscles of the figures, which seemed like petrified representations of pain, and suddenly he felt he had discovered the shattering tragedy in the art of Roman baroque. Was it not at bottom a desperate effort to express and imprison in stone the gloom of Golgotha, vibrant with fear? For behind these heavy masses of stone, which seemed to be gesticulating wildly and expressing a deep inward despair, there was nothing but a naked cross and a red lamp glowing before a tomb. Or perhaps it would be more correct to say a prison, Christ's self-chosen prison. . . . This was the only reality. Everything else was illusion and self-deception. What was it Padre Barnaba had said? "Do not forget, God is invisible, even here in Rome. . . ."

A wave of self-doubt welled up in him. Perhaps Fabian Arnesson was right, after all? Why had he, Thomas Cinnelius, become a priest? Why does an art historian become a priest? To secretly look for new aesthetic values? And when he is asked to bear witness for God he stands up and praises the glories of the world. What was he, actually? An emigrant who had forfeited the right to speak to his own fellow-countrymen; an agitator who tried to catch souls with cheap hypothetical pictures of an earthly Church triumphant; a priest who refused to believe without seeing, and shut his eyes, when offering Mass. . . .

XXII COLLEGIO TEUTONICO

"We have no intention of incorporating you into the great German nation," Doctor Mach had said laughingly a few years before, when he had found living quarters for Thomas in the old German College in the Vatican beside the German cemetery. "But you are not the first Scandinavian to live here, and as an old Wiborger, familiar with German tradition, you can almost imagine yourself among your compatriots."

Thomas did in fact feel quite at home. True, the house was dark and very old fashioned, with rambling stairways and rickety steps, long corridors and creaking floor-boards, but once one was familiar with the confusing lay-out, one came under its charm. Like all old institutions the Collegio Teutonico had developed an atmosphere of its own. It could be icy cold in winter and suffocatingly hot in summer in the narrow little rooms; but the physical temperature did not affect the feeling of ease and comfort. The ruling spirit was free and easy, in fact almost Bohemian. The first commandment in the unwritten law of the College was tolerance towards the thousand little peculiarities that naturally develop in a home where a collection of mature and highly individual bachelors live together. Most of them were German-speaking priests engaged in various special studies; but there was also several permanent boarders such as Doctor Mach, who worked in the Archives or some department of the Curia. Their predecessors rested in the tropically verdant little cemetery among high prelates and prominent Catholic laymen from beyond the Alps under the comprehensive inscription "*Teutones in pace*".

The priests said Mass in the college church every morning before starting their day's work. Thomas shared an altar with three colleagues, following a fixed rota to which he had adhered strictly up to the present. But after his lecture in the Scandinavian Institute he avoided going down to the church while the others were there and only came in to breakfast after they had finished in order to escape awkward questions. As he sat down to his already cold coffee on the fourth morning he found Doctor Mach still in the refectory fiddling with a few crumbs, sunk in thought. It could be seen even at a distance that he had something on his mind.

"We're having distinguished visitors – three Scandinavian artists who want to have a look at the College," he said. "You evidently know them. The name of one of them is Letterman, I believe."

"Why exactly are they coming now?"

"To inspect the church and the Scandinavian graves, and the library, and perhaps to have a little look at us old Papists too. I didn't know that these people regarded us with so much affection. But we must assume it's an effort to make contact, don't you think? I suppose we have to thank you for this friendly gesture?"

"I'm afraid they're putting out their feelers only through ordinary human curiosity."

"That was my first thought too, and I would not have mentioned it if they had not given you as a reference."

"Did they do that?"

"I got the impression that you had told them very eloquently of our goodwill towards them, Monsignor," said Doctor Mach with a little laugh, "and now they want to see how we look at close quarters. That's quite a natural wish. If it's mere ordinary curiosity, there's no great danger."

"What do you mean by danger?"

Doctor Mach became serious. "One cannot appeal to people's deeper interests by tourist propaganda methods, or one scares them off sooner or later," he said. "But of course you know that better than I do. What kind of people are these three? Are they atheists, vitalists, existentialists or what?"

"I don't know exactly, but they all have a certain kind of indifferentist goodwill, if you know what I mean, towards Catholicism."

Doctor Mach looked at him thoughtfully over his spectacles. "You couldn't have expressed it better," he said. "Unfortunately I have had most depressing experiences with this kind of indifferent goodwill. It is only tolerant and understanding until it comes up against a total demand – as in genuine Christianity, for instance." As Thomas flushed but remained silent, he continued dryly: "Have you not noticed that our indifferentist friends like to talk about Catholicism but do not at all like to talk about Christianity? They even incline to play off the two concepts one against the other. In this way they hope to drive a wedge into the Christian front and dodge the absolute demand of religion."

"But everyone knows that the Catholic Church insists on her absolute claims more than any other Church."

"Quite right. But the point is that our indifferentist friends proceed from the view that this claim is not really meant so seriously. From the moral point of view, we must be detestable individuals in their eyes; but if one is morally indifferent too, there's nothing to prevent one from associating with Catholics, provided, naturally, that they are nice, educated people. Of course, the Catholics must be just as indifferent fundamentally. Consequently they are readily recognized as allies against the presumptuous moral claim. If our indifferent friends but understood what we really believe, they would rend their garments. It is very sad."

As he sat there, shaking his head and picking at the bread crumbs on the table, he looked like a bedraggled bird.

"Actually," he continued, "it all comes from the fact that most people have forgotten what the word Catholic really means. It has assumed far too polemical a sound to have the drawing power it should have. That is very regrettable indeed. Unfortunately there are a great many good Catholics who feel that everything is as it should be, since Christ Himself said He had come to bring not peace but the sword. . . ." He stopped short with a comic gesture of horror. "But of course these are terribly heretical thoughts," he continued, "which one should not utter aloud under the shadow of the great dome. Well, have a good breakfast, Monsignor."

He stood up. At that moment the bells of Saint Peter's began pealing so loudly that the stained-glass windows of the refectory vibrated. "Listen to that – even Saint Peter is angry." He laughed, as he disappeared like a scared crow into the narrow corridor, his soutane flapping round him.

The working day had begun long before Thomas arrived in the Vatican City. A little baker's van was delivering fresh loaves to the Pilgrim's Hospice in Santa Marta; a couple of painters were hoisting pails of paint up to the roof of Saint Peter's, and a shining black Cadillac was gliding along the road to the Vatican Palace. From the Swiss Guards' sentry post at the entrance gate a cheerful voice called out:

"Good morning, friend!"

The speaker was a tall, handsome young captain who had joined the Swiss Guard a couple of years ago. He came of an aristocratic Swiss family and was a university graduate and extremely popular. He and Thomas always had a chat when they met. But today Monsignor Cinnelius did not dare to stop and talk to him, for in his mind's eye he saw the three Scandinavian artists at the guards' post, their eyes, sparkling with curiosity, glued to the decorative guards. He walked on, but the three never left his thoughts. He felt as though Letterman were walking beside him demanding an explanation of everything around him.

A distinguished-looking old prelate came out of the canons'

wing and greeted him with a friendly nod. It was Monsignor Grandpierre, an unusually noble character, who had given Thomas much good advice during his years of training at the Vatican. But now he found himself mentally introducing the invisible Letterman to Monseigneur Grandpierre and explaining him in somewhat the following terms: of a highly cultured and aristocratic French family; a legal authority of international repute; consulted as an expert by the French Academy; a very likely candidate for a cardinal's hat. . . .

Feeling quite bewildered, Thomas turned into the Piazza Santa Marta. Two monks in black habits came out from behind Saint Peter's. They were the English and the Spanish confessors of Saint Peter's, and they greeted him with friendly smiles. He made a retreat now and then in their college in the Palazzo del Tribunale, and the Englishman was his confessor. But now the imaginary voice of Letterman, superciliously demanding information about these strange wise men who apparently formed a sort of papal high-court for the examination of matters of conscience, held him back. . . .

'Three stars in the Baedeker,' thought Thomas with a slight shudder. A crowd of Ethiopian seminary students passed him on their way to a lecture, and their white eyeballs rolled as they greeted him. Half-way up the hill in the midst of wonderful green gardens, stood the college which Pius XI had built for them. Here Letterman would probably nod knowingly and say: "A much shrewder way of conquering the black folk than Mussolini ever thought of."

With downcast eyes Thomas walked round Saint Peter's, through Vatican courtyards, and raised his hat, startled, when the gendarmes outside the Pope's personal quarters saluted him. But all the time he seemed to hear Letterman's harsh, mocking voice saying: "You needn't explain anything more. The Americans have a word for all this: 'Biggest in the world, biggest in the world, biggest in the world. . . .'"

His immediate colleague, a little round-headed Milanese priest named Alba, was awaiting him in the office. He looked like a good-natured young peasant, and his most valuable endowment was an excellent constitution, which had proved an ideal basis for a sound Roman training. Monsignor Alba was not one of the greatest intellects in the Secretariat of State, perhaps, but he was moderate and clear-thinking, energetic and patient, and had proved himself a useful and steady diplomat in the delicate political game of the post-war period.

"Yes, the heat has come early this year," he said, greeting Thomas in his singsong voice.

"Do you think so?" said Thomas, who had not noticed that he was perspiring.

Monsignor Alba looked at him intently. "How are you? Don't you feel well?" he asked.

"What do you mean? I'm feeling splendid."

"You have been late several mornings recently."

"Has anyone noticed it?" asked Thomas anxiously.

Monsignor Alba nodded good-humouredly. "How could we fail to notice when our most punctual colleague comes in late on several mornings consecutively. And when he looks badly, too, it is hardly surprising if his colleagues feel a little anxious."

"There's nothing to worry about."

"Of course you're much in demand elsewhere, are you not?"

"What do you mean by elsewhere?"

"With your countrymen, I take it. It's no joke to have to do with Northerners. I know what I'm saying."

He had shortly returned after three years with the Apostolic Delegation in London, and was still full of his experiences of the good and the less-pleasing traits of the Anglo-Saxon character.

"One must know one's job if one has to represent the Church amongst English or Scandinavian people. They're not free and easy as we are down here. They're incredibly critical, and you have to be on your toes all the time if you are not to be vanquished in argument. Their standards in everything are high and strict. Sport with them is not a mere pleasure but almost a necessary condition for preserving their mental and physical elasticity. Do you go in for any sport, Don Tommaso?"

"No."

"Indeed?" Monsignor Alba seemed surprised. "I think you

should, because you apply yourself rather too intensely. You need rest and relaxation. You have certainly earned it."

"I don't need any rest. Besides, it wouldn't make me feel a bit better."

The Milanese smiled – a gentle, clever smile. "It needn't necessarily be football," he said. "One can relax by other means. When I feel tired I go to a little parish priest in Prati and help him with his work. It's the best possible rest. And there are more than enough of such little tasks to be had here in Rome. You only have to apply to the General Vicariate. They are delighted to accept any offer of help. You know, the parishes of Rome are far too big unfortunately. With us in Northern Italy things are much better organized."

His eyes twinkled secret understanding at Thomas as he settled down to work again. Suddenly a familiar rustic sound came through the open window – the cackle of a real, live hen from a roof garden of this amazing Vatican Palace. . . .

Thomas's heart beat fast when he was called to see his chief. The reception-room was a spacious apartment with red damask-covered walls, gilded chairs, and a huge marble centre table. Monsignor Szarnicki was sitting engrossed in the study of a pile of documents, beneath a great oil painting of Jan Sobieski before the walls of liberated Vienna. Now, in his old age, Monsignor Szarnicki, with his full figure, bright complexion, regular features and beautiful white hair, resembled Pius VII more than ever.

"Ah, there you are, my friend," he said, pushing the papers aside. "The Nuncio to the Italian Government has sent a report of your lecture, which has excited considerable comment among the diplomats at the Quirinal. However, the reaction seems to be favourable on the whole. I should like very much to read the lecture. Have you the text, by any chance?"

"I spoke without notes, Monsignor."

"Ah, of course, that was a stupid question." His subordinate's unhappy expression did not escape the Pole. He smiled reassuringly. "It is difficult to speak in such a way as to please everyone," he said. "There will always be different points of view, but our golden rule here is that public pronouncements are to be avoided! It is the duty of the Pope, the bishops and the priests—all in their own domains—to expound the Scriptures, but the secretariat of State is silent. That is our part, as it were, in God's plan."

"Where keeping silent is concerned, I would not mind if my tongue were cut out. But I was asked to speak, and I could not well refuse. I'm not the kind of person you think I am, Monsignor. I haven't the maturity of judgment which is required in the Curia, and I shall never attain it. I'm a convert, and that just can't be helped."

Monsignor Szarnicki was visibly shaken. "But, my dear friend, you are too hard on yourself. You have a good name at the Curia. You should not be upset by such a trifle as this. We live and learn. I suggest that you take a really good holiday, and rest thoroughly. The world will seem much brighter afterwards. I could discuss the matter with the Under-Secretary of State. I am having an interview with him in a quarter of an hour in any case and you can wait for me in the ante-room."

In the ante-room of the Under-Secretary of State there was a continuous coming and going of diplomats, high prelates and other prominent persons from all parts of the world. Thomas had to wait a long time. At last he found a seat between an Indian bishop and a South American ambassador, who were listening with obvious amusement to an Irish Franciscan who was giving a French journalist a graphic account of his adventures in China. Thomas entrenched himself behind a large illustrated volume, but even through this protective barrier his growing anxiety was almost visible. If this was really the cross which he was to bear, he would break down under it prematurely. His first public missionary effort among Scandinavians had proved a wretched fiasco. It was becoming more and more clear to him that he could never again give a public lecture. He simply had not enough strength to break down walls—and still less to build them up.

XXIII SANTO SPIRITO IN GATTAFOGATA

The General Vicariate suggested to Thomas that he should take
the place of the priest of a small outlying parish beyond the Villa
Doria, who was ill. Thomas had never seen such a depressing
region. The little parish had grown up around an ancient Roman
road between the hills, the Via Gattafogata. Two rows of shanties
of indefinite age and a number of miserable barracks, built for war
refugees, formed the periphery. The actual centre consisted of
eight absolutely identical blocks of flats, ten storeys high, which,
owing to dampness, had acquired a hideous mottled appearance
like wartime camouflage. A miserable inn, a shabby hairdressing
saloon and the office of the Communist party formed the hub
of the public life of the commune.

The church, Santo Spirito, stood on a dreary slope rather like
a railway embankment. It gave the impression of a provincial
railway station with its clock in front and its bell on the roof.
Inside too it was curiously reminiscent of a railway station with
its big luggage counter which went by the name of High Altar,
two open compartments which represented side altars, and an
ingenious ticket-office which served as confessional. The architect,
evidently driven to desperation by the ugliness of the surroundings, had hurriedly tried to create a cheap place of transit to a
better world.

There was nothing here to tempt one to contemplate the great-
ness of creation. Via Gattafogata seemed to need a station inspector
rather than a priest. For those who lived around it the church
was a kind of office, where they received the authorization to
reside in this miserable world, the licence to exercise marital
functions, and finally, a ticket into the Great Unknown.

Never before had Thomas felt so wretched as when he sat
here at his counter granting absolution for neglected Easter duties.
The clientele was small and predominantly elderly. Some tried to
get their ticket to heaven on reduced terms. In such cases he had

187

to be strict, for he had no authority to grant rebates. Sometimes, too, penitents put forward claims for proletarian privileges. In such cases it was not difficult to detect the influence of the near-by Communist headquarters. When this had happened repeatedly Thomas decided, like a second Don Camillo, to visit his opponent in his own stronghold. But even before he got inside he met his Peppone.

A little car with the Red Cross on the windscreen was standing before the Communist Party office. A broad-shouldered man with a red bull neck and black curly hair, and wearing a white wind-cheater, stepped out of it. In one hand he carried a small case, with the other he waved a cheerful greeting to the comrades on the steps. When he turned round Thomas recognized Doctor Romolo.

"Good day, Doctor! It's a long time since we've met."

The doctor screwed up his eyes in a comical expression of surprise.

"Hello! It's you, is it? Well, I never!" he cried, giving Thomas a hearty handshake. "How are you? Do you still feel happy in that get-up?"

Thomas noted that his relations with Romolo seemed to be permanently coloured by the fact that the doctor would never take his calling seriously. In Romolo's view Thomas came of a highly civilized race, which had learnt how to put religious super-stition in its place. Hence, as long as he wore clerical attire, he was not only a laughable spectacle but a pathological one too. At every meeting Romolo saw him again as his patient in Bolsena.

This time, however, Thomas decided to accept the challenge, so he assured him cheerfully that he was feeling splendid. "And how are you yourself after all these years?" he asked. "Do you never wish yourself back in Sant' Eusebio?"

Romolo roared laughing. "No, I'm not converted although I spent six months in your monastery. But it did give me a taste for the Campagna. This is my district here. It's not very grand, but it's quite all right."

Obviously he had got on. He had become stout and walked with a swagger. It was plain that he was an important man in this neighbourhood. Just then a dozen ragged youths came out of the Communist office and greeted him with delight. He clapped them cheerfully on their stooping shoulders but suddenly remembering Thomas, he turned to him again and said with a flicker of the old distrust in his small eyes:

"And what about you, Reverendo? – that's what we're to call you nów, isn't it? What are you doing here in this forecourt of hell?"

"I'm spending my holidays here," replied Thomas.

"Holidays? Do I hear you aright?"

"Yes – holidays from my work in the Papal Secretariat of State."

Romolo became quite excited. "But this isn't a health resort," he said. "It's one of the poorest quarters of Rome, if you know what that means. Here people work twenty-four hours a day and still go hungry. No one comes to Gattafogata for a holiday."

"I've come here to work besides."

"Then you're welcome, Reverendo!" replied Romolo, bowing ironically and pointing towards the office door. "I take it you're going to sign on in there?"

"My task is in another field."

"There's only one task here – to procure bread."

"I have a particular Bread to offer, as you probably know."

Romolo became serious all at once. "Is the Pope going to distribute food again?" he asked. "I thought he had given up the deliveries. Please don't try opening one of the Christian Democrat bread depots in this quarter!"

"I'm not speaking of ordinary bread."

"What then?"

"I'm speaking of the Bread of Heaven."

Romolo seemed relieved. "Oh, that's all right as far as I'm concerned; only it can hardly satisfy anyone's hunger."

"That's not its purpose."

"But why do you mention it in this connection?"

"Because it means more than your bread."

"Rubbish!" cried the doctor angrily. "You don't even believe that yourself!"

Thomas was unable to keep his voice from trembling as he

replied: "I think you forget you are speaking to a Catholic priest."

Romolo was going to answer angrily, but after a glance at the other's face controlled himself and said in quite a friendly voice: "Do you know how much bread is consumed in this quarter every day? Or rather, how much should be, if the world were organized on Christian lines? "

"No, I don't."

"I thought as much. And yet you maintain that a handful of consecrated wafers means more? "

Thomas sought in vain for an apt reply but could only think of the old text: "Man shall not live by bread alone."

The doctor shrugged his shoulders irritably. "No," he said, "but he dies if he doesn't get it. You can distribute your consecretated wafers to all who want them. But you cannot feed five thousand people with them as your Lord and Master did. I call that tempting God. I learned *that* much from the Catechism. Domenico! "

A little man in a leather jacket came out of the crowd. His face was rather rat-like, and there were big burn scars on his cheeks.

"Domenico, please fit a new sparking plug for me," said Romolo, and disappeared into the Party Centre.

As Thomas returned to Santo Spirito, Romolo's words were still ringing in his ears. They seemed strangely familiar. Were they not like an echo of his own excited voice disputing with Padre Barnaba about the Blessed Sacrament? The object weighed against it then was a work of art; now Doctor Romolo had thrown physical life itself on to the scales. Moreover, the background here was far more disquieting than it had ever been in the Vicolo dei Pecorai.

True, there was great poverty in Padre Barnaba's parish too, but there never was such an atmosphere of rootlessness and despair. The air of the Via Gattafogata was charged with a diabolical hatred that froze the human heart. It was not easy to preach the message of love in such a spiritual climate. The Madonna of the Shepherds could have had nothing to say to these people. Only a martyr could win the Via Gattafogata to the Holy Spirit, thought Thomas with a shudder as he stood in his poor, cold, ugly church expounding the Gospel of Pentecost to a handful of uninterested parishioners.

Among them was a young girl who did not seem really to belong to the place. She gave rather the impression of being from the country, with her bright colour, strong unruly hair and robust physique which were in striking contrast to the small, fine-featured face. Then Thomas noticed the sensitive mouth, narrow nose and magnificent brown eyes and wondered where he had seen her before.

After Mass she came into the sacristy and greeted him blushing. "Don't you remember me, Father?" she asked. "I'm Assunta from the Vicolo dei Pecorai – Fausto's Assunta. . . ."

Ah, yes, of course! The little portress of Santa Presenza. He had not seen her for several years. Someone had told him that her mother had died and that her father, Fausto, had gone back to his native village.

"This is certainly a surprise," he said, smiling kindly at her. "I didn't know that you had come to this district. How is your father?"

"He's up in the mountains," she replied, blushing still more.

"Yes, so I heard. And I suppose you have work here?"

"No, I'm married."

"Congratulations. May I ask to whom?"

She beamed. "Sor Anacleto's son Cesarino – you know him, of course? He works for a travel agency and drives a big coach right through Italy."

"And when he's away you have to sit at home alone," he said with a laugh. "Still, that's the way it is. Have you any children?"

"Not yet. Our papers are not in order," she replied in a matter-of-fact voice.

"How's that?"

"I'm not yet of age, and we can't get the papers without Father's consent, Cesarino says."

"Does that mean that your father is against the union?"

"Yes, he can't stand Cesarino. He never did like him. He just doesn't understand any modern young men. But he will have to give way."

Thomas had to stop and think for a moment. There was something disarming about the girl's frankness.

"But then you're not married at all, are you?" he asked cautiously.

"I'm married in the eyes of God and the Party comrades," she replied proudly.

"Certainly not in the eyes of God," he said.

"How do you know that?"

"Because God has given us clearly to understand what He means by a marriage. And besides, I have not yet heard that your Party comrades claim to be able to marry people."

Her eyes scanned his face uneasily. Obviously his words had made an impression on her and he had gained the upper hand, so it was a matter now of striking while the iron was hot.

"Where are you living?"

"With a comrade of Cesarino's named Domenico."

"Hm. I think I've met him. Are you all right there?"

She swallowed hard. "It's only for a the time," she said. "We'll have a proper home later on – but only when we have a child."

"You must not think of having a child," he told her firmly. Assunta flushed crimson, but listened submissively without protest to his warnings. Already he felt he had saved a soul. But the next day she appeared unexpectedly in the parish office with Romolo, who seemed somewhat embarrassed.

"You can't expect me to go back and live in the mountains," she lamented, her voice choked with tears. "I simply cannot live alone there. It would be bad for my health."

Thomas did not allow himself to be put off by this. Turning to the doctor he asked: "Is the girl your patient?"

"No, but I'm sorry for her," replied Romolo sullenly. "She's a good girl. Everybody here likes her."

Thomas was already tasting the pleasure of approaching victory as he asked frigidly: "Do you mean the Party comrades?"

"Yes, they too."

"Do you belong to the Party? "

"No, I only act as doctor to the men when I'm needed. But what's that to you anyway? "

Thomas shrugged his shoulders. "If Assunta wants to stay here she must leave Cesarino in any case."

The girl broke into despairing sobs. "Go away from him. Then I'll die," she cried. "Wouldn't I, Doctor? Tell him I'd die! I have no one else to go to. I can't live without Cesarino! "

Thomas looked at Romolo again, this time with an expression of extremely polite expectation.

"Don't you see that the girl is serious? " said the doctor excitedly. "She wants to marry him. She will certainly get their relationship legalized as soon as she can. That is purely a practical matter. There's nothing to be gained by sending her back to the mountains. All that's needed here is a little forbearance, and above all goodwill."

Thomas became frosty. He felt like asking Romolo if he doubted that a priest could have goodwill, but he feared being unable to control his voice. The doctor misunderstood his silence and flushed with indignation.

"This is the first time since the War that I have asked a favour of a priest," he said, "and I'm only asking you to exercise your reputed sense of reality."

"The only reality is God's will."

"Please spare me your magic formulae and keep to facts! "

"The fact is that this child here has run away from her father, and is living with the fellow in an irregular union which is contrary to the laws of God and man."

Assunta burst into tears. "That is not true," she cried. "We love each other. We didn't want to do anything wrong."

"If you did not know what you were doing, your guilt is not so great," said Thomas more gently. "But now you do know that it is wrong. If you still persevere in your sin, you may find yourself excommunicated one fine day."

"What does that mean? " asked Assunta, her voice suddenly very small.

Thomas caught an ironical gleam in Romolo's eyes, and a wave of repressed anger rose in him. This man had a peculiar knack of standing in his way in delicate situations. Pale with agitation, he turned to poor Assunta and explained the matter to her, emphasizing every word.

"It means that you will be excluded from the Church. You will no longer be allowed to receive Holy Communion, or be married in the church. You will be buried outside the walls of the churchyard. But it will be your own fault. Those who do not accept the Lord's invitation while there is yet time will have to hunger for all Eternity, in darkness and cold, when the gates of heaven are finally shut against them. It is only a matter of choosing. . . ."

He stopped short when he noticed the effect his words were having. Assunta pressed her hands over her ears and ran out of the room, weeping loudly.

Romolo sat by the window smoking. There was absolute silence. Thomas avoided his eyes. The doctor seemed to be waiting for something. When nothing happened he stood up and stubbed his cigarette-end in the ashtray.

"That was a grand trump card – that bit about the churchyard walls," he said bitterly. "They must be fine and thick in your heaven."

"What do you mean?"

Romolo laughed. "Do you imagine the girl knew what excommunication means?" he asked.

"I've just explained it to her!"

"That's precisely what you haven't done. The only thing you did make clear to her was that she would remain outside the walls, and the only thing she understood was that she would have to go hungry, not only in this life, but in the next too. But of course you have saved the honour, and the power, and the glory. That word 'excommunicate' has a positively terrifying effect on these simple people."

"The girl is childish and ignorant, and her religious instruction has probably been neglected. But that is not my fault."

"I didn't say it was," replied Romolo contemptuously, "but you knew perfectly well what you were doing."

He went out, got into his car, and drove off without a word of farewell.

⤳⊷⟐⊶⤳

XXIV   THE JANICULUM

The next morning Thomas telephoned Cardinal Norcus's secretary. "May I have an audience with the Cardinal?" he asked.

"His Eminence is away until tomorrow, but I can put you on his appointments list. Is it an official matter?"

"No, a purely personal one. Please make a note that it's about a promise I made him in Orvieto fourteen years ago."

"O.K. You'll be hearing from me."

But on Thursday afternoon, as Thomas was saying his Office in the church of Santo Spirito in Gattafogata, he heard an unusual lot of noise from the back courtyard where the youth of the parish played football. Thomas was going out to ask them to be quieter, but in the sacristy he met a fair-haired young priest who seemed to be looking for him.

"Excuse me for intruding," said the stranger with a strong American accent, "but are you the Scandinavian Monsignor?"

"Yes, I am."

"I'm Milson, Cardinal Norcus's secretary. His Eminence asks if you would care to take a little walk with him."

"With the greatest pleasure," replied Thomas, delighted. "When?"

"Right now. His Eminence is waiting outside in the yard."

Thomas rushed to the window. In the middle of the wildly roaring crowd of boys he caught sight of a tall grey-haired man in a plain black cassock, who was showing a twelve-year-old the correct position to take when kicking off the ball. Thomas ran out past the laughing secretary.

"Pardon me, Your Eminence. I had no idea that you were here."

The Cardinal disentangled himself from the crowd of boys.

"How could you know?" he replied. "It is I who should ask pardon; this was just a sudden idea. The evening is so fine, and as we were driving by, I thought I'd look in and take you out for a little walk before sunset. Don't you think that would be good for both of us? Actually, I have sent my car away so that I shall just have to walk back."

Il cardinal americano was certainly over eighty, but his walk was still sprightly, his back erect, and his eyes had the same boyish expression as ever. He was still a very influential figure in the Vatican and had recently been appointed Cardinal-Bishop of Castelpendente, which gave him a place of honour in the Sacred College.

They walked towards the city along the Via Aurelia Antica, past picturesque country houses, fertile fields and flowery gardens surrounded by high walls. The air was mild and full of the fragrant smell of new-mown hay. Flights of swallows were whizzing through the great park of the Villa Doria, and to the left the dome of Saint Peter's rose, like a fata morgana, directly above the fields and gardens.

"Fourteen years ago Your Eminence was so kind as to give some advice to a young man who wanted to become a priest," Thomas began. "It was after the Corpus Christi procession in Orvieto."

"Yes, I remember quite well."

"Your Eminence was doubtful of my vocation then, and I'm afraid your doubt was justified."

The Cardinal's attention seemed suddenly to be absorbed by an old Roman aqueduct which ran alongside the street.

"That is naturally a matter I should have confessed," continued Thomas. "But I would never have dared to trouble Your Eminence with my private worries if you had not made me promise to come to you in case of new difficulties."

The Cardinal's eyes glanced absently over the younger man's face. "You have a good memory, Monsignor," he said, "but you need not have felt bound to your promise after such a long time."

Thomas could not hide a touch of bitterness as he replied:

"Then I can only beg forgiveness for having troubled Your Eminence."

"But, my dear friend, there's no question of trouble. If there were I would hardly have suggested this evening walk. But I don't understand what you mean. Surely you don't think that I have been harbouring doubts about your vocation all these fourteen years? "

"No, of course not. I expressed myself badly. That's because I'm tired and don't see things clearly. I'm afraid I've made a terrible mistake."

"Well, what's it all about."

"It concerns an old weakness of mine. I have again and again longed to look upon God's glory, and I can no longer blame any 'vision' for this. I see that I have been deceiving myself all these years. That had begun even before Orvieto. It was not God who called me. It was the devil, who worked on my vanity as he has always done. . . ."

"Tssh ! " interrupted the Cardinal, jocosely threatening him with his stick. "The devil doesn't call a man to the priesthood. And apparently you have quite forgotten that I myself ordained you. The Sacrament of Holy Orders was in itself a confirmation of your vocation which holds good even if all your earlier deliberations were dreams and fantasies. True, I did have some doubts at first about your intentions, but remember, please, that you were a complete stranger to me at the time. And now I may tell you I have quietly watched your development since, and it wasn't long before all my doubts had entirely vanished. And as regards this little vanity, well, there are tried remedies for troubles like that. But tell me, what has actually happened? Milson only knew that you had got a short leave from the Secretariat of State. Were you ill? "

Thomas came out with everything. He walked along with half-shut eyes, and spoke as if he were kneeling in the confessional. The Cardinal listened attentively without interrupting him. When the other had finished speaking, he said : "We can go into some church on the way and I will give you absolution. And if there's anything else you want to tell, you can say it then."

They had arrived at the city walls, and with a little exclamation of delight the Cardinal stopped in the open square by the Porta San Pancrazio and pointed his stick towards the massive wisteria-covered walls of the Villa Aurelia.

" What do you say to that, Milson? " he asked. " Have you ever seen anything like it before? Our College would do with a camouflage like that."

They turned left and walked in the direction of the College across the crest of the Janiculum, where Garibaldi looks down from his bronze horse on the capital of United Italy. Then the Cardinal stopped again. " Now let us enjoy the view in the evening light ! " he said, sitting down on one of the worn stone benches under the twelve cypress trees which, according to local tradition Philip Neri had planted in honour of the Twelve Apostles.

It was a glorious evening with exceptionally clear visibility, which gave a wonderful panorama of Latium in the middle distance. Glorious iridescent colours oscillated in the sunlight over the green slopes of the Sabine Hills; and the Alban Hills suddenly seemed incredibly near. On their steep sides toy-like villages suddenly appeared, and above the upper shore of the volcanic Lake Albano, the solitary oak grove on Monte Gentile stood out as distinctly as if seen through a telescope. The reflection of the sun shimmered like light signals from Palombara, Tivoli, Frascati and Rocca di Papa. Far away to the north the classical outline of the Soracte rose from the plain in isolated grandeur.

Cardinal Norcus nodded pensively. " We're lucky to have such weather," he said.

The City of the Seven Hills lay sunk in the great brown basin-like Valley of the Tiber. Beyond the greyish, speckled labyrinth of roofs gleamed the emerald-green fringe of the Roman Campagna, over which the aqueducts ran down from the mountains. The dim, golden-brown shimmer that lay over the mass of buildings at the bottom of the valley seemed as though it rose from the river itself. The sinking sun caressed the warm red brick of the ancient ruins peeping out between the tops of the trees on the Palatine and Aventine, and shone like gold on the windows of San Gregorio Magno, the Quirinal, and the Villa Medici. It seemed hardly credible that this fairyland of light and colour was really a modern city of nearly two million inhabitants.

The Cardinal looked enquiringly at his secretary. "Now, Milson, what do you think of this panorama?" he asked.

Milson fidgeted a little. "Well, it's a marvellous view . . ." he replied.

"You must admit that it's beautiful!" persisted the Cardinal.

"Sure," replied the secretary with palpably forced enthusiasm.

"No, Fred Milson can't appreciate all this," said the Cardinal, laughing. "I know what he's thinking – the streets are far too narrow, the houses are far too old, there's a lot of dirt and disorder everywhere. In short, this cracking-up of Rome is all romantic nonsense! Real beauty is never dirty. Am I right?"

"Yes, that is true, Your Eminence."

Thomas could not help smiling. "The dirt and lack of order are not important," he said. "What you see here, after all, is history itself, and unfortunately, history is not always beautiful. But one should not shut one's eyes to its brighter side because of that. We must learn to see it as it really is. We cannot alter it according to our ideals."

Father Milson became serious. "No, I certainly don't want to falsify history, but I prefer to leave it to the experts and devote my own energy to the future," he said. "Why should what is old be especially beautiful and esteemed? That's something I can never understand. It's quite right for the historian to look back, of course, but why should everyone else do so too? It has always irritated me to see how people here in Rome are systematically trained to direct their minds back to a world which has passed. Is that really wise?"

"But surely we cannot cut off our roots? Rome – after all, it's the foundation on which we are all building. To come and live here and presume to deny history is the same as denying one's own soul – it's moral suicide."

Thomas had become really heated and he expected an equally heated answer, but he got none at all. Milson merely looked at him with an expression of mingled compassion and resignation.

But a pair of clever grey eyes fixed themselves intently on Thomas and a long arm clasped him around the shoulder.

"Now, what if Fred Milson is right and we are wrong . . . ? " asked Cardinal Norcus, with a little laugh. But there was an undertone in his voice that made Thomas sit up.

It was no secret that the Cardinal's life in Rome had been by no means a bed of roses. Wonders had been expected of him; but he had not been able to fulfil all the hopes which his countrymen had placed in the first American Cardinal in the Curia. Rome had proved too strong for him, and he had been forced to compromise. It had been the same with him as with so many other non-Italian churchmen – he had remained a foreigner in the Eternal City, but was looked upon as a Roman in his own country. That is just as it should be, and should continue to be, thought Thomas. In the past Rome assimilated Gauls and Germans; now it is the turn of Creoles and Yankees. . . .

"In what respect may we be wrong? " he enquired cautiously.

"It is difficult to say in a few words," replied the Cardinal. "And however beautifully I might express my thoughts, they would still sound like grave heresy in the ears of a true Roman. But I sometimes ask myself whether the Church herself would not be in a very different position today if this city were not so heavily burdened with history? "

"Burdened with history? "

"Yes, you see, it can hamper the manoeuvring of the ship, as too much ballast does. There are those who think that the whole organization of the Church is suffering from sclerosis of the heart; that is to say, that the museums are threatening to swallow up the Vatican. That is an exaggerated view, of course, but it makes one think. Personally, I value museums very much; but they should not penetrate into the churches. Do you see what I mean, Monsignor? "

"Yes, but . . ."

The Cardinal smiled. "I know. You're thinking that's the American coming out in me. And why not? We American Catholics are reproached with a lack of appreciation for the historical. That may be a natural failing, but it may perhaps have its positive aspect too. Let us take an example from the history of the Church itself. Where would we be today if the Early Christians had allowed themselves to be guided by historical considerations, instead of deciding, as they did, to break with the past and look to the future? They may have overthrown tradition to a greater extent than was good, and smashed up more pagan statues than we care to admit. But at any rate they saved Christianity when the old world collapsed, and a great deal else too, which otherwise would have been irretrievably lost. Am I not right? "

"I suppose you are," admitted Thomas without enthusiasm.

"If, instead of this, they had stuck desperately to the old world, they would have fettered the Church to a corpse, or at least to an organization doomed to death. How would the Universal Church have fared then? Would Christianity have been able to save anything at all of the old cultural heritage? This is the paradoxical lesson which I have learned from Roman history. I know quite well that one should not draw inapt and untimely parallels. But I regard the question in itself as highly topical. Or what do you think, Milson? Have I interpreted your views correctly? "

"Quite correctly, Your Eminence." Father Milson smiled to himself as he wound up his camera, which seemed to interest him more than anything else.

"To me Rome is an example of a city which conquers itself," the Cardinal continued in a quieter tone. "It has an eternal perspective that applies to all – Americans as well as Europeans. But in order to acquire that perspective, one must first overcome history itself, which in this case is only another name for the glory of the world. It is definitely an interesting subject which can always win a large, appreciative and intelligent public. Nevertheless one need not sell one's soul for fireworks on account of it."

Thomas remained silent. He felt that the Cardinal was at last coming to the problems that were worrying him.

"To be quite honest, Milson," continued the Cardinal with a little laugh, "I too have my doubts about the panorama here. It's magnificent, really far too magnificent, and that's just why it has always disquieted me a little. Not a great deal, but just enough to remind me of that mountain where the devil tempted Christ. I sometimes wonder how many may have allowed themselves to be seduced by this panorama to – shall I say – serve strange gods? "

Thomas put his hands over his eyes. "You're right, Your Eminence," he said.

The Cardinal glanced at him. "You needn't take it quite so literally, my dear fellow," he said. "It is merely a little contagion to which even seasoned residents of Rome are sometimes exposed. It lies in the air here, so to speak, and it cures itself in time."

Father Milson had adjusted his camera at last. He stood up and began to walk a bit farther up the hill, as if looking for a subject to photograph.

"I have been wrestling with this problem myself," continued the Cardinal. "There is one solution which I should like to recommend to those who come up here. That is, to reverse the perspectives."

"I don't quite follow you. . . ."

"I mean, to try, for instance, to view this Roman history from those mountains out there. That can be helpful for a change, and certainly less dangerous to one's peace of soul."

"Would that really be different? "

"Go to some simple sanctuary, for instance, from which you don't get too magnificent a panorama. There are plenty of them to choose from. Have you ever been to Santissima Trinità? "

"No."

"That is one of the greatest places of pilgrimage in this part of the country. But foreigners seldom go there because to tell the truth the journey is rather difficult. I haven't been there myself for years."

His eyes searched a blue range of mountains that glistened behind the Sabine hills. Suddenly he pointed his stick towards a little isolated peak on the farthest horizon. "It's in that direction," he said. "The peak which you see is farther off. It's Monte Lino and it's in my bishopric. From here you can see it at most about once in a year."

"Monte Lino? I seem to have heard that name before. . . . Isn't there a town there? "

"No, only a remote little village. It's the highest point in the district but so inaccessible that no stranger ever attempts to climb up to it."

"Monte Lino . . ." repeated Thomas thoughtfully. "I'm almost sure I came across the name in Santa Presenza."

"That is quite possible. It's a really extraordinary mountain. . . . It seems to look right into Eternity. But to see the panorama one has to stay quite a time. The air and light seem to be stronger there. . . ."

"Your Eminence has been there, then?"

"Yes, once, only once, but I should like to be able to spend my whole life there." The Cardinal sat with his chin resting in his hand, his eyes fixed on the little gleaming snow-capped mountain in the distance. The last glorious radiance of the setting sun shone on his grey hair, and the merry shouting of children in the park behind mingled with the murmur of the wind in Saint Philip Neri's tall cypresses.

"It was like a foretaste of beatitude," said Cardinal Norcus. And Thomas noticed that he was smiling to himself as if heaven lay wide open before his eyes.

༺༒༻

XXV VALLEPIETRA

"Come back in a week," said the ticket clerk at the coach station in Castro Pretorio.

Thomas, taken aback, stared at the man's incredibly dirty shirt collar.

"There are special coaches there every hour, but they're all booked up days ago," snapped the man, brushing him off rudely. "Next please!"

The obvious dismay of the little fair-haired priest awakened the sympathy of the bystanders.

"Do you want to go to Santissima Trinità, Father?" enquired a very sunburnt young man who had a cheap fibre suitcase tied with string hanging from his shoulder.

"Yes, I do."

"Why don't you try to join a crowd of pilgrims who have their own coach. That should be possible."

Thomas shook his head. "I'd really prefer to go alone," he said.

The man with the suitcase shrugged his shoulders, but his neighbour said: "It's not necessary to go to Vallepietra first."

"Isn't it?" asked Thomas looking keenly at the broad-shouldered mountain peasant in the thick black suit, who definitely gave the impression of reliability.

"You could get there from Trevi or Subiaco, or Cappadocia. . . . People go to Santissima Trinità from every direction. The walk is somewhat longer, of course, but it's well worth it."

"Many people spend days walking there," said a withered little peasant woman beside Thomas. "I once walked the whole way from Sulmona. There were no coaches then."

Thomas took his place once more in the queue before the ticket office. He found out that there was a coach just starting for Subiaco, and he had to run the length of the coach park to catch it. It was a regular service coach and was almost full up, but he succeeded in squeezing in right at the back.

The June sun was shining hotly over the dazzling white dust of the Via Tiburtina, and the Campagna was ablaze with poppies. The smell of the distant sulphur baths of Aquae Albulae came in through the open windows. In barely half an hour they reached the foot of the mountains. As the coach groaned up the first bends a dark cypress grove behind the olive gardens gradually became lost to view. It surrounded the ruins of Hadrian's Villa, formerly a favourite Sunday excursion of the art historian Thomas Cinnelius.

From Tivoli onwards one noticed the fresh mountain breeze. On the other side of the great dam a new landscape gradually opened up. Dull blue, like naked steel, the waters of the Annio gushed through the stony valley. Hazel and birch trees lined its banks. The road ran between fertile fields, luscious meadows and dark green woodland. High above, on the bare windswept mountain walls, the limestone glittered white as snow in the sun. Horace's country, thought Thomas with a touch of melancholy, as he remembered reading the Eclogues among those vineyards fifteen years ago.

Among those conical hills they passed many little towns he had known well in the past – Castel Madama, Vicovaro, Mandela, Roviano. When the road turned south the panorama widened and the mighty Simbruini suddenly came into sight. Almost on the edge of the horizon the bizarre silhouette of Cervara, clinging defiantly to its steep mountainside, stood sharply outlined. On the other side of the valley lay Anticoli Corrado looking like a mis-shapen, earth-coloured anthill, between loamy vineyards and grey olive-clad hills. The thin curls of smoke rising up from its sloping roofs brought back to Thomas one of his earliest memories of Italy.

He had once spent a warm August evening sitting under a vine-covered pergola there with some Scandinavian artist friends. As they sipped their wine they listened to singing and laughter in the distance, and Letterman said: " This is a very poor town, Cinnelius. It has no cathedral and no cafés, and it's infernally cold in winter. But if all other towns were to shut their gates, Anticoli would always be open to an honest poor devil of an artist who neither sows nor spins. Don't forget that, my learned friend. . . ."

In Subiaco Thomas got out, bought bread and plums for the journey, and started on his solitary pilgrim's road. It was ten o'clock in the morning, and he reckoned it was a good ten miles across the mountains to Vallepietra. Below Sacro Speco the road seemed to leave civilization finally behind and lose itself in a wild and beautiful valley. Thomas hardly dared to look up at the old cave-monastery as he passed below it. He could be there in a couple of minutes. The Benedictines were his friends and would receive him with open arms. Indeed he could stay with them for a week or a month if he wanted to. He could roam through the mountains, browse in the library, and enjoy the primitive frescoes in the cave-church to the accompaniment of perfect Gregorian chant. In short, he could lead an existence ideal for an expert on Catholic art, and his hosts would certainly preserve him from any activity unbecoming to the dignity and comfort of a monsignor. Never-theless he kept doggedly onward.

The valley contracted to a narrow gorge into which the river gradually disappeared. The path wound higher and higher up the wooded slope, and it was midday before Thomas arrived at the little town of Ienne, isolated and dream-like on the edge of the summit. The heat obliged him to stop and rest, so he took a simple meal of salad, boiled eggs and water, and lay down for a good *siesta*. At four o'clock he set out again, but his pace was much slower, for he had to take a steep donkey-track right across the pathless mountain. The sun was already setting when he reached the main road to Vallepietra.

Now he was no longer alone. The road was full of pilgrims, some on horse carts, others riding donkeys, but most of them walking. Each group carried a cross, or else a banner with a primitive representation of the Blessed Trinity in the form of three absolutely identical pictures of Christ. Those who were returning home usually carried musical instruments with them behind the banners, and were festively dressed. The women wore jewellery and magnificent head kerchiefs, the men wore carnival caps and carried artificial flowers, and even the animals were decorated with paper garlands. Those who were on their way there, on the other hand, were penitential in attire and demeanour and the only indication of their destination was a simple little bow in the buttonhole. Most of them were singing interminably long, monotonous songs in ancient rhythms. Part of the way Thomas followed pilgrims from Genazzano, who were tirelessly repeating a primitive hymn to the Most Holy Trinity. Their rough voices hammered the simple refrain on his ears:

> "Viva, viva, sempre viva,
> Quelle Tre Person Divine,
> Quelle Tre Person Divine,
> La Santissima Trinità!"

He was unable to keep up for long with the quickly marching crowd. He fell behind, and the thunder of the heavy coaches which were passing drowned the singing. The traffic became more dense as the journey approached its end. At last, in the fading

light, he caught sight of the lonely little town of Vallepietra
perched on the hilltop.

Along the wide approach to the town an impressive number of
long-distance coaches were parked. He read some of the names –
Viterbo, Rieti, Civitacastellana, Tivoli, Palestrina, Anagni, Frosi-
none, Latina, Velletri, Castelgandolfo, Albano, Frascati, Civita-
vecchia, Tarquinia, Orvieto. . . . Almost all Latium seemed to
have a rendezvous here. He walked on and came on about a dozen
large Vatican coaches that had brought pilgrims from the suburbs
and poorer quarters of Rome. Suddenly he heard his name called.
Among the waiting coach drivers he saw the little fellow with the
leather jacket and rat-like face from the Via Gattafogata.

"Domenico! What are you doing here?"

"I've brought a load of pilgrims here at the Pope's expense.
There are several people you know among them."

"Indeed? Who are they?" Thomas did not seem very interested.

"They went on foot to Santissima Trinità early this morning
but I'm expecting them back here any moment."

"Are you returning to Rome this evening?"

"Yes. Would you like to come with us, Monsignor?"

"No, thank you. I've only just arrived. Do you know if there's
an hotel anywhere in the town?"

The driver shook his head. "There's only a little inn," he said,
"and it's hardly worth enquiring about. If you're going to stay
the night it's best to try and get lodging in the presbytery."

Unfortunately Thomas found the priest himself had gone on
the pilgrimage and his house was crammed with guests. Nevertheless the news of a priest without lodging spread like wildfire
through the town and a little public meeting quickly formed in
front of the church. The majority were in favour of the distinguished visitor lodging with Il *Commendatore*. A delegation consisting of the sacristan, the barber and the publican took possession
of the stranger and conducted him to a little stone villa at the
edge of the town.

The Commendatore was a tall, bald gentleman with a scrubby
beard, and his rough clothing smelt of horses. He was taking
supper with his daughter, and declared that he would be delighted

if his Reverence would share their simple meal. He sent his daughter, a fine young woman of about thirty who evidently kept house for him, down to the cellar to fetch some wine. His elder children were already settled in life, the Commendatore said. He had a little farm in Vallepietra and a very modest practice as a lawyer, which he carried on more for pleasure than anything else, for in this remote place there was not much litigation. Nevertheless he had decided to remain in Vallepietra, for his family had belonged here for three hundred years. He had buried his wife five years ago – she had been a very good wife and had a considerable dowry. He informed his guest of all this while his daughter was serving the meal.

As he filled Thomas's glass he said: "Now you must eat well, Reverendo. You have a strenuous day before you tomorrow. And where have you put up your mule, by the way?"

"My mule?"

"Yes, have you no mule?"

"No, indeed I haven't," said Thomas, almost apologetically.

"Then I must procure one for you at once, Monsignor," said his host, quickly draining his glass and standing up. "Excuse me a moment. I shall go and see if there's one in the stable."

"To tell you the truth, I intended to walk."

The Commendatore plopped down on the chair and stared at his guest. "To walk?" he asked.

"Yes."

"Good. Very good. . . ." The Commendatore scratched his bald head. "But have you ever been to Santissima Trinità before?" he asked.

"No, never."

"You're not an Italian, are you, Monsignor?" he asked, reaching for the wine.

"No, I'm a Finn."

"But you speak Italian perfectly."

"It's kind of you to say so. . . ."

"I mean it. How long have you been in this country?"

"Over fifteen years."

"Fifteen years!" repeated the Commendatore, visibly relieved.

"Then we can understand each other. Now, tell me frankly, do you really want to make the attempt?"

Thomas had to laugh. "I may tell you I've walked the whole way here from Subiaco . . ." he said.

The worthy man seemed terribly upset. He observed his guest with mingled respect, surprise and awe, then, after recourse to his faithful bottle, made another effort to get to the bottom of the mystery.

"I don't quite understand. . . . Aren't there several coaches every day from Rome?"

Thomas nodded. "Yes, I know. But I didn't want to come that way. I'm travelling *incognito*, as it were."

The Commendatore's conflicting feelings suddenly showed themselves in visible mistrust. "But surely that doesn't make it necessary to go on foot, Monsignor?" he said.

"No, of course not. But one can make better progress this way."

"How do you mean?"

"I mean that one should measure a journey in hours and not in miles. That's a wise old maxim. I've made a long journey to get here."

"Yes, to be sure, if you have come on foot from Subiaco," put in the Commendatore with unconcealed irony. "Forgive my curiosity, Monsignor, but why in heaven's name have you taken all that trouble?"

Thomas decided to make himself clearer. "Because I wanted to get as far away as possible from my starting point," he said.

The Commendatore seemed to struggle with himself for a moment, then said: "In that case you chose the right direction. But do you really know the kind of place you're going to?"

"No, I told you that it's my first pilgrimage."

The Commendatore seemed to recover his composure. Looking at his guest thoughtfully, he said: "It may well prove a strange experience for you, Monsignor. I do not know how I should explain it to you . . . Santissima Trinità is not a place of pilgrimage in the ordinary sense of the word. Very few foreigners have ever visited it, and that may be a good thing, for one has really

O

got to know our poor mountain regions to understand its meaning. There are various things which may repel one at first sight. It is what one might call a third-class place of pilgrimage."

"I'm quite sure Christ travelled third class."

The Commendatore smiled, or rather gave a polite, joyless grin that seemed to divide his face into two halves.

"You're joking now, Monsignor," he said, "but once you get up there, you will not joke any more. For then you will find yourself face to face with the poor of Italy. You will meet peasants to whom the loss of a single day's work is a great sacrifice, and labourers for whom the purchase of the necessary food for the pilgrimage is a great financial risk. And yet they come here in crowds year after year, for Santissima Trinità is their very own sanctuary, the temple of the poorest of the poor. . . ."

He took another drink. His guest noticed with some uneasiness that he had taken a great many, so he remarked, to distract him: "How is it that one hears so little about this pilgrimage? And yet it seems to me to concern all Central Italy."

The Commendatore flushed deeply. "Yes, I shall explain that to you, Reverendo," he said. "Santissima Trinità is essentially a pilgrimage of the working people. There's simply no possibility of dragging a cardinal up here; not even an ordinary monsignor."

Thomas felt compelled to protest. "Believe it or not, it was a cardinal who recommended this pilgrimage to me?" he said.

The Commendatore winked and said in a changed tone: "I noticed at once that you understood the situation when you said you wanted to go on foot. I was only afraid it would be too strenuous."

"To tell you the truth I am a little tired and I should like to have a couple of hours' sleep before starting out," Thomas admitted.

"I can believe it. What is your programme for tomorrow?"

"I should like to say Mass up there."

"Then you will have to set out before sunrise. A native can do the journey in one to two hours but a tourist had best allow himself at least three. And besides, you will be tired after today. In short, the route is difficult and most people like to travel by night, when it is cooler. Moreover, to see a sunrise up in the mountains is something well worth while."

The Commendatore emptied his glass and conducted his guest to a bedroom with bright red wallpaper and imitation Chippendale furniture. Along by one wall was a large double bed with a luxurious eiderdown and lace-edged pillow-covers. Thomas stared in astonishment at the elegant mirror, cut-glass perfume bottles and gilt-framed photographs on the glass-topped dressing-table.

"This was my wife's bedroom," his host explained, "and that is the door to the bathroom. Good night, Reverendo!"

The taps in the bathroom were fairly rusty, and there were big gaping patches on the walls where the plaster had flaked off. The bed, on the other hand, was really disgracefully comfortable. However Thomas had only been asleep a few hours when his host stood in the doorway once more, unshaved, but fully clothed.

"It's three o'clock, Monsignor. I think you will have to start."

Thomas was so tired and stiff from the previous day's walk that he had difficulty in dressing.

"I have prepared some provisions for you," said the Commendatore, when his guest came tottering out of the bedroom at last. "You will need them after Mass because the food up there is very poor."

Thomas was beginning to thank him, but the Commendatore interrupted him, saying he would accompany him part of the way.

The night air was cold and fresh and the full moon was just disappearing. The Commendatore marched ahead through the narrow, dark streets, carrying a large lantern. He stopped in front of an old house and shone the lantern on an old stone gateway and the carving of a scorpion-like creature.

"That is our family coat of arms," he said. "The house belonged to my father's brother, who left it to the Holy See."

He obviously expected a complimentary reply, but Thomas remained prudently silent. They marched on to the little old market place where his companion stopped again, shone the lantern on a house, and said:

"This is actually our family mansion. Unfortunately we had to give it up in my father's time. But he saw to it that a considerable legacy for the foreign missions was included in the conditions of sale."

Thomas felt he should express at least official approval, where-upon his companion's spirits rose visibly.

The guest had to view yet a third house. It had belonged to the Commendatore's wife, and Thomas was told that she came of a family very loyal to the Church, numbering two bishops and an abbot among its members.

Thomas reacted as expected, saying in his best curial manner: "The blessings of Providence surely rest on this house."

By the time they left the town the moon had disappeared. The Commendatore stopped and shone his lantern high over the road-way. "Now you only have to keep straight ahead. It will not be too hard at first and you will have daylight soon."

Thomas was going to take leave of him, but the other still had something on his mind. "I hope you will have time to look in on me when you pass through Vallepietra on your way back, Rever-endo," he said. "Then I will show you my father's grave. He was an officer of the Papal Guards and was wounded at Mentana."

"That would certainly be very interesting, but unfortunately I have made no definite plans for the journey home."

The Commendatore remained obstinately standing where he was, and the flickering light of the lantern distorted his friendly smile into a skull-like grin. "You will understand, Reverendo, that our family belongs to the Black Society in this neighbour-hood," he said.

Thomas, who had not forgotten his host's statements, assured him with a good conscience that he understood. And to comfort him for his disappointment, he added: "I am sure that the name of your family is remembered with respect in the Vatican."

The Commendatore seemed satisfied. He embraced Thomas, and they parted.

XXVI SANTISSIMA TRINITÀ

A faint light announced the dawn. Over in Vallepietra a few
sleepily flickering yellow lights appeared, but it was still pitch
dark in the valleys. Only with great difficulty could Thomas
distinguish a few yards ahead the chalk-white road he was trying
to follow. Somewhere in front of him the sound of shrill singing
rose out of the darkness. The simple melody was very similar to
that of the hymn to the Blessed Trinity; but the refrain consisted
of a salutation to the Virgin Mary and her only-begotten Son.
Thomas followed the direction of the singing and soon found that
his road led that way.

The light came quickly and he saw before him a verdant valley
between precipitous walls of rock from which mountain torrents
rushed down noisily and collected into a little river that wound
through the valley. Gardens and fields lay along the banks but on
the whole the district was strikingly treeless and sparsely popu-
lated. Thomas passed by a few sleeping farmsteads and a mill
which was grinding listlessly. Farther up the valley only isolated
herdsman's cottages and sheepfolds were to be seen. The fields
smelled of clover, wild strawberries bloomed by the roadside, and
the whole landscape awakened in Thomas memories of Scandinavia.

As the light increased he could distinguish more and more processions of pilgrims down in the valley, all going in the direction
of a huge mountain that cut off the view to the north. So that was
Monte Autore, where the pilgrimage church was! The path now
led into a pinewood which covered the foot of the mountain. A
steep naked rock-face, which looked impossible to climb, rose
perpendicularly a good thousand feet over the edge of the wood.

Suddenly a piercing white light, like a huge gradually extending
arc of neon lighting, covered the eastern horizon, coming from
some vast isolated mountain walls covered with snow. The sun
itself was still hidden behind the mountains, but over to the east
the vault of the heavens had gradually changed from blue-grey

to a clear azure. A new summer day was coming over the Abruzzi,
and in the valley below a joyful bird chorus joined in the invocations that now rose with renewed strength to the smiling
heavens.

Thomas marched on for a good hour without stopping; then he
decided to take a rest so that he could reach his goal without having to break his fast. He found an ideal spot, where a narrow
wooden bridge led across the river, which had dwindled here to a
pebbly brook. On the bank were a tall cross, a water trough, and
a wooden bench on which he sat down. He took out his breviary,
but he was not able to read much. A philosophical-looking billy-
goat was scraping the ground with his horns at the foot of the
cross, a shepherd came along to water his drowsy herd, and passing
pilgrims stopped to fill their water-bottles and wash their faces
and feet in the brook. In the wood at the other side of the hill
high-pitched women's voices were drawling their continuous
Evviva Maria! and peasant girls, garlanded with flowers, came
out of a clearing and crossed the wooden bridge backwards, throw-
ing stones into the water, as if getting rid of the last of their sins.
Thomas felt himself carried back thousands of years to the morning of the world. Now at last the sun rose above Monte Autore,
and when he looked up at the mighty steep mountain wall, he
could not suppress a movement of astonishment.

The lower half of the mountain was covered with pines; but
towards the middle of the great towering flank, a little above the
tops of the last trees, a row of whitewashed buildings stood out.
Perched on an invisible terrace, they looked like a line of swallows'
nests clinging to the rock face. One of them was obviously the
church; otherwise the whole picture was reminiscent of a Tibetan
lamasery. So this was Santissima Trinità, the objective of the
pilgrimage!

Walking on invisible paths – and looking like ants in the
distance, people were climbing up and climbing down the rock-
face in long columns. A big procession was working its way in
zigzags up from the pinewood – it was the procession from Vallepietra; another, smaller one was coming down slowly from the
plateau in the north, and a third was struggling along a pass-like

depression on the eastern side of the mountain where ran the main highroad of the Abruzzi.

It was seven o'clock before Thomas felt sufficiently restored to start on the really difficult climb. The path became more and more arduous. The spring rains had made gaping furrows. At one moment the climbers stumbled on sharp stones, the next moment they sank in loose sand. The streams had dried up long ago, and there did not seem to be any springs on this side of the mountain. The green patches had disappeared, and the pinewood turned out to be no wood at all – the barren sandy ground was only sparsely covered with stunted trees which neither conserved humidity nor offered shelter. The whole mountain-side was mercilessly exposed to the rising sun that was drawing every drop of moisture from the soil. The air was pitilessly still, yet incredible quantities of dust were rising up from the parched ground and hanging over the roads in white clouds. No, this scorched and scorching country-side, over which birds of prey were silently hovering, was any-thing at all but idyllic.

So Thomas had to stop and take breath many times. At last he joined a crowd of peasants from the Sandal region, who were making the ascent at an easy but steady speed and had a dirty little donkey on to which they invited Thomas to load his baggage.

Now he realized why so many pilgrims preferred to make the journey by night. The sun was already becoming distressingly hot and he found this nightmarish pine-wood definitely reminiscent of Dante's Mountain of Purification. The higher he went the more forcibly this comparison struck him. The whole mountain-side was one single purgatory. His companions of the road toiled up the mountain with bowed heads still singing their hymns as shrilly and monotonously as when they had set out from their homes. This singing was not an expression of joy, however, but a form of penance, and that was why it seemed to have neither beginning nor end. It was endless as the sins of the human race, and each one of these penitents was trying according to his modest strength to shorten his own tally of sins just a little. When one group fell silent for a while, another took up the refrain. It was as though the wild mountain itself were singing, and Thomas was surprised to find himself joining in the song in the end. It was an incredibly naïve story of how Saint Anne helped three orphan girls to pay their rent. The pilgrims sang it monotonously right through with all its refrains, a good hundred verses. But Thomas kept on bravely. Hardly conscious of the sense of the words, he clung to the persistent melody as to a mountaineer's rope.

On the final stretch of the road he really needed this rope. At last he perceived above him the terrace on which the sanctuary stood. It was a natural projection, and ran crosswise along the whole rock face, the outer edge trailing off into a sandy slope. The path led diagonally across the declivity over which dusty-grey bush like pine trees were thinly scattered, like cacti in a desert. The ground between them was trampled by thousands of heavy shoes, and fouled all over with excreta. There was not a breath of wind, and Thomas realized with horror that he would now have to traverse this gigantic latrine.

The whole scene once more recalled Dante's *Purgatorio*. I could never have got through this alone, thought Thomas, and prompted by the sheer instinct of self-preservation, he sang out his litany: "*Qualsiasi favore Sant' Anna vi farà* . . ."

Directly behind the terrace the mountain wall rose about a thousand feet high. The projection itself was some thirty feet wide and could be reached only from the sides, where converged the mountain pathways from various directions. At the foot of the rock face there were a few caves. But what had looked from a distance like a mysterious and beautiful cluster of sanctuaries, proved at closer range to be very unimpressive structures – an ordinary village church with various additional buildings, a few little whitewashed houses, one of them apparently the presbytery, a small police post, and a first-aid depot. That was all.

Meanwhile Thomas had reached the terrace, and he stopped short, astonished. He forgot his fatigue and his thirst, he forgot the dust, heat and smells. He only stood and stared. For on this lonely rock in the middle of the desert of mountains a mass of humanity was crowded as densely as in the main thoroughfare of a modern city of a million inhabitants. The *carabinieri* were marshalling the incoming crowds into long orderly queues that stood patiently waiting their turn to enter the little church. Thomas and his companions from the Sandal country were held back at the police post to leave way for the stream of pilgrims coming out.

The space behind them was quickly crowded with new pilgrims from the eastern approach – dark, thick-set people, slow of movement, with round heads and broad shoulders. They all had the same clear, sharp expression, weather-beaten skins and thick brush-like hair. They wore old-fashioned clothing, incredibly rough shoes, and simple paper flowers in their hats. Coming from the interior of the Abruzzi, most of them had had a long journey on foot. The names of the various villages from which they had come – Anversa, Cleano, Popoli, Pescasseroli, Opi, Cappadocia, Scanno, Tagliacozzo – were written on their simple banners with the three throned figures of Christ.

Thomas's presence did not attract any notice. Many priests had come on foot and were waiting to say Mass in the church or on improvised altars in the open. Thomas sat down on his rucksack and waited. In front of him the newly arrived pilgrims were kneeling silently before the grotto altars where their priests were saying Mass, or sitting quietly meditating, with their rosary beads in their hands. Those who had already made the pilgrimage unpacked their scanty provisions, laid the empty bags or newspapers on the hard ground, and lay down to have a sleep during the hottest hours of the day before starting on the return journey. They had nothing but a few half-withered branches of beech or oak, which they had broken off on the way through the mountain woods, to protect them from the pitiless scorching sun.

Thomas struggled against a feeling of almost physical sickness. He thought of the words of the Commendatore, that Santissima Trinità was a pilgrimage for the common people. What he saw here before his eyes seemed to represent the barest minimum standard of life. If the way into the Kingdom of Heaven was to be like going through the eye of a needle, this pilgrimage should certainly serve as an example.

A Mass had just ended in one of the side grottoes. The priest came out with the Blessed Sacrament and gave the Benediction over the kneeling crowd, who broke spontaneously into a hymn, a popular melody, emotional and lengthy – the Song of Orvieto!

> " *T'adoriam, ostia divina,*
> *t'adoriam, ostia d'amor . . ."*

The rhythm swung out over the mountain-side, died down in few times as if it had been lost among the weary resting pilgrims, then swept through the throngs like wind through brushwood. Thomas listened, strangely moved. All the people around him were singing. He joined in just as anonymously, naturally and sincerely as he had sung of the miracles of Saint Anne. He had got through his " eye of a needle", at least as far as aesthetic demands were concerned. . . .

Meanwhile a report had reached the church that a Monsignor was hidden somewhere among the swarms of pilgrims, and a young priest worked his way zealously through the crowds over to Thomas.

"There's an altar free in the church now, Monsignor, if you would like to celebrate your Mass," he said.

The church was entered by a narrow flight of steps at each side, its inartistic façade crowned by a balcony with a simple iron railing and a triangular gable framing the three figures of Christ. The church itself was built into the largest of the caves, which still retained some of its former atmosphere of a prehistoric place of worship. The only decorations in the low dark chamber were simple frescoes painted directly on the rock.

A passage was roped off around the church, and the pilgrims were being directed through it. They kept as close as possible to the walls, touching the rough stone with their hands, as if even physical contact with the grotto imparted a special blessing. After performing the prescribed prayers they went out the door back-words. They would have considered it disrespectful to turn their backs to a place where the Lord Himself had revealed one of His greatest mysteries.

According to the local legend the Apostles Peter and John had once passed through this neighbourhood on their way to Rome.

At that time the district was waterless and unfertile and a huge snake frequented the ravine-like valley at the foot of the mountain. But while the Apostles were praying, an angel appeared to them, struck water from the rock, and gave them food. The following day they were granted a vision of the Blessed Trinity in heaven, surrounded by the heavenly hosts. The mountain split asunder and crushed the snake. And the Lord blessed the Apostles and solemnly promised that all penitents who made a pilgrimage here would be granted remission of the punishment due to their sins. And His angel announced, moreover, that this mountain valley would be a saving ark for many in times of distress, until the Day of Judgment. . . .

Thomas went up to the altar and said his Mass, but he could hear the tread of the pilgrims' feet behind him all the time. Then he slipped quietly out of the church, hoping to find some out-of-the-way corner in the open where he could eat his provisions and rest undisturbed for a couple of hours. But that proved impossible. Most of the pilgrims had already eaten and were now lying or crouching on the ground asleep under some of the branches which they had dragged with them in such quantities that the whole rocky projection had turned into a dusty copse. There was not even space left between them to put down one foot. Nowhere could he find a square inch of unoccupied shade. So he picked his way onwards in the pitiless sunshine between the sleeping crowds – a tortured looking foreign fugitive with his ridiculous pince-nez. And suddenly he found himself wondering if the eye of this needle were not really far too narrow for him. . . .

The space around the first-aid post at the other side of the church had been turned into a kind of fair. A double row of stalls had been set up along the whole length of the terrace, and all kinds of cheap rubbishy goods were offered for sale – religious souvenirs, holy pictures in crude colours, paper flowers and carnival hats, cycling caps and head scarves, soap, penknives, cheap jewellery and toys – all miserable third-rate goods. The device of the three figures of Christ was used almost like a trade-mark on every imaginable article.

At a stall with picture postcards, prayer-books and coloured rosary beads a girl was standing, longingly fingering a brightly coloured panorama of Saint Peter's Square. There was something strangely familiar about the strong, thick-set figure, stubborn little head, and plump arms moving busily about between the goods on display. As Thomas came nearer he saw he was not mistaken, and his spirits rose many degrees.

"Good day, Assunta," he said. "Are you on the pilgrimage too?"

"Yes, Monsignor," she replied, blushing.

"And how did you find your way here?"

"I came in the coach Domenico drives," she replied, as scared as if she were being questioned by the police.

"Indeed? I met him in Vallepietra as I was coming here. But was he not returning yesterday evening?"

"Yes, he was, Monsignor" – Assunta curtsied quite frantically – "but I stayed to meet someone I know here. He is a priest," she added quickly, as if to avoid further enquiries.

Thomas did not question her further, but passed on with a friendly nod. Behind the market place the terrace narrowed down to a path which wound gently uphill. Here the pilgrims' bivouacs came to an end at last. Feeling desperate, he sat down on the naked rock right in the scorching sun, hanging his legs over the ledge as there was nothing to rest them on. A few feet below him were some bushes growing in a sandy hollow; he wondered whether he might not find some shade under them.

He had forgotten about the *carabinieri* until he heard a voice saying: "There's a canteen here, Eccellenza. It's very modest of course, but there's a table at least."

Behind Thomas was a reliable looking sergeant with a bulldog face and thick neck who, it seemed, had been zealously following him like a bodyguard at a distance.

Thomas tried to refuse the invitation politely, but the astonished policeman replied: "But, Monsignor, you're sitting in a spot that is dangerous!"

The canteen was at the other end of the terrace, in the corner between the *carabinieri'* guard post and the steep mountain-side, and was surrounded by a pergola made of thin branches of beech and elm that divided it into two compartments. In the inner one were a few water butts, a wooden box full of bread, another of bottles of soft drinks, and a rusty field kitchen with a huge pot of soup boiling on it. The outer compartment was the restaurant, with simple benches surrounding a long, deal table. The customers consisted of the little squad of *carabinieri*, an ambulance man, and a few donkey-drivers who had carried the fair goods from Valle-pietra. There was not a single pilgrim.

One of the donkey-drivers reported that about thirty thousand pilgrims had visited the church so far and it would be fifty thousand before the pilgrimage ended for this season.

Thomas was given the place of honour at the head of the table.

"It's more comfortable eating here than out in the open, Reverendo," said the Sergeant. Thomas looked at him more closely. The man seemed familiar to him.

"Haven't we met somewhere before? " he asked.

A flush of pleasure spread over the broad peasant face. "Quite true, Eccellenza, many times. I used to belong to the police detail in Saint Peter's in Rome. I recognized you at once."

Thomas began to unpack the basket of provisions the Commendatore had given him. The result was as startling as a bombshell. He had hardly opened the cover when apricots, plums, tomatoes, chocolate biscuits, cakes, fine cheeses, liver pies and tinned lobster rolled out over the simple table in absolutely shameless profusion. Thomas felt himself turning red. But none of his table companions seemed in the least scandalized by this Lucullan display. There was only understanding and respectful goodwill to be seen in their rough faces, not a trace of envy.

Thomas promptly shared the dainties with his table companions. When the last apricot-stone had been thrown away the sergeant leaned across the table and said with an obsequious smile: "May I thank you for the food, Eccellenza? "

"I'm not an Eccellenza," protested Thomas.

"In my time all the gentlemen in the Secretariat of State were Eccellenza," replied the sergeant, almost offended. "But as you wish, Monsignor. Were you surprised to find me here? "

" Why should I be? "

" I'm glad to hear that, because it's a great mark of confidence
to be posted to Santissima Trinità. Only really good Christians are
considered for the job."

Thomas shut his eyes. If he also begins talking about Mentana,
I'll simply flee, he thought.

" A man is not appointed to the Saint Peter's police detail either
without merit," added the sergeant smugly. And passing his hand
significantly over the long row of decorations on his breast, he
started explaining the most important ones to his respectfully
silent table companions. " I've had four decorations altogether
from the Vatican. You see, they can't appoint just anyone to
watch over the safety of cardinals and ambassadors. I've had most
responsible commissions," he said.

" That's true," agreed his men, who understood that their chief
was leading up to something important and needed their support.
" He's the best sergeant in the whole Corps. No one is a patch
on him ! "

" Be quiet, boys ! " said the sergeant with a laugh. " You see,
Monsignor, how loyal they are. But talking seriously, may I ask
a favour of you? "

" I shall be pleased if I can be of help to you," said Thomas,
becoming more and more uneasy.

" I can certainly say that I have done a great deal for the Holy
See in the past. Now, I know that there's a Papal decoration which
is given to deserving and serious-minded people. When you return
to Rome, would you put in a word for me, Monsignor? When a
man is responsible for keeping order in a place of pilgrimage like
this, he should really be able to call himself Cavaliere, don't you
think? "

Thomas stood up and looked around as if seeking help, and the
sergeant immediately sprang to his feet.

" Forgive me, Monsignor ! " he said. " You won't take my little
request badly, will you? It's always been my greatest wish. . . ."

" I don't take it badly at all," replied Thomas wearily. " But I
shall have to think it over."

" Perhaps you would like to rest a while? "

"No, thank you, I must go now."

The sergeant became anxious. "If you will allow me, I should like to place my camp-bed in the guard-room at your disposal," he whispered. "Perhaps it's not quite regular, but in this case we can make an exception. You cannot very well take your *siesta* out there on the bare rock. . . ."

Thomas thought of the bedroom with the Chippendale furniture in Vallepietra, and hurriedly cut the man short, saying: "No, thank you, I must be going at once."

"It's not possible, Monsignor," objected the sergeant, now visibly alarmed.

"Unfortunately it has to be. I must look around for my companions. We're in a hurry."

"No one sets out at this time of day. But if you wish, Eccellenza, I can procure a mule within an hour to take you to Vallepietra."

Meanwhile Thomas had noticed something. Assunta had just come out of the church and joined a group of pilgrims who had apparently eaten and rested and were now about to set off. He seized the opportunity. "There they are," he cried, "and they're just starting off. . . ."

The sergeant looked at him with unconcealed astonishment. "But, Monsignor, surely you're not going with these people? They're not going in the Rome direction at all. . . ."

"Who said that I wanted to go back to Rome, Cavaliere?" asked Thomas. He immediately repented of his ironical tone when he saw the tragi-comic shock of the sergeant, who now muttered rather crossly:

"Those are not ordinary pilgrims. They're penitents from the wilds – doubtful types. . . ."

Thomas observed the little crowd on the steps of the church. They were obviously all poor mountain folk. They had no banners and no paper flowers, and there was nothing to indicate where they came from. But one thing surprised Thomas very much – they were all barefooted.

Now they started to move, and came past the guard-post. Thomas suddenly gasped. In the midst of the pilgrims he saw a very familiar figure. True, his back was bent, his wonderful lion's mane of hair had turned white, his walk was even more ungainly than formerly. But there was no possible doubt – it was Padre Barnaba.

Thomas turned with a smile to the policeman. "I think you need not worry about my safety, Sergeant," he said. "I shall be in very good company among those people."

⋘⋙

XXVII THE ABRUZZI

From Santissima Trinità the pilgrims wandered out into the mountains, marching for hours through an immense beech wood, their winding path lined by endless lines of dark, naked tree-trunks. They crossed a few scattered clearings gay with forest flowers. Now and then through gaps in the shady foliage snow-covered mountain peaks could be seen glistening in the distance. In the valleys there were pastures, and once they came upon the ruins of a cowherd's cottage by the pathway. Otherwise there was no sign of habitation, nor any trace of cultivated land. Sometimes in the distance the echo of a woodcutter's axe was heard. They met no more people, and the last pilgrims' songs had long since died away in the silent woods.

Thomas had plenty of time to observe his new travelling companions, who meanwhile had put on their shoes again. At first glance they seemed little different from the rest of the pilgrims he had seen at Santissima Trinità, but the striking thing about them was that they did not say a word to one another. They were of magnificent physique, heavy and strong as bears, and with the same rolling gait. Their leader was a broad-shouldered patriarchal-looking giant with flashing eyes. He was followed by a number of men with dark brown faces, glistening white teeth, and sheep-skins thrown over their shoulders. And behind them, with down-cast eyes, walked the rest of the procession, apparently not in any particular order. It consisted of about forty women, girls and boys.

Assunta was walking in the last row with a rosary in her hand. She looked pale and very tired.

Padre Barnaba had at once beckoned Thomas, dropped behind a little, and whispered: "How glad I am to see you, Tommaso. Or perhaps I should say Monsignor? I have heard that you're a very capable priest. You're working at the Secretariat of State, aren't you? Yes, indeed, you'll soon be a *pezzo grosso*, an important man. . . ." He shook his head and laughed. "Who would have believed it. Do you remember how you used to sit in the library at Santa Presenza absorbed in your heavy reading? Truth to tell, I could never have imagined at that time that your life would take such a course."

"Neither could I, for my mind was almost entirely in my books."

"I noticed that. But you couldn't possibly have gone on wasting your life in our old library. And that's why I shut the door on you, although I must confess it cut me to the heart to do so."

"You were certainly right; nevertheless I often think it would have been better for me if I could have stayed with you."

"You can't mean that?"

"Yes, indeed I do, Padre Barnaba. I have missed you terribly."

Padre Barnaba had to turn away. "You shouldn't have," he said. "What am I but an old rag who will end up on the rubbish heap sooner or later."

He had indeed aged. His broad back had become bent, and he suffered greatly with his feet on the difficult mountain paths. He wore an old soutane burst at the seams and green with age; probably a souvenir from Santa Presenza. However, in spite of signs of age he gave a greater impression of strength than ever. With his deeply furrowed face beneath the great white mane, silhouetted against the sky, he looked like the Mountain King himself as he strode over the stony rubble, which shot up every time his stick struck the ground. . . .

Now and then, when the climb became too difficult for the Mountain King, a young man who had apparently remained in the rear to be at hand in case of need came out from the procession to help him. He was a cheerful fellow with extremely

P

expressive, merry brown eyes. Although they had not exchanged a word Thomas felt at once that he had won the boy's friendship.

" He's my personal servant," said Padre Barnaba jocosely. " His name is Marco and he's a nephew of Filippo the deacon. . . ." He stopped short.

" Who is Filippo? " asked Thomas, surprised.

" He's the man who is leading the procession. He's a kind of deacon in the village," Padre Barnaba explained with apparent reluctance.

" What village? "

" Settevetri. That's my parish."

" I never heard the name before."

" How could you? It's very far away," gasped Padre Barnaba wiping the perspiration from his forehead with a dirty handkerchief. " Yes, it was a great joy to meet you, my dear Tommaso. It has done my old heart good. But you must not come any farther with us. You have a long journey before you yet to Vallepietra, and surely you need to sleep in a proper bed tonight, Monsignor? "

" May I not come with you, Padre Barnaba? "

The old man scrutinized him uneasily. " Of course you may," he said, " but our road leads right into the wilds. Where are you actually going? "

" To Settevetri."

" But, my dear Tommaso, you cannot be on the way to a place you have never even heard of before? "

" Why not? I have a good guide in you."

Padre Barnaba slowly shook his head and smiled. " You don't know what you're talking about," he said. " We have a long way before us. You will hardly have a chance of a rest before we get to Castelpendente."

" Good ! Then let us push on to Castelpendente ! "

A new mountain-ridge lay in front of them. As they climbed higher the beech-trees disappeared and a belt of pine-covered mountain began. A cold resin-laden mountain breeze now blew over the heights. They crossed a little pass, and suddenly found themselves standing on the edge of a horrifying abyss. The face of the country-

side had changed in a flash. They were now in the border region
between Latium and the Abruzzi. Behind them rose the steep
walls of the Simbruini and at their feet lay the Roveto Valley,
with its vineyards and oak groves. It was all like an idyllic dream.
Before them towered the first broad gradients of the huge central
massif of the Apennines. The air was crystal clear. A honey-
coloured shimmer lay over the brown mountain sides, and in the
far distance the jagged snow-covered peaks stood silhouetted
against the horizon in hues of greyish white and dull pink.

After a brief rest they started to descend by a tortuous path,
and as the sun sank behind the blue-black mountains in the west
they crossed rapidly through the verdant valley where the Liri
rippled between the poplars. By the time they had climbed a little
way up the next height the last reflections of the sun had disappeared on the crests and darkness was rapidly falling in the
valley. In a vain effort to keep up with the fleeting light they
climbed up another stretch, but it soon became too dark and difficult, and they decided to rest in an abandoned sheepfold beside a
little spring until the moon should rise.

Feeble lights twinkled up at them here and there from the little
hamlets far below. Half-way up the mountain lay a small town
with a dimly illuminated romanesque campanile, embedded
between chestnut trees, the white flowers of which shone through
the darkness.

"That's Castelpendente, where Monsignor Boccaperta lives,"
said Padre Barnaba. "He's Cardinal Norcus's vicar. I suppose you
know him?"

"No, I haven't the honour."

"Indeed? All the same, I'm sure you could put up there for
the night."

"Why should I spend the night there?"

"But we have come such a long way and you must be terribly
tired," said Padre Barnaba anxiously.

"Oh, I can keep going. After all, I'm on a pilgrimage too and I
should like to remain with you. They will hardly expect me to
pay them a visit in Castelpendente in these circumstances."

Padre Barnaba remained silent for a little while, then he asked in a low voice. "Did you tell His Eminence about this journey of yours? "

"Yes, indeed I did. In fact, it was he who told me about Santissima Trinità."

Padre Barnaba only nodded. Then he sat down beside the water trough, broke a bit of dry bread, gave half of it to Thomas, and said in a voice which in the darkness sounded a little more brusque than usual: "I'm very glad that you're coming with us, but don't forget that you're free to turn back at any time. We cannot give you more than two hours' rest now. As soon as the moon rises above Monte Cornacchia we must move on."

The pilgrims lay down on the bare floor of the sheepfold. Marco wakened them shortly after midnight. The night was now at its darkest and the sky full of glistening stars. But the full moon had risen somewhere over the peaceful Campania and was shining down like a little jack-o'-lantern through the pass in the south.

Now Marco took over the leadership. He knew all the paths better than anyone else and had the eyes of a cat. At a steady pace they climbed the stony donkey-track and crossed the little pastures and copses which became less frequent. Then they came to a bare slope, and here the limestone shone so white in the moonlight that it was easier to find the way. The vegetation decreased, and for long stretches there was none at all. Only here and there, between the crags, broom or juniper bushes cast leafy shadows. The naked shimmering slope gradually rounded off high above in the darkness. To the wayfarers it seemed like walking on the disc of the moon. The Roveto Valley became lost to view and nothing but desolate mountain peaks met the eye.

The moon had now reached Latium. From there it was peeping, with visible effort, over the edge of the Simbruini, but it could no longer illuminate the landscape. The darkness became more intense again, and Marco had to set a slower pace. But the going was becoming easier. The treacherous, break-neck pebbly path came to an end; the track was now like a hard sandbed. Gradually the outlines of separate hills detached themselves from the great mountain ridge. Towards morning a dry, cold wind rose in the east, and

Thomas noticed that they were now traversing a great plateau.
The moon had disappeared; the stars grew pale, and the sky turned
ice green. On the eastern horizon a row of red peaks suddenly
blazed up like torches. The sun had risen somewhere over the
Adriatic, and in a few minutes day arrived.

Azure-tinted chains of mountains with dull red crests surrounded the miles of plateau. A vast barren tract, swept bare and
level by wind and water, extended before the eyes of the pilgrims.
It was like marching over an endless steppe in a starless cosmic
space where white limestone ridges stood out like huge drifts of
salt on the pale green slopes that surrounded them.

In the middle of the plateau stood a solitary cone-shaped mountain with a glistening cap of snow. Its outlines bore witness to the
colossal force of a volcanic eruption of thousands of years ago,
which had reached to a height of some nine thousand feet. Now
the solitary giant towered up like a petrified clenched fist stretched
up from the underworld in helpless protest against the powers of
the gods. Thomas recognized it at once and glanced enquiringly
at Padre Barnaba. The old man nodded.

"Yes, that's Monte Lino," he said. "*Il vecchio Monte Lino*, the
old wise mountain. . . . We are trying to get there before
midday."

They rested for a short time, ate their dry bread and washed
their faces and feet in a little brook. Padre Barnaba recited the
Angelus, and also a few other prayers which sounded very archaic.
Then, guided by Filippo, they continued on their way towards the
solitary mountain. But now, in sight of his goal, Thomas suddenly
felt unutterably tired. It was not merely physical exhaustion. An
unconscious tension had eased and the reaction had set in. Suddenly he was perturbed to feel the familiar little shooting pain in
the back of his head, but as it got better when they moved on, he
consoled himself that his torturing old migraines, from which he
had had ten years' respite, were not returning.

After they had been marching for an hour in the fresh morning
air, a man's voice intoning a simple melody in a primitive key was
heard from across the plateau. It brought to mind an Eastern priest
calling the faithful to prayer from his minaret. But here in the

wilderness there was no minaret, and the sonorous voice rose all alone into the clear air like a fakir on a magic rope.

But soon Thomas noticed that this voice was relating something. It was definitely not a song sung merely for the sake of singing but rather a kind of recitative. The vocalized intonation was only used to make it more audible. The basic pattern consisted of a primary melody of five semitones, which was endlessly drawn out. The singer was apparently very far away. Thomas could only distinguish isolated words that seemed to refer to some stray sheep. "*Perduti . . . lost . . . lost*" the voice sang with almost biblical pathos, and then fell silent almost as suddenly as it had begun.

Thomas stole a glance at the faces of his companions, but saw no reaction in any of them. After a while the song started up again, now more audibly. The dialect was difficult to understand and the language was stylized in the manner of ancient folk poetry. Nevertheless Thomas gathered that it was about wind, and weather, and a water-supply. It must be a shepherd sending a message to other shepherds, he thought. And in fact an answer came from very far away in the same monotonous melody, so faintly, however, that Thomas could not catch the words.

But now the shepherd seemed to have caught sight of the pilgrims. "*Tornano i pellegrini*," he sang. "The pilgrims are returning home from Santissima Trinità. They are already halfway across the plateau."

The news met with an immediate response. Distant voices replied from different directions. But not a sound came from the procession of pilgrims.

"The pilgrims are returning home," repeated the first voice. "Assunta is with them too. They have made good speed."

Filippo suddenly turned round and looked at Padre Barnaba enquiringly. The priest nodded. Then the deacon took a deep breath and sang an answer. He had a strong, harmonious voice that must have carried a long way.

"We have vowed not to speak until we arrive home," he sang. "We have walked for four days and we are very tired. All the

same we will break bread together this evening at the Good
Shepherd."

"God be praised! We will break bread together at the Good
Shepherd," confirmed the first voice. "Soon we shall have water
in the well again. . . ."

The sun had now risen high above the encircling mountain
range, and the sky had turned a deep grey-blue. The plateau too
awoke to life. Little birds flew up, butterflies fluttered about the
golden broom, and solitary birds of prey hovered high up in the
air. As the heat increased lizards ventured out on the sunny
rocks, and the torrid air vibrated above the dazzling white limestone ridges. Soon the sun had dispelled every trace of morning
shadows from the flat plateau, which was completely exposed to
its scorching rays.

The pilgrims had now reached a wider donkey-track and they
quickened their pace. Some distance away were sheepfolds built of
unhewn limestone blocks, and on the hills nearest them, the first
herds of cattle. The herdsman waved at them as they passed.
Between the encircling hills were many deep ravines which ran
down to the plateau and formed a network over it like the veins
on a leaf. They concealed little oases of bushes, luxurious grassy
patches and even leafy copses, which had been quite invisible from
the plateau. There was a spring in the middle of nearly every
oasis with a water-trough beside it for the cattle, but most of the
troughs were empty.

The procession had almost arrived at the solitary white-capped
mountain, when Thomas noticed that his feet were failing him.
He saw with forgivable envy that Padre Barnaba, in spite of his
years, was far more able than he was. The sharp pains in the back
of his head had come on again. Was he going to collapse so near
the goal?

He looked longingly up at the mountain. A terraced projection
was distinctly visible on its southern slope, and in the middle of
it, a yellowish-white limestone cliff the shape of a huge wooden
shoe, with a little group of dwellings clinging to its farther end.

"Settevetri," said Padre Barnaba, nodding towards it.

A large valley at the foot of the mountain was partly covered

with green fields and partly with dark green leafy woodland. At
the other side of the pathway little buildings came into sight, but
to Thomas's disappointment they turned out to be only sheds and
cow-houses. A little farther on they passed a white-washed chapel;
not one of the pilgrims made a move to enter it. At the next bend
of the road there was a dried-up well, and half-way up the slope
a donkey was struggling, carrying an apparently empty water
barrel. The pathway had become wider, but it was very steep and
covered with loose stones that made walking a torture. Thomas
stumbled more and more frequently. The back of his head was
throbbing, and he felt sick. But he staggered on with his last
ounce of strength. Suddenly he felt a supporting arm around his
waist. It was Marco.

In this way he stumbled into the village of Settevetri, a few
hundred yards behind the others. His burning eyes wandered over
the miserable little stone cottages. Padre Barnaba was standing at
an open door and beckoning to him. He crossed the threshold as
if in a dream and was led to a bed, where he sank down and fell
asleep instantly.

◦◦◦◦◦◦◦

XXVIII   THE INN OF THE GOOD SHEPHERD

Thomas slept for eight hours without a break. When he awoke
it was evening and Padre Barnaba was standing beside the bed.

"It's time for supper. Would you like to share the pilgrims'
meal? We are all eating together. It's a little thanksgiving feast."

Thomas got up staggering with sleep. He found it difficult to
get his bearings. "It's very kind of you," he murmured. "Of
course I will come with the greatest pleasure."

"Very well. I shall wait outside!" Padre Barnaba walked to
the door, but stopped on the threshold. "I think I should prepare
you for the fact that it is not an ordinary meal," he said. "It has
a sacred character, as it were. Up to the present strangers have
never taken part in it. I'm telling you this so that you may realize

that I am making a great exception of you, dear Tommaso. But after all, you have taken part in our pilgrimage."

When Thomas went out the mountain air hit him in the face like a winter wind. The sun was already setting, the scorching heat of the day was past. Padre Barnaba laid a sheepskin over his shoulders. "You needn't feel embarrassed at this," he said. "We're over four thousand feet above sea level here, and after sunset it's as cold as in your own country."

They stood in a little open square. A young girl – a robust, dark type, with full lips and lively brown eyes under her black kerchief – was sitting at the base of an old roofed well. She stood up, and with a curtsey asked Padre Barnaba to hear her confession.

Thomas had time to look around him. The little market place was obviously the centre of the village. The yellowish-white limestone rocks towered up north and east behind the low line of cottages. Towards the south and west, on the other hand, the square was open, and only a low wall of rough stones, like a breastwork, stood between it and the sharp declivity. Looking over this parapet, Thomas could see the sun rolling with almost visible speed towards a distant bluish chain of mountains, while the snow-covered crown of Monte Lino glowed, ochre yellow and fiery red, high above the village.

Padre Barnaba had sat down on the step of the well. The girl was kneeling beside him, her head leaning against the basin. The scene had an almost biblical character – the white-haired priest, the kneeling sinner, the red glow of the sunset on the old well, and far below in the valley, the evening music of the sheep bells. Two men in dark clothes passed and gave Thomas a friendly greeting. He recognized them as fellow pilgrims. They disappeared into the last house, which was right under the limestone rock face. It stood out a little, was bigger than the others and even had a kind of pergola. Immediately behind the men came two women and a young boy. They all seemed to be carrying some provisions – a loaf of bread, a piece of goats' cheese, or a handful of vegetables.

"Where is the church?" asked Thomas when Padre Barnaba had finished with his penitent.

"At Fontenuova. You remember, the big well we passed early in the morning."

"As far away as that? "

"Our people here in the village have a much longer way to go to their work every day. Up here our standards regarding distance are quite different."

Thomas shook his head resignedly, remembering the hardships of the upward climb. "I don't know how you bear it," he said. "I suppose you have to make the journey several times a day? "

Padre Barnaba nodded. "Yes, it's very tiring," he replied. "Recently I have said Mass down there only on special occasions. But we can talk about that tomorrow. We must join our friends now, for I'm afraid we're a bit late as it is."

He conducted his guest to the house with the pergola, which at close quarters looked like a simple village inn. A wooden signboard with a faded inscription in blue hung over the door.

"*Locanda del Buon Pastore*," Thomas read.

"This is the Inn of the Good Shepherd," said Padre Barnaba significantly as he walked under the pergola.

With much patience and effort something like a garden had been created. The ground was naked rock to be sure, and on one side stood a continuation of the same wall which fenced the market square off from the declivity. Two plain wooden tables, large enough to seat about a hundred persons, were placed alongside this wall. The whole space was roofed over with a simple wooden frame that supported a thin network of foliage, a kind of wild vine which spread high up the wall, and covered the walls of the house.

Behind this pergola there was a small room with a counter, simple tables and chairs and a shelf of glasses, beakers and bottles. Filippo was standing at the counter receiving the foods which Marco took into the kitchen. Padre Barnaba greeted the two men, then sat down under the pergola at the head of the first long table, with Thomas on his right.

The men sat at one table, the women at the other. All remained silent. The mountain was bathed in brilliant sunlight which shone in through the foliage. There was a wonderful view of the plateau, which had recovered its warm, golden-brown colouring once more.

Suddenly the silence was broken by a clear voice intoning the same strange song that Thomas had heard the shepherds singing early that morning. Looking down the table he saw a stout little man with smooth brown hair above a cherub-like face. He was standing there, in his grey sheep-skin coat, with a book before him. The recital seemed to move him deeply, for his face was distorted like one of Van Eyck's singing angels.

The text was from the Acts of the Apostles: "And all that believed were together, and had all things common; and sold their possessions and goods, and parted them to all men, as every man had need. And they, continuing daily with one accord in the temple, and breaking bread from house to house, did eat their meat with gladness and singleness of heart. Praising God and having favour with all the people. And the Lord added to the Church daily such as should be saved. . . ."

There was water, bread and cheese on the tables. Filippo and Marco served up two savoury-smelling roasts of lamb, and Padre Barnaba recited a brief blessing over the food. The old priest sat there with his arms crossed over his breast, and his eyes, radiating kindliness, wandered to and fro among the familiar faces at the tables. Thomas had never before seen him looking so contented. He was like the happy father of a family among his children.

And now he began to speak, quietly and naturally, as though he were only joining in the conversation at the table. He started by mentioning the pilgrimage which had just been made, and recalled Christ's promise to be with His disciples all days to the end of time. The Good Shepherd, he said, must have walked the road to Santissima Trinità many times, first with Peter and John, when He banished the devil from the mountain, and then again with Linus, when the saint struck water from the rock, and finally with all the penitents who had gone on pilgrimage to that holy place down the centuries in order to recover and once more partake worthily of God's graces. Penance gave one a deeper insight into one's own heart. Hence the pilgrim kept silent so that he might hear the Good Shepherd speaking. And when the pilgrim returned and sat once more at the table of the Good Shepherd, his first words must be words of thanks. . . .

Thomas glanced at his companions on the right, a tall deeply tanned man, with a very prominent forehead, sunken temples, and a troubled expression. He was leaning over the table, holding his plate firmly as he devoured his food hungrily. But when his gaze met that of the guest who had come from far away, a merry smile lit up his deep-set eyes. Thomas nodded silently in response. The man understood what he meant – that he felt it an honour to be taking part in a holy meal with this poor community.

When the dishes were empty at last Padre Barnaba broke the silence once more. "Let us give thanks," he said, standing up.

Every head was bowed, all hands were clasped as he prayed:

"Father Almighty, we thank Thee
For Thy Holy Name,
for which Thou hast prepared a dwelling in our hearts,
and for the knowledge of things to come,
which Thou hast revealed to us
through Jesus Thy Shepherd.
Thou, O Lord, Almighty Ruler,
hast created all things for Thy Name's sake.
Thou hast given food and drink to Thy people
that they may eat and drink and thank Thee.
To us Thou hast given food for our souls, and life eternal,
through Jesus, Thy Shepherd.
Thou dost deliver Thy faithful followers from all evil,
and dost perfect them in Thy love.
Lord, assemble from the North and the South,
from the East and the West,
all Thy saints into Thy holy tabernacles
which Thou hast built on the Mountain of Thy glory
through Jesus, Thy Shepherd."

Thomas listened bewildered. The prayer was in the local dialect but its basic pattern reminded Thomas of an ancient text he had once read. Padre Barnaba paused for a moment, then continued in a louder voice, as if he were speaking to a larger congregation:

> "The Kingdom of God is at hand,
> and this world will pass away.
> Let him who is holy come forward!
> Let him who is not do penance!
> Lord, come to us! Lord, come to us,
> through Jesus, Thy Shepherd!"

He fell silent, and a chorus of rough men's voices answered from the table:

"Lord come to us! Amen."

A woman with two children stood up from the other table and left the pergola. Then a little crowd of young people came out of the inner room. They had been waiting there as penitents used to wait outside the church. The girl who had made her confession at the well was one of them.

The little man at the end of the table resumed his recitative. He read the story of the Disciples of Emmaus from Saint Luke's Gospel:

". . . And they drew nigh unto the village, whither they went: and he made as though he would have gone further. But they constrained him, saying, 'Abide with us: for it is towards evening, and the day is far spent.' And he went in to tarry with them. And it came to pass as he sat at meat with them, he took bread, and blessed it, and broke and gave to them. And their eyes were opened, and they knew him; and he vanished out of their sight. And they said one to another: 'Did not our heart burn within us, while he talked with us by the way, and while he opened to us the scriptures?'"

Filippo appeared at the door with a big basket.

"Thanks be to the Lord," he sang in a thundering bass.

"Amen," replied those at the tables.

Thomas was filled with a growing but indefinable uneasiness as he watched Filippo take little rolls of bread and plain glasses from the basket and place one of each in front of each person. Marco came behind him with wine which he poured into the glasses, indistinctly murmuring some greeting, to which the person being served replied. But when he came to Thomas he suddenly stood still and asked in a low voice:

" Will you take part in the Lord's Supper, Reverendo? "

Thomas looked around him alarmed. He had been mechanically following what was being done without even daring consciously to admit to himself what he saw. But now the fact could no longer be denied: What was taking place here was certainly no profane folk-feast, but a celebration of the Lord's Supper according to a very early Christian rite. The catechumens had left the room, and only the community of the faithful remained. And now Marco wished to know where he, Thomas, stood. He looked appealingly at Padre Barnaba, but the old priest was reciting the Confiteor with bowed head, and did not see his dilemma.

Marco, looking embarrassed, repeated the question. Thomas's neighbour at the table misunderstood his silence, and tried to be helpful.

" You do not have to take part if you are not prepared," he whispered. " You could go inside the inn for the present and have a glass of ordinary wine. . . ."

Thomas was seized with a feeling of dizziness. Here was an Abruzzi shepherd standing before him in a poor village inn, asking him solemnly whether he wished to partake of the Body and Blood of the Lord at the rough deal table just as if that was the most natural thing in the world. The centuries whirled to and fro in his mind and he wondered whether he was having hallucinations. Only now did he notice that Padre Barnaba had changed his soutane for a rough dark shepherd's cloak, definitely better suited to the surroundings. Thomas suddenly felt himself to be an anachronism, sitting there in his black clerical attire with his breviary in his pocket. At the same time his apprehension in face of the unknown turned to real terror: How could he dare to approach something forbidden to outsiders? How could he aspire to a right which was not befitting to a person of the twentieth century? Would it not be as sacrilegious for him to receive the

Lord's Supper which was being offered to him here and now as it would have been had he received Holy Communion that time in Bolsena? He shook his head violently in token of refusal, but before he had time to utter a word he heard Padre Barnaba's confident voice saying:

"May the Almighty God have mercy on you, forgive you your sins and lead you to life everlasting."

"Amen," replied the congregation.

Thomas noticed with relief that Marco was pouring out wine for him. He clasped his hands, bowed his head like the others, and listened as if in a dream to what was happening around him. Padre Barnaba had begun to speak again; but his words sounded as though they came from another world across an immense space of time. It was the world of absolute reality which humanity had dreamed of down through the ages, and which he, Thomas, had been seeking all his life. He had never succeeded in getting one step nearer to it by his own efforts, but now it was coming nearer to him without his having done anything to make this possible. Perhaps he too should just sit here quietly and wait – like a child? And suddenly he became aware that he had come closer to the mystery of the Eucharist.

Now Padre Barnaba sang something in a strangely clear voice, and the chorus at the men's table boomed "Amen." But he held the note and continued to sing in a tremolo, like the shepherds on the plateau:

"The Lord be with you!"

And the rough voices answered in the same style:

"And with thy spirit!"

Suddenly the cantor's voice broke forth in a strange, exultant, bird-like tone:

"Lift up your hearts!"

And the answering chorus came like the rush of a mighty wind through a ravine:

"We have lifted them up to the Lord!"

The voice of the cantor rose higher and higher, in a silvery cascade of semitones, to a note of supreme joy:

"Let us give thanks to the Lord our God!"

And with a heavy, earthy pathos the chorus replied:

"It is meet and just."

But the cantor suddenly commenced to descend the strange vocal spiral. And now he sounded almost breathless with suspense as though he had a wonderfully joyful message to announce, as he sang:

"It is truly meet and just, right and salutary, suppliantly to beseech Thee, Lord, the Everlasting Shepherd, not to forsake Thy flock, but through Thy blessed Apostles to keep it under Thy continued protection. . . ."

"Holy, Holy, Holy," answered Filippo's bass, and the chorus joined in like a mighty organ:

"Holy, Holy, Holy, Lord God of hosts, our Shepherd. Heaven and earth are full of Thy glory. Hosanna in the highest. Blessed is he that cometh in the name of the Lord: Hosanna in the highest!"

Padre Barnaba, before whom Marco had placed the bread and the wine, now stood up. Thomas heard him praying for the rulers of the Church and for all Christian peoples. Then he saw him raise his open hands and let them drop again as his lips spoke the words of Consecration.

There was dead silence around the tables. The last rays of the setting sun filtered, tremulously, through the foliage of the pergola and fell softly on the grey head, bent shoulders and clasped hands. A gentle breeze blew in from the plateau, and somewhere in the distance isolated sheep bells tinkled sharply, like drips of water. This was peace. An ineffable, inexpressible, unearthly peace pervaded all. And then the most incomprehensible thing happened. There came One, and took His place in the midst, One whom no one saw, yet Whose presence was apprehended by each and all. Padre Barnaba remained silent, and it was as though time itself was filled with silent dialogues.

Thomas sat as if paralysed, without daring even to look up. The sense of the Absolute, the supreme Reality, was too overpowering. The divine effulgence had unexpectedly approached too close to his earthbound being, and threatened to engulf it. The ground was going from under his feet, and he felt he would die if his world of visions were shattered. His hands closed convulsively over the little bit of bread which lay before him on the table. Then it was as though somebody took hold of him bodily and drew him out of the waves. The ground was under his feet again. He still did not dare to look up, but he became more and more conscious of a deep feeling of security. He put the bread to his lips and his heart became filled with a liberating sense of certainty. What had happened? he asked himself. The feeling of an invisible Presence remained, but now it awakened only calm trust in him. Now he understood that the shadows that had darkened his youth were finally dispersed, the last barriers of doubt had fallen, and he was free to love with his whole heart. At last he had made contact with the Absolute, and the Absolute was measureless love. What he had experienced left him with a deeper feeling of happiness than he had ever felt before. It made him strong.

The sun sank in a blood-red glow behind the mountains. The last glow of the setting sun shimmered through the foliage of the pergola from the summit of Monte Lino. It reminded Thomas of the reflection of a forest fire that he had once seen in his childhood in the distant sky, over the great Karelian forests. Now as then he trembled before an incomprehensible world. Padre Barnaba recited the Memento for the Dead in a low voice. Then he said the *Paternoster*. The response rose up from the bowed forms around him. Gradually backs straightened, heads were raised, and a slight noise was heard along the tables as the glasses were pushed back and the last crumbs of bread carefully gathered up. Meantime, Padre Barnaba again raised his hands and with a clear voice intoned a prayer of thanksgiving.

> "We thank Thee, O Father,
> For the life and the wisdom
> Which Thou hast revealed to us
> Through Jesus, Thy Shepherd."

Filippo answered with a long-drawn-out Amen, and Padre Barnaba continued in the same chant:

Q

"We thank Thee, O Father,
For Thy holy vine
Which Thou hast revealed to us
Through Jesus, Thy Shepherd."

Suddenly Thomas felt himself being gently nudged on the right.
He turned round and encountered friendly smiling eyes beneath
bushy eyebrows. His neighbour had something on his mind. He
flung his arms round Thomas's shoulders and gently touched his
lips to his cheek. This was the primitive Christian kiss of peace.
It had apparently made the round of the table already. Thomas
responded to it in accordance with the ritual.

Padre Barnaba raised his hand and gave the final blessing.
Then he sat down again and looked at the guest by his side with
a quiet smile as if to indicate that he was ready now to explain
everything if required. But Thomas sensed that this was only a
friendly gesture, for the ardent religious joy in the eyes of the old
priest would have simply nipped any troubled questioning in the
bud. Thomas could only nod silently to show his acquiescence.
His heart was too full of joy to desire any explanations.

Filippo came with two smoky oil lamps and hung them on the
pergola. Marco carefully brushed up the last traces of bread
crumbs from the table and ate them. The darkness fell quickly
and moths soon began to flutter around the oil lamps. It turned
almost cold, but luckily the wind had fallen and the rock face
still retained some of the day's warmth, as though the mighty
mountain wished to protect the human beings who had sought
its ample shelter.

Very soon all moved off silently. The Piazza was in complete
darkness. The summit of Monte Lino gleamed palely in the starlight, and a little lamp was burning under the simple wooden
sign-board of the Good Shepherd. The houses stood silent and lifeless. Only the sound of sleeping animals could be heard now and
then from the back yards.

Marco was standing in front of the old fountain with a copper
jug in his hand. Water was gently running into the basin. He
drew a jugful of cold refreshing water and offered Thomas a drink.

"They say," Marco told him, "it was at this spot Saint Linus struck water from the rock to be a sign that grace would always flow down on this village. That is why there's such dismay if it ever dries up. But do you know, it's as deep as a bore-hole."

❦

XXIX PADRE BARNABA'S HOUSE

The following morning Thomas awoke with the same feeling of happiness. As he was very tired he remained lying in bed for a long time trying to sort out the varied impressions of the last few days, putting off going over the events of the previous evening until the last. He recalled his departure from Rome, his walk from Subiaco to Vallepietra and from Vallepietra to Santissima Trinità, his meeting with Padre Barnaba, the moonlight on the mountains, and the morning sun rising over the plateau.

But all the time his thoughts were groping ahead towards Sette-vetri. It was as though everything else had only been a prepara-tion for this sacred meal with the shepherds. And whilst the impressions of the preceding events gradually faded away, the last experience remained and dominated his thoughts. *Pacem relinquo vobis* – Peace I leave you. The consciousness of no longer being alone filled his heart with peace in the same way that knowledge of the mere presence of another person in a house gives a feeling of protection. Monsignor dei Palleschi would have declared that a marvellous, boundless grace had certainly been poured down over the unknown village of Settevetri. But why precisely on Sette-vetri? He asked Padre Barnaba.

"The wind bloweth where it listeth," replied the old priest smiling, as he gazed serenely out of the window through which bright daylight was filling the room.

"But how is that possible? The whole place seems so holy, just as though Our Lord were here among us in person."

Padre Barnaba's smile deepened. "No," he said, "Our Lord is

not nearer to man here than in any other place. But it may be
that the people of Settevetri are somewhat nearer to Him – at
least sometimes."

" Do you mean that they are in some sense a chosen people? "

The question sounded so perturbed that Padre Barnaba laughed
outright. " Heaven forbid ! There are no sects in this village. The
people don't know themselves what makes them different from
others."

" So there *is* something which makes them different? "

" They love their God. But they don't imagine on that account
that they're better than their fellow men. They bear the divine
love in their hearts, and that is why Our Lord is with them
wherever they go. This love is the only treasure they possess, and
it has been inherited from generation to generation since the time
of Saint Linus."

Padre Barnaba's house stood right in front of the fountain on
the north side of the piazza. It had once been whitewashed but
now it was just as weather-beaten and earth-coloured as the others.
It consisted of two rooms and a kitchen which was also used as a
dining-room. The inside was strongly reminiscent of Santa Presenza; the floors were worn, the walls bare and the furniture plain
and rough. It was as though Padre Barnaba had brought a bit of
the monastery with him when he moved to the mountains. But
indeed it was more likely that the monastery in Rome had assumed
something of the atmosphere of this wilderness. The silence, the
solitude, the lowliness – all that made up the innate and specific
atmosphere of Santa Presenza had really come originally from this
remote region where the people lived in solitude before the face
of the Lord.

" Where did you say Mass this morning? " Thomas enquired.

" When we have celebrated the Eucharist at the Good Shepherd
I do not say Mass the following morning. But if you want to go
down to Fontenuova I shall give you the key of the chapel," Padre
Barnaba suggested.

Thomas considered for a moment before he asked:

" To which diocese does your parish actually belong? "

" Settevetri is under the Bishop of Castelpendente. But from time immemorable the parish priests of Settevetri have had the *Linus privilegium*. This entitles me to celebrate Mass on special occasions according to the ancient rite in the Inn of the Good Shepherd, as you have seen. At other times I say Mass in the usual way down at Fontenuova. For in any case everyone is not able to take part in the Lord's Supper up here."

"Do you decide who may do so?"

"As parish priest I have the final word, of course. But the general rule is that no strangers at all are ever invited to the Buon Pastore. And that is certainly the best thing, for otherwise I might very soon be forced to cancel the *privilegium*. I have made a very great exception of you, my dear Tommaso."

But Thomas's head was still in a whirl.

"The rite?" he asked. "Where did the rite come from?"

"From Saint Linus, of course," replied Padre Barnaba, smiling. "Do you think that so extraordinary?"

"Well, to be quite frank I do."

Padre Barnaba shook his white locks with an air of happy conviction. "When you've been here a few days longer you'll no longer find it so. And of course to anyone who has been born here it's the most natural thing in the world. This way of speaking and singing is native to this mountain region. It must surely have been the same in the time of Saint Linus."

"But how can you know that it is all true?"

"Because it was here that Saint Linus sat at table with our Lord."

But doubting Thomas could not be silenced. "It's certainly hard to give historical proof of that," he said.

Padre Barnaba sounded slightly annoyed. "I don't know what you want to prove," he said. "At any rate, this place here is very ancient. Everyone says so."

"Do you think people lived here in the time of Saint Linus?"

"I told you already, didn't I, that the rite has come down to us from his time."

"Can it really have been preserved for nearly two thousand years?"

"Why not? The winds of fashion do not blow here. The words

of the text may have changed a little with the times; that's quite a different matter, however."

"But how could you offer a sacrifice, without even an altar?"

Padre Barnaba smiled. "Did you not see it, then?" he asked.

"What should I have seen?"

"What took place at the table yesterday evening. If you had, you would understand that the love of God is the best altar."

Thomas fixed his pince-nez firmly on his nose. "Human nature . . ." he was beginning to say in his old academic style, but Padre Barnaba interrupted him good-humouredly.

"Human nature has been corrupted – we all know that," he said, "and it has become infected with pride more than with anything else, but here on this poor mountain infection does not thrive. There are plenty of liars and ignorant people in Settevetri, but as for proud people, well they just make sure to go and live somewhere else. And wherever humility reigns in the human heart, the Sacrifice of Love can be confidently offered to God out in his own sunshine. You understand what I mean, don't you?"

"There can also be other reasons for erecting an altar."

"There are as many reasons as there are cities in the world, but I'm only speaking of Settevetri now. Here people may offer sacrifice to God at certain times without a visible altar. And Saint Linus must surely have seen to it that this privilege should not be forgotten. Remember that Monte Lino is his own mountain."

This argument was evidently the deciding factor for Padre Barnaba. Thomas had no wish to argue with him any longer, and indeed before he had time to make a reply there was a knock at the door. Padre Barnaba went and opened it.

"Here's a friend to visit you," he announced with a smile, discreetly leaving the room.

A sun-tanned, child-like face, surrounded by bushy grey hair, appeared in the doorway. It was Fausto. He seemed broader and more unwieldy than ever, but his eyes were moist. He shook Thomas warmly by the hand.

"How glad I am to see you, Reverendo," he said. "Welcome to Settevetri!"

His joy was so obviously sincere that Thomas was touched. "Thank you, Fausto. You're really too kind to a poor tramp."

"You mustn't say that," protested Fausto, "for I have to thank you for bringing back Assunta."

"It wasn't I. She came back of her own free will."

Fausto seemed surprised. "But didn't you come here together? " he asked.

"Only the last bit of the way. When I left Rome I had no idea she was on the way here."

Fausto scratched his head with a puzzled smile. "But it was certainly you who influenced her to make the journey. She would never have come if you had not explained the Lord's will to her."

There was a hidden appeal in his voice which made Thomas feel uncomfortable. "I was only an instrument," he said, nervously adjusting his pince-nez, "and a very poor one indeed."

"All of us are only Our Lord's tools. You have saved Assunta from something terrible."

"We must not judge others," said Thomas, and then to change the subject he asked: "What made you come to Settevetri? "

"Well, you see, I was born in the mountains."

"And are you living here quite alone? "

"Yes. The climate would not have agreed with my wife. She was from Trastevere and needed heavier air, if you understand what I mean."

"Yes, I understand . . ." Thomas assured him.

"I would have liked best to come back here the time Padre Barnaba left San Lino, but I couldn't because of her. You have to be used to the mountains to be able to carry your cross over these roads. My wife was too old to learn our ways. So she went to Our Lord by her own road. I only hope it won't be too hard for Assunta up here. . . ."

"Are you happier here than in the Vicolo dei Pecorai? " asked Thomas gently.

"Ask Padre Barnaba? " replied Fausto in the same low voice.

"Was it he who suggested you should come back? "

"He helped us. Without him we would hardly have got a place to live in up here. You need to have friends in the village, and they don't at all like strangers to stay more than three days. But now we're very happy and comfortable."

"Assunta too?" asked Thomas involuntarily.

A dark shadow passed over Fausto's face. "What can you expect, Father?" he asked. "She's very young, and youth has its sorrows. I can't blame her for wanting to go back to Rome. But there's no use fretting about the old story. She must get used to living up here even if it's hard. There's nothing else she can do. Don't you think so too?"

"As you are her father you must know best," replied Thomas, more worried than ever. "Besides, you can always ask Padre Barnaba for his advice."

Fausto nodded. "The people here will do their best for her, I know. And besides, she has a good friend who will certainly come to her aid."

"Who is that?"

"You know her well, Padre," replied Fausto with a smile. "Nostra Signora dei Pecorai."

"Our Lady of the Shepherds?"

"Yes, indeed. She really belongs to these parts. Didn't you know that?"

"Yes, of course, but I didn't think of it."

"I think she feels more at home here than in Rome," said Fausto. "They say she is seen on Lo Zoccolo at sunset."

"What is that?"

"The green limestone rock above the village. She walks up there and waits for her Son to come down the mountain to the Lord's Supper at the Good Shepherd."

Fausto's innocent smile was irresistible.

"Have you seen her yourself, Fausto?" asked Thomas.

"No, I haven't, but a long time ago she appeared to a few girls from the village. Then there was a little statue erected to her up there. You must be sure to go and see it, Father. It's very like our Madonna of the Shepherds in Santa Presenza."

XXX SETTEVETRI

The characteristic smell of smoke and sun-dried dung hit Thomas
in the face when he came out on the Piazza. It was almost midday. Pigs and goats were ambling about and plastering the cottage
walls with their droppings, and brown, sunburnt children were
playing around the rippling fountain. The little square was bathed
in a penetrating light that gave an almost surrealist dimension to
its outlines. It was like the stage of a natural open-air theatre,
where the huge limestone rocks made the gleaming white back-
cloth, and the picturesque little cottages huddled together formed
an earth-coloured stage on three levels intersected here and there
by lanes cut in the rock like little stairs. High above gaped the
dark mouths of caves.

Thomas did not see a single house which looked like a public
building. One would have to be well acquainted with this strange
miniature community to know how to order one's life here. He
felt irresistibly drawn back to the poor inn. On entering it he
found Filippo inside weighing salt into an old tin box.

"Good morning," he said. "Are you the village shopkeeper?"

"That's far too grand a name, Father," said Filippo, laughing
and pushing the salt aside. "What can I do for you?"

"At the moment, nothing, thank you. I only asked out of
curiosity."

"Unfortunately I have no cigars, and hardly anything else a
gentleman would need. But Marco can get you anything you
want in Castelpendente. Just tell him the next time he's going
down."

Thomas looked around enquiringly. "Do you put up guests
here too?" he asked.

Filippo looked at him sharply. "Yes, when we have to, but
only someone who needs a roof over his head for a night or
two."

"And why not for longer?"

"Because we have no proper guests' room. You see, we have to lend our own beds if we have guests."

"But if somebody wants to stay longer?"

"It just can't be done."

"Can't one rent a room anywhere in the village?"

Filippo shrugged his shoulders. "You had best ask Matteo," he said.

"Who is he?"

"He's our mayor, you might say. Don't you remember – he was with us on the pilgrimage?"

"Yes, of course. I should have guessed he was that. I suppose I should announce my arrival officially?"

"Why should you do that?"

"Because I'm a foreigner."

"A foreigner?" Filippo looked him up and down. "But aren't you dressed as a priest?"

"The dress has nothing to do with it. But of course there are police here, aren't there?"

Filippo smiled roguishly. "You say yourself the dress has nothing to do with it. No, there are no uniforms here. But Matteo will certainly be pleased to see you. He may even be expecting you already. After all, we don't often have such grand visitors."

"Ah, don't make such fine speeches! He knows nothing about me and I know nothing about him. Has he been taking an interest in politics for long?"

Filippo laughed uproariously. "Matteo?" he cried. "He doesn't bother himself about politics. He's a wool merchant and has good friends everywhere."

The village street was of solid rock worn smooth, and so dazzling white that it hurt the eyes. It ran from the north side of the Piazza and was separated from the steep mountain-side in the west only by a close row of cottages, grey with age. Built right on the edge of the precipice, they grew out of the rock, and nothing could be seen between them but open, light-filled space. In good visibility one could see the sun shining on their seven windows from far down on the plateau. Hence, the name of the village, Settevetri, seven windows.

Padre Barnaba had told him that these seven houses, and indeed the whole mountain and its surroundings, belonged to the oldest families in the neighbourhood, who nevertheless lived just as poorly as did the shepherds and farmers. Thomas strolled along the picturesque village street and thought to himself that these dwellings were timeless as the wind and the stars; they had endured through happy and unhappy centuries and would probably survive any future catastrophes of civilization.

Matteo lived in the last house. He was sitting in his kitchen turning a sizzling roast of lamb on a spit before a fire.

"Welcome, Father," he cried. "Have you recovered from the march?"

He was a short, thick-set man of middle age and his full open face was radiant with the happiness of one at peace with himself.

"Please forgive me for coming at an inconvenient time," Thomas said. "I don't want to disturb you."

"You're not disturbing me at all. On the contrary, I must ask you to excuse me for having to keep you waiting. You see, this roast is for you."

The news-service of the village was evidently well organized. Thomas felt quite bewildered.

"You are very kind," he said. "I only wanted to ask for some information."

A broad knowing grin covered Matteo's face. "You needn't worry about formalities, Father," he said. "Any friend of Padre Barnaba may stay here for as long as he likes."

"Thank you, that's very kind of you. I'm on holiday and I'd like to rest here for a couple of days."

"Rest? No one comes to Settevetri to rest. It's far too poor and uncomfortable."

Thomas stared at him. The words seemed all too familiar. But Matteo continued with evident embarrassment: "We really have no place for summer visitors. We would need to be quite differently fitted out to do so. You probably don't know that there hasn't been a single house built here this century. . . ."

"I didn't mean anything like that. I only wanted to make sure that I wouldn't cause you any trouble. . . ."

Two shaggy, dirty-white sheep dogs rushed in from the street without warning. They dutifully bared their teeth at the stranger and then stretched themselves out on the ground, their eyes fixed on the appetizing roast. A tall lanky fellow in high boots, with a pipe in his mouth, followed them in. With a friendly smile he raised his hand to his forehead. On glancing at the thin, dark face Thomas recognized his table companion at the Good Shepherd.

"This is Luca," said Matteo. "He will be of help to you if you want anything. Luca is my right-hand man."

Luca repeated his military salute.

"Yes, indeed," agreed the philosophic Luca, stroking the animals behind the ears.

"Now put your mind to talking reason to Don Tommaso," continued Matteo. "He's afraid the sheep will eat him up because he has no resident's permit. And now he's going to have dinner with us." Saying this, he took the roast from the spit and called out: "Gianni!"

"Here I am," replied a high, clear voice from the next room. A large tray with bread, wine, cheese, salad and cherries appeared in the doorway, and behind it the little man with the cherub's face who had read the Gospel at the Lord's Supper.

"*Il maestro* – the school teacher," said Matteo. "He lives with me."

"Welcome to the house, Reverendo," said Gianni in as loud and distinct a voice as if he were addressing a noisy class.

"Thank you, Maestro," replied Thomas. "Have you been working long in Settevetri?"

"I was born here," Gianni informed him in the same rather unnatural voice, which he seemed unable to lower.

"Gianni is my sister's son," explained Matteo. "He was at the Teachers' Training College in Castelpendente. They were very pleased with him there, I think."

Gianni flushed. He was rosy-cheeked and healthy looking. With his plump hands and dreamy expression he did not really seem to fit into the surroundings. But his uncle looked at him with visible satisfaction as he continued: "He was offered a scholarship so that he could continue his studies. But he had such a longing to come back to Settevetri that he refused it. Perhaps you may think that was unwise; but we who have been born up here look at the matter differently. And Dottoressa Vanna understood him too."

"Who is she?"

Matteo seemed slightly embarrassed. "She's our doctor," he replied, "but to tell you the truth she's more interested in the study of antiquity, and is full of strange ideas."

"Well, after all, it's not wrong to study the past," objected Thomas.

Gianni smiled in a slightly supercilious manner. "When I came back here," he said, "I bought myself a little library of historical works, but I haven't read them all yet."

"A good idea! Is it a fairly large collection?"

"No. But before one can really profit by a book one must be sure that it's true. Don't you think so?"

"Of course," agreed Thomas, amused. "But surely one can assume that it is true."

"Not always. Even the best books are full of lies and hearsay. In order to get a knowledge of real facts one has to learn to think for oneself. And one can do that best of all up here."

"How is that?"

"Because there are no marble statues here to obstruct the view," declared Gianni almost brusquely. "Caesar was never here, nor Garibaldi either. The history of Settevetri is the history of the shepherds. But the history of the shepherds is the history of mankind. And it is true because it had its beginning in Bethlehem."

Thomas stole a glance at the young man. Was he a fanatic? But Gianni only nodded with a little schoolmasterly smile. Then he suddenly found he had to hurry up and lay the table. He took knives and forks out of one cupboard, glasses and plates out of another, then placed the roast on a dish, all in an expert manner. Meantime Luca had got the dogs to move into a corner by the fireplace and had given them some bones to gnaw. The wool merchant took his place at the head of the table.

"Will you please say grace, Father?" he said.

They ate in silence, but Matteo seemed ill at ease. At last he said, turning to Luca: "I'm afraid our guest is disappointed with Settevetri."

"How did you get that idea?" asked Thomas.

The wool-merchant looked at him fixedly. "Tell the truth, Father," he said, "you have surely never before met a mayor like me? But I was only given the title because there was no one else. I'm really not a mayor at all, but something more like the superintendent of a poorhouse."

"Padre Barnaba told me that," replied Thomas. "When I first met him he was superintendent of another poorhouse – Santa Presenza in Rome. I suppose you've heard of it?"

Matteo seemed relieved. "Yes, in the past many people went from our village to Santa Presenza. But life down there has changed so much that no one seems to want to go away from here now."

He stood up, fetched a little black book, and put it down in front of Gianni. "Padre Barnaba has taught us to read a few verses even on weekdays. I think this piece is just right for today."

Gianni stood up and began to read in a solemn chant: "Again, the kingdom of heaven is like unto treasure hid in a field; the which when a man hath found, he hideth, and for joy thereof goeth and selleth all that he hath, and buyeth that field. . . ."

"Yes, we can take the text as a basis," said Matteo, "but it's not easy to direct a whole commune according to it. It's not enough to find the field, I can tell you. It's necessary to be able to till it too. And that's not so simple when one has used up all one's resources to buy it."

As Thomas listened silently without comment, the wool-merchant continued cautiously: "Everyone who lives in the village has some kind of work, to be sure, but there are few opportunities for work up here. And we don't want to have more residents than can find a seat at the table in The Good Shepherd. That is our only communal policy. Am I not right, Luca?"

When Luca nodded in agreement, Matteo continued with more assurance: "Perhaps it's not necessary to keep the matter so secret as the man in the parable did. For very few people go to search for treasure in the wilderness. They have to leave too many things behind them – uniforms, and newspapers, and paper money, and the other toys of mankind. All these things disappear like smoke in the clouds, and only the naked mountain remains. That is what Gianni meant by the truth of life. Isn't it, Gianni? "

" Men build their dream palaces," said Gianni gloomily, " but Our Lord was born in a stable. And the only way to keep on the right path is to follow in His footsteps."

" Amen ! " said Matteo, standing up. " Now let us say good-day to Grandmother."

He led the way into a large room with bare whitewashed walls and shabby furniture. A furrowed face with tawny skin and black, sparkling eyes looked up from behind a little weaving loom by the window. A bent and wrinkled little woman was sitting there weaving an almost luminous cloth of blue, yellow and red.

Matteo's grandfather had been the biggest merchant in the village within the memory of man. He had even had business connections as far afield as Sora. Some of the light from his halo seemed still to encompass his widow. Thomas bowed respectfully at the threshold. It was clear to him that he was in the presence of the widowed queen of Settevetri.

Matteo looked sharply around the room. " Are you alone? " he asked.

" I'm always alone," she hissed at him. " Haven't you grasped that yet? "

Matteo's mother was dead, and *la nonna*, his father's mother, was still the only woman in his life. She kept house for him as far as her strength allowed and never tired of exhorting him to think not only of the future of the village but also of the continuance of his family. But Matteo was definitely afraid of bringing a strange woman into the house and preferred to hire a girl from the village to do the rough work.

" You know Assunta is back again," he told his grandmother.

" Assunta? " she replied in the same tone. " She's feeling badly. The walk was far too much for her. You should have thought of that."

Matteo flushed like a youth. " How could I . . . ? " he began.

" Ah, you men never understand anything. I can only tell you she vomited so much that Fausto and I had to sit with her the whole evening. In the end we had to send for Dottoressa. She gave her some medicine which made her better. As always, you others couldn't guess anything, may the Lord forgive you!"

Matteo shrugged his shoulders and looked unhappy. Turning to Thomas almost apologetically, he said: "This is my grandmother, Father. Would you ever believe that she's ninety-five years old?"

"Ninety-seven," the old woman corrected him. "I was fifty-eight the time of the great earthquake. You can't even remember that."

"Of course I remember," declared Matteo, but he did not sound too sure.

La nonna nodded tolerantly. "You know," she said to Thomas, "he's too young to have had any great experiences yet, but he's the only one left to me."

"Have you had many children, Signora?" the guest enquired politely.

"Eleven."

She looked him over quickly as if she were estimating his weight, then, turning to her grandson, she said: "He speaks Italian very well. Is he a good Christian?"

"But, Grandmother," said Matteo, horrified, "he's a priest!"

"I've never seen a priest wearing such good clothes. What's he doing here?"

"He's a good friend of Padre Barnaba and he came with the pilgrims from Santissima Trinità."

The sparkling black eyes suddenly became tense: "You're Assunta's friend, aren't you?" she asked.

"Yes," replied Thomas as timidly as if he were admitting a fault.

For two embarrassed minutes she scrutinized him before she said: "It's easy to see you weren't born this side of the Liri. Still you seem very clever. Do you understand what I'm saying?"

"Yes."

"And did you also understand what Assunta said?"

"Yes."

"I don't believe it. If you did, she wouldn't be here."

"But she came here on account of her father."

"Now don't try to push it on to poor Fausto! Our Lord Himself said a girl must leave her father and mother and follow her
husband."

"Yes, when she's grown-up."

La nonna screwed up her eyes until only two narrow slits were
visible. "When is a person grown-up?" she said slowly. "I'll
tell you, Signorino. When he feels love in his heart, and not
till then, even if his coat has been made by the best tailor in
Rome!"

❦

XXXI LO ZOCCOLO

In the afternoon Thomas decided to climb the curious limestone
peak which surmounted the village, but he had hardly stepped
out on the square when he met a fair-haired lady in a green wind-
cheater with the hood pulled up. She wore heavy mountain boots
and was carrying a pick-axe in her hand and she had the air of an
obstinate child about her.

"I'm Dottoressa Vanna, Monsignor," she said, smiling at him
in an indulgent, motherly way as she held out a plump hand.
"Are you going up Lo Zoccolo?"

So even one's unspoken intentions could not remain secret in
this little place!

The Dottoressa had an air of nonchalance which did not seem
quite genuine. Her mouth was sensitive, her eyes almost melancholy, and curiously restless as if in search of a definite object
in life, yet fearful of focusing on any living being.

"I have already heard of you," said Thomas without answering
her question. "Aren't you the medical officer of Settevetri?"

"No, not really. It's a purely personal arrangement. One has to
strike camp somewhere. You see, I'm a nomad. But you needn't
look at my equipment with such astonishment." With a laugh
she raised the pickaxe. "I'm not taking it up to the mountain-

R

top, but only to the caves. You've heard about them, of course? "

" I'm afraid I haven't."

" Is that possible? They are the most interesting things to be seen up here – from the archaeological point of view. I heard that you too have studied archaeology? Isn't that so? "

" A long time ago. But I had no idea that discoveries had been made in this region."

There was a touch of triumph in the Dottoressa's faint smile as she answered: " Others don't know about them either, but if you are interested, I'll show them to you. You see, archaeology is my hobby."

She led him along a cool, shady lane that wound like a stairway up to the back of the village. Then they walked along a narrow passage between the last row of houses and a steep rock-face. Stones and rubble made walking exceedingly difficult.

The old caves were now used by the villagers as cellars and rubbish dumps. The entrances were all nailed up with boards, except one that led into a large empty chamber. The floor was the original rock; tools and measuring instruments were strewn around. It could be seen that human hands had been working on the rock walls, and several fragments of grey-brown pottery and bits of metal covered with verdigris were spread out on a cask near the door.

" So far I have only been able to work systematically in this cave," said Dottoressa Vanna dejectedly. " The others are still filled with things I dare not shift; but I'll do them in their turn. Now, I should photograph these things here, of course, but I don't have the equipment. . . ."

Thomas looked around him. The cave was definitely interesting, but the operations in hand were absurdly amateurish.

" Yes, one could win world fame here," continued the Dottoressa. " I can prove that there were people living in this village long before the Capitol was built in Rome. This was a place of refuge in olden times. Under the houses there are remains of prehistoric fortifications, and these caves were apparently places of religious worship, perhaps the oldest in the whole Apennine Peninsula. Do you know what that means? "

"No."

"It may mean that I have discovered a Samnite Delphi. Do you understand? "

He did not dare to look at her, but began showing a polite interest in the pieces of pottery, though he was not expert enough to decide whether they were really of archaeological value.

"I imagine these caves were formerly used as goat-stalls? " he suggested.

She smiled tolerantly. "Most people think I'm crazy," she said. "I've found a gold-mine but I can't work it. After all, I'm only a poor woman without proper authority. I lack money and strength for a task like this. I really need a man to help me, but there isn't anyone suitable for miles around. Little Gianni is interested, it's true, but he's far too simple and ignorant. You are actually the first educated man I've come across whom I could rely upon in this matter."

"What makes you think you could? " asked Thomas, almost discourteously.

"We have a mutual friend in Rome who spoke highly of you."

"Who on earth is that? "

"Don Achille of San Lino."

Thomas felt the blood rushing to his face. "What made Don Achille commend me to someone in Settevetri? "

"If I'm not mistaken he mentioned you as the person he would like best to succeed him when we were discussing the question."

"To succeed him? "

"Well of course he has been made Rector of the Seminary in Aosta. Didn't you know that? "

"I did hear a rumour to that effect, but I should never have expected to have it confirmed to me here in Settevetri."

Dottoressa Vanna smiled her unfathomable smile. "It may interest you to know that Don Achille and I have been friends since our youth," she said. "We used to do a lot of climbing in the Alps when he still had the use of both his legs."

"I admire Don Achille sincerely. He's exceptionally capable."

"A bit too capable," interjected the doctor a little sharply. "It was a misfortune that he broke his leg. Up till then he allowed himself certain human weaknesses."

"He is greatly beloved as parish priest of San Lino."

"I'm glad to hear that. It seems then that some of his old character still survives in spite of all his perfections. Assunta too gave a very good account of him."

"I can well believe that. It's a pity he couldn't have kept her in his parish. If he had, things might have turned out differently for her."

Dottoressa Vanna seemed somewhat surprised. "You're certainly right there," she said. "It was a great mistake to take her away from her environment."

"I didn't mean that."

"I know well what you mean, but I still stick to my view. Assunta is a dear creature, but she does not fit into Settevetri. She has her mother's nature, and she simply freezes to the marrow when faced with too wide a horizon. What she wants is to have a snug home in a narrow lane, with good neighbours around her, and to know that the father of her children is playing cards outside the wineshop in the nearest piazza, not running around the mountains after stray sheep."

"You certainly know her better than I do," remarked Thomas a trifle curtly.

"Well, I wouldn't say that; but I attended her when she was ill and I certainly believe she spoke with sincerity."

"How is she now? I hear the long walk got her down a bit."

"She's getting over it, but she has to be careful in her condition."

"What's wrong with her, then?"

The Dottoressa stared at him, astonished. "It came out that she's expecting a child?" she said. "Didn't you know that? It would hardly be wise to send her on any more pilgrimages this year."

"Excuse me for asking such a stupid question. I should have guessed it was that," murmured Thomas, abashed. "And now, if you don't mind, I'll continue my walk while there's still daylight."

Behind the seven cottages a narrow pathway led up to the

limestone rocks. The climb proved more severe than it had promised to be, and the sun was already setting by the time Thomas reached the top.

Lo Zoccolo was deeply scarred and pitted with holes and ruts, and exceedingly difficult to climb. The rock was quite bare almost everywhere. Only a few miserable shrubs and creeping plants grew here and there in the crevices. The rays of the setting sun still lit up the yellowish rock, but the plateau far down below was already enveloped in a delicate violet veil. It was as though the earth were covering its face with the purple of mourning, while the lonely mountain summit still rose up freely towards the bright sky. Its outline became more and more unreal, and the rugged spikes took on strangely picturesque forms.

A little way off the path stood the Madonna of the Shepherds. She had the same faded blue garment and golden halo as the Santa Presenza statue, but here she was out in the open under God's free heaven, with no protection from wind or weather. Erected on a rock that formed a natural base, she seemed to be looking down observantly on the village. Her arms were stretched out in a motherly gesture, as if she were calling an excited crowd of children to come to her. She was smiling to herself at the doings of man but was too kind to disclose the pettiness of human activities. There she stood in the world of dreams, like an envoy from the realm of reality. Philosophers and martyrs all spoke far too difficult a language for the children of men to understand. She alone had such gentle hands and such light footsteps, that she could move about the world of mankind without destroying its castles in the air or trampling its toy towns. She only opened the discreet door to the sunlit reality. And behind her the birds sang and the wind blew across life's Mount of Purification.

If you do not become as little children . . .

But up there, in the midst of the unearthly stillness, someone was weeping with the abandonment of despair. Thomas went nearer and caught sight of a familiar little figure, which was crouching, shaken by sobs, at the other side of the statue.

"Don't cry, Assunta," he said, hesitantly, "everything will come right in the end."

The girl looked up astonished. For a moment her eyes met his, but then looked away as if into an immeasurable distance.

"There's no need to cry," he repeated. "All is not lost."

"I'm not worried about myself," murmured Assunta, her face still turned away.

"Is there anything I can do . . . ? "

Now she looked at him again, just long enough for him to see the despair in her eyes.

"I'm only worried about Cesarino," she whispered hardly audibly.

"What's the matter with him? "

"He's so violent. God knows what he'll take it into his head to do when he finds out I've gone away."

"Didn't you tell him that you were going home? "

"But he wasn't in Rome, Reverendo. He'd gone on a journey through the mountains. He'll be demented. What on earth shall I do? "

She must be terribly tired, thought Thomas. She should go to bed instead of sitting here torturing herself about things that may not happen. And then, to his surprise he heard himself saying: "You should ask Cesarino to come to Settevetri."

She stared at him, baffled. "But why? He has a horror of Settevetri," she said.

"When he knows you're here perhaps he'll overcome his horror for a few days. Don't you think so? "

"What would he do here? "

"Talk to your father."

Assunta shook her head disconsolately. "It wouldn't be any use," she said.

"I can't imagine that Fausto would refuse at least to listen to Sor Anacleto's son – after all that has happened."

"Father can't stand Cesarino," she said, casting down her eyes and flushing deeply.

"But if you have a good talk with Cesarino first. . . ."

"There's only one person he'll listen to."

"Who is that? "

"Doctor Romolo."

Thomas, startled, began nervously polishing his pince-nez. "Doctor Romolo, how could he get here?"

A sudden gleam of hope came into the girl's eyes. "I have asked Our Lady to show him the way," she said.

A high, clear chant, earnest and monotonous as an oriental hour-prayer, suddenly rose from the village. It seemed to leap up the mountain in spurts as if hindered on its way by the boulders and ledges of rock, and isolated responses which sounded like distant whispers echoed through the crystal-clear air. Someone was singing a message to the shepherds on the plateau and the voice sounded like Padre Barnaba's. Listening intently, Thomas caught the words: "Behold the handmaid of the Lord . . ."

"The Angelus," whispered Assunta, falling on her knees.

Thomas looked down at Settevetri, which lay like a fairy village, bathed in the brilliant, romantic hues of the sunset. He began wondering how the little hamlet and its inhabitants looked in the eyes of the Blessed Virgin – Matteo and his grandmother, Luca and his dogs, Gianni and his books, Dottoressa Vanna and her fragments of ancient pottery. They all had their particular interest in life. Thomas could not help smiling as he visualized Romolo walking up the village street, his small eyes, in which suspicion struggled with an honest inclination to laugh, scanning the line of huddled cottages. Then he realized that Doctor Romolo had preserved in his inmost heart the same child-like confidence in the powers of good which animated this little community. But whilst the humble shepherds of Settevetri placed their confidence in the best of all shepherds, Romolo, like an inquisitive schoolboy, sought his happiness in the mysteries of nature. Was there really such a great difference between the shepherds' road and Romolo's? Were they not striving towards the same goal, the one on the sunny side, the other on the shady one? And perhaps there was also a Madonna standing somewhere by the side of Romolo's stony road as he marched undauntedly along.

When he awoke from his day-dream, Assunta had disappeared. The sun too was gone and only its reflection was left, but he managed to reach Fausto's house before darkness had fallen completely.

"Fausto," he said, " may I give your greetings to Sor Anacleto? "

"Why, of course," replied Fausto warmly. "He's a good fellow."

"And his son Cesarino – may I give him your greetings too?"

Fausto remained silent.

"Don't you think he'll turn out just as good a fellow as his father?"

"It's hard to know."

"They say his friends think a lot of him."

"I can well believe that, but it doesn't make the matter any better."

"What matter?"

"Well, that he's a Communist. He's bad."

"Hm. Does Our Lady say so too?"

"I haven't brought her into this," said Fausto indignantly. "Cesarino certainly has nothing to do with her."

"How do you know?"

Fausto jumped up. "But he doesn't even want to be married in church!" he cried in deep distress.

"That's just why Our Lady is waiting outside. . . ."

"But he – he's even been heard to deny God."

Thomas replied with a forcefulness which surprised even himself. "But what if he has deep in his heart something very precious – something which many have lost? That is, the ability to say 'Yes' to God's greatest gift, namely life, from which, after all, faith, hope and charity spring. It may be only a matter of sowing the right seed and then taking care that it is not suffocated by weeds. Ask your daughter, Fausto, whether she feels ready to do that. And if she says yes, you have no right to refuse your parental blessing. . . ."

Fausto looked out of the window desperately, and clutched his head as though trying to free himself of the intolerable burden of thought which Thomas had thrust upon him. But no, it was not possible to evade the problem. It was as though Cesarino himself had impudently stuck his foot in the doorway, and stood there demanding an answer.

"I'll think it over," muttered Fausto submissively.

"It's more than three thousand feet from here to the summit," said Luca, "but the climb isn't very difficult."

Padre Barnaba laughed. "Not for you, of course," he said, "but think of Don Tommaso's poor feet. Two days' rest are not enough after the long march he has made. He was very tired when he arrived."

"I wasn't used to the mountain air," said Thomas, "but I feel much better already. And we could do it slowly."

Padre Barnaba shrugged his shoulders. "You know best yourself," he said, "but don't forget to come down again. I'll go up a bit of the way with you."

Leaving the village street they took the narrow path up the mountain. Again and again since his arrival in Settevetri, Thomas's eyes had strayed up to the gleaming white summit, visible from every angle, which gave the impression of being a mystical centre of gravity towards which this whole remote parish was drawn.

"There must be a wonderful view from up there," said Thomas longingly.

Padre Barnaba nodded. "Saint Linus thought that too, and that's why he came down again. That's really the moral of the whole legend."

"I never heard about that."

"Of course it's only a legend. But up on the summit you will come across the remains of a little stone hut which has been there from time immemorial. Linus is said to have built it in his youth. He had retired to the wilderness to fast and do penance, as holy men used to do. A few shepherds had led him up there and he was so bewitched by the beauty of the scene that he resolved to remain there always, living as a hermit beneath God's free sky. But one day a lone shepherd, whom no one knew, came to him. He was strong and handsome and he said he had walked all the way from Rome to look for one of his sheep that had

strayed away into the mountains here. When Linus told him of
his decision he shook his head sadly and said that one could not
look into Heaven even from the highest mountain in the world.
It was only pride that drove people up to the mountains, for
Christ Himself lived down below among those who had taken
Him into their hearts. And he succeeded in persuading Linus to
come down with him. But when they reached Settevetri and sat
down to eat, it happened as with the disciples in Emmaus – Christ
revealed Himself to him in the breaking of bread. Since then the
pathway by which Our Saviour led Linus back to the world has
been called the *Passo Santo* – the Holy Path. . . ."

They passed close by the Madonna of the Shepherds, who stood
with her arms stretched out, as if she were beckoning them.

"I usually say my office here," said Padre Barnaba, turning
away in the direction of the statue.

Luca now led the way. He strode on slowly ahead, his pipe in
his mouth. Thomas found the speed almost too slow, but he
noticed that the other had set his pace intentionally to reserve
their strength. The climb was more difficult than he had antici-
pated, as the path was covered with sharp flints. After the first
few bends it became steeper and steeper. Thomas had to slacken
his pace for want of breath, and soon found himself a long way
behind his guide. Violent palpitations of the heart compelled him
to sit down. Luca came back to him laughing but obviously surprised that his companion should have to take the first rest so soon.

Thomas felt almost ashamed. He was still within earshot of
Padre Barnaba, whose white hair and devoutly bowed head could
be seen distinctly beside the little statue of the Madonna.

"Do you come up here often? " he asked.

Luca shook his head. "Only in high summer," he replied. "The
pasturage is poor at this height."

The grassy slopes were parched and brown and the broom was
scantier higher up the mountain. At the next resting place Thomas
could see only occasional tufts of grass and a little moss between
the boulders. He felt slightly dizzy when he looked down. Settevetri looked like an unreal oasis, the flecks of green on the plateau
below like a fata morgana over a desert of salt.

Close to Fontenuova a little bright green square, well fenced
and cared, caught the eye. It was as though angels' hands had
carried it from some more fertile land and planted it on this poor
barren mountain for some mysterious purpose. Thomas could not
suppress a surprised question.

"That's a wheat field," replied Luca solemnly. "We call it the
Agro Sacro."

"And why is it called the Holy Acre?"

Luca smiled. "Because it belongs to Our Lord," he said. "We
get our Eucharistic bread from there."

"Do you mean what we had the day before yesterday at the
Buon Pastore?"

"Yes, indeed. We never use any other wheat for the Holy
Bread."

"Do you raise a special kind of wheat there?"

"It has been growing there as long as I can remember. I don't
know where it came from originally. It yields large full ears of
corn. But the earth was carried up on donkeys from far away in
the Roveto Valley."

"That is most extraordinary," murmured Thomas. He recalled
having read, in accounts of medieval life, that special land was
tilled to grow wheat for the sacramental bread, but he had never
heard of the custom having been kept up to the present day.

"Who cultivates the field?"

"Padre Barnaba actually, but we all help when necessary. It's
a matter of honour to the whole village that good wheat should
grow in the Lord's field."

Thomas stood up. "That would be a suitable task for someone
like me," he said with a quiet laugh. "I would willingly serve as
a labourer of Our Lord if I might work with my hands in His field.
Shall we go on now?"

The path became more and more difficult and now led over
naked mountain strewn with boulders and deeply creviced.

"Be sure never to use your knees for climbing," Luca warned
him.

Thomas hardly heard him, for his thoughts had strayed back to
the little green square below. To sow the seeds from which the

altar Bread would spring. . . . To harvest the wheat which Our
Lord would change into His own flesh. Whoever ploughed that
field must truly have pure hands. He was so absorbed in his
thoughts that he did not notice that the tension in his neck and
the beating of his pulse became more intense the higher up he
climbed. Finally a piercing pain in the back of his head forced
him to stop.

This time he could not ignore the symptoms. His nerves were
vibrating as if from electric shocks. There was a drumming in his
ears and his mouth filled with saliva. In a few moments more the
familiar iron grip in his neck would set in and would not relax
for many hours. He remembered that the doctors had warned him
against air travel, but that was so long ago that he had not thought
of the similar danger in mountain-climbing.

He sat down on the ground, wiped his face with his handkerchief and stealthily pressed a flat stone against the nape of his
neck. He did not want to admit to himself that he was having
this recurrence of his old malady. He looked up longingly at the
mountain top where he could distinctly see frozen snow in the
crevices. There did not seem to be much of it and it was probably
as hard as the rock, but it would certainly relieve the dreadful
burning in his head.

"Have we much farther to go?" he asked to divert Luca's
attention from himself.

"It's a good stretch more," said Luca, glancing suspiciously at
Thomas's handkerchief. "There's a brook somewhere hereabouts
if you'd like water."

The brook proved to be a mere trickle dripping down from a
melting snow-drift above. Nevertheless the icy cold water gradually relieved the strange glow in his head, and the pain. Two
things were clear to Thomas – that he would need all his strength
to come down the mountain again without collapsing, and that he
would never be able to climb right to the top of Monte Lino.

Again he looked upwards. Unimaginably remote from the earth
in its dazzling whiteness and pitilessly cold, the mountain summit
stood outlined against the deep blue summer sky. But below its
shimmering snowfields, the landscape was Dantesque in its horror;

for the summit was encircled by a grey-black stony wasteland
that gave a terrifying impression of bleakness.

With a shudder Thomas looked down, but there was not a sign
of life to be seen down below either; nothing but the usual midday spirals of smoke circling fine as foam from Settevetri over the
great limestone cliff which hid the roofs of the houses. Thomas
felt dizzy. The sight that unfolded before him seemed too much
for human eyes. All around stood the high mountains in menac-
ing columns as though only waiting for a sign to march – stern,
solemn giants, who seemed to question the right of mortals to
climb up into those cosmic regions. In the vivid light a fantastic
variety of enchanting colours, from copper-brown and flame to
blue and lilac, played over their broad naked shoulders. With an
awe-stricken shudder Thomas discerned a shining streak on the
horizon behind the Simbruini in the west. It was the Tyrrhenian
Sea, gleaming like molten gold. Then he perceived just the same
kind of shining streak behind the Maiella in the north-east – the
Adriatic.

Suddenly he felt as though he would suffocate. "Now I'm beginning to understand your legend," he said, looking over almost
appealingly at Luca.

But Luca, who had sat down too and was filling his pipe, took
little notice.

"I think it's time we turned back," continued Thomas. "I
have learned the lesson of the *Passo Santo*."

Luca looked at him uneasily now. "Do you feel better,
Reverendo?" he asked.

"Yes, thank you, I'll be all right once we're down again."

Luca puckered up his face and nodded significantly. "You're
not the first to be taken ill up here," he said. "It's not at all a
healthy place. Indeed, it must have been on a mountain like this
that the devil tempted Christ. It seems as though a demon might
be hanging around here, doesn't it?"

"That's possible," replied Thomas, standing up with difficulty.
"Now I'll try again."

Luca jumped up, visibly relieved. "Perhaps we shall be home
for dinner," he said.

But they did not manage that, for going down was even slower than going up, and Thomas had to rest many times to save himself from collapsing completely. "We shouldn't have climbed so high. It was very foolish," said Luca, full of sympathy.

"Don't say that. No one knows the ways of the Lord."

"Christ will not come back this way."

Luca's positive tone made Thomas smile. "How do you know that?" he asked.

"I don't know, of course," replied Luca in the same serious tone. "There's only one thing we do know for certain, and that is that He will come one day from somewhere or other. We're all waiting for that day."

"Don't you find it enough that He is among you in the Blessed Eucharist?"

"I'm always hoping to be permitted to see Him in the flesh," came the humble reply. "All of us here in the village are hoping for that."

"That sounds as though you were expecting Him any day."

"Well, He said Himself that's what we should do."

"He did not mean it that way."

Luca took the pipe from his mouth and shot a spit out in front of him with military precision. "I know, of course," he said, "that man should not try to fathom the will of God. But, after all, it is to happen some day, and the time is getting shorter year by year. Isn't that so?"

"We do not know how the Lord measures the passing of time in the world."

Luca thoughtfully knocked the ashes out of his pipe. "Marco sometimes brings newspapers back from Castelpendente," he said. "True, I don't understand much of what's in them; but sometimes I think to myself: the Day of Judgment can't be far off."

What could one say to such a statement? The shadow of a smile, like the reflection from a fire alight inside a cave, crossed Luca's dark features as he continued: "May I ask you something, Father? Is it wrong to feel happy at this thought? You know, I don't wish anyone any harm . . ."

It was late afternoon when Thomas tottered into Padre

Barnaba's house. The old priest was quite alarmed. "Oh, my dear friend, you're ill," he exclaimed.

"I'm only tired," said Thomas. "I'll be all right soon."

Padre Barnaba eyed him. "A man in good health doesn't get as tired as all that. Won't you see a doctor?"

"That wouldn't make me any better."

"To neglect one's health, especially up here in Settevetri, is tempting Providence," said Padre Barnaba sternly. Then he disappeared and in half an hour returned with Dottoressa Vanna. "What's the matter?" she asked. "Mountain sickness?"

"I don't think so," replied Thomas. "Anyway, I feel much better already." Seeing Padre Barnaba's enquiring glance, he added apologetically: "It's probably the result of an old war injury."

Dottoressa Vanna examined him quickly. "What did you say it was?" she asked.

"Nothing – a mere trifle."

"Even trifles generally have some medical name."

"I've forgotten it."

The doctor looked appealingly at Padre Barnaba, who said rather sternly: "If you really make an effort you will remember the name."

"The doctors mentioned an enlargement of a blood vessel in the brain," replied Thomas obediently.

"But that's not a war injury, is it?" objected the doctor.

"No, but it was discovered at the same time that I was injured."

She shook her head dubiously. "And have you had no treatment for it all these years?" she asked.

"What could I do? I thought it was healed."

Again she glanced significantly at Padre Barnaba. "Of course if all goes well he can live to be a hundred," she said, "but better not in Settevetri. He must definitely see a specialist as soon as he returns to Rome."

She wrote a little note and stuck it into an envelope. "Give this to Professor Fortunato," she said. "And no more mountaineering without his permission, please!"

Thomas slept the whole evening. Towards nine o'clock someone came in and left a tray with bread, cheese, ham and salad, and a jug of cold water, near his bed. He thought at first it was Padre Barnaba, but when he turned round to say "Thank you" he saw a young girl tiptoeing towards the door. It was Assunta.

"Sleep well, Reverendo!" she said with a smile, looking back over her shoulder.

❧

XXXIII FONTENUOVA

Thomas passed a quiet night. Early in the morning Padre Barnaba came and asked him if he would like to say Mass down in the village chapel. It was the Feast of Corpus Christi.

Thomas had not said Mass since he had left Santissima Trinità. Somewhat surprised, he agreed.

"Of course, only if you feel able," added Padre Barnaba, "but I thought it would do you good after all the mountain climbing."

"Yes, there's certainly nothing better I could do."

"We really can't manage processions in this region, but everyone who can possibly do so will come to church. If you like I shall serve your Mass."

Thomas found the Fontenuova chapel just as uninteresting inside as outside. It had nothing of the archaic atmosphere that seemed to mark the religious life of Settevetri.

Padre Barnaba noticed his disappointment and said: "There used to be a lovely little ancient church here, but it was completely destroyed in the earthquake of forty years ago, and this one was built in a great hurry. Unfortunately it didn't turn out as beautiful as the old one."

Meantime the church had filled. There were sweet-smelling meadow flowers on the altar and the fresh air poured in the open door. Thomas's thoughts wandered back involuntarily to Santa Maria degli Ulivi and he felt almost as tremulous as he had before his first Mass. The words of the Introit were before his eyes:

"He fed them with the fat of wheat, alleluia; and filled them with honey from the rock . . ."

The Feast of Corpus Christi! So the triumphal procession in Orvieto had turned into a lifelong pilgrimage – over paths that had become steeper and steeper, and had finally led him to this poor little mountain chapel. The climb up Monte Lino had been the last stage. Now he was standing like a beggar before the altar, groping with clumsy hands at the door to the Holy of Holies.

When he came to the Epistle he was hardly able to control the emotion in his voice as he read:

"Brethren, I have received of the Lord that which also I delivered unto you, that the Lord Jesus, the same night in which He was betrayed, took bread, and giving thanks, broke, and said, Take ye and eat: this is my Body which shall be delivered for you; this do in remembrance of me. . . ."

It had become deadly quiet behind him in the church as he stood with eyes closed and hands raised. In spirit he was in the Inn of the Good Shepherd once more, waiting for the coming of the Lord. But he only heard Filippo's magnificent voice striking up Saint Thomas Aquinas's hymn to the Good Shepherd. The familiar text now had new and vivid associations for Thomas. He had come a long way, he had fallen and bled, but he felt he had come really nearer to his goal. Up here in the mountains the Lord had passed, and the rough shepherds' voices behind him in the church were rejoicing as fervently and simply as they had once rejoiced around the stable in Bethlehem. The road still led uphill, but now his feet stepped over the stones without effort, and his eyes no longer dwelt on the glory of the world. He offered a prayer for all those who were still struggling along on the dark side of the road of life.

After Mass, Matteo asked to speak to him. Obviously he had something important to say. A little group of men – Filippo, Luca, Gianni and Marco – were waiting outside, all looking equally solemn.

"How do you like Settevetri?" asked the wool-dealer.

"I've never liked any place better," Thomas assured him.

Luca observed him anxiously. "You don't think it was a bit too much for you yesterday . . . ?" he asked.

S

"Not in the least," lied Thomas bravely. "I think one would get used to it in time."

Matteo's face lit up with pleasure. "That's certain. And we would be very happy to have you with us for a long time more."

"And I – I'd be only too glad to stay."

Filippo laid his rough hand on Thomas's shoulder. "We would like to be your friends, Father," he said. "Not many strangers understand our way of life."

Thomas involuntarily passed his hand over the back of his head. So far he felt no danger-signal; but would he be able to manage the climb back to Settevetri without getting a new attack?

Gianni noticed the gesture and took it as a sign of hesitation. "It's true, there's not much suitable for a man of your gifts to do here, Reverendo, but still you needn't be afraid that you would not have enough work."

"We have an old rule that every traveller may stay with us three days if he wishes to," added Matteo. "He needs that time to rest, of course. But after that he must take on some work if he wants to stay on. And it's not always so easy to settle that."

Evidently these men sincerely wished him to stay, not as a townsman on holiday but as a real member of their community. Here association with strangers followed very ancient rules. Anyone who did not participate in the work of the community was not permitted to participate in their agape. So that was the question – the work of the community.

"No, indeed it's not easy," he replied, somewhat perplexed. "I'm afraid I'd make a very bad shepherd."

The wool-dealer's eyes questioned the others. Then he turned to Thomas once more. "May I make a suggestion, Father?" he asked.

"And what is that?"

"You are a good friend of Padre Barnaba, and you see that he is getting old. He would certainly be glad of a helping hand now and then."

"That's true."

"To be quite frank, we would really need a younger priest here, who could come down and say Mass in Fontenuova oftener."

'Let your communication be, Yea, yea; Nay, nay,' thought Thomas. But he only said: "Doesn't the appointment of priests, even in Settevetri, lie with the bishop?"

"Of course it does," replied Filippo, "but there's no great choice."

"Did you talk it over with Padre Barnaba?"

"We shall do so today if you wish. He will certainly be very glad, because he's very much attached to you," said Luca.

Thomas looked around the circle and caught Matteo's eyes. "Some land goes with the chapel too," said Matteo, with a humorous twinkle. "Come and see."

Immediately below Fontenuova they turned off from the road. Marco, singing merrily, ran up to a little hill and beckoned them with an osier rod. Down in a hollow at the other side, Thomas saw the little field Luca had pointed out to him the day before from the mountain.

"*Agro Sacro*," said Luca.

A paved pathway to it led through the brushwood. The sun shone kindly over the slope and a smell of strong earth and growing wheat rose from the ground.

"Up to the present Padre Barnaba has tilled the field," Matteo explained, "but it is gradually getting too much for him. Marco does what he can, of course, but it should really be a priest."

"To cultivate the field?" asked Thomas, surprised.

"Yes."

"But why?"

Matteo shrugged his shoulders. "It has always been so," he said.

"Perhaps it is because the priest has no one else to work for," said Gianni.

"Or because he understands better than we others do how Our Lord likes His bread," said Filippo.

"Or because he is to eat it himself," interjected Luca.

Thomas had to smile. "I think Luca comes nearest to the truth," he said. "One who is not willing to work should not eat. Or what does Marco think? Hasn't he worked on this too?"

Marco seemed embarrassed. "Padre Barnaba is just as good a

farmer as any of us. He has given much more time and trouble to this little field than you would imagine."

"Oh, I can well believe that," said Thomas seriously, "but it requires a special knowledge that not every priest possesses."

Marco nodded towards a niche in the stone wall opposite, in which stood a little wooden statue overgrown with foliage. It looked like a forgotten rustic deity from antiquity. "Ask Saint Joseph. Nothing at all would grow here without his help," he said.

"I shall do that in due course, but first I must speak to Padre Barnaba."

As usual Padre Barnaba was able to answer his question. "There is no official rule that the field must be cultivated by a priest," he said, "but there has not been a priest in Settevetri for a long time who has not done it. And it's not just a matter of the ploughing," he continued laughing. He led Thomas to a large storeroom that smelled strongly of corn. Inside were four huge earthenware jars, a wooden box, and an unwieldy handmill of ancient design. "Do you think you could turn it?" he asked, pointing to the mill.

"I – do you mean?" asked Thomas surprised.

"You can grind the corn whatever way you like, but I can assure you from experience that this mill is the very best kind. Besides, turning it is an extremely healthy exercise for both soul and body."

Thomas looked dubiously at the heavy handle. "I'll take on the work if the doctor allows it," he said.

"Then see that you get your health back," Padre Barnaba advised him earnestly. "If you had shown more of that spirit fifteen years ago I would have been glad to allow you to remain in Santa Presenza. It is just the spirit we tried to foster in our monastery. It is the fruit of humility, work and prayer, and cannot be produced artificially. But I think you have acquired the spirit – and therefore you are welcome to return to Settevetri later."

"Up here it's easier to understand such things. But how have you managed to preserve the same spirit out in the world."

"By dedicating our lives to the presence of Christ in the Blessed Sacrament," Padre Barnaba replied. "But – how few remember that He is still among us all the time! How many approach the Sacrament with pride in their hearts! How many betray His Body and Blood again and again! Have you ever considered how much evil has been caused in the world by sins against the Blessed Sacrament?"

"Perhaps I do understand a little," admitted Thomas.

※ ※ ※

XXXIV   THE GARDEN OF PARADISE

Dottoressa Vanna came again in the afternoon. "So you were about early this morning?" she said, with obvious disapproval.

"Yes, I was down in Fontenuova."

"And you didn't feel any pain?"

"None at all," Thomas assured her, already regretting that he had been so frank the evening before.

"I don't believe you. You must avoid any physical strain whatsoever. I really came to tell you that there will be a mule here in half an hour to take you to Castelpendente."

"Did you arrange that for me?" he asked suspiciously.

"No, a coach ran into a ditch somewhere near the Passo del Diavolo, and the passengers have been roaming about in the mountains. Marco has promised to get them to Castelpendente. He's collecting the mules now."

Thomas decided to treat the matter as a joke. "Do you definitely want to drive me out of paradise?" he asked.

"Yes, indeed I do. This opportunity has come just at the right time."

"For you or for me?"

"For you."

"And what if I refuse to leave?"

"In that case I would ask you not to consult me again. But what would you do here, anyway?"

"What people do in paradise. I could help Padre Barnaba with his rough work, if nothing else."

"That's just what you could not do. Moreover, I should like to tell you that you simply don't fit into this paradise."

"Why not?"

"Because you know too much."

He seemed surprised. "I? What am I supposed to know?" he asked.

"Don Achille says you are one of the most learned men he has ever met."

"Don Achille is somewhat addicted to superlatives. I assure you I've forgotten everything I learned."

She laughed. "I can well imagine that Adam said exactly the same to the archangel before he was thrown out," she said ironically. "But you cannot forget – that is, if you want to preserve your intellect, sinful though it is."

"What do you mean?"

"No quibbling, please! Living here among these people one comes on strange ideas. It is as though they had untilled fields in their brain-boxes whereas we hide away our darkest experiences in ours. Have you ever seen Gianni read a book?"

"No, except religious texts at mealtimes."

"He reads a lot besides, but of course only what is 'true'."

"I'm afraid you're simplifying the problem."

The doctor smiled feebly. "No, I certainly don't do that," she said. "As far as Gianni is concerned there isn't any problem at all. He only reads things which his conscience tells him are clever and good and useful. That is childishly simple."

"You're really malicious."

"Very likely I am. But after all, I'm the serpent in this paradise."

"How is that?"

"I try to lead the young people astray."

He looked at her intently. "How do you do that?" he asked.

"I read with Gianni, for instance – in secret, of course. We hide under a big hazel bush below Fontenuova. I call it the tree of knowledge. You cannot see it from the path, because it's down in a ravine. No one has found us out yet."

"I don't quite understand. . . ."

"You needn't be afraid. We don't read any prohibited books. And if we do chance on anything questionable, Gianni shakes it off like dirty water rather than let it poison his subconscious mind."

"And what do you read together?"

"Mostly languages, he for heaven, I for hell. Presumably Latin is spoken in both places. Gianni only learns for heaven, of course. Once I tried archaeology on him, but our ideas on the subject were too utterly opposed."

"Only a couple of days ago you said he was so ignorant?"

"Yes, indeed, and I wanted to help him to improve his deficient education. But he doesn't show the least interest in scholarly matters; he says, in fact, that the past only interests him in so far as it has a bearing on the future. Do you know what the people of Settevetri mean by the future?"

"No."

"They start out from the same fact as all other reasonable people. It's only the way they look at the matter that is different."

"What fact do you mean?"

The doctor threw him one of her fleeting glances. "That the world is not going to last much longer," she said.

"How do you come to that conclusion?"

"I read the signs in the stars and the dripping of water. They all point in the same direction."

"I thought you said fact," he remarked dryly.

"What kind of a priest are you to want facts instead of believing! The truth is that Our Lord gave us the choice – and we chose to roll downwards. Any child can see that we are rolling faster and faster. I agree entirely with Gianni in this."

"No," said Thomas sternly, "we shouldn't think that. Others will come after us."

"Yes, unfortunately."

"Why unfortunately?"

"Because our natural feeling for posterity these days should be solely one of pity."

Thomas looked away. "Every generation has the same hopes," he said. "That is why there is a Church on earth."

"But surely you don't mean to say that the world has become better since they built Saint Peter's?"

"The task of the Church is not so much to make the world better as to teach people to live better for a coming world."

"No, no!" protested the doctor. "Let us not hide our heads in the sand. You know as well as I do that the end must come one day. In spite of everything the thought of this is rather terrifying for ordinary mortals, but Gianni isn't afraid at all. He is honestly interested, and sees the matter solely from the point of view which he calls the true one – in contrast to us others, who have the doubtful advantage of being able to look down into hell too."

"Now you're indulging in fantasies. . . ."

She gave him a sad little smile. "If you could stay here somewhat longer you would notice that you were living in the company of wise children of nature. It is clear to all of them how things are going with our world and that the end may come at any time. It simply makes an unbeliever shudder. At such moments it's good to have a prehistoric cave in which to hide oneself and one's fears. Call that escapism, if you like. I shan't protest."

Thomas felt the blood rushing to his face. "I don't think escapism is the right word here," he said.

"Perhaps I should mention that I was a novice in a convent before I became a doctor," she said, looking at him challengingly.

"What gave you the idea?" he asked, surprised.

She smiled slightly ironically. "The ennobling influence of good friends," she replied. "You see, I was deeply moved when Don Achille went away to be a priest. I didn't want to do less than he, so I cut my studies short and entered a nursing order. But I hadn't any real vocation so I left again, with the approval of the Superior, of course."

"And how did you land in Settevetri?"

"That was also through Don Achille. During the War, I was working in a hospital in Sulmona, when I met him again. It was a cruel time, and we were both so weary of all the misery – tired to the very depths of our souls. Yes, indeed – even Don Achille. And he spoke so beautifully of Settevetri and maintained that up here one could somehow live a better life. He even hinted that he might possibly retire here after the War. I believed him – as usual. I may, indeed, have believed that I would find at last what he had found in life. . . ."

"And did you not succeed?"

Dottoressa Vanna gazed into the far distance. "Perhaps I too should have had to break a leg first," she said. "Now I have really no calling."

"But why, then, do you live up here?"

"Why? Well, because I like it here. I cannot say that the people here are better than elsewhere but at least they don't concern themselves with impossible Utopias and foolish complexes. And when I become tempted to private ambition now and then, I withdraw to my cave. You understand?"

"Not really. Do you believe in it yourself?"

"In what?"

"That about finding another Delphi? I mean, that it's true?"

"Now you're asking questions just like Gianni," she said, laughing.

Padre Barnaba stuck his head in the door. "Marco is waiting," he said.

"Well, then I'll be going," said the doctor, standing up. "It's been a pleasure to know you, Monsignor Cinnelius. Give my kind regards to Professor Fortunato. And if ever you return to Settevetri, I'll gladly fix you up with a cave of your own, if you like."

Thomas could not help smiling. "You can hardly have two Delphis here, can you?" he asked.

"You will be free to turn your cave into a crypt," she said smiling, and went off.

Padre Barnaba was still standing at the door, struggling pathetically with his emotion. "Filippo has prepared some food for the journey," he said at last.

Thomas did not speak. He seemed hardly to believe himself that he was going away. Padre Barnaba looked at him more and more sadly. "I suppose we must say good-bye for the present?" he said.

"Thank you for the days I have spent here," replied Thomas in a clear voice. "I hope I shall not have to be away very long."

At this Padre Barnaba came up to him and in his awkward way put his arm around his shoulders for the last time. "I shall be looking forward to your coming back," he said. "To be quite honest I don't know anybody I would rather have here than you, dear Tommaso. For a time I had hopes of Don Achille, but that was not to be. And anyway, I'm not at all sure that he would have settled down here very well permanently. He's an ex-officer and he has to have someone about to give orders to. Can you imagine him working on the *Agro Sacro*?"

He could not help smiling at the idea, then he continued more cheerfully: "But you know of course that Monsignor Boccaperta has to decide this matter, and he may make difficulties. It would do no harm to call and see him when you're passing through Castelpendente."

"May I give him your kind regards?"

"Yes, of course. And now, have a good journey! And be sure to come back soon, fresh and well."

He accompanied Thomas out to the piazza. Settevetri lay bathed in the warm afternoon sunshine. On the old parapet green lizards were stretching up their little heads as if to breathe in the mild perfume-laden summer breeze blowing up from the plateau below. A slender whitish coil of smoke was rising from the chimney of the Inn of the Good Shepherd, and a girl with a big copper can on her head was going in under the pergola.

Two philosophic-looking mules, as grey and motionless as if hewn from stone, were standing waiting by the fountain. For all I care they can stand there until morning, thought Thomas; but Padre Barnaba thought otherwise.

"You're starting fairly late," he said, "but you will be able to make up for it in the early morning hours. You will certainly have a rest at Monsignor Boccaperta's."

A crowd of villagers had assembled in front of the house. All the faces were familiar to Thomas. Matteo was the first to speak.

"We're expecting you back soon again, Father," he said. "If there's no other way of getting you, we will send Marco even as far as Rome to fetch you."

"It won't be necessary," said Thomas, laughing. "I'll come in any case."

Gianni took him aside. "May I ask a little favour, Reverendo?" he said.

"Certainly, if there's anything I can do for you?"

"You know, I study a bit on my own," explained the schoolmaster modestly, "and I wonder whether you could hunt up a reliable archaeological history of this neighbourhood. You see, I want to consult some other authorities besides Dottoressa Vanna. I mean real authorities . . ." he said with an apologetic smile.

Thomas looked with curiosity into the young man's guileless eyes and for a moment felt tempted to say: 'Get all this archaeological stuff out of your head, my boy.' But then he remembered the doctor's triumphant smile, and he realized that Gianni simply needed help – reliable help.

"I'll try to find something, though to be quite frank I don't think there's much to study here from the archaeological point of view. In spite of Dottoressa Vanna's discoveries. . . ."

Gianni seemed relieved. "I've been thinking the same for a long time past," he said, "but she's so enthusiastic, and it's often very difficult to decide what is fact and what is fantasy in her assertions."

"We will investigate the caves thoroughly when I come back again," Thomas promised.

Fausto and Assunta were waiting for him at the crossroads just outside the village. They smiled at him as he approached, but Fausto's brown eyes were full of unspoken questions.

"But you'll be back for the wedding, won't you, Padre?"

"The wedding?" repeated Thomas, surprised. "Is it to be so soon?"

Fausto's face clouded. "There's no sense in putting it off," he said. "Padre Barnaba has promised to marry them in the summer. It will all be very quiet, of course, because we can't rise to a big celebration here."

"I'm glad you have your father's blessing, Assunta," said Thomas, shaking hards warmly. "Does Cesarino know yet?"

"I've written to him, but if you meet him, Father, please give him my greetings."

"Of course I will. And may I ask where the young couple are going to live, Fausto?"

"In Rome, of course," replied Fausto. "But who will help her?" he suddenly asked, his eyes fixed on Thomas, full of anxiety.

"In what way?"

"I mean with her religion. Who will see that she gets Holy Communion in case of need? Cesarino won't trouble about that. And when Don Achille is gone, there will be nobody at San Lino's whom she knows."

Thomas looked from father to daughter. "I shall look after her," he said.

Down in the plain he looked around him. The sun was almost exactly in the west. The first fine shadows of evening were falling, and the little village lay around Lo Zoccolo's white feet – a narrow, silver-grey spangle set with seven glistening stones.

"*Ecco*, Settevetri," said Marco, pointing with a smile to the seven windows which shone in the sunlight like lighthouses.

⚜

XXXV CASTELPENDENTE

Monsignor Boccaperta received Thomas the following evening. He was a heavily built man with an angular face and short-cut grey hair. His large brown eyes gazed at anyone he happened to be speaking to with dove-like gentleness not devoid of a certain cunning. It was not possible to meet those eyes. At most the suspicion of a smile told that they had fixed upon their object, even before the victim knew that he had exposed himself to scrutiny. When caught they quickly assumed an expression of wide-eyed, innocent wonder, like those of a slightly wounded roe.

His intuitive knowledge of human nature enabled him to find the right word quickly. On occasion he could speak his mind very freely, and this candour made him most popular throughout his

rural bishopric, although it had caused him quite a bit of trouble
in his dealings with the Roman Curia.

This time, however, Monsignor Boccaperta seemed unable to
find the right word at once. He fidgeted in his chair, ran his first
finger around inside his collar, and let his eyes wander in an even
wider radius. At last he knocked the ashes out of his pipe and
asked: "What about taking a little walk before supper?"

Castelpendente lay on a broad comfortable ledge of mountain,
at a point where the valley seemed to stretch out longingly
towards the open plain in the south. From ancient times the town
had been a main centre of that district and it still had traces of
antique Cyclopean walls. On the highest point stood an old
stronghold of the Guelphs, its jagged outline giving the impression that it had been hewn straight out of the rock. With its
cathedral and plain town hall, Castelpendente was a true replica
of a little medieval mountain town. The modern part, dating from
the turn of the century, was spacious but quite commonplace.
Its centre consisted of a large market square with arcades, behind
which were shops, bars and cinemas. A wide high street led down
to the coach station and continued from there as an asphalted
motor road zigzagging right down to the valley. At its highest
part it formed a pleasant promenade between luxuriant chestnut
trees. On reaching this Monsignor Boccaperta slackened his pace
and asked how Padre Barnaba was getting on.

Thomas saw that the bishop wanted exact information.
"Mentally he is still astonishingly fresh, but otherwise he has
aged considerably and probably he is no longer able to do as
much as he used to."

"Yes, it's a hard life up there," said the Bishop, "much harder
than here." His vagrant gaze strayed over his companion.

"What made you settle in Italy?" he asked gently.

Thomas had a vague idea that the other was preparing to turn
his flank, as it were, so he decided to play for safety. "I really
cannot say that I have settled in Italy," he replied. "I have merely
lived in Rome for several years."

The Bishop laughed outright. "People are always wanting to
cut Rome out of Italy," he said. "They failed to do it with

halberds and swords, so now they are trying with sophisms. Rome, they think, should be poised somewhere between heaven and earth, anywhere at all but in this country. Yet the fact remains that Rome is only a little wrinkle on the face of Italy, and what is more, a most unhealthy one, because it lies below the level of the Campagna."

"You misunderstand me," protested Thomas. "I only meant that I haven't had any fixed domicile up to the present."

The Bishop's guileless gaze wandered over the mountains, where the shades of evening were already spreading their azure veils between the olive woods. "And now you have lost your heart to our part of this country?" he asked.

"That is certainly true, but the problem lies deeper."

The Bishop's eyes ceased to wander as if they had found something to fasten on. "Please do not think I am disregarding that! But you people from the other side of the Alps have such a strange and at times positively fatal inclination to confound your romantic feeling for the beauties of nature with more serious sentiments. There have been certain sad cases of well known and clever people who could not distinguish between vespers and sunsets. I take it that is not the case with you."

"Definitely not."

"Well then I must ask you something else. You say you feel unable to bear the responsibility of your work in the Vatican. For what work, then, do you think your natural gifts fit you?"

Thomas flushed. "It is not a question, in my case, of choosing between several fields of work. I have simply found one of the original founts of Christianity, a fount which is still flowing and producing the purest water that a modern person could ever be privileged to taste. It is an historical wonder."

Monsignor Boccaperta looked worried. "If it were as simple as that . . ." he murmured.

Thomas was beginning to feel desperate. "But I'm not proposing to take anyone else's place," he said, "and I'm not irreplaceable in Rome. I am only going there now to consult a doctor."

"And that done, you propose to exchange your silk Vatican soutane for a mountain shepherd's cloak, eh? Very nicely conceived, but it rather smacks of romanticism to me. I have no authority to nominate hermits."

"At Settevetri I found Christ again after I had believed I had betrayed Him. And I want to go back there as soon as possible to devote the remainder of my life to Him as completely as I can."

The Bishop gave a rapid triple shrug. "Strictly speaking, you already dedicated your life to Him when you became a priest," he said. "Now you're asking for something else – an advance instalment of eternal bliss, as Peter did on Mount Tabor."

Thomas stared at the ground in silence. Suddenly he raised his eyes and looked into the Bishop's face with that clear blue gaze of child-like sincerity and deep earnestness only to be seen in Nordic eyes, and said clearly and distinctly: "For me, at any rate, it is a vocation."

Monsignor Boccaperta remained silent. They had left the town behind them and reached the end of the tree-lined avenue where the motor-road went down the mountain. At the turn stood a crassly modern brick building, four storeys high, surrounded by weathered stone walls. It was the new diocesan seminary which the Bishop had built in an old monastery garden. The chapel bell was ringing for the evening service, and a group of pale, slim youths in fresh and neat-looking soutanes were streaming through the iron gate. The youngest were still children with merry, playful eyes, the oldest precociously serious youths with a bad colour and darkening chins. Monsignor Boccaperta replied to their deferential greetings with a friendly grunt. His eyes, which had glanced sharply and observantly over his charges, now fixed themselves earnestly and almost reproachfully on Thomas.

"Don't you believe that these also have a vocation?" he asked.

"I should not dream of doubting it," replied Thomas. "Please understand that I am speaking only of my own experience in Settevetri."

"And you consider that this experience gives you the right to go back there for the rest of your life?" asked the Bishop with suspicious mildness.

"That depends on you, Monsignor."

"Let us suppose that I send the whole seminary to Settevetri.

The young people would probably come back having had even more overwhelming experiences."

It was Thomas who was silent now.

"We are nowhere told that the faithful at large should experience the rare grace of direct access to the original founts," the Bishop continued. "Had that been the case, Christianity could never have penetrated beyond the frontiers of the ancient world."

When Thomas still remained silent, the Bishop, slipping his arm familiarly under the younger man's, went on: "I can assure you that it's rather embarrassing to have an 'original fount' of this kind in the middle of a modern bishopric. It produces a mass of problems, and not only of an administrative nature. As long as Santa Presenza existed there was always a suitable priest to be found for Settevetri. But when Padre Barnaba drops out I really do not know of any suitable successor for him. If you are counting on succeeding him, you must settle the matter with the Cardinal in Rome. For this is a question not of individuals, but of principles."

"Pardon. . . ?"

"Yes, indeed, principles. You know, of course, that Santa Presenza was founded long ago by people from the Monte Lino neighbourhood. Conversely, the pastors of Settevetri were recruited for centuries from the Brotherhood. But now it is necessary to decide upon analogous qualifications, and I am not at all sure that a subjective experience in the place itself could be regarded as a decisive factor in an applicant's favour."

"I did not ask to be made parish priest there, but only to be permitted to make a sacrifice."

"What do you propose to offer? Your impaired health? If that's the case, don't apply for Settevetri, because your sacrifice would amount to suicide. One needs a strong heart and good nerves to survive conditions there. Padre Barnaba was an athlete in his youth. I have not many boys in my seminary with the physical qualifications which his successor will require. In this case private vocation plays a secondary part."

"Are there also private vocations?"

For the first time Monsignor Boccaperta lost his composure.

"Very seldom, and we do not care to speak of them," he replied.

"Why not?"

"Because Settevetri is not a place of pilgrimage," replied the Bishop brusquely. "I would immediately suppress any attempt to make it into a Lourdes or a Loreto. And I am convinced that anyone who looks into the situation would agree that I am right there. Or do you feel called upon to tell your experiences to all and sundry in Rome?"

"Most definitely not."

"Luckily the people of Settevetri are a silent, reserved race themselves. And the occasional strangers who come to Monte Lino are astoundingly blind. Most of them hardly glance at the village. It would remind one of the old legend of the heliotrope – you know, the magic stone which made its owner invisible."

But Thomas would not give up. "And what do you do with those who have received a private call, Monsignor?" he asked.

The Bishop had recovered his composure and he answered with a smile: "I place them in the service of Saint Linus."

"In Settevetri?"

"No, my friend. In my own cathedral. But of course I can also send such a priest to San Lino's in Rome later on. Don Achille will be going north, and the parish needs other priests in place of the former Fathers of Santa Presenza."

"What does being in the service of Saint Linus mean?"

"It means sacrificing one's own ambitions completely and living and dying almost anonymous, just as did the first successor of Peter. Serving Linus means serving the principle rather than the person."

"What principle?"

"The Holy Spirit and the love of man."

"That is what I have been always looking for," said Thomas a trifle polemically.

"Must one really *look* for it?"

Thomas cast down his eyes. "I have lived a lonely life, Monsignor," he said. "I have never had duties to living persons; nothing but desk duties."

"I thought so much when you said just now that you had

T

nothing to do in Rome except consult a doctor. But in Settevetri there are no desk duties, nothing but live personal ones."

Thomas suddenly remembered something. "Yes, there is one personal matter that I must see to in Rome," he said.

"That sounds a little better. I would not care to send a foreigner straight from a desk in the Vatican to Settevetri. If you really wish to go there eventually, then you must work for a time in an ordinary Italian parish – even if you feel no particular vocation for it. But first of all you must fulfil your personal obligations in Rome. Indeed, I feel it may be that Our Lord looks upon attention to them as the greater sacrifice."

Thomas bowed his head in silence, then he said: "Would you put in a word for me with Saint Linus, Monsignor?"

"I shall certainly do so," said the Bishop, "and the best advice I can give you at the moment is to offer Mass at his tomb here in Castelpendente in the morning. If you wish to, I shall have the crypt opened for you."

"Thank you very much. I'd like to do that."

They walked slowly back to the town. The sun was already sinking behind the mountains to the west, blue-black as thunder clouds, while a deep red glow still rested on the slender clock tower of the cathedral.

Monsignor Boccaperta looked Thomas over with a smile. "You know of course that the archaeologists are not quite certain that the traditional tomb of the saint is authentic," he said.

❦

XXXVI THE CATHEDRAL OF SAINT LINUS

The old piazza of Castelpendente was situated high up on the mountain-side with an open view to the south. It was not much bigger than the courtyard of the castle, and the rough paving had not been renewed for centuries. The outer side was protected by an old breastwork which formed part of the medieval defences. On the inner side stood the cathedral, and opposite it the Bishop's palace. Between them was a row of modest houses with steep steps and low-arched gateways between which ran dark vaulted passages. In the middle of the piazza stood an old, insignificant-looking fountain.

The cathedral was one of the earliest Romanesque buildings in Central Italy. Two weathered stone lions, hardly recognizable as such, watched over the sombre, massive façade, with its old marble portal. The dark interior was astonishing. Heavy, ungraceful columns supported the low vaulted ceilings, and the walls were a veritable picture-book of frescoes. The unknown painter had followed the conventional plan on the whole – the story of the Passion in the choir, the heavenly Jerusalem over the vaulted ceilings, the creation of the world over the front entrance, and the life-story of the patron saint along the walls of the nave. True, the painter's knowledge of anatomy and sense of perspective left much to be desired, but he more than compensated for these deficiencies by his irresistible delight in colour. Such was the skill and power of his brush-work that even now, after many centuries, the frescoes glowed like magic fire when the cathedral was lit up.

When Thomas was on his way to say Mass in the morning he was utterly astounded to see an old acquaintance leaning over the fountain, drinking water from the hollow of his hand.

He decided to take the bull by the horns. "Good morning, Cesarino," he said cheerfully. "What brings you here?"

Cesarino staggered back as if he had got a blow on the chest. His foot slipped on the wet paving and he had to put out his hand to stop himself from falling full length. "What's that to you?" he snarled, scrambling to his feet.

"I'm sorry I startled you, Cesarino. I didn't mean to. . . ."

"I wasn't startled at all. I was only thirsty," he answered sullenly.

"I'm glad to see you, anyhow," continued Thomas undeterred. "Are you going up to the mountains?"

"No, I'm only collecting the passengers I drove into a ditch," he answered insolently.

"I heard about that mishap, but I didn't know you were the driver."

"Where did you hear about it?" asked Cesarino suspiciously.

"In Settevetri."

"You were in Settevetri?"

"Yes, I left there yesterday, and Assunta asked me to give you her greetings. . . ."

"Spy!" hissed Cesarino stepping back a pace and clenching his fists so tightly that the knuckles showed white.

For a moment Thomas thought the young man was going raving mad as he stood rolling his eyes like a bull about to charge. But the same instant the sound of voices came from the cathedral, a little group of tourists came out on to the piazza, and Cesarino disappeared as if the ground had swallowed him.

Thomas stood there bewildered, trying to collect his thoughts. He held his fingers under the water and was so fascinated by the rainbow shimmer that he did not hear footsteps behind him until someone gripped him by the arm and said: "Good heavens! It's Don Tommaso!"

"Beata Veronica!" he exclaimed, just as startled as Cesarino had been a moment before.

She stretched out her arms and stood on her toes, radiant with joy. Only his soutane saved him from an embrace. He retired cautiously behind the fountain.

"You don't know how glad I am to see you, Monsignor! I knew you were on holiday, but how could I ever have imagined we should meet here? What colossal luck! Are you on a coach tour too?"

"No, it's more like a water-cure," he laughed, drying his fingers in his handkerchief. "But what brings an eminent scholar like you to this remote corner of the world?"

"Oh, it's perfectly wonderful!" she exclaimed fervently.

"What is?"

"You can ask that? It's perfectly marvellous! I'll come back here again and write a long article about it. At home they have no idea of the treasures hidden away in this region."

Thomas looked down into the valley. "Yes, it's certainly beautiful here, much more beautiful than in Rome," he said.

"Bah! Don't make silly comparisons," she snorted. "I don't mean the landscape. I mean the frescoes, of course!"

Thomas noticed the drops of perspiration on her face, and his old love of teasing suddenly awoke. "What frescoes?" he asked.

But she was far too excited to be damped so easily. "The frescoes of the life of Saint Linus, what else! What do you think of them, Don Tommaso? After all, they're just in your line. . . ."

"I haven't even looked at them yet."

She gasped for breath. "Is that possible? Aren't you interested in them, then?"

"I am, certainly, but I don't venture to study them without special preparation."

"Why is that?"

"Because we find it so hard to understand them. They were painted in an age very different from ours."

"Difficult to understand?" she repeated in an almost affronted tone. "No, I can't say I find them so. These primitive Italian masters had an incredible gift for making themselves intelligible to everyone. They possessed a secret: they knew the way to the original founts."

"To what?"

"To the original founts of Christianity and of art. They had only to draw from them. . . . Hence their sincerity and freshness, their natural sureness of touch, their heavenly purity. . . ."

"Pardon my question – but what do you know about these original founts?"

Even his air of bewilderment did not damp her.

"I? Nothing, of course. The secret has been lost to us."

"Do you mean to say that the original founts of Christianity have been lost?"

"I don't know. Perhaps we have become too sophisticated. But there's an extremely interesting monograph on primitive Christian art in the Abruzzi which . . ."

"How on earth did you get here?" he interrupted her almost brusquely.

"We are on a pilgrimage to the old churches of Central Italy.

The C.I.C.I. you know – the *Confédération Internationale des Catholiques Intellectuals* – organized it. We had a wonderful tour – Greccio, Rieti, Antrodoco, Aquila, Bominaco, Popoli, Sulmona, Anversa, Scanno. . . . Actually, we would not have come here at all if the driver hadn't lost his way and driven the coach into a ditch right in the middle of the wilderness. We have been wandering through the mountains since, like real brigands, on hired mules. It might have ended badly, but luckily we found a guide who showed us a direct path up to Monte Lino. Wasn't that exciting? "

"Did you actually get up to Monte Lino? "

"Ugh! Yes! It was an utterly unnecessary detour. We climbed right up to the village itself – what's this it's called? – but we didn't dare to spend the night there. It was simply too horrible! "

"How? "

"I have never seen any place so wretched – dirty, primitive, depressing in the extreme. Not a single pretty house, not an interesting face in the whole village. And the food was almost uneatable! "

"Did you take supper there? "

"Yes, unfortunately we had to. We couldn't get away in time. But not in the *osteria* – it looked too awful. We took our food in the open on the mountain. That was definitely better."

"I suppose so . . ." murmured Thomas.

At last Beata Veronica noticed his depressed air. "You mustn't think I judge people by what they set before me," she said. "No, it was something else which repelled me about – Settevetri – yes, that's the name of the place. Just imagine! There wasn't even a decent church up there. We rustled around and enquired everywhere, and in the end we found a poor old priest – the queerest old creature you could imagine – who looked like a runaway monk. He showed us a dilapidated little wayside chapel quite outside the village. That was all. No, I'd prefer to forget Settevetri, thank you! "

"Yes, let's not talk of Settevetri . . ." agreed Thomas, and his gaze wandered very far away. "Well, I must go and say my Mass now, so good-bye! We shall see each other again in Rome."

The cathedral was built over a cave which had been hewn out of the rock in pre-Christian times. This crypt was a small, longish chamber with dripping wet walls which still showed traces of primitive rock drawings in red. The altar, a marble trestle devoid of all ornament, had been erected much later, but it failed to dispel the atmosphere of a place of pagan worship which still pervaded the low vaulted chamber.

In the middle of the north wall was a railed-in niche about seven cubic feet in circumference containing an ancient stone sarcophagus. Before it stood a vase of withered meadow flowers. This was the reputed tomb of Saint Linus.

Thomas immediately noted the similarity to Santa Cristina's and many other vaulted crypt tombs. But he was not scandalized now, for he had come to realize in the interval that Our Lord does not mind what instrument He uses when he wishes to play a beautiful melody. All that is required is a pure and humble heart to grasp it. The function of the tomb was not to clarify historical associations but to facilitate contact between God and the questing hearts of men. Nevertheless Thomas was not completely satisfied.

If they had really brought the body of the saint back to his native mountains, why precisely had they laid him to rest down here? And why are so many great saints hidden away in dubious crypts as though Catholics still feared persecution? Linus should be high up on his own mountain among singing shepherds and grazing flocks, in God's open sunshine, as a promise to all erring wanderers in the valley of the shadow of death. . . .

Thomas found a young seminarist waiting down in the crypt to serve his Mass.

"Paolo Bracciaferro," murmured the young man, dropping on one knee and kissing Thomas's hand with that gay servility characteristic of the Neapolitan.

Young Paolo proved the perfect acolyte. Everything was exactly as it should be, each action was perfectly timed, and he himself moved about the altar as lightly and discreetly as a dancer. His voice was well modulated, musical and ideally impersonal, and he succeeded so completely in de-materializing himself as it were behind the liturgy, that Thomas felt at times as though he were alone at the altar.

And yet he was not alone. Cesarino was still so present to him that he decided to offer his Mass for him and Assunta.

As he raised his hands over the missal he thought he heard Fausto's rough bass growling the Amen somewhere in the distance, and during the Preface the singing of the shepherds on the plateau seemed to echo through his own voice. A tremulous presentiment told him that the Holy Presence was near, just as indubitably and overpoweringly near as he had experienced it in the midst of the simple circle around the rough deal table under the sun-flecked pergola of the Inn of the Good Shepherd. A feeble sound floated in from the bell tower as he spoke the words of Consecration. He genuflected, and then, with eyes wide open, raised the thin white Host above his head.

He had attained certainty: the Holy Spirit had laid a Victim into his hands, a Victim which bled unceasingly and invisibly. He himself participated in this sacrifice, not only as recipient but also as co-victim. He had offered Christ upon the altar thousands of times, but now he knew that Christ had raised him up to Himself on the Cross and that he, Thomas, would one day be permitted to discharge his part of the sacrifice with his own blood.

Book Four

SANTA PRESENZA

֍

XXXVII   AUGUST 1954

As soon as Thomas was appointed parish priest of San Lino, he moved into Santa Presenza. Don Achille had left Padre Barnaba's old cell respectfully untouched as a memorial to the last member of the Brotherhood of the Holy Presence. The room, which was as bare and austere as a mountain hut, but lofty and therefore cool in summer, seemed still to preserve something of the spirit of the old priest, and also a certain odour of masculinity – a curious mixture of boyish carelessness and meticulous tidiness such as one finds in the cabin of an old seaman.

Thomas had inherited all the old household equipment – the *prie-dieu* and the desk, the solid bed and the cupboard that held everything; also the rickety desk chair, the cracked shaving mirror, the roughly patched sheets, the simple metal crucifix, the gaudily coloured oleograph of Christopher Columbus on board the *Santa Maria*; as well as eight wall hooks for his outer clothing, and several towels, rosaries, and other things.

But the greatest treasure of all was the handwritten commonplace book, yellow with age, that lay on a special shelf in the cupboard. With its simple maxims and meditations written down by long-dead Brothers of Santa Presenza for the edification and guidance of their colleagues and successors in their daily work among the faithful, Thomas soon discovered that this book was his greatest resource in his pastoral work. Moreover, it taught

him much about the spirit which had animated the defunct
Brotherhood. Sometimes it gave him the impression of being a
direct continuation of his conversations with Padre Barnaba in
Settevetri.

"That pride which brought about the downfall of Lucifer is
also the most dangerous stumbling-block for a poor monastic
brother," he read. "We must eradicate it in ourselves and in our
own community, for there is nothing that harms us more in the
eyes of the Lord. As cockle spreads among the wheat, so does pride
spread among even the most pious Christian communities, and
the bigger the field, the greater the danger. He who stands nearest
to the altar must beware that he does not hide the Most Holy
from those who stand behind him. And those who are within the
Church must not fail to make way for those who stand waiting
outside. While communities have lost their faith in the Sacrament
because they have no longer kept the tabernacle before their eyes."

Here the writer had set a full-stop, perhaps because he had got
tired; the old-fashioned writing was not that of one used to wield-
ing a pen. About a century later another hand had taken up the
same theme in a bold, almost exuberant-looking script:

"It is not wrong to be proud to stand as near to the table of
the Lord as we do. But we must not allow this just pride to turn
into arrogance when we go out among our fellow-men. Think of
how easily a splinter of wood cut from the statue of a saint turns
into a magic talisman as soon as it leaves the church. The pride
of Christians has propagated falsehood and superstition in the
name of the Holy Spirit; it has collected gold and riches to hide its
failures; it has built prisons and palaces, and mobilized armies and
fleets, all on the pretext of smoothing the way to the Kingdom of
God. The Brothers of the Holy Presence would do well to meditate
day and night, morning and evening, on the difference between
the will of God and the will of man, so that arrogance may never
lead them into misusing His Sacrament for unworthy ends. . . ."

Since his return from Settevetri Thomas had avoided his old
friends lest he should expose himself to obtrusive questions. The
Secretariat of State had given him leave of absence for an indefinite
period. But sometimes as he sat, with aching head, alone in his

dead monastery, he felt as though he were sitting huddled in one of Dottoressa Vanna's caves.

Moreover, Professor Fortunato took an extremely serious view of his case. "She should really be locked up, that woman," he growled on first examining Thomas. "However, it's a good thing she sent you to me. Mountain-climbing is definitely out for a long time to come."

"What do you propose to do with me?" asked Thomas apathetically.

"I should naturally prefer to operate, but unfortunately it is quite possible that some important cerebral centres might suffer secondary effects if I do so."

"And what would that mean?"

"At the worst a deterioration of certain mental capacities," replied Fortunato, "and of course that is not very pleasant. Where were you intending to spend the summer, by the way?"

"In the Vicolo dei Pecorai."

"Hm! It can be frightfully hot there."

Fortunato was right. But as it happened, the great heat made a merciful barrier against intrusion. The Lane was generally silent and empty all day, and the scorching Piazza delle Pecore formed another zone of safety which no one without good reason was willing to cross. Life had receded to minimal visibility, but it still went on with its mysteries, big and small, hidden behind Venetian blinds and hermetically sealed windows. Priests and doctors still had a certain right to see in.

One day, when the sky was yellow from the *sirocco* and the dust was whirling in spectral pirouettes over the Piazza delle Pecore, Fortunato dropped in unexpectedly on Thomas.

"Well, how are you today?" he asked.

"I could be better. Some days it seems particularly bad."

"You should be careful in this weather; otherwise it could end badly for you."

"Well, we're both defenceless against the weather."

"Yes, but you could allow me to operate while there is still time."

"God has given me my brain and I propose to keep it whole even if it chafes a bit at the edges."

The doctor shrugged. "I have warned you," he said.

The next morning when Thomas went out the weather was ideal. He felt quite restored and blamed his bad turn completely on the *sirocco*. It was the hour when foreigners lie in bed and only real Romans are up and about. In any case moneyed folk and all other disturbers of the peace of the world had left Rome for the hot season, and Thomas had the feeling that the people left at large around him were all old friends.

By the time Thomas had finished his morning programme the heat had increased. Nevertheless he ventured the last lap, right across the open square, in the murderous glare of the sun. He knew that he would come home bathed in perspiration, with hammering pulses and gasping for breath – but that was simply the price of his happiness. He knew it was a higher price than that paid by his colleagues in neighbouring parishes, but he accepted this as penance for his spiritual pride. Later, as he sat in Padre Barnaba's poor cell after a cold sponge down, his heart overflowed with almost Franciscan joy. And this time the pain in his head did not come back.

Towards evening life moved out of doors again, and the streets turned into a great communal home where all broke their bread and drank their wine in unity and innocence of heart. Thomas crossed over to Sor Anacleto's for a little chat, just as Padre Barnaba used to do. He had discovered that this was an important part of his pastoral activity. Sor Anacleto knew everything that went on in the parish and was able to give him a good deal of valuable information. Also many people were glad to consult the priest on matters which could not well be discussed either in the confessional or in the parish office. Thus, Padre Barnaba's table had become a little institution born of years of experience and a deep awareness of the various problems of the parish. Basically these were the same problems that Don Achille had tried to solve by his ambitious Catholic Action programme. But he had never allowed himself time to discuss these things quietly over a glass of wine, so spirits in the Vicolo dei Pecorai had risen several degrees when a black soutane had shown up again at Padre Barnaba's table and people could once more count on getting a kindly word of personal advice.

This evening Sor Anacleto got out his best wine carafe. "A special vintage," he said with a grin, pouring out two glasses brimful. "*Salute, Reverendo!* How do you like it in San Lino?"

"How *can* you ask such a thing?" replied Thomas with a smile which went straight to Sor Anacleto's heart.

"It's grand to hear you say that! Do you remember the first time you sat at this table? It was before the War, of course, and we talked about . . . Now, what's this we talked about? Ah, yes, I think I told you about my mother, didn't I?"

"Yes, that's right."

The innkeeper could contain himself no longer. He drew his chair close up to Thomas and whispered into his ear the secret with which his heart was bursting: "What do you think? Cesarino is getting married!"

"Splendid! When?"

"Tomorrow – but don't tell anyone."

"Why not?"

"He doesn't want us to. Perhaps he's ashamed of his comrades knowing. Of course it will be a hole-and-corner wedding, but what can we do? We would have liked a proper wedding for our only son, but perhaps it's better this way for Assunta."

"Where are they being married, then?"

"In Settevetri."

"But won't you and your wife be there?"

"No, we shan't," said Sor Anacleto. "You see, the journey would be too much for Michela, and of course I can't leave my business. But we are going to have a little celebration for the couple when they come back here – only within the family circle, of course," he added uneasily.

"I understand. Are they going to live with you?"

"No, but I expect I shall have to find them a home somewhere. Naturally I would like them to settle down in the Vicolo dei Pecorai. I will want someone here to give me a hand later on in my old age."

"Is Cesarino still with the coach company?"

"No, they sacked him that time after the accident. He's driving a tram now. The young scamp will take any job that puts wheels under him. Young people have queer notions nowadays."

Thomas could not help smiling. "Ah, there's no great harm in that," he said reassuringly. "It's only a childish malady they grow out of."

Sor Anacleto listened almost suspiciously, as if he wanted to make sure that the priest's words rang true. "I only hope you're right," he said, "but it's a wretched malady anyhow. Cesarino was so on edge all the summer. It's a pity Don Achille has gone away."

"Did Cesarino like him?"

"No, not specially, but Don Achille was so strongminded, he would have brought the boy to his senses."

"So you think . . . ?"

Sor Anacleto threw him a cautious glance. "Of course I'm exaggerating a bit," he said, "for neither you nor I can do anything about it, really."

"Perhaps not by compulsion, but . . ."

"You're right there," admitted the innkeeper penitently, "but there must be other ways. You must get to know Cesarino better and then he'll get used to you, so to speak. He's a good boy at heart, but he's hot-tempered and suspicious. It may take a lot of time, Reverendo."

Thomas's eyes had wandered up to the little Madonna in the wall-niche of Santa Presenza. "I'm prepared to wait," he said.

The night remained warm, and the people of the Vicolo dei Pecorai stayed out of doors until very late. Thomas too remained up a long time. He sat in his room reading the old commonplace book of Santa Presenza and learning the art of herding Peter's sheep while he listened with half an ear to the thousand little noises in the street below.

"You will probably have plenty of trouble there," Cardinal Norcus had said when he had suggested the post of parish priest of San Lino's to Thomas. "The Communists of the parish regarded Don Achille as enemy number one. I should not be surprised if they hold high carnival now he's gone."

"I'm not afraid of them, Your Eminence," replied Thomas.

The Cardinal smiled. "Neither am I. The Romans are essentially good-hearted and up to the present Communism has not made them malicious. But they have to be met with their own weapons, if you understand?"

The feast of Saint Linus was at the end of September. Thomas had sung the High Mass in the morning and afterwards held the traditional reception for the San Lino Circle in the Bishop's Residence. Don Achille had always organized a little parish party to take place after the evening service, but this time the cinema proprietor Ettore had got in first and announced a big Communist rally in the neighbouring quarter. Thomas wisely refrained from trying to compete with him and contented himself with illuminating the church. The evening devotions were well attended and passed off normally, although crowds of young men wearing red ties marched around the piazza, their arms around each others' shoulders, chanting a sort of litany-*cum*-lament demanding bread, land and peace. When Thomas crossed over later to drink a glass of wine with Sor Anacleto, he found the *osteria* full of people. A man was sitting alone at Thomas's regular table, watching the goings-on in the piazza with obvious enjoyment. It was Carlo Romolo.

Thomas's first reaction was a spontaneous wave of pleasure – he had met a friend again after a long time. He noted automatically that his old opponent looked still the same. His thick hair was slightly grizzled, but otherwise he seemed almost more youthful than ever. He sat laughing boisterously at the goings-on – a wild horde of boys had opened an entirely non-political offensive against Pietro, the stout porter of the Palazzo Terrasanta, and a fierce scrimmage was going on in the market-place. It ended in one miscreant after another landing into the fountain with the black marble goats, to the accompaniment of shrill screeches. Romolo was childishly happy. Obviously his heart was with the wild boys who threw pebbles at property owners with the same glowing conviction with which their big brothers in the Party headquarters threw stones. And over on Santa Presenza the little plaster Madonna stood in her glass shrine, with her wreath of electric lights round her head, smiling down as kindly as her big sister up on Lo Zoccolo.

"Good evening, Doctor. It's nice to see you here," said Thomas.

Romolo looked up. Thomas knew only too well the dark shadow which spread over the doctor's features, and the testy expression with which the screwed-up eyes looked him over as if they were trying to nip in the bud any sign of a smile. But this time Thomas's good nature won, and Romolo laughingly capitulated with a placating handshake.

"The pleasure is entirely mine, Monsignor. Nice here, isn't it? Sit down and have a glass of wine with me!"

"With pleasure," said Thomas taking a seat.

"Quaint place, this. I suppose you're spending the remainder of your holiday here?" said Romolo pouring out a glass.

"I've been parish priest here since the first of July."

Romolo stared at him open-mouthed. "What?" he exclaimed. "You're no longer in the Vatican?"

"No."

"But how's that? Monsignori are hardly underpaid?"

Thomas said nothing and Romolo immediately regretted his tactless remark. "I imagine you feel better here – better than in the Via Gattafogata, eh?" he asked.

"It was a bit too hard for me out there."

Romolo smiled to himself. "I noticed that at the time. I'm sure it's much easier here. All the same you still look very poorly. How do you feel, actually?"

"Thank you. I could feel better. If I can't keep on I shall probably come to you."

Romolo took on a bantering tone. "You're welcome. I promise you I won't cut out your immortal soul," he said.

"That's almost more than Fortunato dared to promise," replied Thomas laughing, "but of course you have known me since the affair at Bolsena."

"It was only a trifle that time," murmured the doctor.

"It's no more than that now either. All the same – one gets older and the spasms of pain get worse with the years."

But the mention of the great brain specialist's name seemed to have destroyed all Romolo's desire to joke. "I would willingly help you now too if I could, Monsignor, but I don't practise in this neighbourhood. I only came here to visit Assunta out of friendship."

"How is she getting on?"

The doctor shook his head. "She'd have been better in hospital a while longer, but unfortunately Cesarino insisted on having her home. She is still very weak. If I had known she was pregnant I would never have consented to her doing that mountain pilgrimage in the spring. But you had forbidden her to think of having children, so the poor girl didn't dare to admit her condition for fear of being excommunicated on the spot."

Thomas flushed. "How is the child?" he asked.

"It was a miscarriage. Didn't you know?"

"I didn't even know she was home," answered Thomas dejectedly.

Romolo seemed astonished. "That's strange," he said. "She spoke of you several times, and that made me think you had been to see her."

"Did she speak of me?"

"I think she must have asked Cesarino to fetch you."

Thomas looked away with a sad little smile.

"But you will surely visit her?"

"I most certainly will. But there's somebody who doesn't want me to."

"You mean Cesarino?"

U

"Yes."

Romolo made an impatient gesture. "Isn't the old quarrel buried yet?" he asked.

"Cesarino has forbidden me ever to set foot in his home."

"How childish, when Assunta wants so much to speak to you. . . ."

"Cesarino has had a good Communist schooling. He has declared that he doesn't mind a bit if Assunta sees me in church, but he won't have a priest visiting his home. He has sent me word that the worst will happen if I show myself there."

Romolo was visibly embarrassed. "Well, Cesarino has his principles. Besides, he naturally considers you largely responsible for his misfortune. Perhaps you could try to have a sensible talk to him about that? But the main thing is to spare Assunta any unnecessary excitement while she's ill."

"Nothing else?"

"No, I'm only speaking as a doctor," said Romolo suddenly frigid.

Thomas laid a placating hand on his arm. "Please let us not start the old quarrel again," he said. "I must ask another priest to go in my place."

"But it's you she wants to see."

"What she really wants will help her just as well from the hand of another priest."

"Even I know that much, but if you don't want to lose face I advise you to bring the woman the Sacrament yourself since she must have it."

Thomas smiled. "Thank you. I only wanted to hear it from you."

Romolo looked up, surprised, then he laughed. "Go in peace, Don Tommaso! You even have my blessing this time!"

Sor Anacleto, who had been hovering around the table with a worried face, signalled enthusiastic agreement behind Romolo's back.

When a twelve-man chorus took up its stand later in the evening in front of the Palazzo Terrasanta, Thomas went to his room and lay down. But dancing went on in the Piazza half the night under fairy lights, and hoarse voices bawled the everlasting war-song:

> "*Vogliamo pane,*
> *Vogliamo terra,*
> *Vogliamo pace*
> *E niente guerra . . .*"

When Thomas dropped into an uneasy sleep at last he dreamed he was in Vallepietra and the clericalist Commendatore was knocking loudly at his door and calling in that he must come at once to reach Mentana before the Reds attacked. He protested sleepily but the Commendatore kept on hammering so hard that Thomas feared he would burst in the door; and now he was shouting that the way was difficult and Assunta was waiting. Dazed with sleep, Thomas tumbled out of bed, turned on the light and opened the door. Sora Michela was standing outside, in tears.

"You must come, Monsignor. Assunta is so restless, and she's calling for you."

"I'll come at once. Where's Cesarino?"

"I don't know. Out somewhere with his comrades."

"Go and prepare Assunta while I fetch the Blessed Sacrament from the church."

It was nearing two o'clock, and the Vicolo dei Pecorai was dark and deserted. Sor Anacleto was awaiting him at the gate with a little lantern, and now raced on ahead with a speed he never showed in daylight. Thomas had to ask him to go more slowly. Anxiety for his sick daughter-in-law was obviously not the only reason for this haste.

At last the innkeeper stopped before a narrow door at the end of the Lane, and swinging his lantern to and fro like a magician, said: "It's in there."

Thomas threw an astonished glance through the doorway. It was so low that one had to bend down going in, and it seemed more like the entrance to a coal-cellar than to a dwelling-place. But right at the back a feeble light showed from a yard window.

"It's really an old warehouse," explained Sor Anacleto nervously, "but it wasn't easy to get a roof of any kind over them in a hurry."

He went on ahead towards the little room in the yard. The lantern light glanced over the characteristic surface of an antique brick wall. The whole house was obviously built over an ancient ruin. Thomas could not refrain from asking: "Have they been living here long?"

"Assunta was here only a few days before she went into hospital," said Sor Anacleto, visibly ashamed, "or she would have asked you to come to her long ago. She thinks a lot of you, Reverendo." As he spoke he turned round and shone the light back on the entrance.

"Are you waiting for someone?"

"No, but I thought I heard steps," he muttered evasively, opening a door. A bright ray of light streamed out into the yard and was reflected in a little pool of water before the threshold. They stepped into something like a prehistoric cave, but it was warm and very roomy. It contained an enormous double bed, a charcoal stove, some simple kitchen equipment, and a splendid radio set. The walls were decorated with brightly coloured and stirringly worded election posters. What appeared to be rock drawings peeped out here and there between them. These were at least as eloquent in their primitive way as the posters.

Sora Michela was waiting beside the bed. From the pillows a pair of black eyes, full of fear, stared out towards Thomas.

"She wants to make her confession," whispered the mother.

"Where's Cesarino?" asked Sor Anacleto almost inaudibly. When she only shrugged her shoulders he withdraw discreetly to the door with his lantern but kept running out every minute to see that the way back was still clear.

"You must not hesitate to send for me when you want me again," said Thomas to Assunta when the fear was gone from her eyes at last. "I promised your father that I would help you, and of course I know the way here now."

But Assunta's eyes became filled with a new uneasiness as she stared at the door.

"We had best let Assunta try to sleep now," said Sor Ana-

cleto nervously, "and I'm sure you're very tired too, Monsignor.
I will see you home."

"Oh, no, thank you, that's not necessary. I'll find my way all
right."

In the outer doorway, beyond reach of the light from the
window, a heavy figure stood waiting, swaying like an angry
bear. It was Cesarino. With tousled hair and holding a stone in
his hand, he was reeking of wine and proletarian hatred. . . .

"You blasted spy!" he hissed.

The next morning a *carabinieri* who had patrolled the environs
of San Lino's after the great festival was over, reported that he
had heard a strange cry from the Vicolo dei Pecorai. But he could
see no one except the new parish priest, who was leaning against
a doorway holding his shoulder, and he had told him it was only
a cat that had cried. As he noticed he was in very great pain the
carabinieri had helped him home, but the Reverendo had made
him promise firmly not to investigate the strange noise any
further.

⚜

XXXIX ALL SOULS' DAY

There were great crowds at the tram-stop near San Lorenzo-Out-
side-the-Walls. A gigantic flower garden had suddenly sprung up
from the asphalt of the market square. A human stream, which
became broader and broader, flowed through the great gates to the
big cemetery, where it gradually divided into thin streams between
the rows of graves. For it was the Day of the Dead, when the
people of Rome make a pilgrimage to the Campo Verano to light
a candle or a lamp on the graves of their relatives.

With an involuntary shudder Cesarino stubbed out his cigarette and stuck the butt carefully behind his ear. The doors
slammed and the heavy green tram started lumbering along.
Rolling past the fortress-like walls and dark cypresses of the
cemetery, it turned with a screeching clatter into the University

City with its clinics. Cesarino listened with a feeling of relief to the noise in the over-crowded tram. Better an over-load of live people than an empty car full of ghosts. If there really was an underworld the entrance was surely somewhere in this region of death and sickness.

One should indeed visit one's dead today. Cesarino had many a good friend behind those gloomy walls – comrades of his school days, of the piazza, of the Party. . . . They had always left him in peace, which meant that they were pleased with him. And he would leave them in peace too if this blasted tram company did not oblige him to pass by the cemetery several times a day. It was a hard lot for an expert driver who had driven long-distance coaches over the great highroads of Italy.

Cesarino's mother had grown up in the porter's lodge of the ducal palace of Del Pilastro in Naples. Duke Cesare, tall, handsome, an ideal specimen of manhood, possessed a villa in Sorrento, a town house in Rome and another in Paris, as well as a ruined castle of Norman origin in Apulia, besides the family palace. He had married an American heiress and he bred the finest racehorses in all Southern Italy. It had been Sora Michela's girlish dream one day to name her first-born son after Duke Cesare. The dream had come true, but this baptismal gift was destined to blight the entire youth of her son. To try to bring up a snotty-nosed urchin in the Vicolo dei Pecorai on the model of the far-away ducal ideal was really too fantastic. Her efforts only resulted in giving the boy an instinctive hatred of Duke Cesare. As he grew older he came to hate dukes in general. When the noble image continued to haunt Sora Michela's house, Cesarino himself fled in sheer despair to the farthest edge of Rome. However, one cannot escape one's destiny. A few years later he found himself back in a dark hole in his native Vicolo dei Pecorai, but he hardly knew himself how it had all happened. It was not a very happy start for a marriage, though his mother, who still lived in a world of illusion, declared that this home of his was just as good as her childhood home in Duke Cesare's palace.

Cesarino stared down from his driver's seat, his eyes dark with bitterness. His ungainly form was almost eloquent in its silent

pathos. The powerful rump with the muscleless arms, the rebellious red bull-neck under the curly head of hair, the low, rugged
forehead always bent down, the round shoulders which looked as
though shrinking from the threatening lash – he seemed the
reincarnation of a Roman galley slave as he sat forged to his seat
in the Outer Circle tram.

Viale Regina Margherita was the most monotonous street on
the whole line. Only beyond the Via Salaria did the character of
the town change. The side streets became lighter and airier;
modern luxury houses appeared. Cesarino felt still more repelled
by this region, for dukes and capitalists lived here. Evidently some
well-known preacher had been speaking in San Roberto Bellarmino
because a lot of smart-looking people were streaming out into the
Piazza Ungheria ! The detestable pack ! If it were not the Day of
the Dead he would have liked to run his tram over one of those
well-fed swine. But there was enough death in the air today. He
clanged his signal fiercely and tore along in a hurricane of noise
towards the Zoo. Villas, parks, museums – all deserts where healthy
bodies dry up. Only at the terminus near the Belle Arti was he
able to draw breath and take out his cigarette again for a miserable
four minutes.

More repugnant sights opened up on the other bank of the
Tiber – wide middle-class avenues, endless blocks of flats, smart
shops, and to crown all, the Vatican. After Cesarino had piloted
his tram through the teeming crowds of shoppers on the Viale
Ottaviano, he suddenly came on his wife, wearing a thick black
veil and clasping a small metal crucifix in her hands, standing
waiting at the tram-stop on the Piazza Risorgimento. She got into
the tram.

Assunta had put on weight since her illness, and was getting
more and more like her father. She was as dark as an Arab girl
and her sharp lively expression betrayed the fact that she was
rapidly acquiring all the traditional toughness and obstinacy of
the Roman working woman.

"What are you doing here? " asked Cesarino suspiciously.

"I was waiting for your tram. I want to go to Mother's grave."

"Where have you been? "

"To get a crucifix blessed by the Pope."

"Who's that for?"

"For us, of course!"

"Don't you dare hang it over my bed!"

"You can't get out of having it over you!"

"I tell you this: it shall not come into my house even if a hundred Popes blessed it!"

"All right, I won't bring it into your house, but you will lie under it one day whether you like it or not!"

"Oh, will I! Where will that be?"

"When you join Mother and me on the Campo Verano."

He slammed the doors and started the tram, clanging the signal wildly. He felt as if a dark cloud had rolled up suddenly from the Vatican and cast a cold shadow over the lively, crowded city. The mere sight of the crucifix made him shudder.

"How did you manage to get that blessing?" he asked roughly after a while.

"Don Tommaso gave me a letter."

"I thought so! That fellow sticks his nose into everything!"

"I asked him for it myself. What would he get out of it anyway?"

"You never know. Why do you think he sits evening after evening gaping at the piazza, if he gets nothing out of it? Or why do you think he goes snooping around back yards . . . ?"

He crossed the Via della Conciliazione without casting a glance at Saint Peter's in the background. A beggar was sitting on the Victor Emmanual Bridge fingering a rosary and slyly watching the passers-by. One of the spies of the priests, of course . . . !

"That Don Tommaso has been on your heels from San Lino to Gattafogata, and from Gattafogata to Settevetri, and from Settevetri back to San Lino," continued Cesarino furiously. "I know the type. Fellows like that come into the kitchens and get the housekeeping money off the women when the men are out, and go around dressed like women to put chaps off giving them a sock on the jaw! But I won't miss my chance another time."

"What's that you're saying?" asked Assunta, horrified. "Surely you wouldn't think of attacking a priest?"

"I think what I like . . . Pah! It's enough to give a fellow a pain in the neck – all this grave-visiting! You'd think the whole city was turned into a cemetery!"

Assunta looked sharply at her husbanad. "Listen, Cesarino," she began. "I know you can't stick Don Tommaso, but you're all wrong about him. He's a good man. I was mad with him once, too, and I thought he was bad, but he's not. He means well by us, I know he does. We wouldn't be married yet but for him."

"Don't talk rot!"

"But it's true. When he saw how we love each other, he became quite different to me. And anyway, it was he who persuaded Father to consent to our marriage."

A sudden twitch in Cesarino's red neck betrayed the fact that a new thought had bored its sharp claws into his poor dull brain. He tried in vain to shake it off. "Consent indeed!" he muttered. "I don't need any consent to love anyone I want to."

"Perhaps you don't, but I do. And Don Tommaso has really done everything to help me. He even spoke kindly of you, a lot more kindly than you deserve. . . ."

Cesarino went crimson. "Nothing but soft talk!" he muttered. "Stop your blather, anyway! Don't you know it's forbidden to talk to the driver?"

She stepped back into the tram, and he shook himself like a wet dog. The banks of the Tiber lay deserted and lonely. This was the region where Thomas waited for the tram when he went into town now and then. Cesarino forced the pace for the last lap and drew with a sense of relief in front of the waiting queue on the Via Arenula. As he drove over the Garibaldi Bridge a faint whiff of lysol floated over from the Tiber island. Suddenly he caught himself wondering whether he should not have offered to take Don Tommaso to hospital that time. But God knows that might have cost him, Cesarino, his job. . . .

The familiar noisy scrimmage of people getting on and the monotonous shouts of the conductor at last jerked his mind back to the present. His spirits rose as he ploughed his way through the incredible throngs in Trastevere, where the trams almost touched the stalls, and children, dogs and cyclists swarmed in front of the wheels. Clanging cheerfully, he forced lorries and handcarts to get out of the way, and crossed the Tiber for the fourth time. In the Via della Marmorata fresh crowds were standing waiting to storm the trams, and throngs of people were rushing out of the Via Ostiense like packs of wolves. Along the Appian Way, past the Palatine Hill and the Colosseum, he drove like a triumphant conqueror. At the Lateran he jumped off, bought a bag of roast chestnuts, and gave Assunta a handful, saying magnanimously: " Very well, we shan't quarrel about a miserable foreigner like that ! "

" Don Tommaso is no foreigner ! "

" Surely you can't say he's a Roman? "

" He has the heart of a Roman. You can shake hands with him without any misgiving the next time you meet him."

" He certainly won't come to the house to see me," muttered Cesarino as he slammed the doors, " but I'd be very glad to drive him to Campo Verano if you asked me to," he added, grinning at his grim joke. In fact, the whole conversation had made him more uncomfortable than he dared to show. He had found it a hard job to explain that cry in the night to his terrified family two months ago.

❦

XL   CHRISTMAS DAY

A pale rose shimmer beyond the mountains announced the dawn, but the Campagna still lay shrouded in darkness, and the valley of the Tiber was covered with an undulating sea of mist, from which the cupolas of Rome's churches stuck out like gigantic bell buoys. And from these buoys came a thin peal of bells as though a slow swell were passing over the sleeping sea. Now the day came quickly. A moment more, and the sun of Christmas Day climbed, poppy-red, over Tivoli.

But the morning light filled only lifeless streets and empty squares. The Venetian blinds on the shop windows were still down. Only here and there a church door opened hesitantly, almost unwillingly. The whole town was still resting after its long vigil during Midnight Mass.

A solitary priest was walking along the Via San Teodoro below the Palatine Hill. His small, crooked figure with the flapping soutane cast a shadow like a caricature from the last century against the flecked grey wall. He was moving slowly as though the long walk caused him infinite pain. It was Thomas on his way to say the Christmas morning Mass for the San Lino Circle.

While many doubted whether he was physically able for the charge of a parish, all had been agreed that he would make a splendid successor to Don Achille as director of the San Lino Circle. But the shy little priest with the tired, somewhat absent expression had dedicated himself with such passionate energy to his parochial work that he had not convened a single meeting of the San Lino Circle since the annual reception on the feast of Saint Linus.

Fortunato had been furious with him the whole autumn, though for a different reason, to be sure. "You look very badly, Don Tommaso," he had remarked every time they met. "You're burning the candle at both ends."

"Candles are meant to be burned," Thomas had said, "and I don't want mine to be so chopped down that I can't see by it any more."

The more the doctor warned, the more reserved the patient became. It was clear that he feared another examination, and he categorically refused to have one, though the pains in his head were drawing a veil over his eyes more and more frequently. When they became too dreadful he went to a little chemist's shop where the pale, bilious-looking proprietor, who suffered from stone in the kidney himself, slipped a packet of pain-killing powder into his hand with silent sympathy. Thomas never found out what the stuff was, but it helped him over the worst attacks.

There seemed to be something wrong with his left shoulder too. He found it difficult to raise his arm, but when asked, blamed it on rheumatism, and generally kept his hand in front of him, stuck under his soutane. Sometimes an attack of giddiness obliged him to go to his room, and when he reappeared he always looked more tired than before. But when anyone asked how he was, he replied with unfailing optimism: "I think I'm a bit better, thank you." And when anyone said that he should take a holiday, he only smiled, and replied cheerfully: "We shall see, perhaps at Christmas. . . ."

A few days before Christmas Sora Michela had asked him if she should get out the Crib.

"What should I do with a Crib?" he asked her, rather at a loss.

"Padre Barnaba and Don Achille always set it up at Christmas –for the children, you know. . . ."

When he only shook his head wearily, she got desperately uneasy. "You should really go away somewhere for a good rest, Reverendo," she said.

"Where would I go?"

"Where you would be well looked after – perhaps to your own country. But – I suppose it's very far away?"

"Yes, it's much too far away. And anyhow I'm very well looked after here."

"We do our best to make you feel at home, Reverendo," she said with a grateful smile. "All the same, we all like to be with our own folks on the big feast-days – everyone does."

Thomas's contact with his relatives had dwindled in the course of the years to a few Christmas cards which turned up with clock-like regularity. From his former fellow-students in the College of the Propaganda he only received occasional greetings, and he knew precious little about their activities in that enormous harvest-field of the Lord known as Scandinavia. But they all had something which he had not – a home to which they could go on this feast of the Holy Family; where they could get out their modest cribs and set them up lovingly, making them look like little flowering gardens. And in their churches they had children around them, children of their own race, who spoke their own language and who would one day continue their work. But he could have no part in this future, and in his distant lost home-land no one made cribs.

His eyes turned in mute appeal to Sora Michela. It was clear that she understood his distress, for she said with a motherly smile: "I'll help you to set up the Crib, Reverendo."

On Christmas Eve Felix Letterman had turned up in the Vicolo dei Pecorai. He was wearing a bright red beret, a white woollen scarf and a blue-black, long, loose overcoat, and the inevitable pipe stuck out like the beak of a bird. This was his usual winter get-up, and he looked rather like a woodpecker in it.

Thomas was genuinely delighted to see him again. "Happy Christmas, Felix! What brings you to this neighbourhood?" he asked.

"I was passing and I thought I'd pay his Reverence the pastor a visit. My pious daily help tells me one should visit the sick and the poor on Christmas Eve. How are you getting on?"

"Very well, thank you. Lots of work. And you?"

"Rottenly, thank you. Too little work, I suppose." He slouched across the small office and examined the portraits of the Popes with a quizzical expression. "*Roma aeterna*, indestructible as her idols!" he said. "Well, well! So this is where Monsignor Cinnelius lives and works, day in, day out. But let's hope you will celebrate Christmas with His Holiness and your fellow monsignori in the Vatican?"

"No, I shan't."

"You won't? Well then come and eat your Christmas ham with your fellow Scandinavian expatriates in the Cultural Institute."

"No, thank you. I'm celebrating Christmas here in the Vicolo dei Pecorai."

Letterman scratched his head. "Well, I call that true wisdom, Don Tommaso! I too prefer to keep clear of my fellow country-men at Christmas. I can't stand these solemn sacrificial meals. I'm an honest pagan, and when I see a pig's head crowned with a wreath, and with an apple in its snout, it nearly makes me vomit. If you wouldn't mind I'd much prefer to come over here tomorrow and drink a glass of Olevano with you. And we'll eat

a few dried figs with it, as we used to do long ago in Anticoli."
"You'll be very welcome indeed."

It is said that the early Christians of Jerusalem commemorated
the birth of the Saviour three separate times between the night
of Christmas Eve and Christmas morning. They celebrated the
first Christmas Mass in Bethlehem at midnight. Then they walked
back to Jerusalem to celebrate the great Christmas Mass in the
principal church there. But on their way they rested in the Chapel
of the Resurrection. There, at dawn, they celebrated the Eucharist
for the second time, together with the shepherds of the neighbourhood. This was the original second Christmas Mass, the Mass
of the Shepherds. And it was the only Christmas holiday away
from his parish which Thomas allowed himself. . . .

The Via San Teodoro lay deserted, like all the other streets, but
the grass was already shooting up through the red-brick ruins of
the Emperor's Palace on the Palatine Hill. The first rays of the sun
were feeling their way shyly through the leaves of the evergreen
oaks on to the ancient ruins of the Magna Mater Temple on the
south-west corner of the hill and lighting up the remains of the
legendary settlement of the shepherd-king which the old Romans
had preserved as a memorial of the origin of their city. Directly
under the Temple a Christian church rose almost obtrusively above
a row of old and very dilapidated grey houses. It was called Santa
Anastasia and its patroness was an obscure Eastern saint who was
regarded as symbolizing the mystery of the Resurrection.

This, then, was the site of the cult of the everlasting morning.
In the Middle Ages the Pope, after celebrating the first Mass of
Christmas in Santa Maria Maggiore, used to walk to Santa
Anastasia carrying a lighted torch. And the Brothers of Santa
Presenza had also chosen as a matter of course to celebrate a
Christmas Mass in this church. Pious local patriots, too, assembled
here from time to time in order to celebrate the birth of the Divine
Light near the spot which, according to tradition, saw the dawn
of Roman history. Otherwise, not many of the faithful took the
trouble to come here to attend the Mass of the Shepherds in this
archaic setting.

The San Lino Circle, which also fought tenaciously for the preservation of ancient traditions, had become greatly reduced in the course of the years. Thomas greeted the old friends – the professor of chemistry, the poet, the historian, the philosopher, and a few others. In the bright morning light they all looked very old and worn. He looked in vain for a young face among the little group. Will this Circle also die out for want of successors, as Santa Presenza has done? he thought.

Avvocato Tartaruga, who held his hand clasped for a long time, had become very shaky. "I am so glad that you have been able to give us this morning, Monsignor," he said. "One can understand only too well that you must dedicate all your strength to the parish work in your first year as pastor. So this Mass here is a little change for you too, I suppose? "

"Indeed it is."

A fresh wind suddenly blew over the hilly square in front of the church. As Thomas looked up at the old buildings, with their semi-underground workshops and crumbling masonry, and the green wooded hill rising above them, he felt transported back to the Abruzzi. The dawn was rapidly becoming brighter. Today the Light of the World will stream over us, he thought. And from the gardens of the Palatine his thoughts strayed out to the Campagna, and from there into the mountains. At this same hour Padre Barnaba had probably gathered his friends around him and was reading the simple text of the day to them: "And the shepherds said one to another . . ." There was certainly a big crowd under the pergola of the Inn of the Good Shepherd today, for of course all the people of Settevetri sat down to table together on Christmas Day.

Beside the members of the San Lino Circle the church was almost empty. When Thomas had read the Gospel he turned to the circle of aged faces which were looking up at him in the morning light, and said:

"'To win the world, we need neither wisdom nor eloquence, but children to whom we can teach our prayers.' This is a text from the old commonplace book of Santa Presenza." And, visibly moved by his theme, he continued: "Where are all the children

today? Today all the churches in the world are gathering the
children under their roofs, but our Circle is becoming smaller
from Christmas to Christmas, and the young men – they are not
here. We must find our way back to the world of the child if we
are to have anything at all to say to those who come after us.
And we must learn, above all, to listen, as children listen,
to each other. In this way we shall teach the children too
to recognize the presence of Christ among us. This is the
heritage of Santa Presenza, and there is no other way to the
future. . . ."

After the Mass the friends crowded around to wish him and
each other a happy Christmas. Tartaruga invited Thomas to breakfast, but he excused himself on the plea of parochial duties. Before
starting back to his parish he sat down with his breviary in a
corner of the cold, empty church and became lost in ever more
distant memories. From the plateau of Monte Lino his thoughts
strayed farther northwards, and soon were wandering wistfully
between glistening snowdrifts into snow-covered forests over
which the pale light of the Finnish Christmas morning was only
now beginning to dawn.

His holiday – his own special Christmas holiday – was very near
at last. He breathed a sigh of deep contentment. He had offered a
secret sacrifice and now he felt convinced that it had been accepted
and would surely in some way help his own country. This thought
rushed through his mind like wind through the crowns of high
trees. Nevertheless he perceived once more the threatening murmur of the great tidal wave lying in the depths of his soul, the swell
of which could make his environment tremble around him like
the cardboard wings of a stage. He had to force his thoughts to
concentrate on the present. He was not yet ready for the home-
ward journey. . . .

He fetched his overcoat from the sacristy and wondered where
he could get some milk for his coffee at this hour. A few men
from the near-by quarter were standing about in the piazza,
enjoying the peace and leisure of the holiday morning.

One of them called out "Happy Christmas, Reverendo ! " with
a smile of recognition. Thomas hesitated and stopped. The small

form, sharp nose and blotchy red face seemed familiar. "Haven't we met somewhere before?" he asked uncertainly.

"Don't you know me? I'm Domenico of Gattafogata. How are you getting on in San Lino, Reverendo?"

"Very well, thank you. Have you moved to this district?"

"Yes, I couldn't have stuck another winter in Gattafogata, not for anything! Tell me, how's Cesarino? I don't suppose he's a tram driver still?"

"Yes, he is. Why shouldn't he be?"

"I know he didn't like it. All the same, driving a tram is safer. At least he can't drive it into the ditch."

"I don't think we should hold that little mishap against him. I'm sure he does his best."

Domenico's grey-blue eyes opened wide with surprise. "None of his comrades blamed him for it," he said. "After all, it's only natural for a fellow to lose his nerve when he finds that his girl has gone off without a word while he was away at work."

"What do you know about it, then?"

"Everything. Didn't they live with us?"

Thomas had to look away.

"I met Cesarino not long afterwards," continued Domenico, "and he seemed nearly off his head. I can't imagine what would have happened him if he hadn't got Assunta back. And it's a good thing they don't have to live like gipsies any more. The doctor didn't approve of it at all."

"What doctor?"

"Romolo, of course. He always said Assunta should have a home in Rome where she grew up, and if she didn't have it she'd surely make off again one day. It was a great relief to them when you became parish priest of San Lino's. The doctor at once advised Assunta to go back there."

"What? Doctor Romolo?"

Domenico nodded with a roguish grin. "I know you two were often at loggerheads, Reverendo," he said, "but Dr Romolo has a great regard for you all the same. He said to me once that he was glad to shake hands with you for all you're a priest. And

X

anyway, he knew that you're Assunta's true friend and want to help her."

"Indeed? And what did he think that I could do for her?" asked Thomas.

"Baptize her child in the first place," grinned Domenico. "Of course it went wrong the first go, but who could know that would happen. Let's hope she'll have better luck next time."

Thomas shook his head. "I would do that willingly, very willingly. But after all, that lies with Our Lord."

Domenico came a step nearer and stuck his first finger into the priest's top button-hole. "Have you a crib in San Lino?" he asked.

"Certainly."

"And who did you set it up for – for yourself?"

"I didn't set it up myself, and I'm sure the woman who did it was thinking of the children in the first place."

Domenico nodded significantly. "That's just it," he said. "But in Gattafogata we have no crib. There's no one who has a care for things like that, and that's why the children don't thrive there."

"There may be something in that," admitted Thomas guiltily.

"It wasn't your fault, Reverendo. Someone should have thought of it long ago. To make a good crib costs time, you know, a lot of time. There are people who devote their whole lives to that art."

"Indeed . . . ?" murmured Thomas, perplexed. Had he not heard those same words in a different connection not long ago?

Now Domenico pressed even closer up to him and continued in a confidential tone: "My father used to carve wooden figures, and when I was a child I used to help him paint them. There wasn't much money in it, but it was the happiest work I ever did. You should have seen his workshop before the Feast of the Three Kings! You wouldn't find kings like his in the whole town!" He screwed up his eyes and winked at Thomas with the knowing air of an expert. "But as I say, to put a good crib together takes time. It's not enough to choose beautiful figures – they have to suit each other. And besides they have to grow into their surroundings, so to speak. Do you know, it can take years before the children get to know the crib really well."

"Unfortunately I have had far too little experience of children in these matters," admitted Thomas helplessly.

"Didn't you have a crib, then, when you were little?"

"No, but now I know whom I can come to for advice when I need it. A happy Christmas, Domenico!"

He went back to San Lino's. Sora Michela had kept her promise. The crib had been set up in a corner of the church according to all the rules of the art. Thomas viewed it with completely new eyes. The core of the whole thing consisted of a dozen simple wooden figures. With their robust naturalness and crude colouring they were not without charm. Apparently an old Brother of Santa Presenza, who was gifted with an understanding of children, had carved them many years ago. Some commonplace plaster figures, mass-produced stuff, had been added later, but both colours and figures were now the worse for age and wear – a camel had broken a leg, an angel had lost a wing, the group in front of the crib had been singed and blackened by candle flames, and the whole manger required to be repainted.

Thomas was cautiously fingering the damaged figures when he heard Sora Michela's voice behind him again. "The cribs in Naples – you should have seen them, Reverendo! When I think of the one in the Palazzo del Pilastro when I was a child . . ."

He sent her to fetch brushes and paints, brought the damaged figures into the office and set about restoring them. He was so absorbed in his work he did not notice that Letterman had come in until a fine whiff of strong tobacco-smoke hit him in the nose.

"What in the name of heaven are you up to there?" asked Letterman.

"I'm painting," said Thomas abashed, looking over his pince-nez.

"So you're going back to art?"

"No, I'm only touching up these crib figures."

"A sensible occupation at last!" exclaimed Letterman, leaning over him and nodding approvingly. "I note that his Reverence takes the matter seriously."

"What do you mean by that?"

"I mean what I say. Your faith has vanquished all the cunning

and snares of the devil. I have always doubted whether you would
hold out, but now I give in, as the great hunchback gave in to
Peer Gynt: 'He was too strong, because dolls were on his
side. . . .' Forgive the slight variation."

With gentle force he took the paint brush from between
Thomas's fingers. "You must dip a little deeper into the paint
pot," he said. "Surely you shouldn't be stingy with colours in the
house of the Lord! Red, blue, yellow, then red again – that's the
way, you see! Even a Sicilian cart-painter would be pleased with
that. In these latitudes people have an eye for bright colours. Have
you ever thought what one could make of a crib with Scandinavian ingredients – bright red huts, poison-green pine trees; and
snow, and gnomes, and all the rest? Theoretically, a Scandinavian
crib should be far more magnificent than most. . . ."

"I believe you've missed your vocation," laughed Thomas.

But Letterman went on painting. When the faded and scratched
old manger had been restored to its former glory he laid aside his
paint brush and said with a melancholy sigh: "I see I'm not the
only one in this town who has hidden his light under a bushel."

Then he got up, produced the bottle of wine he had brought
and poured out two glasses.

"I'm sure I've never admitted to you that I took off my hat to
you in my own mind when I heard you had decided to settle down
in the Vicolo dei Pecorai. I'm not a Catholic but I'm one of that
universal brotherhood who go through life barefooted. We have
many members in your Church too, I'm sure of that. We're a
kind of invisible mendicant order and we make our vows direct
to the Lord of the sparrows. A happy Christmas to you,
Monsignor!"

❧

XLI ASH WEDNESDAY

After the morning Mass Thomas took a little vessel of blessed
ashes and marked a cross on the forehead of each of his flock. His

head felt as though it would burst and he was afraid he would faint in the middle of the ceremony. But he was able to slip into his room afterwards, and when he had rested a little, he took out the commonplace book of Santa Presenza and read:

"Brethren, it is written: 'If thy right eye offend thee, pluck it out and cast it from thee . . . and if thy right hand offend thee, cut it off, and cast it from thee; for it is profitable for thee that one of thy members should perish, and not that thy whole body should be cast into hell . . . !' If someone imagines that his natural gifts destine him for something higher than his brethren in the faith, he must be sharply reproved, and if he persists in his folly, he must be removed from our community and relegated to servile work until he accepts once more with humble heart the truths of love, and no longer seeks to be exalted above his brethren who have remained poor in spirit. If you have the presumption to believe that God the Father loves your head particularly, you should carry a water-pot on it, and if that does not cure you, you must pray that He may lay you prostrate, and that you may rise up with few and good thoughts instead of many and bad ones. . . ."

In the afternoon Thomas went to Santa Sabina to take part in the great public procession with which Lent opens there. He had never once missed it in all the years he had lived in Rome. The Brothers of Santa Presenza used to hold a similar procession in their time. But they wore black cloaks and pointed cowls with only two slits left for the eyes, and walked barefoot in a long procession through the town with an enormous wooden cross at their head, to remind all Romans, tired from their carnival revels, that the time for penance had come.

At the other side of the Circus Maximus the gloomy cypresses on the Aventine Hill stood out like the outline of a cemetery. But behind them the spring glory of the public gardens began, and looking down the streets one could see the red blossoms of Judas trees. The air was heavy and moist after a brief spring shower.

Smart cars were parked in double rows in front of the old basilica of Santa Sabina. The great doors stood wide open and the church was full. Thomas suddenly found himself in his old milieu once more – papal prelates and high Church dignitaries, scholars and artists, diplomats and politicians. And he actually noticed a few faces from the Scandinavian colony in the throng. He felt uncomfortable. Why should I show myself in this company? he thought. All these people have come here to have their heads sprinkled with ashes – in order to give an example; but I am only an unlucky misfit of no publicity value at all. I should have come masked in a penitent's cowl. . . .

The lights fell in bars, like the mighty shadows of an organ, on the spacious middle aisle, where the black-and-white conventicle of Dominicans, looking like a living pianoforte keyboard, sat encircled by the white marble choir. The last hymn of the evening service had just died away and a big black cross appeared at the top of the centre aisle. The monks left the choir and took their places in processional order behind the cross which now began to move slowly forward. The first notes of the ancient litany floated like a bugle call over the multitude, but soon they took on a deeper tone and spread in ever-widening circles over the sea of people, awakening a mighty rolling swell at each new invocation.

Thomas had taken cover behind one of the pillars. The procession slowly passed him by out into the street, and the voices gradually faded away. The church emptied. Thomas waited quietly in his place, but when he ventured out at last to join the tail of the procession, he came unexpectedly on Monsignor Szarnicki.

"So we meet again at last, Don Tommaso!" he exclaimed, obviously delighted to see him.

The Polish prelate's cold hands held Thomas's longer than usual as he asked: "When are you coming back to the Vatican?"

"I don't know," replied Thomas, alarmed, "but I should much prefer to remain at San Lino's. I haven't been there a year yet."

Monsignor Szarnicki laughed. Thomas had never noticed so much warmth in his laugh before. "As long as Cardinal Norcus is alive you certainly have nothing to fear," he said, "and he seems to be vieing with Biblical records. I may say, moreover, that more than one of your former colleagues in the Vatican would willingly change places with you, Don Tommaso. Our Lord means well by you."

"I don't quite understand what you mean, Monsignor," murmured Thomas, getting red.

The Pole's smile became a trifle bitter. "You know very well what I mean even if you don't care to admit it. A priest without a parish is like a married woman without a home of her own. And it's even harder for us foreigners than for the Italians in the Curia, because we can never have the safety valves, as it were, which they have in the parishes of Rome alongside their desk work. I am, and always will be, an immigrant, Don Tommaso – I was nearly saying unlike you."

"Aren't you being rather too pessimistic, Monsignor? After all, you hold an important position. . . ."

"An important position. . . . Well, yes, I suppose you could call it that. I sit in a gilded armchair, enjoy the best of health, and am very well looked after by my friends. But my own country is closed to me, and I seem to hang directly from Our Lord's finger."

"But haven't you got your historical studies . . . ? "

"Yes, I still have them," answered the Pole briefly.

When they left the church at last the front of the procession had already reached the pretty little Piazza of the Knights of Malta at the other end of the street and was moving downhill past the Church of Sant' Anselmo. They followed the procession in silence in the fading light of evening whilst the litany spun out its endless theme of hope and sorrow. When they got back to Santa Sabina the choir was imploring protection from sudden and unprovided death. Once more they entered the dark basilica, where the air smelt stale and vitiated, and heard the last Pater Noster fading away like a half-suppressed sigh over the silent multitude, which then began gradually to disperse.

Monsignor Szarnicki tried to resume the interrupted conversation in a lighter vein. "Wouldn't you like to work in our library again sometimes? " he asked. "I mean on your own studies, as a change from your parochial cares? "

Thomas shook his head earnestly. "I can't see why the parish priest of the Vicolo dei Pecorai should pursue private studies. Not a soul in my parish would be one bit better for it."

"Hm. But there are surely other points of view."

"Certainly, but I am speaking of my own. I have given up my scholarly interests."

An enquiring smile flitted over the other's features. "Do you know that in Santa Presenza you're literally living in an unprospected gold mine? When you're really settled down, we shall look into its history more closely. It is actually virgin soil, and you may make finds that could also be of benefit to your sheep in the Lane of the Shepherds."

Thomas was a little shaken. "Of course, you're right, Monsignor," he said. "I have sometimes thought that myself. Put that way, it no longer seems a mere hobby but a duty. . . ."

"Every honest historian fulfils a duty."

"For me it never became a duty in that sense – rather the contrary."

"How's that?"

"The library was only a place of escape – a pretext for shirking my duty."

Monsignor Szarnicki knit his brows. "I still cannot follow your train of thought," he said.

Thomas drew his hand across his forehead. The hammering in his temples was disquieting. "I have come to realize, Monsignor," he said, trying very hard to steady his voice, "that a cross awaits us at the end of every road which Christ has walked. It confronts an honourable scholar sooner or later on his path. But when I got to the point where I saw the cross shining between the book-covers, I took fright. My love was not strong enough to enable me to carry it. I was too cowardly even to lift it up. I turned back." And while the older man looked at the ground in silence, Thomas continued nervously: "A scholar must seek the truth – the truth, even if it shatters his ambitions. Otherwise he is only a charlatan. But at the time I was looking for something else."

Monsignor Szarnicki still remained silent.

"Do please understand me," continued Thomas almost pleadingly. "My mind was probably unable to cope . . ."

Monsignor Szarnicki nodded. There was kindness and affection in his eyes as he answered, in a strangely hoarse voice: "Perhaps

I did wrong in trying to push the cross on to you. It was simply that I needed to train in a successor in Archives."

After a pause he asked quite abruptly: "Did you know that Boris is dead?"

"Boris? No, I had no idea."

"He went to build a town in Venezuela – you knew he was an architect – but the climate was too much for him. . . . Well, I must go now, I'm afraid. I have a conference with some of my colleagues – we have to discuss the contents of a good eight pounds' weight of papers. And may I ask you for a memento in your Mass, Don Tommaso?"

With a smile and a warm handshake, he said: "Anyhow, I shall soon come back again to visit Nostra Signora dei Pecorai."

The first weeks of Lent passed by. Then Thomas covered over all the pictures and statues in his church with the purple garb of penance, and locked the door to the bell-tower.

❦

XLII   HOLY WEEK

Palm Sunday

Thomas had several attacks of faintness during Lent. By the time it was nearly over, he was very tired. Passion Week had been strenuous, and when he came into the church early on Palm Sunday morning, there was already quite a crowd waiting outside the old confessional. As the morning passed it grew so big that he soon had the feeling that he must have heard the confessions of his entire parish. But the hoped-for penitent for whose sake he had really come to the Vicolo dei Pecorai was still missing.

Sor Anacleto came with the palm branches which were to be blessed this morning; it was now time for the procession. Thomas had rehearsed the ceremony thoroughly with his acolytes and choirboys, and everything went according to plan. The solemn procession which wound its way around the market square and the marble goats which seemed to be dancing with joy at the coming of spring, was only as long as in Don Achille's time. but the cross felt heavier than ever to carry, and Thomas felt the pains in his injured shoulder becoming more and more acute. When he stood once more on the broad steps of San Lino's, and gave the three dramatic knocks on the closed door, his feet were almost giving way under him, but he succeeded in leading the symbolic triumphal procession up the aisle. His temples were hammering as he ascended the altar steps and began to sing the High Mass. Almost as if in a dream he heard the familiar grating of chairs behind him as the people took their places. By the time he had read the Epistle his whole shoulder was in agony. He wiped the perspiration from his forehead while the choir sang, with painful clarity, the Lament:

"I am a worm, and no man; a reproach of men, and despised of the people. All they that see me laugh me to scorn; they shoot out the lip, they shake the head, saying, 'He trusted on the Lord that he would deliver him: Let him deliver him, seeing he delighted in him.'"

Thomas forced himself to continue, and tried to persuade his sinking heart that the text itself would carry him along as the waves carried Peter. But as he read the long Gospel of the Passion he knew he was on the verge of collapse. The words danced before his eyes, he felt stabs of pain like dagger thrusts in his neck; his surroundings sank in mist and thunder, as if waves were breaking over him.

He regained consciousness in the afternoon, and found himself lying in bed utterly exhausted. Sora Michela was sitting beside him darning socks. He realized at once what had happened, and asked no questions. She met his weary gaze with a compassionate smile.

"You have to rest completely now, Reverendo," she told him. "The doctor says you must not stir on any account."

"What doctor?" he asked apathetically.

"One of Cesarino's friends who was there at Mass. Romolo his name is and he says he knows you."

Thomas lay still and shut his eyes to hide a happy smile. With a searching look Sora Michela left him, believing he had fallen asleep.

In the evening Professor Fortunato came.

"How did you know that I . . ." began Thomas, astonished.

"I was notified. It seems you've had a little collapse?"

"That's putting it rather strongly. I was probably overworked."

"I have no doubt whatever of that."

After a brief examination Fortunato shook his head with a puzzled air. "Something has happened here since I saw you last," he said, pressing his thumb on the painful shoulder. "What was it?"

"I fell on the stairs some time ago and sprained my shoulder."

The doctor pressed so hard that the patient could not suppress a groan. "When was that?" he asked.

"In September."

"And you didn't go to a doctor?"

"No."

"Why not? You must surely have realized that it was a serious matter. A person in your state of health has to take every care to avoid complications."

"That's just it. If I had felt stronger, I might have gone to you."

The stern eyes of the doctor rapidly measured the little cell, then remained fixed on Sora Michela, who was standing in the doorway, visibly alarmed. "Did *you* know about this?" he asked her roughly.

"I noticed the whole winter that Don Tommaso looked bad," she said, covered with confusion, "but he wouldn't hear of me getting a doctor to him. And he was always so cheerful. . . ."

Fortunato could no longer contain his indignation. "Do you know it's a sheer miracle that he has kept going until now?" he said.

"Good God! Is it as bad as that?" she whispered, almost speechless with dismay.

"As bad as that? Do you know that the shoulder joint is severely injured, and several other things are wrong as well? He should have had medical attention at once. God only knows what it looks like inside the shoulder."

"Yes, He certainly knows," said Thomas coolly, "but you don't have to scold Sora Michela about it."

The Professor gave him a searching look. " Well, I shan't worry you with any more questions," he said, " since it's plain that you do not wish to discuss the matter from the medical standpoint. But actually the shoulder is not the worst. As a friend, I can only advise you to have an operation, and the sooner the better ! "

" I shall discuss it with my physician in ordinary," said Thomas jocosely.

" Who's that, pray? " asked Fortunato, surprised.

" His name is Carlo Romolo."

" Aha ! The chap who sent me to you. You never mentioned him before. How do you get on with him? "

" Well, at least he has promised not to operate away my soul."

Fortunato shrugged his shoulders. " I am still at your service if you want to consult me," he said, " but if you insist on going your own way, I shall not attempt to dissuade you any longer."

Thomas became suddenly uneasy. " Just one question, Professor," he said. " Do you think that way of mine will be much longer? "

The Professor looked away. " It's impossible to tell without a closer examination," he said. " I can merely repeat that in my opinion the situation is more than serious."

" Forgive me," murmured Thomas. " I suppose I'm too inquisitive."

Fortunato grasped his hand. " I want you to know how often your friends of the San Lino Circle think of you, Don Tommaso," he said, " and I hope you will let us know if you want any help."

" Please remember me to all the old friends. I'm sorry that we have not been able to come together as often as I would have wished."

Sora Michela noticed with a sinking heart that the Professor quietly made the sign of the cross as he went away. But Thomas only smiled and turned to the wall, and his face gradually took on an expression of great peace.

Monday

Every time Sora Michela looked over at Thomas in the course of the night, she found him lying with his eyes wide open. The shadow of a smile still lay over his features, but he answered her questions only briefly and absently. She thought he found it hard to sleep, so she decided to leave him, and did not come back until nearly ten o'clock in the morning. She found him sitting on the edge of his bed, trying to dress. He met her horrified remonstrances with the same faint smile.

"Didn't you notice that the Professor gave no orders at all? I'll say Mass now. It's a bit late perhaps, but that can't be helped."

Sora Michela became embarrassed. She tried to reply but no sound came from her lips. Then she disappeared. When Thomas reached the sacristy he saw the reason for her embarrassment. A strange priest was standing there putting on a surplice. He turned round, startled.

"Oh, Monsignor Cinnelius! You're up!" he exclaimed. He was a lanky young man with sloping shoulders, a bluish tinge on his cheeks and chin, and dark sad eyes. His freshly shaven tonsure was almost blatantly visible. Thomas just stopped himself in time from asking what the young priest was doing in his sacristy, and only said, civilly but hesitantly: "Haven't we met before . . . ? "

"Yes, indeed, Monsignor. I served your Mass in Castelpend-ente last year. I was a deacon at the seminary at that time. My name is Paolo Bracciaferro."

"From Castelpendente . . . ? How extraordinary! "

"Yes, I was ordained at Christmas, and now I've been sent to Rome for special studies."

Thomas could not get over his astonishment. "A priest from Castelpendente here in the Vicolo dei Pecorai . . . ? " he murmured.

"Well, you see, Saint Linus is our patron too . . ." answered Don Paolo, apologetically. "The Vicariate sent for me early this morning. There was no Mass yesterday, I understand? "

Thomas stared before him dreamily. "Yes, that's right," he said after a pause, turning to go. But he stopped on the threshold, took Don Paolo's hand and, pressing it, said: "Welcome to San Lino, dear friend! "

Sor Anacleto was waiting in the office. Deeply embarrassed and with almost a touch of aggressiveness, he explained: "I chanced to meet the parish priest of San Carlo ai Catinari yesterday, and he said it would be best to apply at once to the Vicariate. Here's the medical certificate."

Thomas glanced at the paper. "Unable to discharge his official duties," he read. He knew only too well the name of the signatory –"Carlo Romolo".

"I have also notified your friends of the San Lino Circle," added Sor Anacleto, "because I thought you would like me to. Professor Fortunato came as quickly as he could, but he wouldn't change what the other doctor had written. . . ."

"No, why should he," replied Thomas, laying the certificate on the table. "It was a perfectly clear case of failing to say Mass." Then, seeing the silent plea in Sor Anacleto's eyes, he added with an effort: "You acted quite rightly."

There was a knock at the door and Don Paolo came in. He too seemed ill at ease. "I'm awfully sorry that I didn't have a chance of seeing you as soon as I arrived, Monsignor," he said. "I thought you were asleep and I didn't like to disturb you. Otherwise I would have told you at once that I had been sent to take your place while you're ill."

"That's quite all right. Now I can go back to bed with an easy mind."

"I'm glad that you're better today."

"Thank you, dear friend, but I don't think the Vicariate would consider me well enough yet."

"It's not the Vicariate but the doctor who decides the question."

Thomas smiled. "Neither of them does, actually," he said. "But all the same it's good that you're here. You must tell me about Castelpendente – a little later perhaps."

He took Don Paolo by the arm and led him up to Sor Anacleto, who was standing in a corner, looking like a penitent executioner. "Sor Anacleto, I believe this is a good young man. Look after him well for me," he said.

Then he went back to his cell and lay down on his bed fully dressed. Unable to discharge his official duties . . . he thought. What now? What do they do with a discharged priest?

The darkness of Gethsemane, filled with the frightened voices

of his old doubts, descended on him. Was it all illusion? Was his
life a failure, his vocation self-deception? Were his spiritual
experiences in the mountains nothing more than disordered fancies
and illusions? And his effort to don the mantle of Padre Barnaba
– was that too nothing but caprice and self-deception? The tree
shall be known by its fruit. . . . What results had he to show
for his work in the Vicolo dei Pecorai? It had only revealed to him
his own pitiful inadequacy. His task as shepherd of souls was to
help others. Had he really done this? Had he done anything at all
for which a single being could thank him? Don Paolo seemed to
be winning the hearts of the parish straight away. One had only
to look at Sor Anacleto's face to see that the young priest had
been able to achieve immediately a contact and an understanding
which he, a foreigner, could never hope to win.

A sudden pain in his neck, which felt strangely stiff to the
touch, forced a groan from his lips. Before he could stop it, it
turned into a cry. Sora Michela came running in.

" You called, Don Tommaso? "

" Did I? "

" I thought you were calling for the doctor. . . ."

" No."

At midday he tried to get up but his legs would not hold him.
Sora Michela brought him a plate of boiled rice. Assunta took
over the vigil during the *siesta*, and Don Paolo sat with him for
an hour in the afternoon. But Thomas was too tired to talk. He
slept almost the whole evening.

Meanwhile things were becoming lively down at the outer
door. Many parishioners came to enquire for the invalid. By the
afternoon gifts began to flow in. Finally Sor Anacleto had to stay
in the office to receive the tokens of sympathy with due formality.
The porter Pietro came with a breast of pheasant, the barber
Alessandro brought a bottle of Ceseno wine, and the cinema
proprietor Ettore a real Roman Easter lamb. Others brought
Bologna sausage, artichokes, crabs, cuttlefish, cherries and black
cigars.

Visitors from distant parts of the town also came and knocked
on the door of Santa Presenza – old Tartaruga, who seldom stirred

out of doors these days; a skinny Scandinavian in a red beret, who
handed in a bottle of wine and a bag of dried figs; a monsignor
from the Vatican with a German accent, and another with an
American accent; a little nun from the Brigittine convent with a
huge bunch of red roses; and finally Monsignor Szarnicki. He
alone was allowed to see the invalid. To all the others Sor Anacleto
said with the tactful manner of a man of the world: "Don
Tommaso is resting, but I shall give him your greetings and tell
him you called. I'm sure he'll be very pleased."

Tuesday

Thomas awoke late and felt rested, but a treacherous feeling
of tension in his temples warned him not to attempt too much.
So he was easily persuaded by Sora Michela to remain in bed.
After all, it was very comforting to know that Don Paolo was
in the house.

Carlo Romolo turned up in the forenoon. He walked in with
assumed nonchalance, but there was a tense expression in his face
which Thomas had never seen there before. He was obviously
trying to control his emotion. "A tedious business, this, Don
Tommaso," he said, discreetly laying his bag at the end of the
bed.

This was only an introduction. Thomas remained silent, waiting for him to continue, but Romolo, misinterpreting his silence,
said with a forced smile: "I'm not going to bother you with
questions. I only looked in for a minute, because, after all, it's
really my fault that you're lying here. I'll be off immediately."

"No, please don't. I'm so glad you were in the church when
this happened to me."

"I was passing by, and as I had never been in your little church
before, I went in out of mere curiosity. One cannot say it's
beautiful, but it's rather out of the common."

"And so you happened on my Mass. . . ."

"I didn't know that you were officiating."

"I'm all the more pleased, then. I hope you will come again."

The doctor deliberately misunderstood him. "I have asked
Professor Fortunato to take over your case," he said. "You see, I

can't compete with him, least of all if it's an aneurism, as he says it is."

"It is not only he who says so, and in any case I'm not his patient."

"What? You don't mean to say that the great Professor has passed you on to someone else?"

"Yes, he has. At my express wish he has passed me on to my ordinary doctor."

"I haven't the honour of knowing him."

"Oh yes, you have. His name is Carlo Romolo."

The doctor gave a start, but the distrust in his narrowed eyes quickly gave way to genuinely bewildered astonishment. "What do you mean by that?" he asked. "Haven't you anyone else who could look after you?"

"Why should I? I have done without a doctor for fourteen years, and I knew that you would come back sooner or later."

"You're probably a bit delirious," muttered Romolo, looking round the room with a perplexed air. "Have you taken your temperature?"

Thomas could not help smiling. "If I had known you were coming today, I would willingly have done so."

Romolo opened his bag in silence and stuck a thermometer into the patient's mouth. Then he turned back the bedclothes and examined the ailing shoulder as thoroughly as was possible. His eyes had become small and black again; there was no longer any aggressiveness in them, however, nothing but puzzled concern at the sight of something which he could not understand. He took Thomas's temperature again, examined his heart, and checked his blood-pressure, all in a routine manner. But when he broke silence at last, his voice was curiously tense.

"Please tell me how this happened," he said.

It was now the patient's turn to be puzzled: "Is it really necessary?" he asked.

"There are two things definitely wrong with you – first, the aneurism in the brain which Fortunato explained to me; and secondly, the injury to the shoulder. This latter is not necessarily very grave in itself, but it can bring on a new collapse in the

Y

brain at any time. I must know how you got it, so please . . ."

"Very well," said Thomas resignedly, turning away his face. "I had an accident."

"When?"

"On the feast of Saint Linus."

Romolo scribbled a note. Suddenly he looked up. "What date was that?" he asked.

"The twenty-fourth of September, the evening you and I met at Sor Anacleto's."

Romolo put down his notebook. "Can you be sure of that?" he asked.

"Don't you believe me?"

"Of course – but I don't see how all this fits together."

"You know this is a confession, don't you?"

Romolo flushed crimson. "Call it what you like. The obligation of secrecy is as absolute on me as on you. Only I don't understand why you didn't seek medical attention at the time."

"I had my reason for that."

"What was it?"

"Must you know that too?"

"It doesn't interest me personally at all, but I may possibly have to produce some sort of reasonably credible medical certificate."

Thomas turned his eyes away again. "Our friend Cesarino was the cause," he said, "and it was on his account that I wanted to avoid a medical report."

As the doctor remained silent, Thomas realized that he would have to be more explicit. "You see, Doctor," he said, "the matter would have inevitably led to police investigation. Cesarino would have been charged and everything would have come to light. There are things which simply have to be hushed up."

"So you tried to shield Cesarino?"

"I suppose you can put it that way. But there were other things at stake too."

Romolo made a curious grimace. "Then tell me in God's name what he did!" he snapped.

"He assaulted me," answered Thomas calmly. "Of course he did it in a moment of great excitement. But he could never have denied the fact if charged. He might have been sentenced for assault and battery, perhaps even for sacrilege. You know what that means?"

Romolo made no answer.

"You know little Assunta, and Sora Michela, and Sor Anacleto. They have only their Cesarino and they set all their hopes on him. They look upon his Communism as a kind of childish ailment, and we can ignore it in this connection. The most important thing is the home which he has founded and which is the centre of their little world. But if Cesarino were sent to prison for assaulting his own parish priest – on his way from a priestly duty, moreover – it would wreck the little home completely, and a lot more besides."

Romolo still remained silent, and the invalid continued in a lower voice. "You see, that whole circle is really a delicate little plant in a big desert, and a scandal like that could have incalculable consequences. What do you think the people of the Vicolo dei Pecorai would say if they knew what Sor Anacleto's and Sora Michela's son had done? No, Doctor, there are things about which one must keep dead silent."

When Romolo reacted with only a faint shrug, Thomas continued almost in a whisper: "Of course he didn't know what he was doing. He really only wanted to take revenge on me and not on Our Lord. So I decided to try to pay off my part of the reckoning in this way."

"You don't mean to say that . . . ?"

"I mean that my shoulder is only a private matter which is really of very little consequence in this whole business."

"But it's incredible!"

"How?"

"That you should have gone around six whole months in this condition. Surely someone must have known about it and helped you . . . ?"

"No one helped me," answered Thomas wearily. "You must believe me. I haven't opened my lips to a soul about it. Well, you have heard my confession, Doctor. Now write your report, and let your servant go in peace."

Carlo Romolo stood up. "Promise me at least that you will remain in bed until I come again." Saying this, he tore up the page of his notebook and went out.

Wednesday

Very early in the morning Don Paolo came and asked whether he could be of any help. He was full of friendliness and obviously pleased with life – there was plenty to do in the parish but he found the work a joy because he saw how fertile the spiritual soil was. He had just held the day of recollection for men which Thomas had arranged for, and the results proved that it was definitely a good idea. He had also found very helpful the meditations which Thomas had put together from the book of Santa Presenza.

"Did you see Cesarino?" asked Thomas.

"Who's he?"

"Sor Anacleto's son."

Don Paolo pondered for a moment, then shook his head. "I don't think he attended the day of recollection," he said. "Sor Anacleto came alone each time."

"No, Cesarino certainly wasn't there," said Thomas wearily, "but be friendly to him if you see him in the piazza over Easter. And if he asks for me, say I'm being very well looked after."

When Don Paolo was gone, Thomas tried to read the Gospel of the day, but reading lying down tired his eyes, and the letters swam before them. Suddenly he could distinguish neither colours nor shapes; objects became glassily dispersed and the walls of the room seemed to rock and fold inwards and outwards like the wings of a stage. Suddenly came a voice from the door – a voice so strong and sure that it promptly put a stop to the flight of things visible and restored order to the mental scene like the crack of a whip.

"How are you today? A bit tired, eh?" said Romolo. Laying down his bag, this time on the table, and seating himself on the edge of the bed, he continued in his free and easy way: "I have

consulted Fortunato again. It's no good, we must get you into
hospital for further examination."

"Yes, yes, I know," murmured Thomas, "but there's not all
that hurry."

"It's hard to say, but one thing is certain: you will have to
have this operation sooner or later."

"And you, Brutus!"

"What's that?"

"You promised, didn't you, to spare my soul."

Romolo's compassionate smile betrayed only too clearly that
the jest was a trifle out of place. "My dear Don Tommaso, it's
simply a matter of life and death," he said.

"There is another alternative."

"Which alternative?"

"The old and usual one. You will surely have heard of it in
elementary Christian doctrine."

"Will you accept medical help or will you not?"

"Could we not wait until after Christmas?" pleaded Thomas,
but noticed his error at once. "I mean Easter," he corrected himself with a smile.

Romolo relented. "Very well, if it means so much to you. But
you must definitely remain in bed, no matter what."

"I will try my best."

"Is there someone looking after you here?"

"Oh, yes, two people, in fact – Cesarino's mother and his wife."

Romolo's eyes suddenly glittered. "Does Cesarino know that?"
he asked quickly.

"Presumably."

The doctor stood up and walked to the window, his hands
behind his back. "I hope he hasn't given you any trouble since?"
he asked.

"No, not so far."

"You say not so far. . . . Do you fear anything in particular?"

"No, it's not that; but you know he's a very hot-tempered
fellow, and one can never know what he may do if he sees me
again."

Romolo threw an astonished glance over his shoulder. "How

would he see you now? You surely don't expect he'll visit you? "

"I don't, really, and yet – I haven't quite given up all hope.
I believe I'd be glad if he came."

Romolo shook his head. "That would be anything but good
for you," he said.

"I don't really mean that he should necessarily visit me," said
Thomas resignedly. "Don Paolo could help him just as well."

"Help him with what? "

"Well, he could bless his home at Easter, for instance. Apart
from that Cesarino will not want to see a priest inside his four
walls, but I'm sure he'd want his home sprinkled with holy water
at Easter like everyone else. If only for that reason he will not
break completely with the Church."

"Well, I must say you're easy to please ! "

"I'm content if I only know that the contact is not completely
broken. Sooner or later there comes a time when one needs this
contact. People want to be baptised, married and buried by a priest
if they are not to appear worse than others. When it comes
down to family matters Cesarino really isn't a Communist at
all."

"I suppose you're right, and . . ."

"And that is the secret bond between us. I would rather cut
off my hand than have this bond broken."

Romolo was standing by the bedside again, fingering with
assumed indifference the book which lay beside Thomas. "It's nice
that Assunta is looking after you," he said. "Have you something
to read? "

"The Gospel of the day."

"In other words, good reading for the sick," remarked Romolo
ironically, laying down the book.

"Yes, to be sure, and written by a doctor too."

"What did you say? "

"Saint Luke was a doctor, you know."

Visibly amused, Romolo took up the little book again. He had
obviously never looked at the Gospel from that angle before. "I
have never given myself time to study these things," he said.
"Perhaps one should do so if only to be able to deal with you

priests and not to be talked into heaven-knows-what by you," he added with an amiable grin.

"Are you as scared of us as all that?"

"I only mean that everyone should keep within his own domain. Naturally, there are many things between heaven and earth which science cannot explain. We doctors know that just as well as you do, but we keep clear of things we don't understand. You priests should do the same."

"You're quite right. If only you doctors would see your limitations too."

"Naturally there are also doubtful borderline cases," said Romolo less confidently, "but that doesn't alter the general rule. When you consult a doctor you must follow his instructions. That's perfectly simple."

"Very simple. And when you consult a priest, you should listen to his advice. That's almost simpler."

Romolo came up to the bed and pressed Thomas's hand. "Let's not break our heads over these problems any more now," he said. "At any rate, my instruction is this: Remain in bed and if possible refrain from giving other people advice. Good-bye!"

At the door he turned round again and said, with a grin: "If you do that, I'll read Luke," then disappeared with his old booming laugh.

Towards two o'clock Assunta brought Thomas his dinner. Sor Anacleto had prepared a real feast from the gifts of the parish. Thomas noted with horror the variety of dishes. "Why all this luxurious food?" he asked. "You know Lent isn't over yet."

Assunta made a deep curtsey. "Doctor says you must eat well, Reverendo," she replied.

He stared at her, astonished, then laughed and said: "Very well, then pass me the breast of pheasant. After all, I've promised to be obedient."

"*Buon appetito!*" she said, and remained standing beside him, overflowing with sympathy, until he had finished. Then she curtsied again, and whispered, blushing: "May I ask you something, Reverendo?"

"Of course, but the doctor mustn't know."

"Yes, he has forbidden us to trouble you without necessity, but . . ."–she blushed still more deeply–"This is something that only you can answer."

"And what is it?"

"We're expecting a child in the autumn, Reverendo," she continued in an almost inaudible whisper, "and I'd be so happy if you could baptize it. Or perhaps–if you can't do that–I mean –if the doctor–perhaps–doesn't allow you, may we at least call it after you?"

Did she really have to ask that, he thought when she was gone. Sor Anacleto's dainty dishes suddenly left a nasty after-taste. By the evening he felt very sick.

Maundy Thursday

In the afternoon Thomas received Holy Communion from the hands of Don Paolo, who had previously said the only Mass of the day down in San Lino's. After Mass the Blessed Sacrament was brought to the little side-altar which was symbolical of Christ's tomb.

Sor Anacleto had decorated the Altar of Repose with the most beautiful flowers which could be bought in the Piazza delle Pecore, and surrounded it with a temporary barrier before which the people could kneel. Sor Anacleto had a great many other things to see to on Maundy Thursday; for instance, the big feast for the old poorhouse inmates. This was a custom dating from the days of Santa Presenza, when the Father Superior himself used to wash the feet of the poor.

When evening came Thomas could not resist slipping down to the church in spite of Romolo's prohibition. The high altar was stripped bare, the red lamp was extinguished, the tabernacle was gaping open and empty, but people were moving in an unending procession past the brilliantly lit Altar of Repose. Thomas sat down near the door and began to read his office. Don Paolo was hovering in the background within call. Strange how quickly he has made himself at home in the parish, thought Thomas. At that moment someone who wanted to unburden his conscience came up to

Don Paolo, and the young priest promptly seated himself in
Padre Barnaba's ancient confessional just as if he had been doing
this all his life.

No one came to Thomas. The worshippers passed him by in an
endless stream, yet no one ventured to speak to him. He felt an
outcast. . . . The smell of the flowers, heavy and intoxicating,
filled his nostrils as he sat with bowed head reading the Psalms.
His lonely soul was overwhelmed once more with darkness and
grief as he read:

> I am counted with them that go down into the pit:
> I am as a man that hath no strength:
> Free among the dead, like the slain that lie in the grave, whom
> thou rememberest no more: and they are cut off from thy hand.
> Thou hast laid me in the lowest pit, in darkness, in the depths.
> ....
> Thou hast put away mine acquaintance far from me......
> I am shut up, and I cannot come forth. . . .

Thomas waited on steadfastly as if he were waiting for something. Was not Maundy Thursday the great day of reconciliation
in the early Church, the one on which the penitents, holding
hands, walked in solemn procession, with the bishop at their
head to lead them into the church once more?

Ten minutes before the church was due to close a familiar
figure appeared. Romolo – Romolo at last! He genuflected hurriedly
at the door, made an almost invisible sign of the cross, and looked
around hesitantly. Thomas half stood up as though to make his
presence known. Actually he was not at all surprised, for he had
been secretly waiting for this moment ever since his return from
Settevetri.

The doctor came straight towards him in his somewhat clumsy
way and Thomas noted that today his expression was bright and
open and devoid of the usual mistrust. He waited full of tension
for his first word. Had he not been imagining to himself for
almost a year what it would be? But Romolo only nodded, and
frowned with a slight air of interrogation, then turned to Padre

Barnaba's confessional, and knelt down opposite the grille behind which Don Paolo was sitting.

Thomas remained standing, his hand half raised as if to give a sign. Should not he have heard this confession? Had anyone else thought so much about Romolo, prayed so much for him, suffered so much for him? It almost seemed to him that he had wrestled for Romolo's soul at the cost of his own life. Therefore a share in Romolo's confession of faith was his, and could not be taken from him without cutting into his living flesh. But meanwhile Romolo went on quietly with his confession, and Thomas sat down again, not without a little stab in his heart.

At last Romolo emerged from the confessional, walked up to the Altar of Repose, and knelt down. Thomas looked at his bowed head and clasped hands, and wondered whether Romolo had really recognized him just now, or whether he had thought he was sitting in his confessional as usual. But before he had decided the matter the doctor rose from his knees, walked calmly up to him, and asked him how he felt.

" I was going to look in on you when I'd finished here," he said, " and it gave me quite a shock to see you in the church. You must be more careful. I trust you have not been hearing confessions too? "

"No, I haven't," replied Thomas. And suddenly he found he had nothing to say. He was reduced once more to the status of a patient, an invalid unable to fulfil the duties of his office in his own church.

But then he realized that this was meant to be. His own prestige had to recede. God Himself and not he, Thomas, had brought Romolo back.

He returned obediently to his room and lay down, and was almost glad when he felt the pain in his head coming on again; but he was so tired that he dropped into a light sleep in spite of it. He dreamed that Fausto came into his cell grinning all over to announce a visitor. There was a sound of heavy footsteps downstairs, and Padre Barnaba walked in, gave him a thick frieze cloak, a rope to tie round his waist, and a pair of hob-nailed boots for the roads that he was to walk from now onwards. Waking up,

Thomas felt a sensation of unspeakable peace, stretched himself and fell asleep again, this time deeply in spite of the constant pressure in his neck.

Good Friday

When he awoke early in the morning he wondered why he was lying in bed when everyone else was up. As soon as he got out of bed his pulse began hammering more rapidly, but he persuaded himself that the fresh air would do him good. So he dressed slowly and walked carefully down the stairs. Once outside he did actually feel better. It was the coldest hour of the morning, and the air was as pure as in January.

Not a soul was to be seen anywhere. He heard an indefinable noise in the distance. It was heavy and light at the same time, like the drumming of rain on the pavement. But there was no rain. Suddenly a shaggy, dirty-white sheepdog appeared on the Piazza delle Pecore, stood and looked suspiciously at the solitary man, gave a warning growl, and then disappeared again. The next moment a sheep put its head round the corner of the Palazzo Terrasanta. A second, a third, a fourth followed. Then, as if at the touch of a magic wand, the whole piazza was full of sheep – dirty, slow-moving mountain sheep. Bewildered by the strange surroundings, they crowded together; the dogs which were encircling them seemed just as shy and lost as they. It was a whole herd on its way to the mountains from its winter pasturage in the Campagna.

Thomas stood motionless in order not to scare them by any incautious movement. The familiar sharp smell was wafted towards him. He closed his eyes and gave himself up to the mental pictures conjured up by it and the trample of light hooves. Suddenly he thought he heard his name being called. When he opened his eyes he saw a sunburned shepherd coming towards him, laughing joyfully.

" Marco ! "

" Good morning, Don Tommaso. The spring has come."

Thomas found it hard to realize where he was. " Marco ! But where have you come from? " he exclaimed.

"We had the sheep with Fausto's friends in the Campagna over the winter, and now we're taking them home again."

"Then it must be a long time since you left Settevetri?"

"No, I've come straight from there, and here . . ." he drew a crumpled letter from his sleeve – "I have a letter for you from Padre Barnaba."

"For me?"

"Yes, indeed. I came this way specially to give it to you."

"How is Padre Barnaba?"

"Quite well, but you know he's not as young as he was, and the walk down to Fontenuova is getting harder and harder for him."

Thomas nodded with an understanding smile. "And the *Agro Sacro*," he asked, "who tills it for him now?"

Marco shrugged his shoulders. "Fausto does what he can, and Saint Joseph looks after the rest," he said. "But of course no one can say his Mass for him."

Thomas drew his hand over his eyes. "Tell me what it looks like – up there – now, at Easter . . ." he murmured.

"More beautiful than ever, Father. The pastures are wonderfully green already, and it's getting warmer every day. In two weeks we'll be celebrating the Feast of the Good Shepherd. You know . . ."

"Come in, Marco! Stay here! I need you . . ." pleaded Thomas in a low voice.

But the shepherd only laughed. "I can't stop this time," he said. "We have to be at home for Easter, you know."

"For Easter? Impossible! Today is Good Friday."

"Why should it be impossible? I came from Sora in a big lorry, and we're taking the sheep as far as Castelpendente in it. This evening we will start the climb to the mountains, and we'll be home tomorrow. Come back with us, Don Tommaso!"

He looked expectantly at the priest, and a smile lit up his tanned face. Then he walked a step nearer to Thomas, laid his hands gently on his shoulders, and leaned his bristly cheek against the priest's. It was the age-old kiss of peace of the Good Shepherd.

" Good-bye, Don Tommaso, and come back to Settevetri soon ! "

The herd started moving again. Now the animals trotted across
the piazza and down towards the banks of the Tiber, shimmering
at the bottom of a narrow street. Thomas watched them fading
into the morning mist like a vision. Marco was walking right
behind them. Once more he turned round and waved a last good-
bye. When Thomas raised his arm to wave back, such a sharp pain
shot through the injured shoulder that his farewell wave turned
into a distorted gesture. He slipped into the church which Don
Paolo had just opened. As he knelt down at his *prie-dieu* he
realized that he was still holding the letter from Settevetri in his
hand, but it was too dark to read it in the empty derelict church,
so he slipped back to his room.

" My dear Tommaso," wrote Padre Barnaba, " I am beginning
to feel tired and would need someone to turn the handmill for me.
I discussed the matter recently with Monsignor Boccaperta and he
suggested the parish priest of San Lino's, whose name of course is
Don Tommaso. . . ."

A hot wave of longing flowed into Thomas's exhausted heart,
bringing back a whole cascade of past impressions – the smoky
smell of the open hearths, the tinkle of the sheep-bells, the chirp-
ing of the grasshoppers, the break of dawn, the stars shining down
like great eyes on spectral mountain peaks, and, most vivid of all,
the simple faces around the deal table in the Inn of the Good
Shepherd, and the soft yellow light from the oil lamp which
swung gently in the evening breeze. . . .

Thomas remained in his room. When the service began down in
San Lino's he followed it in his missal. He dutifully read one after
another the great Petitions – that the Lord might banish disease,
ward off famine, open prisons, loosen bonds, grant to travellers a
safe return, give back health to the sick, and guide mariners into
safe harbours. And he imagined he could hear from below a faint
echo of the Saviour's Reproaches, which the Franciscan nuns were
singing :

" *I raised thee up with mighty power:*
And thou didst hang me upon the gibbet of the Cross."

Thomas knew that in the old days of Santa Presenza the whole monastery became a house of the dead, as it were, on Good Friday. Darkness filled the great rooms, and the corridors were silent and deserted as catacombs. At the hour of early Matins the Brothers gathered around the fifteen brown mourning candles in San Lino's and quenched them one after another, then retired to the accompaniment of loud noises which echoed down from the ceiling to symbolize the trembling of the earth at the Crucifixion. The tabernacle stood empty, the Holy Presence had disappeared from the earth, and their monastery had become bare and cold as a lifeless ruin. The Brothers spent the rest of the day alone in their cells calling upon the Lord to lead them, in His mercy, out of this Egyptian night. . . .

Late in the evening Thomas took the old monastery commonplace book and read:

"For the Holy Presence is hidden from the eyes of men behind seven seals. None can perceive it with his mortal eyes unless it be that he treads the same road which Christ has trodden. Only beyond the grave shall we discern the Holy Presence in its full reality. What we may think we have discerned already in this life, was but a fleeting vision, born of the yearning of our restless hearts. But you must not despise your yearning for that reason, for it may be the saving of your soul."

Holy Saturday

Thomas had a long night. When Don Paolo came up to him in the forenoon he found him still asleep, and Sor Anacleto once more resumed his watch on the outer door to turn away any visitors who might come.

Thomas dreamed that he was wandering with Marco and his herd over the high plateau of Monte Lino. It was late in the night, and the stars were big and shining. The limestone peaks were white as icebergs in the moonlight. A choir of rough voices singing an Easter hymn rose from the plain below. The shepherds of Settevetri were watching and waiting out on their pastures for the passing of the Good Shepherd just as Fra Farfalla had watched in his garden at Santa Maria degli Ulivi.

"Night reigns over all the earth," a penetrating voice lamented right beside the dreamer's ear; and in the distance a tremulous trio replied:

"The Good Shepherd is passing over the mountains. The Good Shepherd is leading His sheep to the holy pastures. The Good Shepherd was in the realm of death but He has vanquished death."

In the same monotonous chant the first voice continued:

"Why are we born into this world if not to be redeemed one day? Can anyone have greater love than the Good Shepherd, who has given his life for His sheep?"

And far away in the distance, like a trembling echo, the words came down the mountainside:

"O happy guilt, that merited so great, so noble a Redeemer! O truly blessed night, in which Christ arose again from the tomb."

And now, like the thunder of subterranean waterfalls, the words resounded over the whole plain:

"The night shall be bright as the day . . . a holy night which banishes our misdeeds; washes away our sins; gives back to the fallen their innocence; and to the sorrowful their gladness; drives forth hatred; gives harmony and peace, and brings the pride of tyrants low. . . .

"O truly blessed night, O night on which heaven is wedded to earth; the things of God to those of man!"

Then the sun rose over the mountains and the white brow of Monte Lino appeared like a flash of lightning over the horizon. The larks mounted into the clear air, the snow glistened in the ravines, and the bleating sheep crowded down into the slopes where the young grass was sprouting up, green and tender. Marco lifted his head high and intoned a new theme in his strong young voice.

"As the hart panteth after the fountain of waters, so panteth my soul after thee, O God," and Thomas realized that he was listening to part of the Easter Vigil Service. Now the singing ceased. Thomas had the feeling that the singers were waiting for his response. He tried to call out "*Dominus vobiscum*", but his voice would not obey him. The brighter it became around him the more completely Marco and his herd became lost to view, and the more difficult he found it to follow the antiphonal singing of the shepherds, which was starting up afresh around him. Finally he found himself standing all alone on the road, listening to the last echoes of Marco's voice fading into inaccessible distance.

Suddenly a strong bass voice behind him asked his name in an authoritative tone.

"I'm Don Tommaso," he answered hesitantly. The voice sounded strangely familiar. Whose could it be?

Now it asked, still more imperiously: "Have you renounced your false gods?"

"Yes," he answered.

"And Satan and all his works?"

"Yes."

"And all his pomps?"

"Yes."

Now came a dry laugh, which Thomas must have heard many a time long ago, and the voice continued: "Of course these questions sound like a lot of horrible clichés, but actually they are part of the official formula. Now let us try to express ourselves more simply: Did you stand up and follow the Lord when He passed by?"

Thomas went on struggling desperately with his tired memory. The voice became more and more urgent: "Did you love your fellow-beings in your daily life, or did you hide your heart in the desert?"

"I certainly tried my best," he murmured, "but my strength was not always sufficient. . . ."

But the voice kept on: "Did you bear testimony before your fellow men to the Holy Ghost, the Holy Catholic Church and the Communion of Saints? Or did you seek the forgiveness of sins, the resurrection of the body, and life everlasting outside, on paths of your own?"

Now at last Thomas knew who was speaking to him. "Dom Andrea!" he cried. "Is that really you?"

"Yes, it is I. I only wanted to know whether you were remembering your baptismal vows?"

"Don't question me! I have promised to obey my doctor, and soon I shall no longer be the person I was."

He seemed to hear the contemptuous snort of the old monk in the darkness. "Who told you that Our Lord wants you as you are now? If He crops your ears, no doubt He does so because He considers them ugly as they are. There is no reason to believe that a former art historian should necessarily have more beautiful ears than a terrier."

"You're just as downright as ever, but I'm not worrying about my ears. I'm only wondering whether I'm doing right."

"The doctors are always right – or almost always. And when it's a border-line case between the medical and the ethical, you can ask Don Paolo for advice."

"Why precisely him?"

"Because he's your immediate superior," snapped Dom Andrea.

The words remained hanging in the air like a faint sighing of the wind and when Thomas looked around him he noticed that the summit of Monte Lino had come quite near. He himself was standing a little way from Fontenuova, staring up expectantly at Settevetri, which was shining like a spangle against the bone-white skin of Lo Zoccolo.

Dottoressa Vanna was standing in the mouth of a cave at the foot of the rock-face beckoning him like another Circe. "Why are you torturing yourself for nothing?" she called down to him. "You are not going to reach the summit. Better come up here quickly and hide your head in my cave before Fortunato gets hold of it."

Thomas looked around for help. Marco and his herd had already passed the most dangerous part and were now high up on the mountain path, which had suddenly become covered with climbers. The voices down below on the plateau fell silent. In their stead a clear, calm, powerful voice rose up from Lo Zoccolo. It was the Madonna of the Shepherds herself, who was now singing a hymn, and somewhere in the far distance a triumphant pealing of many bells arose in answer. Thomas grasped their theme without effort. It was:

"There is no way to the truth except through love."

A bicycle bell clanged outside in the Vicolo dei Pecorai, and

Z

when he opened his eyes he noticed that it was already midday. Someone was opening the outer door of Santa Presenza, vigorous footsteps sounded in the hall, and Romolo appeared in the doorway, sullen as a thunder-cloud.

" So you're awake? "

" Yes, I'm awake."

" And how do you feel? "

Thomas tried to murmur some conventional words, but evidently his eyes spoke their own language because Romolo's grim expression became milder.

"I really must scold you severely," he said. "You know you are seriously ill and must obey my instructions. We cannot have any repetition of your Maundy Thursday escapade."

Thomas, on his part, desired nothing more ardently than to speak of what had happened on Maundy Thursday, but the doctor saw no reason at all for discussing his visit to San Lino's. The fact that he had made his confession was entirely his own affair. The fact that he had not done so for two decades was likewise his own affair. None of his friends would see anything in the least sensational in what he had done, and it would have no influence whatsoever in his relations with them – though perhaps it would on his relations with God. But that too was and remained entirely his own private affair. Suddenly Thomas realized that he had exaggerated fantastically in his own mind the significance of what he had observed in the church.

"I was here yesterday evening," continued Romolo, "but you were so tired that I didn't like to waken you. Instead I went to Fortunato. You will understand that I cannot take responsibility for your case if you will not obey my instructions. . . . Fortunato agrees that you should come into his clinic on Monday. After that you will be his responsibility. I hope you can be ready by then."

Thomas shut his eyes. "May I have a few words with Don Paolo? " he asked.

Easter Sunday

It was still dark when Thomas came down to the sacristy. Sor Anacleto, who had just opened the church doors, stared at him,

horrified. "Surely you are not going to say Mass, Monsignor?"
he gasped.

"Should I not be allowed to do so before Romolo takes me
away? It will be my first and last Easter Mass in San Lino's."

Sor Anacleto took out the vestments with a hangdog expression,
then rushed from the sacristy muttering something under his
breath. Now he's gone to fetch Romolo, thought Thomas. But
after a few minutes Sor Anacleto reappeared and announced he
would serve Mass himself. This was an extremely rare attention,
and Thomas realized that it was the good innkeeper's way of
showing how devoted he was to his former pastor though circumstances had obliged him to transfer his services to a successor.

The air was still extremely vitiated after the great Midnight
Mass which Don Paolo had celebrated for the parish in accordance with the restored Easter liturgy. When Thomas went up to
the altar to say his Mass the church was empty. As he recited the
Confiteor he heard someone coming in from the street, and when
he turned round to pronounce the absolution he saw two figures
kneeling humbly in the background – Sora Michela and Assunta.
And behind them he caught sight of a third figure lolling care-
lessly over his chair-back like a boxer on the ropes. It was Cesarino.
Sor Anacleto had summoned his whole family to Don Tommaso's
last Mass.

Another text would fit in here, thought Thomas. "Not seven
times, but seventy times seven times. . . ." The sullen face of
Cesarino looking furtively towards the altar would not leave his
mind's eye. What did the fellow want here? Had he really made
his peace with God, or was it sheer effrontery that brought him?
It was impossible to know. Anyhow it was not up to him, Thomas,
to decide whether Cesarino really wanted to come one step nearer
to the Sacrament or not. Only one thing concerned him at the
moment – to hold out.

It cost him such visible effort to mount the altar-steps that Sor
Anacleto's eyes followed him, full of anxiety. Having recited the
opening psalm he stood for a moment swaying in front of the
open missal before he succeeded in whispering: "Lord, have
mercy on us!"

Sor Anacleto's response: "Christ, have mercy on us!" came short and quick as if he were trying to hurry the Mass in order not to be caught in this impermissible action.

The first light of dawn fell through the dome into the apse. Thomas felt an inclination to shut his eyes. How would he get through this new day? As the Mass progressed his feeling of exhaustion became more overpowering. When reading the Gospel of the day he did not dare to try to think of the meaning; and the *Credo* loomed before his aching head like a pyramid of responsibility and obligation. He found himself confronted with a task of superhuman weight. Christ had left all this to His priests as a heritage, and now he, the weakest of them all, was to hold in his trembling hands the Risen Saviour of the world.

"The earth trembled and was still when God arose in judgment, Alleluia," he read.

If several priests were at the altar to share his burden, it would be easier. For one priest alone it called for superhuman strength to bear this grace and pass it on. But he dared not fail. He would have to go through to the end, even if the effort broke him. If he could take up his cross again for one week, for one day, or perhaps only for one hour, it would help Cesarino, and Sora Michela, and all sinners.

Outside the sun had risen. At the very moment that Thomas bent over the Host to speak the words of Consecration a shaft of sunlight shot through the dome. Suddenly it became bright all round him, bright with a radiant, vivid, liberating light. He was overwhelmed with a feeling of peace. The ultimate reality was approaching, it was already upon him, it had risen. He took the Host in his trembling hands and murmured:

"This is My Body."

And now he began to try, very cautiously, as if It were a tiny bird that had fluttered down – to raise the little Host above him. But suddenly a faint red seemed to suffuse the white wafer, filling it with a mysterious life which pulsed through its fine texture like blood. Lamed with fear, Thomas fell on his knees. The paper-light Host weighed like lead in his hands. Behind him Sor Anacleto rang a shrill alarm with his little altar bell.

And the church bell . . . thought Thomas. Why doesn't he
ring the church bell too? For the Lord has come down to the
earth, and His footstep is so mighty that it must shake the whole
city, as it once shook Jerusalem. . . . But silence still reigned all
around, only the light became stronger and stronger, and finally
it grew so strong that everything seemed to become translucent,
and he could distinguish the outlines of only the nearest objects.
Sor Anacleto moved like a shadow round the altar; the other
figures drifted into an unreal distance. Would the glowing Hosts
be visible through their bloodless, glass-like forms when he gave
them Holy Communion . . . ?

After the Mass Thomas fell silently on his knees before the altar.
He looked as though he were waiting for something. Sor Anacleto
knelt down beside him, casting anxious glances behind, but as
soon as he began to shuffle nearer to him on his knees, and
ventured a slight cough as signal, Thomas collapsed completely.
Sor Anacleto and his son carried him up to his cell.

He recovered consciousness only after several hours, but he did
not speak. He just lay still and waited. The little room was bathed
in light. It penetrated the walls and ceiling, making all solid
surfaces and shapes translucent. Colourless forms, unreal as the
figures in a dream, moved before Thomas's eyes, exchanging unimportant words about hospital and an operation. He did not listen
to their talk, for he was still waiting for the bells to announce the
arrival of the ultimate, the absolute reality.

Gradually all the unimportant things around him faded away,
the shadows grew pale, the illusory world dissolved. Through torn
curtains of cloud a drawbridge came down from heaven and hit
the earth with such force that he sat up bewildered. The whole
world is going to pieces, he thought. And at the same moment he
heard the bells of San Lino's suddenly beginning to peal as if an
earth tremor had started them up. Then he realized that they were
announcing the restoration of the Divine Presence; and soon their
message was re-echoed by the eager peals of the near-by churches.

He sank back on his pillows, smiling. The people around him,
the cell, the monastery, the Vicolo dei Pecorai, all sank into
mysterious depths. The many-voiced murmur of the city faded to

an indistinct whisper at the bottom of a great abyss. The only sound that now rose from its depths was an ever-increasing clanging of bells.

He knew each one of them – the Chiesa Nuova and Sant' Agnese, San Lorenzo in Damaso and Sant' Andrea della Valle, San Carlo ai Catinari, and Santa Maria sopra Minerva, and many others he had listened to countless times from his cell. But from the point on which he now found himself he seemed to hear the bells of all the churches of Rome at the same time, and they sounded as they had never sounded before. From the Capitoline Hill Santa Maria in Ara Coeli had started up a jubilant fanfare which swung down to San Marco and Santi Apostoli, and was carried on by them to the Piazza del Popolo, until the whole Corso was ringing and singing like an invisible festival procession. The bells of the Resurrection clanged between the ruined columns of the Forum, and their echoes danced over the blossoming meadows of the Palatine; they were flung back by the mighty walls of the Colosseum, and became lost like a whisper in the quiet monastery gardens of the Coelian Hill. From the ancient churches on the Aventine a subdued accord rang out. It mingled with the peals from the campaniles of Trastevere, and floated, clear as the song of larks, over the Janiculum Hill. Far off, on the Pincian Hill, Santa Trinita dei Monti took up the refrain, and its echo reverberated like the thunderous organ music of the sea from the great basilicas in the east – Santa Maria Maggiore, San Giovanni in Laterno, Santa Croce in Gerusalemme. And finally the mighty bass of the great bronze bell of Saint Peter's rose above them all, announcing to the whole world that the only way to Truth is through Love.

And while the bells of Rome rang out the Easter tidings, Thomas Cinnelius quietly crossed the bridge into his heavenly home.